Banshee Born

A. M. Megahed

authorhouse

AuthorHouse™
1663 Liberty Drive
Bloomington, IN 47403
www.authorhouse.com
Phone: 1-800-839-8640

First published by AuthorHouse 05/11/2011

ISBN: 978-1-4567-4741-1 (e)
ISBN: 978-1-4567-4740-4 (sc)

Library of Congress Control Number: 2011906935

Printed in the United States of America

Chapter 1

Exploding magma splattered across the carapace of the arachnid shaped machine. It slowly crawled up the steep, spiraling ramp gouged into the pit walls, its articulated legs making unsteady progress with each tentative stride. Another tremor shook the cavern hurling more rocks down the narrow shaft. For a moment the CyberLinked Vehicle tottered precariously on the ramp's edge. The CLV responded like a pirouetting ballerina, avoiding the precipice and the boulders that disappeared into clouds of vaporizing mercury and splashed into the flaming pool hundreds of meters below. As the tremor subsided, the CLV fired its small thrusters, hurtling the last forty meters up the abyss to land with a jolt on the rim of the shaft. The right foreleg collapsed on landing, sluing the vehicle sideways. The pilot deftly fired his thrusters again, lifting the CLV a few meters closer to the uncertain safety of the cavern exit. The twelve ton machine hesitated for a moment, then began a limping walk to the tunnel and escape. It passed the abandoned equipment left by the fleeing peds, and entered the narrow confines of the unlit passage, its single remaining infrared spotlight piercing a path in the stygian darkness. The CLV worked its way steadily upward, past rock strewn debris only hesitating at a rock slide with a protruding armored limb. Like a dung beetle working a manure heap, the machine carefully rolled the debris away with its upper digging arms. Carefully it inspected three uncovered bodies, picked up the two least damaged, and continued on its way.

The compact machine stopped and cleared a cave-in every few strides, its body narrowly working its way past some of the larger obstructions. Finally a tumbled wall blocked the tunnel. The spot light traversed the barrier, like a giant searching eye stalk. Then with infinite care, the CLV fired bursts from a small laser in its left lower mandible, drilling three small holes. From the right primary limb it extruded three charges of plastique into the holes. The CLV gently backed down the tunnel around a curve, placed the bodies beneath its torso and crouched down like a giant insect laying eggs. Moments later a loud explosion shattered the silence. The vehicle picked up its delicate packages, and headed back up the tunnel. Through a cloud of billowing dust a small opening appeared in the granite wall. Laboriously the machine cleared a larger opening and then continued its steady progress.

Passing one last barrier, the CLV walked into a hive of activity in a small cavern. Scores of machines and armored peds were busily repairing damage and treating survivors. Portable halogen lights created wavering shadows amidst the scurrying men and machines. It placed the injured peds on a Red Cross marked gurney. Other peds began loading the bodies into an ancient life support tank. The limping machine continued across the cave into another upward slanting tunnel mostly free of debris and relatively well lit. Minutes later it entered a giant cavern with a tame mercury pit bubbling in the center. The machine limped to one of a half dozen metal doors carved out of the rock. One of the doors slowly opened. Worn out, it backed into the repair bay and shutdown.

Alessandro Watanabee Kane adjusted his respirator, then his pressure suit; standard procedure before exiting his *Termite* mining CLV. He never deviated from good safety procedures. One of the reasons he was still alive after four years of jacking a CyberLinked Vehicle in the Banshee mines. Wiping the sweat off his face he completed the final entry of the harrowing shift into the log, "Traces of crystal bearing corundite and molybdenum were identified via laser spectroscopy twelve meters above the lava pool." He would have preferred lying about the find, the new pit would be a killer, but the computer had already logged the strike.

Quickly slipping out of the cockpit and resealing to avoid mercury and acid contamination of the *Termite*'s internals, he shoved his way past the A shift peds rushing to burn their few vouchers on the *Strip*. Alex did not blame them for their indifference to the death and destruction below; life was cheap in the mines. Catching Chief Tech Solomon McDuff outside a repair bay, he flashed in handspeak, "Meet me in the Control Room." They walked together across the L shaft third auxiliary tunnel ignoring the molten mercury fumes bubbling up from the pit and casting a lethal haze across the neon lights. Reaching the CR lock together, McDuff slotted his ID. The pressure doors opened with the hiss of escaping air. They entered the habitable portion of the mine complex through the lock together, ignoring each other until they completed decontamination. McDuff yanked off his respirator and snapped "What the Hell is wrong with your Cilvee now, laddie?"

Alex ignored McDuff's tone and calmly replied, "I want the coolant system flushed, she's running hot, the left leg actuator is damaged and the reactor energy output is down to 86 percent. Also the one centimeter drilling laser is out of alignment. I want them all fixed this time Duffy. I nearly bought it in the new pit because of that faulty actuator!"

McDuff snapped back, "Laddie ya'r Jacking a blasted twelve ton *Termite* CLV, not a CombatDroid. We do the best we can with what we've got!"

Alex stared at McDuff like a cobra ready to strike. Beads of perspiration began trickling down the forehead of the senior tech. Unnerved, McDuff back pedaled, in a wheedling tone, "We do the best we can Alex. The boys and I will flush the coolant, align the laser and maybe we can repair the actuator. We don't have the parts to fix anything else. The GenClone renegades keep intercepting our supply shuttles, and the mercs get first priority on what does get through. The company does na' care about our survival, Laddie, bein' we're all cons."

Alex angrily snapped, "You may be a Lifer Duffy, but I'm third generation Banshee. I have the right to leave this planet anytime I want! I'm not responsible for what my ancestors did!"

McDuff apologetically replied, "Sorry Alex, I forgot. I hope you do leave someday. You'd be the first to ever leave this Hell hole. The Company will na' easily let go its best *Termite* Jack, or let the outside world find out about conditions here."

Surprised by his own outburst, Alex relented, "Fix what you can Duffy. I'll come in early next shift to check the repairs." He stared at McDuff a moment to reinforce the not so subtle warning, then turned and left the CR through the primary lock leading further into the inhabited sections of the mines.

He overheard with his unnaturally acute hearing Duffy whispering to one of his subordinates, "That one really gives me the willys, did you hear what..."

Walking back to his quarters, Alex pondered; Duffy was right, the Corporate reps would never want witnesses to leave Banshee and its convict operated mines. They had an ideal setup. The Imperial Coalition shipped down its criminal scum, ten kilometers below the surface of the deadliest planet in known space and in return laser crystals and heavy metals went up at almost no cost.

The cons worked the mines until the 1.4 Earth normal gravity, the deadly fumes, the background radiation or the unstable planetary crust managed to kill them. Only those with valuable technical skills, or freaks who adjusted to the deadly environment, survived more than a few years. Alex was the descendant of such freaks.

He could trace his ancestry to the likes of Condor Watanabee, CombatJack turned serial murderer, and to Mustafa Ibn Khalid the legendary assassin. Neither of them held a candle to his most infamous ancestor, Lucinda Kane, His grandmother! The mad heiress to the Binghampton fortune had poisoned the water supply on Mojave, killing thousands on an insane lark.

His progenitors all had two things in common; they had committed terrible crimes, and had managed to produce viable offspring on Banshee. A world where female convicts were supposedly sterilized on arrival to prevent giving birth to hideously deformed babies. The high background radiation and the abundance of toxins made a normal birth very unlikely. Of course the haphazard medical facilities didn't even manage to properly sterilize the inmates. Alex had the dubious distinction of being the leader of the thirteen surviving native born people of this demented world, the Nats of Banshee. Most sane women aborted rather then giving birth to a Banshee freak. Of course women and sanity were both rare in the mines. For reasons incomprehensible to most, some women took their pregnancies to term. The results rarely survived more than a year.

As he turned the final corridor to his sleep cubicle, Kyla Watanabee, his cousin and the only other Nat who was not outwardly a freak of nature, interrupted his bleak thoughts. "Alex we have to speak," she said with a frown.

"Sure Kyla, what's fresh?" Kyla hesitated, the way she always did when something serious was on her mind. Kyla was the most important person in Alex's life. Thrown together for the first time in the company of their mad grandmother they had felt a mutual need from their first moments together. As children sometimes will, they instinctively recognized their shared reality; sanity in a sanitarium for the criminally insane.

Alex had spent most of his life trying to protect Kyla from the harsher realities of the mines with limited success, while Kyla tried to keep him from being callused by the soul eating environment, probably with even less success. For all the travails of their youth, somehow she remained cheerful and supportive, both to Alex and to many of the mines other inhabitants. She had an incredible capacity to overlook peoples' faults and find even the smallest grain of goodness in the most depraved of men. Kyla was universally liked by the saner population of the mines, and the fantasy object of most of the peds. She went to great pains to cover her natural beauty, wearing oversized pressure suits, not wearing the limited make-up available, and clasping her auburn hair back in a severe bun. It didn't work, she was still the most desirable woman on Banshee.

She spoke hesitantly, "I think I'm in trouble. The Slashers cornered me down in medical, they were making pretty insistent noises about initiating me. Thank heaven Blossom wasn't there."

The thin pink scar bisecting the entire left side of Alex's face flared red. In a barely controlled rage he uttered, "It's about time I dealt with Violet Blossom and the Slashers. Where are they now?"

Kyla surprised and scared by his response begged, "Please Alex don't do anything rash. I can deal with it for now. The only reason I told you was I thought you would hear about it from someone else." In an ingratiating voice she continued, "You know how people exaggerate these kinds of encounters."

Alex still furious responded, "You can't exaggerate about the Slashers, they're the worst collection of perverts and homicidal maniacs in the mines, and that monster Violet Blossom makes the rest of them look like tame cockroaches. You know I've been working the angles on Blossom and his boys. He wouldn't have hit on you if he wasn't planning to make a move on all the Nats."

Kyla pleaded, "Alex, please, we have plans. We don't want to ruin them just to deal with the Slashers. They're big trouble."

Alex with gritted teeth responded, "Where are Blossom and his boys now?"

In a furtive whisper she replied, "Please don't do anything hasty Alex. Let's just keep working on our plan to escape."

"Not enough time, we deal with the Slashers now or they pick us off one at a time," Alex replied.

She hesitated before answering, "They're in Leadhead's."

"Go get Tona and Mercury and meet me at the D corridor compressor at 0200 hours." Kyla knew better then to argue with Alex when his facial scar turned blood red.

Alex enraged walked quickly to his standard 2x2 meter cubicle and entered to the chirped greeting of Mamba. The flying Himalayan mini-chameleon flapped from the blanket covered stone slab bunk to his shoulder. She coiled her tail around his arm and tucked her head into his shirt pocket, looking for treats. She gobbled the soy protein saved from dinner, as she slowly changed to the steel gray color of his tunic. Her small frame became nearly invisible as the colors matched perfectly. Mamba swirled around his upper torso, her instincts directing her to find more food before her upcoming hibernation phase. Reconciled to the fact that nothing else was available, she returned to her perch on his shoulder to nap.

Alex smiled at the antics of his symbiot and then laughed out loud. Mamba could always lighten his mood. What a life, eat and sleep, and if there isn't any food, sleep some more. All that rest saved up so the minicham could generate one lightning strike with her poison barbed tail, protecting herself and her master.

As he stroked her frill to the gentle rhythm of her chirps, he recalled his first encounter with Mamba, a scared, starving eleven years old, scampering for food in an abandoned shipping module.

He remembered his wonder at seeing the first animal other than the rats and cockroaches of the mines, curled up beneath a buckled side wall. Curiosity overcame his natural caution, so he crawled underneath the corroded metal plate and picked up the tiny unmoving creature. As he stroked the soft scales the minicham had snapped awake, burying its tiny teeth in his finger and licking the welling blood. He had fallen over backwards in surprise, banging his head against a protruding edge.

He'd regained consciousness to find the Minister leering down at him. The excommunicated disciple of the Church of Purity, and the terror of Alex's youth, was holding him by his torn tunic. He recalled small details of that scene as if it were yesterday. The twisted smile on the pockmarked face, three gray hairs growing out of the large mole on his left cheek, individual strands of long greasy straw colored hair hanging across the bulging brow. The blue handled butcher knife with Hasaki 22 inscribed along the blade.

The words the Minister had shouted still gave him chills. "Another Banshee abomination expunged my Lord, let me back into thine grace..., no, no, I must. It is the Lord's will, I must, I must!"

Alex remembered the knife rising and then slashing down towards his throat. He recalled a flying streak striking at the Minister's eyes, the horrible howl of agony as the Minister grabbed his face and staggered around the confined space of the module. The demented mass murderer finally toppled over, stone dead.

Mamba nipped his palm and licked the blood clean, breaking Alex from his dark reverie. Alex worried about his wide mood swings. Recently they had become more pronounced. Banshee was going to kill him yet if he didn't control them better. He shrugged and gently tucked Mamba away in his unzipped pocket while subvocalizing, "Get ready girl, we've got a job to do." This was not the time to dwell on his failings.

Alex then worked his way underneath the steel desk imbedded in the rough granite rock surface. It was getting harder to squeeze under lately. He was getting big, almost 85 kilos now. It was a lot of weight for the mines. Heavy people died quickly in the 1.4 G gravity. His increasing bulk hadn't slowed him down yet.

Releasing a small clamp in the rock surface he opened a hidden flap and withdrew a cloth bundle, containing an illegal, homemade laser pistol, a vibroblade, and six crystal throwing stars. He hid them in the numerous pockets of his pressure suit. He turned, cycled the entrance and headed quickly for D corridor. Those he passed on the way moved aside. You didn't last long on Banshee unless you recognized trouble when you saw it, and Alex armed and moving purposefully was big trouble.

Chapter 2

Twenty minutes later, Kyla, Tona, Mercury and Alex met near the compressor, where the sound would prevent any *pickups* from overhearing their conversation. Mercury was the last to arrive. He pulled out a homemade cigar of dubious composition, and asked "Well what's so frakking urgent this time Grub, you going to get us into more trouble?"

Alex whispered, "Keep it down." As he furtively looked around. "We're going to have to warn off the Slashers and Violet Blossom, now! We have to remind all the cons not to screw with Nats, ever!"

The immense Tona undoubtedly the biggest person in the mines, spoke in his incongruously high pitched voice, "What do we do, Kyla?"

Kyla responded "Do what Alex tells you Tona." Tona never did anything without Kyla's permission. Tona had an angelic face on top of an incredible mountain of muscle, with the intelligence of a five year old. He survived in the mines because he was nearly indestructible and Kyla did his thinking for him. Alex barely tolerated Tona. He never had much use for those who couldn't take care of themselves. It reminded him too much of his mother.

The cadaverous Mercury on the other hand was short, barely 160 cm tall and hideously deformed from a fall into a mercury pit. The only member of the Nats who wasn't native born. Mercury was also only the second convict that Alex respected. Merc's incredible reflexes and his pre-Banshee military training easily compensated for his lack of size in the brutal world of the mines.

Merc had become Alex's mentor after Alex risked his life extracting him from the mercury pit. Their relationship was always strained. Merc wasn't sure he had wanted to be rescued and Alex wasn't happy longing for the inaccessible universe described by the ex-CombatJack and TripleNull master. However, Alex was an excellent student of this martial art and with his Banshee musculature, his Cilvee pilot reflexes and a controlled rage in combat, he was the most dangerous of the four, even without Mamba.

As Alex surreptitiously handed Kyla the laser pistol, he explained his simple plan. "Kyla cover the main entrance. Merc watch the back entrance and the bartenders. Tona, don't let anybody near Kyla. Let me deal with Blossom and the rest of the Slashers."

Merc sarcastically replied, "Great plan Alex. Step aside General Deip, the most brilliant strategic mind in known space is vacationing in the salubrious environs of Banshee. The Slashers must be terrified of the cunning..."

Alex cut him off, "Let's go."

Tona finally understanding Alex's instructions exploded, "Nobody hurt Kyla, nobody!"

Kyla pointed to the overhead lights and gently said, "Shhh Tona. *Pickups*."

They crossed the tunnel, shoulder to shoulder, Merc expounding sarcastically all the way about the brilliance of Alex's strategy. Beneath the derision there was an edge of worry. Finally Merc stopped them and emphatically whispered to Alex, "This isn't the extent of your plan, Grub!" He always called Alex grub whenever he was worried. "This isn't the Cutters or the Doomslayers, these are the Slashers and Violet Blossom! Your rep and the minicham won't do it here!"

Alex replied, "Violet and I have been on a collision course for months now. You know me Merc, I don't take chances. I've thought this out." Turning to Kyla he continued, "Besides, we don't have a choice."

His voice rising, Merc said "Grub, let's get some of the other Nats and Marco in on this, its crazy going into Leadhead's with just the four of us. We need more muscle."

Kyla vehemently agreed.

Alex snapped back in a whisper, "Keep it down." Then looking at the overhead lights he added, "Anybody who wants out can leave. I covered all the angles, and this is our least risky play. You're going to have to trust my judgment on this one."

After a pause, Merc said, "Let's go."

As they continued down the tunnel, Alex's curiosity got the better of him, "Merc, why when push comes to shove do you follow my lead? You don't owe me anything and you're better qualified to lead then I am?"

A quirky smile appeared on Merc's face as he replied, "Charisma Alex, the power to command loyalty from people, even those who don't like you. I'm here because I don't have it, you do."

Alex almost asked Merc the one question you don't ask in the mines; why he'd been sentenced to Banshee. Alex didn't ask, respecting his mentor's right to privacy.

When they arrived, Kyla cycled the big lock to Leadhead's while Alex and Merc smoothly moved to the sides of the entrance, their movements matching those of a professional combat troop. They had more than enough fighting experience to qualify, enhanced by Mercury's professional training. Even Tona took his standard position behind Kyla without comment. Alex observed the smooth inter-play of the others with satisfaction. Since they had become a team four years ago, they had handled every threat the mines threw at them with deadly grace. Now the convicts treated Nats with a respect second only to the Slashers.

They entered the loud smoke filled lounge. Peds crowded the long metallic bar across the back of the room. At an isolated corner table, a dozen Slashers in their dripping knife emblazoned tunics lounged with the corpulent form of Violet Blossom presiding in his armored wheelchair. A couple of corporate weasels, the universally despised convicts who received better perks by spying for the corps, sat strategically at an adjacent table. The noise subsided as people slowly drifted away from the long anticipated confrontation.

Blossom's voice carried across the room, "My companions, look yonder, the delicious Kyla enters. No doubt she has come to express her desire to join our *August Body*." The mounds of fat shook as Blossom chuckled. Even some of the Slashers blanched at the demented joke. It was no secret that Blossom was a convicted cannibal.

Violet had been a corporate executive until his hideous crimes were discovered. The most feared man in the mines, his enemies had a mysterious way of disappearing. The speculation was that they ended up in his stomach. He was also rumored to still have connections in the corporation supplying him with the contraband he dispensed to his allies like some medieval lord.

With two throwing stars tucked away in his left palm and his crystal ring adjusted for maximum damage if he threw a punch, Alex drifted over to the Slashers, all his senses on alert. Time seemed to slow down at moments like this.

As he neared the table, Alex spoke softly to Blossom, "Hey chuckles, they're looking for something big enough to plug a geyser downside. Why don't you do something useful with yourself and volunteer?"

The Slashers rose as a group exposing a wide array of edged and clubbed weapons. Alex noticed the Weasels shifting position to avoid the anticipated violence. Blossom adjusted his wheelchair so the right arm faced Alex and chuckled, "Come gentleman, Mister Kane was just making a little joke, nothing to become excited about."

Alex moved to his right placing one of the Slashers between him and the hidden right arm slug gun. Slipping his right hand into his unzipped pocket, Alex yelled the command, "Coil hold," as he hurled Mamba at Blossom. The minicham wrapped herself around Blossom's neck, the barbed tail poised barely a centimeter above his left eye. Blossom froze, knowing well that an agonizing death was only one command away, and startled by the attack on his home turf.

The strike occurred so quickly the Slashers had no time to react. Calmly Alex pulled up one of the abandoned chairs and sat down surrounded by the stunned gang.

Alex spoke mockingly in corporate doublespeak "Well Blossom I have a business matter to discuss with you concerning one of *my* associates. It seems you're attempting a hostile takeover. Given the circumstances I might have to initiate a poison pill defense." Almost as if to emphasize the point, Mamba began hissing in a barely audible tone, laced with menace.

Blossom the port stain on his face darkened to the shade of his name, replied in a hoarse whisper, "You and that bitch will beg for death before I get through with you!" His voice rising into an insane howl, "Get this frakking thing off me, now!" All pretense of civilization was gone.

Alex leaned across the table deliberately placing himself in the path of the hidden slug gun. Staring unwaveringly into the unnerving violet blotched face barely centimeters away; he whispered, "Lankar, Freeport post office box 567-187." Alex then raised his hand and removed the still hissing mini-chameleon, placing her on his shoulder facing the rest of the Slashers. Leaning back he watched as the color slowly drained from Blossom's face.

The Slashers growing restive at the lack of response by their leader, began making threatening noises until Blossom waived them away. Finally breaking the silence he remarked, "It would seem we do have some mutual interests to discuss."

Alex took that as his cue, rising from the chair he leaned over and whispered again, "You and I have nothing in common chuckles. All you need to keep in mind is, if any harm comes to me and mine, certain documents automatically get routed to your corporate partners." Quickly turning he walked towards the port. The Nats fell in behind him as they cautiously withdrew from the now silent bar. The nonviolent outcome surprised the patrons who had moved away from the upcoming rumble.

Alex took one quick look back before the port cycled shut. The Slashers were milling around uneasily. They had to be wondering why their dreaded leader had backed down before the Nats on his own turf. Blossom was going to have to assert his authority hard to keep control of the Slashers. Worse he would want revenge against those who had undermined his authority. How long would the threat of exposure to his partners keep the Blossom in check?

As they headed down the tunnel towards home territory, Alex thought just another threat in the mines. There would inevitably be a final confrontation with the Slashers. Probabilities and options for dealing with the threat whirred in his mind. He was always looking for the edge. That was the difference between life and death on Banshee, and his ability to figure the angles placed him near the top of the heap. His lips nearly twitched into a smile with the thought. Top of a heap all right, a heap of shit.

The rest of his team surreptitiously glanced his way as they headed into safer corridors. Finally Mercury spoke, "Alex are you going to explain to us what happened back there."

Alex replied, "Later"

Kyla trying to placate the tension between the two most important men in her life spoke calmly, "Why don't we go to Papa Joe's. I think you at least owe Mercury an explanation"

Tona uncomprehending, blurted, "I'm thirsty."

Alex smiled at Tona's total oblivion to the tension in the small group and replied, "Okay, I have to relieve Brandy in 3C for the rest of his shift. Why don't I meet you at Papa Joe's at 1900 hours. Stay together and tell the rest of the Nats to be on their toes."

Merc answered, "OK, but don't be late Grub."

They split up moments later, Alex heading for the main up-shaft lift station, while the rest headed for Papa Joe's.

Merc put his arm around Kyla as they watched Alex walk away, "Sometimes I think I've helped create a monster. That boy doesn't understand his own abilities, or limitations."

Kyla looked into the scarred visage and spoke softly "Mercury you know I love you, but Alex is the only family I have. He and I have taken care of each other for as long as I can remember. So please try to get along."

"Maybe I envy that cousin of yours. I envy him your affections and I envy his abilities and self confidence. Any other place but Banshee and he would go far." Merc looked down, "Kyla it hurts to know you went to him with your problems first. It hurts even more to know you were probably right. I couldn't protect you from the likes of Blossom. I once thought I was a tough man but the brutality of this place overwhelms me."

"That's why I love you Merc, you still feel, you still care about people. Don't you ever get as tough and ruthless as Alex. He's Banshee born, Banshee tough. He had to be tough enough for the both of us." She looked down as her voice dropped, "I never did hold up my part. He isn't a monster Mercury, he loves me and Mamba and he feels a great deal of responsibility for all the Nats, even you." They turned and headed to Papa Joe's, a beautiful young woman and the lithe horribly scarred ex-CombatJack.

Chapter 3

Alex entered uplift 12 heading for level B. He hated the slow ride up the shaft in the exposed cage only slightly less then the downward trip. The endless passage of the fused black basaltic rock reminded him of the billions of tons of earth between him and the surface he had never seen. He understood Mercury's claustrophobic episodes more than he would care to admit.

The eyes of the others in the uplift seemed glued to the solid floor of the cage. No one spoke. Alex thought, if it was hard on him it must be worse for those who had spent most of their lives in open spaces.

The cage finally arrived at B level, the highest point in the mines a convict could go, only six kilometers from the surface. Alex followed the peds and a few techs out into the arena, the largest open space in the mines. Everyone looked up at the hardened Duraplast galleries on A level overlooking the arena. The mine guards spent their three month tours of duty almost exclusively on A level.

Even more fascinating to the cons, was the great central shaft with its massive double locks. It was almost a ritual to look at those two tenuous contacts to the inhospitable surface when one arrived at B level. Everyone perked up at the proximity to the surface. Alex heard snatches of conversation as he worked his way to the 3C.

"You can't survive out there without the heavy armor, the pressure and heat would kill..."

"...Empire mercs are getting the tar beat out of them up there, by the new CombatDroids the GenClones are..."

"...Hope the GenClones do. I'll have a better chance of getting topside."

"I hear the Slashers and those Banshee freeborn freaks are going at it. The Blossom will..."

The innumerable infantile plans for escape by the cons amused Alex. The latest rumor that the GenClones of the Genetic Purity League might free them, for being enemies of the Coalition was one of the most idiotic. Mercury had fought the GenClones. He had outlined to Alex in graphic detail, the brutal way the GPL dealt with hard core criminals. GenClones believed they were the apex of human evolution and euphemistically talked about expunging the genetically inferior. Banshee miners would be right at the bottom of the GenClone genetic scale. Besides evacuating even a small percentage of the miners was impossible. Not when everyone would need a one ton environmental suit to survive the twenty bar pressure and 120 degrees centigrade temperatures on the surface. Not when the only exit topside was through a five meter wide shaft armed with remote sensors and weapons pods along its six kilometer length.

No, Matsui Mining and Manufacturing Inc. had thought of almost everything to insure no convict ever escaped, and no one had ever escaped, yet!

Alex arrived at the 3C keyed in his code and showed his ID to the Weasel guard. The surly guard carefully examined it before remarking, "You're not scheduled to be up here."

Alex ignored the guard and the overhead cameras and walked into the control room. Even a Weasel had to be careful dealing with a provisional 3C rated tech. Another month logged in and he would receive his tech 2 rating, entitling him to additional vouchers and perks. He would miss his *Termite* once he got a new billet, but he would be that much closer to working his and Kyla's way off planet.

Alex walked over to Brandy's station and waited to be noticed. Finally the old 3C jock looked up from his terminal array. His eye's focused a few seconds later. Brandy carefully disconnected his CyberLink from the small implant at the base of his skull while saying. "Ah Kane, right on time." Brandy staggered out of his chair, sweat drying on his face as he dropped his CyberLink in his slovenly storage drawer.

Alex ignoring Brandy's manner asked, "What's your status?"

Brandy replied, "Some seismic activity down near the new Q shaft, the repair crew was sent down after some damaged sensors. Ah yes, output from the N shaft L tunnel is declining, Ahem, you may have to determine a better direction to drill. A simple task, I'm sure a novice like you can work it out. Everything else is in the computer logs."

Alex sat in the Command Control and Communications module as he withdrew his own CyberLink from the drawer marked Kane. He began the routine log on procedure while scanning the displays for all the critical information Brandy hadn't passed on. The turnovers were getting progressively worse. He immediately addressed a number of small errors and then checked the situation in Q shaft. Finally he spoke, "Okay I'm logged on, you are now formally relieved."

Alex attached the CyberLink Relay to the neural tap at the base of his skull and initiated the link sequence, when he noticed Brandy hadn't left. "Well?"

"Kane, ah, I was wondering if you could advance me my ten percent early this month?"

Alex paused and stared back fixedly. Finally he replied tersely, "No."

Brandy in feigned outrage snapped back, "Why you ungrateful whelp, after all the time I took to train you, to teach you the intricacies of the 3C, this is how you repay me. I ought to withdraw your access rights."

Laconically Alex replied, "Your call."

Brandy licked the moisture off his upper lip, then turned and left dejectedly. They both knew that without Alex's relief, Brandy's inadequacies would have been discovered long ago. Alex didn't really have to pay for the extra log on time in the 3C module anymore. Without Alex, Brandy would have already lost his tech license, and the vouchers to feed his Dreamweed addiction, but Alex had struck a deal with Brandy two years ago, and he never defaulted. It was one of the ways he reminded himself that he was not a con but a freeborn man. He had developed his own rigid ethical code to distance himself from the convicts. A code most people would have found brutal and difficult to understand.

Alex continued his CyberLink start up sequence. The female computer generated voice requested his authorization and password.

He mentally responded in the CyberLinked reality "Kane, Alex, ID code 362472lEX, password Beau Geste."

The computers inanimate voice replied, "Think of a mist of water flowing from a fresher onto your face." After a moment of severe disorientation the disembodied voice replied, "Sequence complete" and the virtual world of cyberspace exploded into Alex's mind. Alex was one of those rare and valuable individuals that could handle the information overload of a full spectrum CyberLink.

After quickly reviewing the situation he began relaying the series of orders required to keep the section of the mine that was his responsibility operational. He adjusted the output of compressors and refrigeration units to maintain the habitable portions of Q shaft. He would have to watch it the rest of the shift to bring it back to acceptable parameters without over stressing the equipment. Brandy wasn't even doing the routine work well any more. So he conducted a complete diagnostic of all the remote sensors and found two subsystems off line. The next two hours kept him busy correcting that, and dealing with myriad other details.

Finally he addressed the issue of the N shaft L tunnel ore strike. He reviewed the geological data on what had started out as a promising source of laser crystals. He hologramed the region, imaging known pockets of crystal in red stars on his 3D display. It became ridiculously easy to determine why the strike was failing. Alex never could understand why the 24 other 3C operators claimed it was difficult to operate a 3C and particularly difficult to locate crystal. All you really had to do was look at the virtual time 3D dispersal pattern and correlate it versus conventional ore configurations.

With time remaining in the shift Alex decided to risk hacking into some of the corp computer systems again. With infinite patience he carefully wove his way past the sophisticated virtual reality defenses into the computer's security sensor array. He decided to check on the Blossom. The fat toad wasn't in any of the monitored locations. His last sighting was outside his cubicle on B level.

It had been an incredible stroke of luck to catch Blossom's unauthorized transmission, double crossing his corporate partners with one of their competitors. He was apparently feeding information about mine output to the General Robotics conglomerate in exchange for credits in a numbered bank account. Someone in corp communications must be helping him. Blossom must also have an escape plan or the credits wouldn't do him any good. Alex grinned, not that they would do him any good anyway. Alex had intercepted the access code, and sent his own unauthorized transmission, moving one hundred and eighty thousand C-bills to an account in his and Kyla's names.

The account number had temporarily neutralized Blossom and given Alex the funds to buy passage off planet for him and Kyla. Now all he had to do was find a way to the shuttle landing bay 300 meters from the top of the main shaft during a scheduled landing.

Wandering through the virtual reality world of the main security computer, he accessed the surface sensors scanning the closed shuttle bay doors and the fort. Alex was always fascinated by these remote visions of the surface. Matsui security, the Empire CombatJacks and the flight control personnel spent their three month tours of duty in the massive reinforced Duracrete fortress. Even the double indemnity pay and the luxurious appointments of the fort couldn't get anybody to stay longer than that on Banshee voluntarily.

A bay door in the fort slowly opened and a mixed company of CombatDroids marched out. CombatDroids were the ultimate extension of the CyberLinked vehicle, man's latest and deadliest killing machines. Operated by virtually linked CombatJacks, the 24 to 72 ton bipedal machines were powered by inexhaustible Warm Fusion Batteries, WFB, and equipped with electromagnetic deflection, EMD, shields and composite collapsed carbon armor, more commonly called cubed armor. Combined with multiple phased array lasers, particle cannons and missile carrying weapons pods, CombatDroids were nearly indestructible and unstoppable. They had displaced aircraft and even StarFighters as the dominant weapons of land based warfare. The invention of high powered phased array lasers and improved line of sight targeting systems had recently shifted the advantage to ground based weapons systems. StarFighters once the dominant weapon were now just flying target practice for a modern CombatDroid unless the pilot was very skilled.

Covered with a dark matte protective coatings, the Empire Droids blended into the background in the weak red light. The backdrop of massive flat slabs of granite dwarfed even the giant CombatDroids. The limited light that filtered through the clouds of concentrated sulfuric acid and the haze of corrosive dust rising with every stride, draped them in vague wraith like shadows.

The 24 and 32 ton *Nimrods* and *Strikers* were the most effective of the Empire CombatDroids on Banshee. Very fast and equipped with Scoop/RamJet thrusters, they could avoid CLV killing earthquakes, and maneuver easily across the fractured polar surface. They did not have the punch of the GenClone SuperDroids, but compensated by launching lightning strikes from ambush and withdrawing before the GenClone Jacks could react. They let Banshee itself do most of the killing for them. Even small breeches in armor, or radiator ruptures could destroy a CLV in the corrosive atmosphere and the heat of the surface.

Alex had accessed combat reports indicating that three out of four GenClone Droids destroyed were the result of equipment failures rather then combat. The secret of Droid survival on Banshee was to avoid even minor damage. Recent reports indicated the GenClones were learning this lesson. They had modified one of their highly advanced SuperDroids into a new fast maneuverable variant with advanced electronics, capable of turning the tables on attempted ambushes. Empire forces had designated it the *Warlock* because of the magical way it appeared and disappeared.

Heavier units began to exit the fort heading towards quadrant four. Curious, Alex switched to the remote security sensors in that sector, and was surprised to find all the monitors off-line, someone must have switched them off. Treason? He switched to the delicate seismic monitors. There were no earth tremors. However the sensors were recording very low level vibrations. At first Alex was baffled, then he thought, those must be combat vehicles, big ones and lots of them. They were heading for the fort.

Alex was concerned, their plans were ruined if the GenClones took the fort. He began to switch between remote sensors hoping to evaluate the upcoming fight. His concern decreased as he determined the GenClones couldn't take the Empire forces. In fact their attack didn't make sense. Then in sector five a strangely armed tracked vehicle appeared. The massive machine had two tubes and two downward facing phased array lasers installed on arm mounts, instead of more conventional missile launchers.

The tank entered a small depression. Alex panned the remote camera around, and watched as it stopped and fired both giant phased array lasers strait down. A billowing plume of dust rose slowly into the air. This doesn't make any military sense. What were the GenClones up to?

After a few minutes the lasers stopped firing and two giant torpedoes were lowered into the newly drilled holes. Alex snapped up in his chair almost losing his Link. Those were massive demolition torpedoes. He started running a program to determine the effects of such an explosion on the mine. The results were shocking. The charges were above the tectonically active main polar fault line directly above the new un-reinforced Q shaft. A properly sized explosion could set off a series of quakes, completely destroying the mine and the fort.

The GenClones did not want to capture Banshee, they wanted to cripple the Empire's laser manufacturing facilities! Alex watched a moment longer as the vehicle hurriedly departed the scene. Frantically trying to determine a course of action, he began issuing a sequence of illegal commands. First, ordering the Nats mining equipment prepared and sent to the L tunnel CLV bays. A series of other orders followed. Cold-bloodedly he rejected notifying the corporate authorities. Once those charges went off nothing could save the miners.

Alex quickly and regretfully shut down his station. He would miss the high of cyberspace. Then he draped his outer tunic over his arm and tucked the state of the art CyberLink headset beneath it. He removed a fuse from underneath the console and headed for the exit.

The ugly weasel stepped in front of him and asked, "Where the frakke do you think your cruis'in, your shift ain't done yet Techy?"

Holding up the fuse Alex answered, "Blown fuse, orders were to take it down personally."

The surly guard grunted, "I never heard of them leaving a station unmanned."

Alex with growing anxiety at the delay replied curtly, "Check with security."

The guard accessed his terminal then turned with a puzzled expression on his face. "Strange, yo'se got clearance."

Alex calmly slotted his ID into the port and walked out of the 3C. Once out of sight of the glaring guard, he picked up his pace. He pushed his way through a milling crowd in front of a stopped elevator. He authoritatively snapped, "This shaft has a malfunction clear out while maintenance runs a diagnostic." Fortunately no one asked for his authorization as he stepped into the cage. Quickly he overrode the security lock he had just placed on the elevator then shorted the regulator. The elevator began plummeting down into the bowels of the earth. He hit the terminal velocity of 145 kph in 22 seconds. He estimated emergency brake activation in 1:55 minutes. He hoped they worked.

Whispering "...52,53,54,1:55" He pulled the red emergency stop switch and crashed to the ground. The G force, the showers of sparks, and the ear bursting shriek of tortured metal momentarily stunned him. The sturdy guide rails twisted like taffy as the cage bounced from one side of the shaft to the other. The cage shot by a half dozen L level tunnels before it slowed.

Alex unsteadily stood up in the madly careening cage and watched as the supporting cable fraying under the tremendous stress. He forced open the twisted metal door with his Banshee developed strength, and waited for the next tunnel. Timing it perfectly he hurled himself through the opening onto the last landing, hip rolling onto the tunnel floor. Moments later a section of cable snapped back up the elevator shaft and the screeching metal sound stopped. The cage had finally broken free of its restraints.

Brushing himself off he walked past some gawking bystanders, with the off hand comment about the notoriously slow elevators, "Those elevators really are getting too fast." Mamba peeked out of his pocket, and yawned. Alex happy to be alive spoke to his minicham, "Sorry if I disturbed your nap Chirps but we got problems." The minicham stretched and began watching its surroundings intently.

Arriving at the CR, he interrupted a struggle between a half dozen Nats and some guards. Merc swore, "Put your hands on her again and lose it Weasel."

Alex shouted, "Chill!" And surreptitiously hand signaled the Nats "Danger." Turning to the agitated guards he explained, "This team has been selected for a priority one mission." Then facing McDuff, "Is the equipment ready?"

The short bull headed head Weasel shoved his face into Alex's and said, "I never heard of a priority one and who the hell are you anyway?"

Alex, after scanning the group replied authoritatively, "Check your orders, and where the hell are the rest of the peds you were ordered to fetch?"

Alex snapped commands at the Nats while the guard checked his orders. He suddenly became very cooperative. "Sorry, ah, I didn't know what a priority one meant." He mumbled "You think they'd warn you about frakke like this."

Alex ordered the guards to find the rest of the Nats; Bilbo and Mildew the deformed twins were missing as was Crazy Eddy.

As the guards left two muffled explosions shook the CR. The Nats cycled the inner lock and entered the decontamination lock. Alex came last.

As he stepped in McDuff asked with a frown "What's going on laddie and what were those explo'sins? My ol' mam never raised no foolish sons, you're up to somethin', com'on Alex you can tell old Duffy."

Alex hesitated. There was no love lost between him and McDuff but they did go back a long way. Finally he said, "Get your boys into armor and head for the quad 4, K tunnel connector." He then sealed the inner lock and adjusted his pressure suit as the port slowly closed. He had given Duffy a chance if he moved fast. He shrugged, it wasn't his problem, as he turned and looked at the six expectant faces, he had his own responsibilities.

As the group left the CR heading for the CLV bays, Alex outlined the situation. Hella and Lulany the giant inseparable cousins, began their incessant chattering as soon as he finished. The only time they ever shut up was in a fight or in their mining suits. Their fighting skills and the vouchers they brought in as top rated mining peds made them valuable members of the Nats. Alex generally avoided them outside of business because he couldn't stand their sleazy humor and constant sexual innuendoes. His grandmother had instilled much of her prudery in him. Curiously the twins earthy vocabulary never seemed to bother Kyla, but then Kyla got along with nearly everyone. The others ignored the cousins incessant chatter.

At the bays, Kyla and Merc crammed into Merc's *Termite* cockpit. The cousins and Tona climbed into their armored pressure suits and the forever silent Marko mounted his eight ton *Carver* drilling rig. Marko was born without ears or a real mouth. Mercury said his head resembled a bowling ball whatever that was, with three small symmetrical holes for breathing and eating in the smooth lead colored hairless head. For all the other peculiarities of his face, it was Marko's flame red slope sided eyes that gave even the hardened cons of Banshee the chills. Marko had survived into adulthood because his appearance was so disconcerting people avoided him. Alex had seen people ignore Marko even in the heat of a fight simply because they couldn't bear looking at his alien face. Alex liked Marko more then most and rarely gave his bizarre appearance a second thought.

They were equipped and heading across the cavern when the first big tremor hit. The far end of the cavern split open like a ripe melon, and molten rock burst through the newly formed crevice. It hit the mercury in the central pit sending a superheated silver cloud billowing towards the madly fleeing Nat's.

Alex ordered the suits into the K tunnel connector. The peds went first followed by Marko in his *Carver* then Mercury's *Termite*. Alex reached the tunnel entrance last and yelled on their private frequency, "Move it, I'll block the entrance!" He fired his anchoring pitons into the cavern walls and hunkered the *Termite* down as the pressure and heat wave hit the tunnel and him. The piton cables held the sturdy *Termite* in place like a giant metal spider in its web. The brunt of the storm dissipated its energies against the CLV before entering the tunnel.

Alex took one last look back into the cavern upon a scene of utter destruction. The heavy duty Duraplast of the CR had dissolved under the intense heat and corrosive atmosphere. The lava was already buckling the vehicle bay doors. Alex thought poor McDuff never had a chance. The Nat's chances weren't much better. Alex hastily released his cables and chased up the passage way after the wavering lights of the others. Molten rock splattered at the CLV's retreating steps.

The armored group slowly made headway up the crumbling tunnel, staying just ahead of the rising lava. The temperature in the cave rose steadily to 135 degrees centigrade, exceeding the safe operating limits for a mining suit. The radiator in Tona's old battered suit began to fail. No matter how many times Alex and Kyla had tried to impress upon him the importance of proper maintenance Tona never took good care of his suit and it was costing him now. With his childish voice he wailed "Kyla, Kyla its hot, Kyla hot, hot."

Kyla, fear in her voice responded, "Tona don't panic, keep drinking water from your bottle, and shutdown, Mercury and I will pick you up, and hook you up to our coolant system."

Tona plaintively, "The water it's hot Kyla, it's hot."

Alex in horror snapped, "No, Tona don't drink the water, shutdown all your systems except life support, we will pick you up. Switching to a private channel, "Merc pass him by, I'll take care of him, your coolant systems are already overworked with the two of you. And Kyla stay off line, your voice will just confuse him."

Kyla in a panic replied, "Alex he's hurting, I can..."

Angrily Alex replied "I said stay off line, we have enough problems without arguing over everything." The channel went dead. He reached Tona's collapsed suit and tapped in to his readouts. He hesitantly turned the suit over and looked into the face plate, to his horror Tona was still alive. The still wriggling man-child was slowly being steamed alive in his own fluids. There was nothing anyone could do to help. Deliberately he aligned the 1 cm laser with the face plate and fired. Then he picked up the armored suit and continued on his way his face impassive.

Kyla desperately shouted, "Tona, Tona can you hear me,... Alex what's his status."

Alex trying to remain calm replied, "He's unconscious. I said I would take care of it, now please stay off line. Alex out." As he switched off the channel he whispered "I'm sorry Kyla, I'm sorry."

Two hours later the arduously slow climb finally ended at K level. The main cavern in K bay was also abandoned, only scattered dead and some equipment remained. Parts of the ceiling had collapsed and a molten lava pool was slowly spreading across the chamber. The group skirted the lava and headed for the main elevator shaft. Hella proclaimed, "If we get out of this I will never put on a suit again, I think I'll start servicing the men. Some of them aren't half bad, ah!" She tripped and started sliding into the lava in mid-sentence.

Alex dropped Tona's suit and deftly scooped up Hella. Unfortunately Lulany also reached out to rescue her cousin, and stumbled in fatigue, taking a nose dive into the lava pit. Molten rock splattered the survivors. Hella's screams reverberated through their private channel as they all watched the receding ripples in horror. Hella struggled to escape the grasp of the *Termite*, screaming "Let me go, let me go, Lulany hold on, I'm coming."

Sobbing Kyla kept trying to comfort the frantic surviving cousin, "Hella calm down please calm down. She's gone Hel, she's gone and there's nothing we can do."

Alex was stunned for a moment, the fatigue of the long day and his feelings of inadequacy combining to wear him down, until his usually sublimated anger at the inequities of his universe burst forth, renewing his resolve to go on. He interrupted the others callously, "Enough, lets go!"

Out of habit and fatigue they obeyed his orders, until Kyla noticed Tona's abandoned suit. "Alex, you're forgetting Tona."

Unemotionally he replied, "He's dead, he's been dead for hours; keep moving." And in a lower tone, "Just keep moving." There was no response.

Reaching the still secured emergency elevator shaft from K level to A level, Alex began setting a huge plastique demolition charge at the armored entrance. After checking the charge pattern carefully, he joined the others behind some fallen debris. The explosion rocked the chamber. With a feeling of déjà vu, Alex led the others through the dust cloud to the small newly formed opening in the shaft. The emergency exit shaft on K level was the only one that went directly to A level, and the only one with steps spiraling up its sides. Fortunately the steps were just wide enough for a CLV, and were still in relatively good condition despite the continuing tremors. The team made good progress.

Arriving at A level, they heard the sounds of combat down some of the tunnels. Apparently the few surviving cons had gotten a hold of some weapons, and were trading fire with trapped corp security. Alex led the remaining Nats in a circuitous route avoiding the fighting while heading for the far end of A level. Another major tremor hit the mines. Charging past the falling rock they arrived at a great crack in the earth.

Alex, with a wolfish grin on his face yelled on their private frequency, "I was right, the quake has created a crevasse leading from this portion of A level all the way to the surface along the North Polar fault line. We have a chance." He hoped his statement was true. Hella in anticipation ran into the bottomless crevice only to be knocked off her feet by another giant tremor. The ground split open beneath her and she tumbled to her death thousands of meters below with a shouted, "Oh frakke, I always screw up, what a bitching way to ..." Silence. Only the three CLV's remained.

Alex heard Kyla sobbing before her comlink switched off. Without comment the troop advanced across the newly opened fault using pitons and thrusters. Clinging to the steep sides of the fault with gripping limbs, their headlights marking the way, they began the seemingly endless climb up the tortured surface. Tired beyond feeling, beyond anger, trapped in a nightmare of death and hopelessness, they continued the unsteady climb to an uncertain future.

Marco's *Carver* lost its grip during one of the innumerable tremors and tumbled to its doom. Marco went to his death as silently as he had lived. Alex was the only person who knew that Marco was capable of speech. He had deferred to his mutated friend's request to never reveal his secret. A great sadness flowed into Alex as he contemplated the inability of the intelligent but deformed Nat to communicate with an uncaring universe. The thought was soon forgotten in the nearly unendurable fatigue.

Mercury began making incoherent sounds as the heat and the concentration required to keep his overworked CLV moving took its toll. Drenched in sweat, Alex kept exhorting Merc on, while wishing he had Kyla in his own *Termite*. There was no chance for rescue if either of the CLV pilots failed, and Kyla couldn't possibly operate the *Termite*. He now wished he had shown her how. He stayed closer to the other CLV than was safe, believing he might be able to intercede in some way if Merc took a fatal misstep.

Kyla gasped in a resigned whisper, as she came on line, "Alex if Merc and I don't make it you have to go on alone."

"No, no, we're all going to make it, Merc watch your step!" Alex shouted as the other *Termite* began to slip. Alex frantically hurled his *Termite* sideways and reached out a secondary limb to stabilize Merc. For a moment the two CLV's tottered over the seemingly bottomless pit, then Alex fired his last working piton and reeled them both in. Desperately afraid of the danger to Kyla and nearly panicked, he started swearing at Mercury at the top of his hoarse voice. Kyla finally managed to calm Alex down, and get Merc moving. A little later, Kyla came on line again, "Alex, listen to me, if we don't make it you have to promise me, you will go on, you will be a testament to all the Nats."

Alex replied resignedly, "Its okay Kyla we're getting out together and that's final" They argued back and forth in intermittent bursts, whenever they had the energy. Finally Alex relented, worried that even the energy of the conversation would critically fatigue Kyla. He had never broken a promise he made to his cousin but he had no intention of leaving her behind.

Alex noticed a shadowed feature to the left of his head-lights. It dawned on him slowly that an external source of light caused the shadow. Increasing the magnification of his cyberscreen and narrowing the focus down to 120 degrees looking straight up, he saw a dull red crack. Hoarsely, he shouted, "The surface Kyla, Merc the surface, look up ahead!"

With renewed hope they carefully worked their way out of the crevice, their way lit by the cloud shrouded setting sun. Kyla whispered in wonder, "It's so beautiful, its so big." Incongruously she giggled then started crying, "I never really believed there was a surface, deep down I thought the rock went on forever."

Alex felt the same wonder as he pulled up besides the other *Termite*. Looking over into the adjacent cockpit his wonder turned to concern. Even through the splattered Duraplast he noticed Merc's condition was bad, Kyla was holding up better. He spotted the fort, most of it already destroyed by the man-made quake. "Merc let's get to the fort. Merc move it! Kyla get him moving."

A mumbled response, and the other *Termite* unsteadily began moving, like a bug on too much Dreamweed. Alex followed, thinking time was running short, both the Droids and their riders were operating well beyond their limits. Working their way slowly around the fort they finally arrived at a relatively undamaged bay door.

Suddenly a *Warlock* SuperDroid appeared from the other side of the damaged fort, its hunched over shape dwarfing the oncoming *Termites*. It aimed its center torso NPC and fired a bolt right at the lead *Termite*. Alex screamed "No!" At the top of his lungs, his face a grimace of agony. He watched helplessly as the bolt hit Merc's CLV dead center. Overriding the red lined emergency alarms, Alex fired his thrusters, hurling himself straight at the oncoming *Warlock*, in a blinding rage. The *Warlock* didn't move or fire at the charge. The tiny mining CLV crashed into the *Warlock*'s cockpit depleting the EMD shield with shear inertia and then collapsed to the ground snapping one of its forelimbs. The *Termite*'s emergency override shutdown the old fission core before it exploded. Alex sat helplessly and awaited the *Warlock*'s death blow. The *Warlock* seemed to hesitate for a moment and then toppled forward right next to the mining machine in a shower of blue sparks.

A long while later it dawned on a paralyzed Alex that the enemy pilot was dead. The hasty shot by the SuperDroid's pilot had overheated the *Warlock*'s reactor resulting in an engine shutdown. Both vehicles had tumbled to the earth after the improbable attack of the *Termite*. Incredibly, a small crack he observed in the enemy CLV's face-plate had proved to be the lethal blow.

Alex sat dazed and uncaring in the CLV, slowly cooking in his own juices. Mamba kept rubbing up against his face trying to gain his attention. He ignored her. Alex knew what he would see if he managed to return to Merc's *Termite*. The *Termite*'s heat monitors suddenly flashed yellow. For a moment he hesitated, then slowly and deliberately he reactivated the fission core. Alex managed to disentangle his damaged CLV, from the *Warlock* trailing broken limbs and fiberoptic circuits, sparks flying from his damaged actuators. He hesitantly limped back to the other *Termite*. Ignoring the warning lights flashing on his board, he reached his friends and watched helplessly as the last of a red haze of blood vaporized from the shattered cockpit.

An indeterminate time later, the persistent chirping of Mamba, finally got the attention of the shocked CLV pilot. Alex slowly regained interest in his surroundings, noticing for the first time the persistent alarms and red lights blinking all over his boards, warnings of multiple system failures. He started his CLV moving to the bay door, cycled the huge portal using the stolen command code, and started to enter. He noticed the nearly undamaged *Warlock* at the entrance. He grabbed it with his remaining forelimb and dragged it into the bay as the giant lock slowly closed behind him. He never looked back at the other CLV left on the giant plateau. He knew if he looked back he wouldn't be able to go on. He had never broken a promise to Kyla, and he wasn't going to start now.

Chapter 4

He awoke many hours later. His body complaining of the abuse it had received the previous day. He climbed off the floor and looked out of the small operations room into the darkened bay below, barely seeing the outline of the two crumpled CLV's. He sat back down, placing his face in his hands, as he vividly recalled the events of yesterday. Mamba kept nibbling at his fingers and chirping to gain his attention. Somehow she knew the terrible pain Alex felt, and wanted to help.

Alex cried, "It's just you and me now chirps, just the two of us." Finally he rose, walked over to the only working console and began accessing information on the status of the fort. It didn't look good. The surviving corps and CombatJacks had evacuated the site. Ninety percent of the fort was non-operational. In fact, other than this bay and a secured area at the heart of the massive structure, the fort was dead. Its primary infrastructure was completely destroyed. Only the auxiliary life support and power systems were up, with only enough fuel for a few more days. Alex leaned back in his chair and sardonically laughed. It looked as if he'd escaped from the frying pan into the fire. At least Kyla had seen the surface before...

First things first. He needed to find food and water. He began putting on his pressure suit, when he noticed a major tear in the tough fabric. Checking the emergency lockers, he found all the suits gone. He was in big trouble if he couldn't leave the small habitable area of the fort. Looking out into the bay again, he spotted the *Warlock*. He fetched a laser cutter and headed to the Droid. Quickly he cut out the cracked portion of the Duraplast cockpit. Time was important, the heat in the bay was still at a dangerous level and his suit wasn't much protection. He noted the damage from a laser hit on the cockpit. His successful attack on the CombatDroid had been blind luck. The *Termite* had struck an already weakened spot, causing stress failure. Hoping the pilot's pressure suit wasn't seriously damaged, Alex reached in and released the hatch.

He looked at the desiccated face of the dead pilot with revulsion. The intense heat and pressure of Banshee's atmosphere had vaporized all the moisture from the body, making it barely recognizable as human. Alex noted that the face-plate was up. Stupid, had it been down the pilot might have had a chance to seal the breach caused by the attack. He had heard that some GenClone warriors would rather die then lose a Droid. It looked like this pilot had taken that goal to his death.

The suit was still intact. He dragged it out, unsealed it, and flushed the dried flesh out with green coolant. Returning to the operations room, he began an elaborate clean out and inspection of the suit. It was a marvel of GenClone technology, combining the properties of a cooling vest and a semi-armored pressure suit. He removed the unit insignia and the name tag, J.L. Krushov. He noted the incredible apparatus for collecting and recycling the pilot's waste fluids into potable water. Donning the suit with Mamba in his pocket, he hooked up an air tank, grabbed a lamp and headed through a functioning lock into the bowels of the fort. His search through the shattered facility proved successful. He found stores of still usable air, water, food and spare parts.

During the rest of the day he gathered the supplies into the bay. Some of the food he'd found was remarkable to a man who'd only eaten fortified concentrates and soy protein. He had never seen frozen vegetables or fresh fruit before. His first naranji brought a sigh of pleasure, until he remembered Kyla wasn't there to share this incredible new experience with him.

At the end of the day he broke into a secured area at the heart of the fort using a laser cutter to breach the lock. Inside there was a luxurious apartment and a backup control center. Real animal hides covered the chairs. Disgusting. The carpet was made of natural fibers and the holo prints on the walls were signed by famous artists. He found a richly clad dead woman sitting in an armchair with a small laser hole in her forehead. He recognized her as the mine manager. An opened and plundered safe was behind her desk. The console on the desk was active and logged into the mine manager's account. Out of curiosity he sat down, broke the computer codes and began rifling through her personal files. He'd been right there had been treason. It appeared that some senior Matsui executives, led by a Superintendent Hojo, and Empire government officials had assisted the GenClones. They were smuggling stolen laser crystals to the GenClones, and were planning to make a killing when crystal production was destroyed on Banshee. Alex thought, some of these business men are worse than the most degenerate convicts. Thousands had died for their greed.

He also found evidence that Matsui had been evading Empire taxes. Alex down loaded the information onto a memory disk, as always, looking for an edge.

Inspecting the desk, he found a delicate release mechanism inside a hidden drawer. Alex carefully triggered the device; a hidden Hippola laser pistol popped out of the bottom of the drawer. He tested the superb weapon then replaced his holstered GenClone machine pistol with it. Taking a longer look into the drawer, he discovered a false back. Behind it lay a cache of expensive, gem quality crystals. It seemed the manager was skimming jewels from the mines as well. Alex pocketed the stones. Nothing surprised Alex anymore when it came to human greed. He continued his search of the living quarters. The only other useful items he found were some gourmet foodstuff in a freeze locker. Bagging everything, he headed back to the repair bay.

For the next two days he gathered supplies and tried to figure a way off planet. The simmering anger directed at the world of his birth was back. He decided he wasn't going to let Banshee kill off the last of its native born. He concluded that no one was returning to the North Polar mining complex. There was nothing left to salvage and a great deal of risk involved from the continuing tremors caused by the newly active fault. He did discover in the files that there was one other facility on the planet, an automated research station at the South Pole. The University of Terranova Geologic Department ran the station with financial support from Matsui. The facility was visited approximately every six months for re-supply and data downloading. The next shuttle could be arriving soon. The unanswered question, was how to cross the thirty thousand kilometers from Pole to Pole, across Banshee's lethal equatorial zone. The only option was the *Warlock*, and that was a long shot, but he had promised Kyla and owed Mamba, so he would try.

Alex spent the next few days moving the *Warlock* onto a repair platform and fixing all the superficial damage. His biggest problems were breaking through the security system needed to upload his CyberLink and repairing the damage to the cockpit electronics. He was making progress on the latter except for the communications grid.

The forty ton SuperDroid was remarkable. An ultra light Warm Fusion Battery ran the Droid giving it nearly unlimited power and a maximum speed of 120 kph before engaging the Overdrive Circuitry. The ODC could increase speeds to an unstable 252 kph for short bursts. It also carried a GenClone quality Artificial Limited Intelligence. The ALI had the most advanced electronic jamming, communication and electronic counter-measure programs available. It also processed the data from a sophisticated sensor array and automatically operated the all points defense system. The APDS consisted of twin retractable pindle mounts each with a 10 MM Infrared phased array laser and a 10 MM sliver cannon. It was capable of engaging up to four incoming projectiles simultaneously and had a retarget/recharge rate of 6 seconds. The CombatJack could also use the pindle mounts against infantry. Since the AI revolt of 2320 all artificial intelligences, even the limiteds, were hard wired to self-destruct rather then risk harming a human. This left the Jack to operate the APDS offensively as well as targeting and firing the main weapons. Twin turrets mounted 40MM lasers, two one ton weapons pods mounted in the left and right torso and the powerful 80MM Neutron Pulse Cannon located on the main turret in the center torso gave a wide range of offensive capabilities. Both pods were equipped with cheap but effective direct fire missiles. Only 2 DFM rounds were left in each pod. The delicate and expensive NPC didn't have the power of the proton cannon, nor the range of the electron cannon, and it had a slower R/R rate. However the NPC was the only weapon capable of punching through an EMD shield with a single shot, making it the best anti-Droid weapon available.

The *Warlock* looked like a StarFighter slung between two massive legs. Quad leg mounted thrusters gave it a 210 meter jump capability in normal gravity. The Droid was one of the fastest, most maneuverable in its class. Its 1.6 CM Cubed armor, and standard 7.2 CM equivalent EMD shields gave it superb defensive capabilities. The result was one of the best recon and fire support Droids anywhere.

Alex was familiar with the changing nature of ground warfare since the introduction of the first CombatDroid in 2372. 25th century warfare was no longer a battle of competing electronics and air and space forces, though they still had their roles. Point defense systems, phased array lasers, the EMD shield and the ALI generated electronic soup of the modern battlefield had neutralized both indirect fire weapons and air power. Mobile ground forces became the main instruments of aggression and defense for the competing empires of man and combat had once again become a test of human prowess epitomized by the CombatJack.

Still recovering from his ordeal he found repairing the *Warlock* fatiguing. It was probably for the best. Keeping busy kept him from dwelling on the past.

He jerry-rigged components from the mine manager's office intercom to partially repair the communications system giving it a limited range. Days later he broke the code, gaining access to the ALI. After hours of minor adjustments, he finally aligned the system with his CyberLink. Entering the cleaned out cockpit, he fired up the *Warlock* for the first time. CyberLinking with an ALI was the equivalent of a powerful drug. Only one percent of humans could handle a full spectrum CyberLink like the mine's 3C unit, and only 25% of those could handle the additional sensory burden of an ALI linkage, without becoming either addicted or suffering permanent neural damage referred to as flaming by Linkers. So he entered the virtual reality of ALI enhanced cyberspace for the first time with a dry mouth. It was an incredible rush. He initially felt the usual disorientation. It lasted longer than normal but when it was complete he sensed a nearly perfect interface with the sophisticated GenClone ALI. Some Jacks gave their ALI's personalities and voice response. Alex thought this an indulgence preferring the mind expanding sense of oneness with the ALI practiced by the Cyberman school of thought.

For hours he practiced only the simplest movements, until he felt a degree of comfort. Finally he moved the giant Droid out of the repair dock and across the bay awkwardly. Four times the size of the *Termite* Alex was used to piloting, he found the task of just walking the *Warlock* daunting. He practiced simple maneuvers until he developed a degree of comfort. The marvelous on-board systems of the *Warlock* continued to amaze him, making his old CLV look like a collection of junk. He shut down hours later with a splitting headache. ALI linking was a tremendous strain on the mind. It took lots of painful repetitions to develop the neural pathways that minimized the strain and improved a CombatJack's response time.

The next day Alex ran a diagnostic on the fort's remaining systems. The auxiliary power supply was starting to fail. He estimated he had only another couple of days to finish preparations for his trek across Banshee. He started work on the last and most critical modification to the *Warlock*. He had to remove the NPC, and mount a combination storage bay, sleeping module on the underside of the Droid. The bay would have to store forty days supply of spare coolant, food, water, critical spare parts, and air processing equipment. Alex found a damaged two ton life support tank that proved ideal. Hastily he welded the structure to the Droid's underside. He managed to put a small functioning lock between the emergency escape hatch in the cockpit belly, and the opening to the tank. After loading all the supplies, there was only a coffin like space left for sleep and exercise.

He tested the new configuration and found the module's weight slightly unbalanced the Droid. The *Warlock* moved like a pregnant woman. Alex hoped the problem would resolve itself once he started consuming the supplies. There wasn't much choice, everything packed away was critical to survival. The supplies needed to keep a Droid and its pilot in the field for forty days was discouraging. Alex had no illusions, his chances of successfully trekking from pole to pole were remote. So even after his preparations were complete he hesitated to leave. He spent his last days at the fort reading and practicing continuously on the *Warlock*. His CyberLink time increased steadily.

The blare of warning horns signaled his departure. Hours later the *Warlock* cruised south at nearly 75 kph across the fractured surface of the North polar plateau. The Droid made good progress, skirting obstacles too big to cross. Alex gained confidence the first day. He covered nearly one thousand kilometers, and survived a medium quake without mishap. On his second day he tested the thrusters he needed to traverse obstacles on his route based on the topographic map extracted from the fort's computers. He fired the thrusters to span a small fissure. The *Warlock* arched 190 meters into the air, effortlessly clearing the fault. Alex however misjudged the landing and crashed to the earth with a jarring impact. He was surprised when his frantic efforts to keep the Droid upright succeeded. A diagnostic test showed all systems were still nominal. Though Alex already dreaded the headache that would result from his mental gymnastics.

Alex, always up to a challenge, continued using his thrusters the remainder of the day without further mishaps. His confidence in his piloting skills increased with every successful jump.

Five days later and five thousand kilometers south of the pole he reached the edge of the great shelf and looked down into the great basin four kilometers below. The view was spectacular. A patchwork of bubbling mercury rivers glittered in sharp contrast to the black basaltic rock. Geysers of super heated heavy metals erupted hundreds of meters into the vermilion tinted atmosphere like giant monochrome mushrooms. Across the plain giant white buttes of calcified granite jutted up, looking like the fingers of giants trying to rip the earth's fabric apart. To underscore the illusion a tremor staggered the Droid. Alex skillfully maneuvered the *Warlock* away from the precipice and looked down on the scene again, first with wonder then with growing concern. He caressed Mamba while he evaluated the situation. They had made good time so far covering about a sixth of the trek in five days, but he was using his supplies at a faster rate than expected, particularly the cooling fluid and water. Of greater concern was the heat level of his Droid. It was three days since the heat monitors were green. The Droid's heat stayed in the yellow range even when left at idle during his short naps, and spiked into the red every time he used his thrusters. The outside temperature on the plateau was a balmy 114 degrees centigrade, well above the boiling point of water in the thick atmosphere. Temperatures in the basin would be fifteen degrees higher even if he managed to avoid the super heated geysers.

He shrugged, there wasn't anything to do but go on. First he would do his calisthenics and catch some sleep. Alex eased out of his harness and idled the giant machine. Then he crawled through the emergency hatch into the tank. It was a good thing Mamba wasn't sensitive to the odor of his unwashed body. The sour smell of unwashed human pervaded both the cockpit and tank. After twenty minutes of exercise, he fell asleep knowing Mamba would warn him of upcoming tremors with frantic chirps. Her ability to sense quakes had already saved their lives twice on this voyage.

He awoke from another restless sleep, and started down the cliff. Night descended as he reached the bottom. He picked up the pace, working his way around the geyser fields and the occasional granite outcrop. The Droid made steady progress throughout the night. At dawn Alex noted massive dirty gray-yellow clouds to the East. They filtered out the rays of the rising sun, leaving a shadowy gray murk in their wake. The *Warlock* moved in a world of stark black and white, like a monochrome hologram, with mercury rivers and occasional white granite buttes contrasting with the gray basaltic rock that dominated the landscape. Even Mamba grew despondent after watching the dreary climate through the Duraplast. She jumped down from her perch on top of the CyberLink and slipped into his cooling suit hoping for some relief from the mindless heat. Alex's mood matched his minicham's even though they made good progress south. On a subliminal level they both anticipated the terrible ordeal ahead. The clouds that overtook them that evening fulfilled their expectations. A torrent of mercury and concentrated sulfuric acid droplets drenched the *Warlock*. Only the specialized fluorosilane coating prevented serious corrosion of the Cubed armor. Alex contemplated running out the storm until stones began raining down from the sky. He turned west and accelerated to 120 kph. This barely kept him ahead of the oncoming storm front. A noise like frying soyprotien magnified a million fold washed over the fleeing Droid. A bolt of lightning flashed through the sky delineating the scene of incredible mass destruction in the rear monitors. Sheets of rock and mercury rain crashed into the planetary crust pulverizing the tortured surface. Pebbles began pinging off the carapace of the *Warlock*. His EMD shield was nearly useless against uncharged particles so Alex didn't bother activating it. Instead he fired up the ODC accelerating towards a great white butte to his left. The heat alarms clamored. He overrode the warning and continued hurtling towards the lee side of the great granite block. Any hesitation now or misstep spelled certain doom. Traveling at 252 kph across the uneven surface while the storm front malevolently beat down on him took all the skill and concentration Alex could muster. Barely able to detect the surface before the charging Droid, each stride became a juggernaut. Only the growing rapport between man, ALI and machine and the pilots remarkable reflexes prevented the nearly unavoidable misstep.

For once Banshee relented, the lee side of the butte had a large overhang cut out of its face by a mercury stream. The Droid slowed then slid to a stop underneath the flimsy protection of the overhang, just as the heart of the storm overtook them. Alex shutdown all the external sound sensors. It didn't help, the world disintegrated around the Droid, the vibrations from the atomizing rock shook the Droid and deafened its occupants. Alex hunkered the *Warlock* down as close to the granite surface as possible and began screaming in a mindless rage "Not yet you bitch, not yet, you're not going to get me yet," until he collapsed. An interminable time later the storm passed. Alex awoke from the most restful sleep in a week, renewed he marched onward. Each step of the *Warlock* generated a billowing cloud of fine dust from the powdered surface. Sardonically he thought, "well, at least now he could explain to the geologists the source of the always pervasive dust".

Over the next week he made numerous detours to avoid storms and geyser fields, dancing his way through tremors and rock slides. His progress south slowed, while his skills at operating the *Warlock* steadily increased. For thirteen days he was CyberLinked to the giant machine almost every waking moment. Banshee's myriad threats frequently interrupted his intermittent naps. He was groggily awakened from one of these naps by the frantic chirping of the minicham. Even after he linked with the *Warlock*, Mamba remained unsettled. Alex walked the Droid forward in a haze, ignored Mamba's fluttering. His reflection in a broken glass sensor cover perversely pleased him. The black cooling suit hung on his gaunt frame like a sack, his uncombed white hair fell down his face in greasy locks, while facial hair grew in patches over his narrow gray haggard face. The fixed stare from the black eyes burned with feral purpose. He thought his hue matched that of Banshee. A grimace of a smile covered his face as he contemplated the irony.

He inspected his on-board systems. Other than the yellow heat light everything surprisingly was still green. He blessed the *Warlock*'s designers even if they were GenClones, he doubted any other machine could have held up as well. His biggest concern was the steady erosion of his armor and its corrosion resistant coating to the pitiless dust laden wind. If he ran into an acid storm now, it would be serious trouble. He looked ahead and to his surprise the monotonous monochrome of the great basin was broken by a red glow to the South. Steadily the Droid worked its way up into the foothills. The glow turned into incandescent flame as he approached. Climbing one of the larger outcroppings he looked out upon the great north equatorial barrier range. A third of the towering mountains in his view were active volcanoes, spewing out magma that flowed in ruby rivers into a great cleft in the earth. The external heat rose to 145 degrees, ash and intensely hot dust hazed the air. The pass shown on the topological map was a lake of molten rock totally impassable. The only other possibility was a fault traversing the range 1500 kilometers to the Southeast. He turned the Droid in that direction and walked parallel to the range without any display of emotion. He didn't have any other choice. Banshee had deceived him again.

Two days later he reached the fault. It was filled with molten lead. Mercury vapors bubbled from the metallic sea condensing on the cliff walls. The quicksilver reflected the red haze from the surrounding volcanoes creating a surrealistic world of sparkling silver and red. Mamba stared fixedly through the Duraplast fascinated by the interplay of light. Alex spotted a mercury slicked shelf running along the right wall of the cleft. As always Banshee denied him options, if he didn't cross here his supplies would run out long before he reached the south pole. He started working his way towards the shelf, using his thrusters conservatively to cross fractures and scale sheer cliff walls. He made it to the ledge. His heat alarms were ringing again. He flushed his radiators with the diminishing supply of coolant.

Carefully the graceful Droid placed each step on the slick surface of the narrow shelf. Delicately it jumped over rivulets of molten rock and mercury flowing down into the black sea below. As the crevice narrowed, the heat increased. Twice tremors and the slick surface slew the Droid dangerously close to the cliff's edge. Both times the skill of the pilot avoided certain doom. At the narrowest point of the fault, the ledge ended, continuing on the other side almost 200 meters away. In the heavy gravity of Banshee the jump was at the extreme range of the *Warlock*'s abilities. With only a slight pause Alex walked the machine back a few paces, then lunged forward while activating his ODC. The giant treads spewed dust and droplets of quicksilver backwards, as they gouged their way forward. Alex fired the thrusters at the last possible moment, hurtling the *Warlock* in a giant arc across the rift. The Droid landed awkwardly on the edge of the path. Alex scrambled for footing while leaning forward, using the CyberLink exclusively to control the movements and maximize his chances. Momentum hurled him into the cliff, he twisted to take the impact on the right arm. The Droid continued its nearly uncontrolled run down the ledge, sparks flying from the scrape of cubed armor on stone. Alex dared not stop on the slick surface. He placed each step precisely so he wouldn't plummet to his doom.

Finally he managed to slow the Droid. The ease with which he had managed the suicidal jump surprised Alex. He was getting extremely good at piloting his SuperDroid. The ledge widened and gently dipped down to the shrinking metallic sea below. Passing by an arroyo washed away by molten lava, a blazing blue reflection from the exposed surface blinded him. He stopped and saw a wall studded with blue gemstones. He reached up with his undamaged mechanical arm and dug out a crystal the size of a human head. The gem looked bottomless, cool azure light seemed to originate from some source other then Banshee. Alex carried it with him out of the fissure.

Hours later the *Warlock* walked out of the mountains into the southern foothills. Alex idled the machine disconnected his CyberLink and collapsed into a fit of shaking. Mamba nipped his hand and chirped encouragingly. The symbiot's saliva seemed to renew him. This trip had verified something Alex had always suspected. Mamba's bite contained a substance that reinvigorated its host. The effect was much more noticeable as his condition deteriorated on this exodus. Mamba had used the nips cautiously ever since an over playful bite in their youth had Alex jumping off the walls. He trusted the minicham's judgment as to his needs. Their lives were far to intertwined for him to do anything else. This trek had strengthened that bond even further.

Later he recovered the gemstone. On closer inspection the stone was even more intriguing. Its radiated blue light was soothing, almost hypnotic. Alex would study the crystal the rest of the trip as a counter to the harsh bleached reality of Banshee.

Mamba was frantically batting his face and chirping. Alex waived at her, "Go away you flying snake, I need some sleep." The minicham was persistent. Finally Alex got up yelling "Okay what's wrong now." Climbing into the cockpit he reviewed his readouts. Nothing was wrong as far as he could tell. Since he was up, he decided to fire up the engines and move farther away from the barrier range that was now just a glimmer in the distance. Mamba wouldn't calm down.

They made good progress across a very flat and smooth plain of volcanic rock. It was the best terrain they had traversed since leaving the polar plateau. The only problems were the ground's excessive heat and the occasional quake. Mamba's agitation if anything increased as they progressed south. A tremor hit, it didn't go away. The ground to their left suddenly sundered and a molten sea began eating its way across the plain. Alex dodged right and accelerated to full speed. Another crack appeared in the plain ahead. He broke left and managed to cross a land bridge, just before the two rifts met. More cracks appeared in the crust. Alex dodged his way around the bigger ones and leapt over the smaller ones that blocked his path.

The land shook and fractured across his entire sensor range. Alex found himself on a floating island in the middle of a molten sea. He jumped across a lava gap to another crumbling chunk of land surrounded by lava. His progress now consisted of fleeing across smaller and smaller crusts of earth and jumping across larger and larger rivers of molten rock. His heat alarms sounded, as the outside temperature steadily rose. He had to keep running and jumping. The alarms began the clamor of imminent system overload. Alex overrode them and flushed fresh coolant from his emergency stores into his radiators. The displaced coolant flashed into green vapor as it hit the super heated air. For just a moment his heat monitor flashed yellow then rose back into the red.

On the horizon he spotted a gray haze. He veered towards it and jumped across another pool of lava. He slowed down to let his thrusters recharge as he rushed towards another gap. The islet's edge hissed with escaping carbon dioxide and vaporizing sulfuric acid as it hit the flame red sea. The land crumbled before him as he jumped to the next decaying plot of crust. Slowly the gray haze transformed itself into a low basaltic plateau, steadily being undercut by the lava sea. He crossed the last islet between him and the potentially stable land only to see a lava gap before him that was well beyond the jump capability of his Droid. Desperately he tried to find a way across the gap. Again he flushed spare coolant through the radiators to prevent a reactor shutdown. Drenched in sweat, Alex shook with the tremendous concentration of trying to keep the *Warlock* upright and moving on the super heated unstable surface. The Droid moved like the proverbial cat on a hot tin roof, bounding left and right to avoid fissures and geysers of super heated mercury. Alex watched another section of cliff collapse into the molten sea and slowly sink. It gave him an idea.

He ran parallel to the cliffs until a particularly large undercut promontory appeared. Turning towards the cliff and activating his ODC, he reached the edge of the floating crust. Then he simultaneously fired his thrusters and launched the paired DFM's from each pod launcher at the cliff base. Arching through the sky Alex estimated he would land in the lava sea at least fifty meters short of land unless his plan worked. The missiles exploded at the base of the overhang, for a moment nothing. Then the promontory slowly toppled into the sea directly into the *Warlock's* path. With a stupendous splash the section of cliff shattered the lava sea and began to sink. The Droid smashed through the wall of skyward bound lava and landed awkwardly on the edge of the sinking gray hump. He scrambled up just ahead of the encroaching sea, finally reaching stable footing and jumping again. Landing on the cliff he took three strides and froze.

Chapter 5

Alex sat dazed. He had made it across the lava sea only to have his engine overheat a few steps from relative safety. There was nothing to do except wait for the machine to cool down and hope the cliff didn't collapse before he could move. Looking at the 3D rearview he saw nothing but a ruby red ocean all the way to the horizon, where there had once been seemingly stable land. Suddenly he started laughing hysterically, as he recalled the name of the plain on the topological map. Mamba looked at him quizzically. Finally in a scratchy voice he said "No I am not crazy, yet. Its just funny, Sea of Tranquillity."

He disconnected from the Droid and crawled down into the tank. Lately he felt vertigo every waking moment not hooked up to the CyberLink. He felt incomplete un-hooked from the ALI. He was becoming more an extension of the machine rather then a human being. Alex had spent more time at a Droid's controls over the past four weeks, then many CombatJack spent in a lifetime. If he didn't have more serious things to worry about, he would have been concerned about what the endless exposure to the CyberLink was doing to his mind. He cracked open a cryogenic air cylinder to cool the living area and provide oxygen while life support was down. There was more room in the tank, over two thirds of the supplies were already consumed.

He found himself surprisingly alert. Laying there unable to sleep and unable to control his fate; he recalled his childhood, recalling vague memories of his mother and her endless army of male friends. Only three people had made an impression on Alex in his youth. His mother wasn't one of them.

First there had been big McDuff. For many years he had been a regular visitor to their cubicle. Usually he would leave with a big smile, while Alex waited outside in fear of the gangs that roamed the tunnels. McDuff would make some remark like "Laddie come along an' I'll sho' you a real man's job." Alex would tag along after Duffy as he went to work. He would fetch things for the talkative Scotian, while the maintenance tech explained his work. Alex had liked the big man and absorbed the knowledge like a sponge. When his mother had died Duffy had stopped coming around, inexplicably to the small admiring boy. Alex was sorry that McDuff had died in the mines. The man had many faults, but Alex had to acknowledge he had benefited technically if not emotionally from the big Scotian.

The second man he recalled was Paul, the "Carver" CLV jock, a small dark wiry man with a surprising sense of decency beneath the rough exterior and permanent frown. Paul spoke little and didn't act friendly, but he let Alex stay in his cubicle while he was with his mother. He had sensed the boys fear of the tunnels and their inhabitants. The CLV jock's cubicle had been a source of endless fascination for the young Alex, filled with Droid paraphernalia and literature. Paul had reacted to the boy's interest in his profession by teaching him the rudiments of running a CLV, even taking Alex in the Carver on some of the safer mining runs. It would be years, after Paul's death in a mining accident, before Alex learned of one last kindness the melancholy little man had done for him. Paul had paved his way for training as a CLV pilot with the corporate talent evaluators. The last time Alex cried, was when he heard of the small brooding man's death.

The third and most important adult in his life, was his indomitable grandmother. She had been the grand dame of the mines for many years. Her crime and sex, her pre-conviction wealth and her longevity, made her the reigning celebrity in the convict community. She had used her notoriety to gain power among the peds.

Alex remembered his nervousness every time his grandmother sent for him. She always demanded to be called "Dame Lucinda," and required her visitors to demonstrate excellent manners. Once a huge miner had picked his nose in her presence while Alex and Kyla were there. She had taken a stool and smashed him over the head, her only comment, "Children, remember bad manners and bad grammar cannot be tolerated. One must maintain standards," as her ped guards dragged the prostate man away. It was at his grandmother's, that he had met Kyla. Lucinda decided that her two grandchildren must become gentle persons; and what Lucinda Kane decided happened. So every day for several years the two of them would trek to Lucinda's for "lessons in etiquette." In her lucid moments she gave them detailed lessons in outdated Imperial court manners, politics, literature and art, as well as speech and language. During her progressively worsening fits, Kyla and he would prevent their grandmother from swallowing her tongue or otherwise doing bodily harm to herself. Both children had feared their insane grandmother and her harsh discipline. Still they had loved her and she them, each in their own strange way. Her protection had made their young lives tolerable. They had not fully recognized its value until after her death. Death, the ever present enemy in the mines. Alex thought he had long become numb to its voracious presence until the death of Kyla.

Alex snapped out of his reverie as his Droid shivered from another tremor, and headed back to the cockpit. The air was stifling, a normal human with less tolerance for heat would have passed out. Another section of the cliff had collapsed into the magma sea. Strapping himself back into his harness, he waited for his heat indicators to reach start up tolerance levels. Finally he fired up the engines and headed south. He had passed the great barrier range, crossed the unanticipated lava sea; and the map indicated he was well past the equator. Something had changed, he felt he had come to an accommodation with Banshee. He stopped hating the world of his birth. It would continue to test him, but as long as he remained vigilant, he inexplicably believed it would not kill him.

Seventeen days later, a sleek SuperDroid limped across the great southern plateau, heading for a small installation near the south pole. The machine finally reached a bay door and stopped. A small armored figure climbed out of the cockpit walked to the external door lock and cut through with a laser cutter. The door opened. The suited figure staggered back to the Droid and climbed slowly back into the cockpit. The Droid walked into the bay and the doors shut.

Chapter 6

Alex awoke the next morning disoriented. He was lying on a cement floor. Where was his Droid, where were the dwindling supplies in the cramped tank? He staggered up, so weak he could barely support his weight in the heavy gravity. He leaned against a wall and smiled as he suddenly recognized his surroundings. Mamba fluttered over and landed on his shoulder. "Well girl we made it." She chirped a nonchalant response, almost as if to say I never had a doubt. Alex was still in terrible shape. He had been without food for four days and without water for two, as well as suffering from sleep deprivation. The trek across Banshee had taken forty-four days and covered at least thirty-six thousand kilometers. He wasn't surprised when his chronometer indicated he had slept twenty-one hours.

He wandered through the small emergency habitat in the complex back to the tiny galley. He found some emergency rations and wolfed them down with glasses of water from a tap. He had found the galley and its life giving water yesterday and then collapsed. Refreshed from his ordinary meal, he wandered through the rest of the complex, finding a well-stocked station, with enough supplies to keep him alive for months. There were three small sleep cubicles a large lounge area, a small library with real paper books and an excellent computer console. Also a large well-appointed fresher, in addition to the galley, and the entrance, with its lock leading to the storage and equipment bays. Outside the habitat was a geological monitoring station with a variety of remote sensors. The library terminal also accessed the data collected by the station so visiting scientists could monitor Banshee in comfort.

Returning to the lounge he decided he needed to clean up. He no longer could bare his own stench, and suspected it would take a heavy duty detergent to make him presentable again. He entered the fresher and decided to waste water on the sinful pleasure of a bath for only the second time in his life. In the mines sonic cleaners were the norm, water was far too precious a commodity to be wasted on washing convicts. He soaked in the small bath for over an hour, using a fragrant bar of soap to scrub himself clean. The water turned murky with the accumulated grime of his trip. Mamba decided to join him fluttering in and out of water in feigned terror. Alex laughed at her antics. She surprised him by turning out to be a good swimmer. He discovered in his random studies that the mini-chameleon's home world of Himalaya was also a desert world.

After wiping himself down he decided to finish the process by shaving his beard and trimming his hair. He inspected himself in a full length mirror after his toilet and saw a tall gaunt young man whose most notable features were slightly slanted piercing black eyes and long white hair. His body hair had been white since birth. In other respects he resembled his grandmother, strong dimpled jaw, flared hooked nose with high cheekbones in a broad angular face. The puckered scar bisecting the right side of his face went from the temple to his Adams apple in a jagged line. It wasn't that noticeable he thought unless he got angry. He didn't have a good frame of reference to evaluate his appearance. However he knew people immediately recognized him as dangerous. Kyla used to tell him he was cute in his youth but even at nineteen no one had thought of him as cute in a long time.

He spent the rest of the week cleaning and repairing his equipment. The good food and exercise coupled with lots of sleep slowly returned his strength and endurance. Alex had decided to rearm the *Warlock*, in case he needed it to persuade the next supply mission to take him along. He had brought most of the components for the NPC assembly with him, and the well-stocked bay had all the additional parts needed. Alex used a fragment of the bluestone to replace the damaged original NPC modulation crystal.

The remaining repairs on the Droid took longer than expected. Banshee had slowly eaten away at the sub-systems. Alex replaced three actuators and repaired most of the armor. He also replaced key electronic components. He found a state of the art O-micron 4002 communications system in stores, and replaced the *Warlocks* failing jury rigged comlink. The corroded surface of the Duraplast cockpit also had to be ground smooth. Finally he decided to repaint the Droid in the black and green of the Wolcott Rangers, a mercenary unit that had been serving the Imperial Coalition on Banshee. This would fit in with his cover story of a stranded CombatJack piloting a captured GenClone Droid.

After the repairs were complete, he took the *Warlock* out on the polar shelf to test and calibrate its weapons. The range and accuracy of the NPC surprised him. After some initial calibration of the targeting gear it proved to be devastatingly accurate. His concern about the jury rigged crystal turned into pleasant surprise. The bluestone crystal provided slightly more power and a quicker R/R then the standard configuration. Alex had serendipitously discovered an upgrade to NPC technology.

Weeks passed and no relief ship showed. Alex started having nightmares about the trek across the equator. Kyla's or his grandmother's face would appear in his dreams imbedded in lava, mouthing unheard screams for help or begging him to join them. He buried himself in the small library, reading dull treatise on geology and paleontology after exhausting all the other books. He also spent a great deal of time in the *Warlock*'s cockpit. Its familiar presence and solidity somehow comforted him. Even though he tried to convince himself it was to check the on board systems. Worst of all Mamba had finally entered her long delayed hibernation. Alex for the first time in his life was totally alone, a whole planet to himself.

He awakened from a restless sleep in the lounge to a strange sound. He looked up and saw three people cycle through the hatch and started removing their armored suites. He sat quietly while the two men and a woman discussed their mission.

The bigger man said "Dr Tsay the data you require can be accessed through the terminal in the library over there. Hanna check the inventory and equipment, and determine what is salvageable, we don't have much time."

The smaller man responded "It is truly a shame. I have long wanted to study this most intriguing of worlds, and now that I am here, I only have enough time for a perfunctory examination. Though, I must say this gravity would become most debilitating if we were to stay long."

Hanna looked up saw Alex and froze for a moment, finally she spoke, "Dr. Saporand, who is that?"

Alex froze speechless at the sight of the first humans he had seen in months. He recovered, stood up and walked over to the stunned trio, "Let me..., Ah, introduce myself," as he bowed formally, "Alex Kane, CombatJack with the Wolcott Rangers at your service. I have long anticipated your arrival."

Saporand asked, "What are you doing here young man, how did you get here?"

"My story is long, I would gladly relate to you the events that stranded me here, but I gather you are in a hurry."

Tsay anxious to get to his long anticipated work replied, "You are correct, we only have 24 hours before the shuttle departs. I must get to work, but I look forward to hearing your no doubt fascinating story. We should wait until time is less pressing. If you will all excuse me," As the dapper little man walked to the library.

Hanna with a piercing look at Alex responded, "OK, we can wait, I need to salvage what I can from this installation, before the university abandons it. Dr. Saporand please notify the ship of our unexpected visitor."

Alex, silently blessing his grandmother's training in etiquette replied formally, "Can I be of service Madame or is it Miss, I am quite familiar with this installation and its resources."

Angrily Hanna snapped back, "It's Blount, Dr. Blount to you mercenary. I was director of geologic research on Banshee until you and your GenClone playmates wiped out Matsui's facility on this planet. Now we have lost our funding. She replied bitterly. "Come along I can use your muscles if nothing else."

Alex thought strike one for grandmother's training. It apparently didn't work with irate scientists. He spent the rest of the day with Hanna Blount, inventorying and collecting the most valuable supplies. They loaded everything into the scientist's modified APC. Alex learned the station was to be moth balled and the system abandoned. Neither Matsui nor anyone else could afford the capital to re-open a mine this close to disputed territory. There wasn't enough convict labor anyway. Alex was lucky, he would be leaving on the last shuttle to visit Banshee for a long time.

The large heavily armed Horatio class shuttle surprisingly belonged to the Empire military. Alex learned that this stop was just a detour from a diplomatic and scientific mission to the Vegan Republic, which was the reason for haste. The StarShip was discharging its Khalid-Nagoya Coils in preparation for the next stellar hop without delay. The invention of the K-N Coil in the 22nd century had started humanities great exodus from old tired Terra. It was unlikely, but the military nature of the ship might expose his cover story. He hoped its personnel weren't familiar with the Rangers.

They stopped and ate lunch together and discussed their activities. Dr. Tsay expressed great excitement about Alex's trek across Banshee. He plied Alex with questions about the topography and geology of the world. Alex answered as best he could until he noticed all three of them staring at him with puzzled frowns.

Alex uncertainly asked, "Have I said something inappropriate, if I have I apologize. It's been a long time since I have been with people."

Tsay replied, "Not at all Alex, it's just incredible that anyone could succeed on such a trek, and your knowledge of the geology of this planet is remarkable. It far exceeds that of many supposed experts in the field."

Alex knew his mine centered world view had tripped him up. He was demonstrating knowledge not expected of a CombatJack. He would have to be more circumspect, "It's a hobby of mine Doctor." Then changing the subject, "Hanna," she was now letting Alex call her that, "I can use my Droid to recover some of the remote seismic and heat sensors if you'd like."

"No we don't have time and there isn't much room on the shuttle. By the way, Captain Hohiro probably won't let you bring that Droid along, he has some serious weight restrictions."

Alex went cold inside, the idea of leaving the *Warlock* behind was inconceivable. For months it had been home, more then that it was almost an extension of his being. Emphatically Alex replied, "I am not leaving Banshee without the Droid."

His expression made the others flinch back. Dr. Saporand finally broke the silence. Querulously he said, "Mr. Kane, you do understand that this is not our decision, you will have to convince Captain Hohiro and the mission commanders. Unbelievable, every time we turn around we have another problem!"

Grimly Alex responded, "Then I better speak to him," as he got up to fetch his pressure suit.

Dr. Tsay in a conciliatory voice recommended, "You could use the intercom."

Alex replied tersely, "No, I think this should be face to face."

DR Tsay going out of his way to help offered, "Then let me accompany you, I need to down load some data into the ships systems anyway."

They donned their armored pressure suits and marched across the monochrome terrain to the shuttle *Kilaminjaro*. Entering a small port, they removed their suits and decontaminated. Once they were in the ship proper, Alex asked a waiting crew member to see the captain. The crewman replied "He's on the bridge." Alex asked how to get there and was directed to the main elevator.

Quizzically Tsay commented, "You are aware, of course, that you have to request permission to visit the bridge?"

Alex uncertainly asked, "How do I do that?"

"You can use the intercom on the elevator, since we are already here," Captain Hohiro agreed to see them on the bridge.

When they arrived, Alex and Dr. Tsay politely bowed to the Captain and a superbly dressed attractive middle aged couple. They were introduced to Alex as Her Excellency Ambassador Debra Alcorn and her husband Colonel Jacque Bayard of the Vegan Republic. The usual introductory amenities required by polite Bukharan Imperial society followed. Alex was pleasantly surprised that the norms of upper class society in his grandmother's day were still acceptable in the present. Alex finally got around to the point of his visit "Captain Hohiro, I am informed that there may be some difficulty in bringing my Droid along. I am willing to do whatever is needed to convince you otherwise."

The immaculate captain replied, "I am afraid Mr. Kane that you have been informed correctly, there is very little room left on the *Kilaminjaro*, certainly not enough to take on a medium sized CombatDroid."

Alex desperate to keep his Warlock argued, "But Captain, I am piloting a SuperDroid of radical new design." Including the ambassador and her spouse in his conversation, "Surely Vegan scientists will want to examine it. You could be losing valuable intelligence about GenClone technology if my *Warlock* is not brought along."

Colonel Bayard exclaimed in surprise, "You're piloting a *Warlock*? How did you come into possession of the GenClone's newest SuperDroid? They have been giving us fits in the border conflicts, and as far as I know we haven't been able to capture one yet."

Telling part of the truth Alex explained "I captured it when the North polar mining complex was destroyed. I was left behind for dead in the hasty evacuation, as was the GenClone pilot of the *Warlock*. After I recovered I ran into the *Warlock* in my damaged Droid, and a lucky shot with my surviving phased array laser cracked his already damaged cockpit."

Hohiro inquired, "How did you get from the North Pole to here Mr. Kane?"

Alex hesitatingly replied, "I walked."

Tsay, as some scientists often will, expounded, "A truly incredible trek, even the best, most durable remote sensors sent into the equatorial zone of this planet have failed. I must say that the more I here of your story the more unbelievable it becomes. It is hard to credit a human even in a Droid could survive the deadly environment for the amount of time required."

The others suddenly all looked at him with suspicion. It had suddenly occurred to all of them simultaneously that they might be looking at a GenClone spy. Alex understood their disbelief of the most truthful part of his story. Even he sometimes doubted the ordeal of crossing Banshee, not to mention his possession of a SuperDroid. Alex didn't know what to say to extricate himself.

It was the Ambassador, who rescued the situation. "Whether Mr. Kane's story is believable or not, I believe the *Warlock* must be brought on board for evaluation. Captain Hohiro, I will sacrifice the load of Iberian wine for the Vegan court to permit room, if that is acceptable. I am sure The Republic would prefer a detailed analysis of a *Warlock* over Duke Leton's most generous gift. I do recommend that this young man be disarmed and confined to his quarters until we confirm his story. Possibly you have someone on board familiar with the Wolcott Rangers who can question him?" Turning to Alex before the Captain could reply, "You do claim to be a member of that mercenary regiment, don't you Mr. Kane."

Alex hesitated then spoke uncertainly, "Ah yes, though I only recently joined?" He had never been a convincing liar and looking at the faces around him it showed.

It was Dr. Tsay who completely discredited his story,"I find it hard to believe young man, that any CombatJack would be unfamiliar with the layout and procedures of a military shuttle." Turning to the others in explanation, "He had to ask directions to the elevator, and had to be told he needed permission to enter the bridge. Though I must say if you are a spy you are a remarkably incompetent one. That ridiculous story about crossing Banshee."

Tripped up by the truth, Alex laughed. He considered editing his story, but doubted anything he said would be believed. Looking at the hostile faces around him he explained, "Whether you believe me or not, I mean no one on this ship any harm, nor do I have any goals other then to leave this world with my possessions."

They ignored his remarks, while the Captain ordered guards to disarm and accompany him to secured quarters. They took his laser pistol and ceramic knife in a cursory search. They missed the throwing stars and Mamba. Then the guards escorted Alex to a cubicle with his arms hand cuffed behind his back, at least the *Warlock* would be brought along, and Mamba was carefully tucked away inside his inner pocket. He wouldn't be leaving anything of value behind on Banshee.

Chapter 7

Alex was confined to his room for hours. He finally fell asleep until awakened by the roar of engines as the *Kilaminjaro* left Banshee. He got up once the acceleration decreased, and asked the guard posted outside his door, to see someone in authority. Disconcertingly, a little while later Colonel Bayard, himself walked into the cubicle. Politely he asked what Alex wanted.

"Colonel, this may be a strange request, but I was hoping to see Banshee from space during departure." To his surprise the Colonel agreed to accompany Alex to a view port. They walked silently together, with the guard following a discrete distance behind, to the officer's lounge. Alex's first look outside unnerved him. A small gray red ball receded from the shuttle. The planet itself was nondescript, but the endless expanse of star studded space was breathtaking. He leaned against the wall and almost fell from a severe case of vertigo. Feeling for the first time in his life the immense size of the universe and his own insignificance. He had lived on a world that confined the human body and spirit. Even Banshee's surface with its short horizons and permanent cloud cover, always limited one's vision while forcing humans to encase themselves in protective armor. The usual confidence with which he faced life faded, as he thought, nothing on Banshee had prepared him to deal with this.

He looked away to see the Colonel staring at him curiously.

"If I didn't know better I would think that was your first view of space."

Alex didn't want to lie, "If you stayed on Banshee for a while Colonel, I think you would find space disconcerting." Unable to contain his curiosity he asked "Do people get used to looking at that, do they get blasé about such immensity?" He waved his hand at the view port.

The Colonel replied, "Hard to say, each man has his own reaction. Some shrink from it choosing not to see, others try to make it into something understandable, others let it overwhelm them, most just choose to ignore it." As he nodded towards the few occupants in the lounge all with their backs turned towards the view port. "What is your reaction?"

Alex surprised himself by answering with his true feelings, "I just feel small and insignificant."

The Colonel laughed, until he noticed Alex's angry reaction "I wasn't laughing at you Alex, I find it amusing because it has the exact same effect on me." He smiled, "I never have admitted that before, not even to Debra. I believe it to be the reaction of everyone when first they look into the heart of space. People have an immense capacity to gloss over what they do not understand, so most of us find some way to explain our true feelings away. I am still curious as to why you haven't?"

Alex chose not to answer, instead he asked, "Colonel, I again would impose on your charity, is there any chance I can check on the disposition of my Droid?" Alex wasn't really worried about the *Warlock*. He just felt a profound need to be somewhere familiar, the Droid was the only thing available. More and more he felt out of his element, in a universe even more uncertain then Banshee.

The colonel accommodatingly agreed, "Certainly, as long as you are willing to answer the tech's questions about its performance."

With some anxiety Alex replied, "yes I'll answer technical questions," with the emphasis on technical, "they aren't doing anything to the *Warlock* are they?"

Bayard leading the way to the Droid bays said, "Let's go see". Another larger CombatDroid was in the storage bay next to the *Warlock*. Alex was not familiar with the design.

Bayard noting Alex's gaze commented with a smile, "My Droid, one of the new *Raptor's*. I lost my old *Renegade* in the fighting on Neuvo Leon against the GenClones. With just a note of pride in his voice he continued, "President Houston himself awarded me this Droid for my services."

Alex commented distractedly, "Its impressive." But his attention was mostly focused on the *Warlock*, and the Techs working on it, "What are they going to do?"

"Let's go ask"

They walked up to one of the techs and the Colonel made introductions. Chief tech Robart Fuller was a slender old balding man who looked ten years past retirement. Alex found out that Fuller was a family retainer, who had served three generations of Bayards. Alex, would learn that Fuller was a wizard at CombatDroid field maintenance.

Bayard asked, "What do you think of the SuperDroid Robart and what are your plans?"

Robart in an odd lilting accent replied, "Well now your lordship, I haven't had a chance to do a complete inspection, but given her size she doesn't have enough firepower for my taste. She won't last long in a stand up fight, but she sure would be hard to catch in a chase. Fuller turned to Alex and asked, "What did you do to the NPC mount, it looks like a retrofit to me?"

The tech was very observant. Alex thought he had removed all traces of the modifications, "I replaced the mount with a combination storage locker and life support tank for the trek across Banshee. I needed a place to sleep and store supplies for many weeks if I was to survive, and didn't foresee much use for a NPC. What made you notice?"

Fuller, with a knowing smile, replied, "Secrets of the trade Mr. Kane, Secrets of the trade." Turning towards the Droid and looking at the NPC turret admiringly, "You do very nice work, I doubt most of my boys would have noticed." As he pointed to various parts of the Droid, he expounded on his other observations, "You rigged the emergency hatch from the cockpit so it accessed the tank, very innovative. You lost armor and lots of it to corrosion, that planet of yours must have a very nasty environment to chew Cubed armor like that. Your thrusters need to be realigned, they look like they have a thousand plus hours on them. You must be one jumping fool Mr. Kane."

Alex sardonically answered, "I didn't have much choice Mr. Fuller. The ground had this curious habit of falling away from beneath me." With a raised eyebrow Alex asked, "Anything else your cursory exam revealed to you chief tech?"

Robart now in full discourse replied, "Well, I haven't confirmed it yet, but I believe your crystal matrix internal structure is close to fatigue failure." Looking at Alex knowingly, "Someone put a tremendous amount of distance, at very high temperatures on this Droid, to do this kind of damage. How far was that trip you say you took?"

Alex looking at the *Warlock* in surprise answered, "Oh, About thirty-six thousand kilometers give or take a few. I didn't even know a crystal matrix could suffer fatigue failure"

Bayard in surprise asked, "You're not trying to tell us that Alex really did cross the entire breadth of Banshee in a Droid, are you Robart? And by God stop calling me your lordship or I will retire you this time."

With a toothy grin Fuller replied, "Well Your Colonelship,

I heard that harebrained story about the lad over here crossing Banshee in this Droid, and decided to do a little investigating of my own. I can't say I'd bet my life on it, but by gum I'd bet my life savings. That Droid recently covered a whole lot of territory on Banshee, or a very similar world, if there is such a thing. All you have to do is know where to look, I don't know the truth of your story Mr. Kane but Droids don't lie. I would consider it an honor if you would tell me about your trek sometime over a beer, it must be a humdinger"

Alex now worried about the status of the *Warlock* asked, "Can you replace the damaged structure Mr. Fuller"?

Fuller replied, "you can call me Robart, Mr. Kane, and yes we'll repair it, it'll take a couple of days. Do you want me to upgrade the 40MM lasers to Vegan Four-forties it shouldn't cost to much, and will give you the fire power to do some damage?"

Alex hesitated a moment looking speculatively at the *Warlock*, "Only if you can upgrade the targeting software as well Robart, and I would consider it an honor if you would call me Alex."

The chief tech in amusement responded, "Oh, I think we can swing an upgrade to the targeting software as well, but it will cost you fifteen thousand C-bills, Mr. Kane."

Bayard interrupted, "Go ahead and make the modifications Robart. I will arrange for funds."

"Certainly your Lordship." Fuller turned and walked away shaking his head and talking to himself, "Can't pay the boys, but enough credits to help strays... Wait till I tell them, can't believe it myself, fatigued crystal matrix, never thought I'd see the day. Have to write it up,..."

Bayard, slightly embarrassed at the overheard remark, "My chief tech is a bit eccentric. He is indispensable, a true genius at keeping CombatDroids performing at their peak and he knows it. There shouldn't be any problems with the..."

Interrupting, Alex blurted out "Colonel, I am grateful for your offer, but I do have funds and can afford the maintenance of my own equipment. I don't care to be beholden to anyone even a gracious jailer such as yourself."

Surprised by the outburst Bayard responded formally, "Certainly sir. On the issue of your freedom, I momentarily forgot about your status. I cannot unilaterally release you, but I am sure that both Captain Hohiro and my wife will agree to give you the freedom of the ship once I have communicated the facts to them. They both have great faith in Robart and his technical expertise."

They returned to Alex's quarters amicably. The Colonel asking leading questions about the journey across Banshee, and Alex describing many of the wonders he had seen while avoiding the specifics of his ordeal. Alex felt inexplicably reticent, about the trek, somehow it did not feel right describing the intensely personal journey to the Colonel. It would have made him feel naked; at the same time he didn't want to appear distrusting of Bayard.

Alex was resting in his room that same evening. He had still not received word from Bayard, and he was becoming concerned. A knock on his door. He got up and opened it. Ambassador Alcorn and Colonel Bayard walked in followed by Dr. Tsay. There were none of the usual amenities, all four of them stood around uncomfortably.

Colonel Bayard with a concerned look on his face said, "Alex, Captain Hohiro after hearing about the evaluation of your Droid, gave me complete freedom to decide your fate. Debra and I were on our way here to apologize for your treatment and offer you our hospitality for the remainder of this trip, when Dr. Tsay raised an unsettling possibility"

They all turned and looked at the nervous doctor. Tsay nervously spoke, "Ah, well, I believe in the evidence, so you did cross Banshee in that CombatDroid. But there remain some unanswered questions."

Alex in a controlled voice asked, "What would those be doctor?"

Tsay pontificating, "In the Colonel's haste to exonerate you he forgot about your unfamiliarity with shuttles. Unlikely for a CombatJack, as you claim to be. I consider myself a man of deductive reasoning and there are other pieces of the puzzle that concern me. For instance your surprising familiarity with the geology and mineral structure of Banshee."

Alex worriedly asked, "I am afraid I don't understand why that would be a concern Doctor. After all I did spend a great deal of time on the surface." The Bayards remained silent observers to the interplay.

The Oriental sermonized, "It has been in my limited experience, with apologize to the Colonel, that CombatJack are obsessed with their martial skills and ALI linkages. They generally have little or no interest in mundane subjects." Looking straight at Alex, "You on the other hand, have demonstrated a practical knowledge of the geology of Banshee. The kind of hands on knowledge usually associated with miners."

Alex, trying to be nonchalant asked, "Not all CombatJacks are alike, why should my knowledge of mineral sciences be of concern?"

Tsay with a look of excitement replied, "Because as you probably already suspect, I don't believe you are who you claim. Using Razor's axiom, I can only conclude that you are an escaped convict miner. Ah, as for your skill with Droids, it probably derives from piloting a mining CLV, I am informed they use those in the North Polar mine."

Alex replied bitterly, "Did use them Dr. Tsay."

The good doctor's discovery of at least part of the truth didn't surprise Alex. He had always felt that life in the convict mines must leave indelible scars on a person that all could see. He remembered watching new convicts come to Banshee tough, self satisfied or delusional; believing their sentences just an interlude until some elaborate escape plan could be devised. In the end they all had the fatalistic lost look of abandoned children even the mad ones when they let life penetrate their walls of unreality. He laughed "I am not a convict Dr. Tsay, but you are very close to the mark."

Bayard interrupted sardonically, "Ah, I suppose now you will tell us you were unjustly imprisoned?"

Ambassador Alcorn in a reasoning voice said, "Jacque has taken a liking to you Mr. Kane. If you tell us the truth we may be able to help. I would advise you not to continue your deceits. Only those committing the most heinous of crimes are sentenced to the living death of Banshee. Though I may not totally approve of Imperial justice, I feel an obligation not to let loose a murderer or worse on the universe."

They all looked at Alex expectantly. It occurred to Alex, that people had a morbid fascination in truly vicious crimes, in the mines the more dreadful the crime the higher the status of the convict. He had built his own reputation for brutal toughness by taking down some of those with the biggest reps. He wolfishly smiled, the ambassador and the doctor flinched while Colonel Bayard stared him in the eyes. A very tough man Alex thought,

That smile had unnerved some of Banshee's meanest.

Finally he spoke, "I won't decry my innocence Doctor, it doesn't matter any way. I believe in the fairness of the Ambassador." As he turned to Alcorn and raised an eyebrow, "You will off course verify my presumed guilt in the Imperial archives, by cross referencing my retinal pattern against those for convicts sentenced to Banshee."

Tsay, with a self congratulatory grin, "You expect your patterns not to be there? But you are familiar with the Empire's criminal record keeping system, some what incriminating in and of itself, wouldn't you say. I believe you are playing for time Mr. Kane."

Bitterly Alex replied, "Dr. Tsay you are an intelligent man, but this universe and the strange events that occur in it, are bigger then your so called deductive reasoning. Check the records, at the next Worm Whole Transmit facility. He was tired of the charade with these self satisfied bureaucrats, "Then let me free with my Droid. Oh by the way, you are correct I am not a member of the Rangers.... I would like to retire now."

Bayard coldly said, "After your rest, you will be escorted to medical for a retinal imprint and a physical."

Alex sat on his bed as the others left. He had seen the anger in Bayard's expression, at Alex's deception. He told himself he didn't care. He should have known that Kyla and Mamba were the only true companions he would have in life. No one could accept him, knowing of his ancestry, or of the things he had done to protect himself and Kyla on Banshee. What was a man but his parentage and his deeds. What did that make him? What was he? There were no answers as he slowly drifted to sleep.

The next morning Alex awoke to Mamba's fluttering greeting. The end of her hibernation lifted Alex's spirits. "Great to have you back old girl." She chirped wildly as he caressed her frill.

The door opened and two guards came into the room. Alex quickly tucked Mamba underneath the bed with the whispered command "Hide." The larger crewman said, "we were ordered to escort you to medical." They hand cuffed him and escorted him to a medical facility and a Dr. Laura Irwin.

Dr. Irwin took a retinal imprint in silence. Then she escorted him to an examining room shooing the guards away. As she went about her preparations she spoke to Alex with a friendly smile, "I here you are rumored to be some terrible escaped convict?" To his surprise, she removed the handcuffs. It didn't make sense to leave a potentially dangerous criminal alone with an unprotected female doctor, unless she wasn't alone! Alex looked around surreptitiously for hidden pickups. He smiled, they didn't even hide them very well and then responded, "It doesn't seem to disturb you Doctor?"

Irwin looking down answered, "Nope, I don't approve; sending anyone for any reason to Banshee is a great evil. That world is a living hell. The combination of gravity radiation, pressure and poisons is a slow torturous death; and if you managed to escape good for you." Glancing up, "Off course, you would know the conditions there better than I." Alex made no comment. "Would you please strip down to your civvies."

She looked up with a gasp as Alex stripped to his underwear. "Scripture, how did you get all those scars!" Dr. Irwin immediately regained her composure commenting with a strained smile, "I thought the one on your face was bravado."

Alex hadn't thought much about his old scars and burns. Everybody in the mines carried scares from mining injuries or the vicious gang warfare, and the limited medical facilities weren't used for cosmetic surgery. His scares were more elaborate then most because of his innumerable fights to protect Kyla. All this raced through his mind as he shrugged. There really was no way to explain life in the mines to an outsider.

The good doctor examined the scar on his face, commenting, "A little corrective surgery and you wouldn't be half bad looking."

Alex mumbled a noncommittal reply. He didn't trust the Doctor, or her supposed friendliness. He noted her puzzled expression as she poked, prodded and sampled various parts of his body. An interminable time later she finished and he returned to the cubicle. He wanted something to read, but his stubborn pride didn't permit him to make further requests of his jailers. He decided to do some I Chin stretches, he hated feeling helpless but there was nothing he could do to improve his situation except wait. At least he had the minicham. She buzzed out and flew around him chirping quietly as he did his Mantras.

For two days he was left to himself. Meals were brought regularly, and someone decided he could access a computer terminal during his confinement. Alex found out the shuttle was to rendezvous with the StarShip *Hokaido* in eight days at a safe discharge distance from the sun. Discharging a coil near a gravity well was suicide and a StarShip was too expensive to waste hauling materials to and from a planet. StarShips were nothing more than giant MC drives a fusion power plant and a series of docking ports for in-system shuttles and StarFighters. Even the crew lived in a detachable pod. StarShips rarely ventured into the unsafe discharge distance of four AU's from a system's primary. So shuttles of many varieties did all of the in system hauling. The *Hokaido* was scheduled to make four transits all the way to Vega IV Capitol world of the Powerful Vegan Republic. He thought the choice of transit systems interesting. It was not the most direct route and skirted Fringe space. The remote barely explored region of space 300 light years out from earth.

On the third day a delegation showed up at his door consisting of Dr. Tsay and Dr. Irwin with the Bayards. He thought what now, as he let them in.

Colonel Bayard got right to the point, "Mr. Kane, you are still an enigma to us, turning to Dr. Irwin for further explanation Your medical results seem to dispute our conclusions."

She scrutinized her electronic clip board a moment then clearing her throat she began, "In 25 years of practicing medicine, I have never seen stranger results then these.

Alex asked sardonically, "Am I about to die?"

Dr Irwin replied, "No, in fact, you are in incredibly good health. You have the densest musculature and the densest bone structure I have ever seen. Your cardiovascular system, liver, lungs, and most remarkable of all your neurological systems all operate above conventional human or even GenClone norms." Looking down at her electronic clipboard, she continued. "The remarkable configuration of the myelin sheath surrounding your neurons has doubled the speed of synaptic transmissions, and it shows in your reflexes. Your body seems to have super efficient systems for removing heavy metal toxins and radiation induced free radicals. Just incredible! Either your body, faced with the hostile environment of Banshee mutated to a more efficient form, which I consider improbable, or someone is conducting genetic experiments to build a superman. Not even GenClone genengineers have succeeded in improving human physical performance this much. Besides you don't exhibit any of their trade mark gene splicing techniques. You wouldn't care to explain, would you Mr. Kane? I personally don't believe you are an escaped convict, but I have no idea what you are."

Alex stood silently a moment. He had always known he was quicker stronger and healthier than those around him. Mercury had commented on it more than once during training. However the idea of being the product of genetic manipulation didn't make sense, he knew how he had come into the universe. He finally answered with a question of his own," Would anything in your tests indicate hypersensitivity to pain?"

"Yes, All your senses would be hyper-activated with the faster transmission along your neural pathways"

Alex nodded this explained much, "when I was young I was considered a crybaby. Scratches and bruises others in the mines would ignore would disable me with agonizing pain."

Dr. Tsay, "Ah, you admit to being a convict!"

"How did you overcome this intolerance to pain?" Bayard asked, while gesturing at the savage scar on the left side of his face, "I presume you must have."

Alex shrugged, he might as well tell the truth, "I didn't, Mamba did."

Tsay spoke next, "Who or what is Mamba?"

Alex responded by whistling the "come" command. The mini-chameleon flew from her hiding place beneath the cot landing on his shoulder with a chirp as Alex answered. "Mamba"

Irwin in surprise, "A Himalayan minichameleon one of the rarest creatures in the universe.

They supposedly cannot live away from their Landwhale symbiotic hosts for more than a short time, and they have a very poisonous stinger. How in the world did you acquire it and why is it still alive?"

Alex thought a moment and saw no harm in answering the questions asked, "I found her hibernating in an abandoned shipping module in the mines years ago." Mamba nipped his ear and licked the drop of blood welling out, "Her nips enable me to tolerate pain. I believe they have some other beneficial effects as well; and obviously she derives nutrients from the blood she consumes."

The others were both startled by this revelation and slightly revolted at the vampirish relationship between the two of them. Dr. Irwin just nodded with excitement, "Of course, that would explain the unusual complex proteins in your blood stream. They probably stimulate production of endorphins that reduce pain. Still that doesn't explain the rest of your physiological abnormalities."

Alex considered a moment and finally decided to tell the truth. "I was born on Banshee, my grandparents were convicts sentenced to the mines"

Tsay pontificated, "My understanding is that all women sent to the mines are sterilized, quite barbaric. How could they give birth?"

Alex with a twisted half smile responded, "As hard as it is to believe the sterilization is not always effective. I also would disagree with your judgment Doctor It is more barbaric to let anyone give birth on Banshee, given the conditions in the mines. Most of the Banshee born died in agony shortly after birth. Those that survived longer had to cope with serious birth defects and the hostility of the inmates in an asylum for the criminally insane, not to mention the loving care provided by their convict parent." Everyone was quiet for a moment as they tried to digest the reality of life for a child in the mines.

Irwin commented, "Not really all that hard to believe. There have been a number of suppressed investigations into the inadequate medical facilities for the Banshee convicts. I would not be surprised if the sterilization program was as negligent as all the other medical services. It would explain your physiological anomalies. You may just be a successful mutation to the harsh environment on Banshee. In fact that makes the most sense given the data available."

Alex seeing an opening said, "Imperial records will show I am not a convict. Again I believe in your honor Colonel; and expect to be released with all my property as soon as I am exonerated. Alex really wasn't sure what they would do now. His only knowledge of how the Vegan elite operated came through conversations with his mad grandmother and Mercury. Neither one a completely reliable source.

Bayard hesitatingly replied, "The pieces are beginning to make sense to me Mr. Kane. I believe the present version of your story as far as it goes. Under the circumstances I would suggest that we give you the freedom of the passenger quarters excluding militarily sensitive areas." Looking at the other members of the delegation, "I would also recommend that we keep this knowledge to ourselves. It would be a serious embarrassment to both the Imperial Coalition and Matsui if this were to become widely known."

Ambassador Alcorn agreed, "You are right off course dear. Keeping this quiet will also benefit you Mr. Kane. Knowledge of your background and ancestry could arouse prejudices, making it difficult for you to live without harassment on even the more enlightened worlds."

Alex sarcastically answered, "Your concern for me Ambassador is very reassuring. I don't need your help, just let me off at the next civilized stop."

Bayard hesitantly responded, "Mr. Kane, no I mean Alex, I find myself in an awkward position. I feel responsible for making you distrustful of us, yet I am concerned about letting a man loose with a CombatDroid, who hasn't been taught the constraints of civilized society. I am afraid I can't let you just go, any harm you inflicted on others or to yourself would then be a least partially my fault.

Alex went cold inside. He stared fixedly at the Colonel and said without expression, "I will not be imprisoned again for just being who I am Colonel. If you're afraid of me and the damage I can do just try it."

Bayard staring back angrily snapped, "Your tough but your just a kid so don't push."

Alcorn soothingly interceded, "If I may make a suggestion dear. Why don't you take him on as an apprentice CombatJack in your battalion. You get the services of a SuperDroid and a skilled warrior, and Mr. Kane gets training and legitimacy. Wait Mr. Kane please let me finish! A standard apprenticeship in Bayard's Brigadoons is two years. I am sure my husband will agree to release you from any further constraints after you have completed your training. An apprenticeship I might add that many a Jack would give a great deal to get."

Bayard and Alex starred at each other for a moment. Finally Bayard spoke "That's acceptable to me."

Alex thought it through. He didn't seem to have a lot of options that wouldn't make him an outlaw again. Besides he needed time to acclimate to this strange new universe, and Bayard was committing to training and supplying him with credentials in a useful profession. Mercenaries were common throughout known space. Hundreds of independent worlds and confederations could not afford to purchase and maintain high tech CombatDroid forces. CombatJack mercenaries mostly equipped with Terran surplus equipment supplemented lower tech planetary militias in numerous conflicts. Even the more advanced nations like the Vegan Republic, the loosely bound Confederation of Independent Planets, and the totalitarian Imperial Coalition found it cost effective to hire mercenaries to supplement their national armies at times. The great nations could use mercenaries in situations where national armies were politically risky. The Brigadoons in fact were under long term contract to Vega and were often sent on missions outside the 64 systems ruled from Vega IV. Alex reviewed these facts in the moments before he replied "I can live with that."

Alcorn in relief turned to her husband and added, "Dear I think we will need an explanation for the good captain. Might I suggest we hint to Hohiro, that Mr. Kane was a Vegan agent investigating the combat on Banshee. Given the rapprochement between the Coalition and Vega, I am sure he won't press the issue." Looking at the others, "Dr. Tsay and Dr. Irwin, I trust in your discretion in this matter."

They discussed the details for a few more minutes and then they left, taking the guard at Alex's door with them. Alex had the freedom of most of the shuttle, and after signing a few documents later that day officially became a member of the Brigadoons.

Chapter 8

His apprenticeship began the following day. The Colonel assigned him to assist the techs in the maintenance of the two CombatDroids. He was also given the Operations Book for the Brigadoons. The archaic thick written tome contained everything he needed to know to perform his new duties. The Colonel requested he memorize it and assigned a Major Paul Decampe to oversee his training. Major Decampe, the Colonel's aid and confidant scheduled a crash training program for the three weeks remaining in the voyage. The Major was crippled in a Droid duel. The loss of his left arm and damage to his back made it impossible for him to jockey a Droid. Alex was to learn it didn't make him any less of a task master.

The next three weeks passed in a whirlwind. Alex learned everything from the layout of a shuttle to appropriate conduct at a military ball. The Major even arranged for dancing lessons. Most importantly Alex had to learn the battle operations manual for the Brigadoons. When Decampe wasn't grilling him, Alex spent time in the shuttle's single CyberLink simulator testing in increasingly more difficult scenarios. He spent his so called spare time with Chief Tech Fuller tearing down and totally rebuilding the *Warlock*. He found out his tech training was spotty. Fuller knew CombatDroids and their maintenance like the back of his hand, and he tried to impart as much of that knowledge as possible to his trainees.

He did notice the docking of the *Kilaminjaro* with the StarShip *Hokaido* and the hyperlight transit, only because it was part of his training. The Major escorted him up to the control room and reviewed the whole sequence with him. Alex wanted to better understand the principles behind the Chen-Malik drive. The Major found the request inappropriate. He responded by stating, "Your training to be a CombatJack not a scientists." Alex suspected the Major just didn't know enough to explain, so he used some of his very limited free time to seek out Dr. Tsay and ask him for the principles of the drive. The good Doctor didn't know either.

Tsay explained, "I am sorry Alex. Frankly I have never met any of the few individuals who can explain the intricacies of the CM drive. Humanity is in an interregnum, mighty Sol system once the center of civilization is in decline. Most of its 16 billion people now live on negative income tax at subsistence levels. Terra's resources which once launched hundreds of StarShips every year have turned inward dissipated on a population addicted to drugs and cheap CyberLink entertainment, while the colony worlds waste their resources in interminable border feuds."

Alex thoughtfully asked, "I always heard Sol system was an invincible bastion of human technology and social justice."

Tsay dedicatedly replied, "Oh Sol system is still the greatest power in the human sphere, but the torch is being passed. GenClone genengineers have surpassed even Terra's scientists in modifying the human genome and in building better CyberLinked vehicles. Bukhara, New Rome, Vega and the GPL are all building a few StarShips now. Still most of Humanity lives under repressive regimes with limited access to education. The interminable wars fought by the colonies are really the beginning of a transition to a new order. The big question is who will replace Terra's leadership. Until that is decided mercenaries like yourself will be in great demand."

Alex left Tsay thoughtfully. A really devastating war could turn humanity into a scattering of system bound civilizations. He began to understand the need for the Universal Articles of War. If Terra no longer had the will to intervene an unrestricted war could result in total disaster for the species.

After the Transit his workload decreased, and that question came back to haunt Alex. He knew he wanted to keep the *Warlock*, but at the same time he wasn't sure he wanted to be a CombatJack mercenary. He began wondering if he would have chosen this career given a choice. Alex had spent his whole life fighting and again he was drifting into a violent profession. He dreamt of Kyla and his grandmother. They didn't seem to be angry about being left behind anymore. But after each dream he awoke in a sweat, vaguely feeling they wanted him to do something important. He just couldn't grasp what it was. After a while he decided to ask Colonel Bayard if there were alternatives to joining the Brigadoons. The Colonel granted him an interview.

Alex walked into the Colonels office and gave the smart salute he had recently learned and stood at attention. The Colonel returned the salute from behind a massive real oak desk and then formally asked, "At ease Cadet, what is it you want to discuss?"

Alex uncomfortably said, "Colonel this is awkward for me. After learning what I have about the Brigadoons and their illustrious history I appreciate what a great honor you bestowed on me by offering me a posting."

Bayard interrupted Alex with a raised eyebrow and asked, "But?"

Alex replied, "Colonel I am not sure I'm cut out to be a CombatJack. I might be better suited for another profession."

Bayard turned to a terminal built into the desk and scanned some data. "Alex do you know what I am looking at?"

"No sir"

With a sigh the Colonel spoke, "These are your training records. They're remarkable. Your simulator trials indicate you're already as good a pilot as any member of the Brigadoons. Major Decampe tells me you have progressed in three weeks farther then some trainees have in six months, and chief tech Fuller informs me you're already better then most of his tech assistants. I already know you're a survivor with a great deal of unorthodox combat experience." Pausing, "Alex you could be a great CombatJack given some more training and experience. A single CombatDroid with a pilot like you is worth a couple of conventional armored infantry regiments in combat. I know we have been driving you hard over the past few weeks, but we're only looking out for your best interests."

Alex surprised by Bayard's forth rightness replied, "It isn't the training regimen sir. Compared to Banshee it is manageable." An understatement, "I just... I just think its time for me to get away from all the killing all the violence. My life has been one endless war just to survive, and now I am drifting into a profession where I will be fighting for things I don't even understand. There must be other options. Maybe I could become a scientist or merchant trader or even a tech. I feel I ought to at least make the choice."

Bayard with a fixed stare commented, "Alex, you may not recognize it yet, but you're not cut out for civilian life. You have the instincts and temperament of a warrior. Do you really think you can quietly stand by as the future of humanity is decided by Droids on battlefields across known space? There is no place where you can crawl in a hole and escape the upcoming conflict. It's only a matter of time until the temporary truce carved out by the Treaty of Terranova ends and the GenClones continue their aggressive expansion. The Brigadoons will stand for civilization and order, we must help hold back the endless dark of the GPL's genetic meritocracy. They must be stopped before they impose their genengineering on all of humanity. We need man like you to stand with us if we are to succeed."

Alex looked at the Colonel with new understanding, This man's usually calm demeanor covered a powerful commitment to a cause. Bayard believed the GenClones would destroy his vision of civilization, and had to be stopped. Alex wasn't sure he agreed with the Colonel's goals. The GenClones were clearly more technologically advanced. However a person of Alex's dubious genetic background would have very little opportunity in a society that predetermined status via genetic mapping. In their stratified culture genetically enhanced clones ruled the roost. He also agreed with the Colonel's analysis. He wasn't cut out for a quiet life. Deep down he knew that. "All right Colonel I'm on your side with reservations for now."

The Transit took them to an obscure uninhabited system simply designated as K-5467A on the star charts. They were meeting another StarShip carrying the majority of the Brigadoon's 1st battalion, returning from the fighting on BluePearl for a well-deserved rest and refit on their home world of Normandy. Alex found this out as he watched a Horatio and a Leviathan class shuttle dock with the *Hokaido*. Alex, the Colonel, Madame Bayard, Fuller and Major Decampe transferred to the massive 8000 ton Leviathan class shuttle, *Bayonne*, the Brigadoon flagship that evening. A party celebrating the reunion of the Brigadoons with their commander was in the main lounge.

The raucous greeting of the Colonel by his command surprised Alex. The Colonel had an easy camaraderie with his officers and troopers. Alex was very uncomfortable as a dozen CombatJack jostled around him toasting the Colonel and Ambassador Alcorn. The future success of the Brigadoons and damnation to the GenClones were liberally toasted. The only time Alex had seen these many people packed together was during the incessant Banshee gang wars. He eased himself out of the crowd and finally found some space against the far wall of the lounge. He noticed the palms of his hands were sweating. Alex smiled at his absurd nervousness. He was warier then if this was a rumble between the Nats and Bloods. His mind kept telling him to get ready to fight, and suppressing his combat reflexes was a strain. He wished Mamba was here. He shouldn't have left her back in his quarters. Her presence would have helped. The Colonel was right, he didn't fit in polite society. An elbowed tap on his arm broke his concentrated indifference.

Turning Alex saw a tall slender blond man with captain's bars, looking like a cutout from a recruiting poster. The young officer snapped a greeting, while carrying two over filled drinks in each hand, "Hey newbie why don't you mingle and get acquainted with your fellow Jacks. Here have a blowtorch," as he handed over one of the drinks. Alex took the glass hesitantly, balancing it expertly in the low gravity generated by the slow acceleration of the ship. He didn't dare drink it. Alcohol and most drugs gave him migraine headaches and other neurological side effects that were equally unpleasant. He surreptitiously poured the drink into a planter when he thought no one was looking.

"Not very neighborly pouring an offered drink away like that."

Alex turned and saw a very young attractive female lieutenant in an elegant dress uniform staring at him. Flustered that he had been observed unknowingly, he haltingly replied, "I didn't want to be rude by turning the drink down. I'm allergic to alcohol. I'm Cadet Alex Kane and you are?"

The young women answered, "I know who you are, and formalities aren't required here Alex. I'm Bridgette. Campy says you're one hotshot pilot on the simulators, almost as good as me." Just as quickly as she made that remark she changed the subject "So how do you like your fellow Brigadoons so far?"

Having trouble following the conversation Alex responded "I really haven't had the opportunity to meet anyone except for the Colonel and Major Decampe. Who is Campy?" It occurred to Alex that the only conversations he had ever had with women, were with his relatives; Kyla, his mother and grandmother. A woman in the mines never just walked up to someone and started a conversation, unless it was a proposition and she had protection in the vicinity. Alex smiled again as it just occurred to him he was needlessly scanning the crowd for her backup. He wondered if this woman was unnerving or he just wasn't used to dealing with young beautiful women.

"Major Decampe silly!" As she threw back her stylishly cut blond hair with violet highlights and burst into a disconcertingly horsy laugh, "We all call him Campy, not to his face off course. That wouldn't be nice, he's such a dear. So how did you get a posting with the Brigadoons? Everybody is being quite mysterious about your background they won't even tell me, not even Robart. The old fuddies. So why don't you tell me? What's so amusing. You aren't laughing at me are you?" As she frowned.

Alex froze with his mouth half open. He didn't even know where to start. The returning captain who had offered him the drink saved him by asking. "Bridgette you aren't giving the newbie the third degree already. Give the poor fish a chance." Turning to Alex, "Don't worry about Bridgette she confuses the hell out of everyone. Even the Colonel gets that glazed look sometimes when dealing with her." He and Bridgette both laughed while he put his arm around her and stared at her possessively. "I just don't know why we all put up with you Bridge. By the way I'm Stanislaw Bouchard, my friends call me Sting." As he reached out his hand in greeting. Alex shook it.

Bridgette faking a pout not very successfully replied, "You interrupted me just when I was about to break this iron willed newbie cadet. Now how do you expect me to figure out if he belongs in the Stingers?" Turning to Alex she asked, "I hear you're riding a *Warlock*? What's it like? Is it as good as they say?" The bewildering conversation continued with Alex trapped as an unwilling participant. He tried responding to the barrage of unrelated questions fired at him by Bridgette, while trying to make some sense of the conversation.

By the time Bouchard escorted her away Alex was drenched with sweat. He had finally figured out that the Stingers were a specially formed light to medium Droid company commanded by the captain. Apparently Bridgette commanded a lance in the same company. Though he hadn't quite confirmed that. The Stingers were apparently a scouting and quick strike company, specifically designed to get behind enemy lines and disrupt supplies and delay reinforcements. He couldn't imagine Bridgette commanding anything especially a combat lance. How could her people make sense of her orders. He decided he would have to avoid the Stingers even though Bouchard seemed capable enough.

This was further reinforced when he saw Bridgette give a big hug and kiss to the Colonel and then lock arms with him. The Colonel had a big incongruous smile on his craggy face. Totally unprofessional he thought until the Ambassador also joined the little group. A light went on in Alex's head. The resemblance between the two women was remarkable. Bridgette was obviously the Colonel's daughter.

The party grew louder as liquor was freely consumed. After a while Alex sneaked out and returned back to his quarters aboard the *Kilaminjaro*. He lay down on his cot with Mamba fluttering on his chest. Well he had never fit in at the mines so why was he so surprised that he didn't fit in with total strangers. After contemplating the evening for a while, he finally shrugged and turned over to sleep. It was trite but he was who he was. There was no changing that, and if the universe didn't make room for him and what he was, he would carve out his own niche. He had done it in the mines and he could do it out here. With that resolve he slowly drifted into a restful dreamless sleep.

The next day the Colonel and his whole contingent including Alex transferred to the *Bayonne*. Fuller coordinated the difficult transfer of Droids in space. Alex helped, mostly by staying out of the way. Alex found out he was sharing quarters on the *Bayonne* with another trainee, an Ensign Brandon Flanders. They met in their cramped cubicle. Both men were busy and after hasty introductions returned to their duties. Alex was rushing to the Droid bays to run a check on the *Warlock*. He wasn't really happy about sharing quarters, but he knew the *Bayonne* was crowded. At least Brandon didn't seem to mind sharing his quarters with the minicham. His response to being introduced to Mamba, had been to comment, "I used to share my bed with my dog Blowfeld I don't mind pets." His remark seemed to offend Mamba.

At the Droid bays, he saw a bewildering array of CombatDroids and equipment. He found the *Warlock* positioned between a 48 ton *Katana* and one of the new 32 ton *Ghostrunners*. Techs were scurrying all over the place rearranging equipment and the Droids to trim the weight distribution of the giant shuttle.

Alex joined Fuller and his staff. Fuller quickly assigned him to check out the *Warlock*'s on board systems. Alex fetched his CyberLink and climbed into the cockpit for the first time in a week. It felt good to link again with the mighty machine. He spent half the morning running diagnostics on the ALI and interface systems, and assisting the techs by making adjustments and relaying data. Disappointed when the task was completed, he rushed to change and join the Major for more classroom training at 10:00 hours.

Three other trainees and Major Decampe were already there when he arrived. Brandon arrived moments after Alex. This was the first time in a classroom with other cadets for Alex. The Major began reviewing a history of Droid combat without bothering with introductions. The major emphasized the new tactics developed to counter GenClone SuperDroid technology. The Major droned on about the last great war;

..... The only advantage the Anti-GenClone Alliance had after the defeat of the 1st Imperial Coalition on New Alexandria in 2410 was the coordinated fire of whole combat units, versus the GenClone preference for single combat. By bringing multiple Droids, and massed armored infantry to bare on one SuperDroid, GenClone technological superiority could be overcome.

Flanders asked, "But aren't the GenClones changing their tactics to respond to this?"

Decampe replied, "Yes, we saw it on Terranova. The GenClones are beginning to imitate our tactics at least to the extent of coordinating fire at the small unit level. The Vegan Republic tacticians believe we can overcome this by using coordinated fire at the battalion and regimental level. Even though we continue to improve the performance of our Droid equipment, we still need to bring larger forces to bare at each engagement, if we intend to defeat the GenClones in the field.

Alex agreed with the principle the Major was espousing, but the reality might be difficult to achieve. CombatJack were notoriously independent and weren't likely to permit a commander to pick their firing strategy for them or coordinate effectively with infantry. Even more important from Alex's prospective was speed. In general the GenClones had faster Droids then the fragmented alliance worlds, which made it difficult to bring overwhelming numbers against the GenClone units.

His *Warlock* or the traditional GenClone medium Droid, the *Werewolf* would both be nearly impossible to trap, because of their speed. GenClone Jacks weren't stupid, given an untenable position they would withdraw until reinforcements arrived and then counter attack. He raised this concern with the Major. The discussion that followed didn't satisfy Alex's concerns. The class's conclusion was the GenClone warriors wouldn't withdraw because of their arrogance. This at least had been their response to date. Alex had his doubts.

Training continued the following week, while the StarShip discharged its coils. Alex grew familiar with his fellow trainees. Big laconic Flanders outwardly friendly and soft spoken was the best strategic thinker in their class with a remarkable intelligence. Alex immediately recognized another person driven to succeed by his own internal demons. Both Alex and Brandon were naturally introspective, keeping their own councils and studiously not discussing their respective pasts. Flanders was the only other trainee with his own Droid, an ancient *Scout*. No one knew where he had acquired it. Brandon had joined the Brigadoons on Terranova as a reservist during some of the most intense fighting. He had proved himself an able CombatJack and was proving out as the most able of the trainees. Even Alex recognized the innate leadership skills of the lanky senior trainee. The other members of the class generally followed his lead except for Alex of course. Alex never followed any ones lead, though he did admit the big guy made an acceptable roommate.

Things went smoothly until Alex and the other trainees began rigorous combined operations training on the sophisticated set of simulators aboard the *Bayonne*. Alex was far and away the best pilot technically, consistently out scoring Claudia Bovary, who always came in second, much to her chagrin. In the combined ops tactical planning simulations, Alex's scores dropped drastically, while Brandon's soared. When given command of the sim lance, Alex understood the tactical situations on the displays as well as anyone, but he couldn't communicate the orders that he thought were the appropriate responses. Worse yet, according to the Major, he couldn't take orders, often deviating from instructions to the detriment of the virtual reality lance. Alex was frustrated; he'd never failed at any task and he could not understand why his experience commanding the Nats didn't translate into effective leadership skills. There wasn't much of a difference as far as he could tell.

After another grueling session, the trainees stepped out of the simulator. Major Decampe strode over to Alex and began another verbal tongue lashing of his performance. Listening intently, Alex couldn't understand why he was scoring so badly, and the Major's diatribe didn't help. Why couldn't he command effectively?

The Major and the other trainees continued to believe Alex was trying to use his superior piloting skills to hotshot the sims. Alex knew better, but he couldn't understand what he was doing wrong. He recognized his actions were alienating the others.

Alex decided he needed to talk to someone and the obvious choice was his roommate, Brandon. Though taciturn, the big pilot was the least judgmental of the trainees. Alex caught up with him as they entered the locker room and politely asked, "Brandon, can I speak to you a minute?"

In his well-modulated voice, the quiet giant answered, "Sure Alex, what's up?"

Alex intensely replied, "Brandon, do you believe I'm hot-dogging it in the sims?"

Brandon bending over to unlace his boots Tersely responded, "Yes."

"Why, what am I doing wrong?"

Brandon stopped and looked at Alex appraisingly. Finally he said, "You really don't know what you're doing wrong, do you?"

"No, I really don't!"

Brandon replied, "OK, I'll try and make this as clear as possible. You either aren't obeying orders or when you do, you take them so literally, that you end up making a mockery of the commanding officer. It seems like you're trying to make fools out of the rest of us! That isn't the way a combat unit works."

Alex with a wrinkled brow replied, "I understand what you're saying but that still doesn't tell me what I'm doing wrong. If I don't do what I'm told, I'm not a team player, but when I follow instructions exactly, I'm not using initiative. I need more specificity to change my behavior!"

Brandon frowned as he deliberated on Alex's response. "OK, let's get specific; in today's sim you were ordered to take the right flank and watch for an enemy scout Lance. When the *Katana* and the two *Battleaxes* came out of the arroyo on the left, you stayed in position until Claudia ordered you to help! By that time it was too late, we'd been slagged!"

Alex snapped back, "But I was obeying orders like you and everyone said I should!"

"Come on Alex. You saw we were in trouble, yet you waited for Claudia to send you a command. You know what it's like in the middle of a fire fight, there's no time to send out orders for every little detail."

Alex asked, "So you're saying I should deviate from orders if the situation calls for it?"

Brandon sounding a little uncertain for the first time replied, "Yes, to a certain degree."

Alex training to determine the crux of the problem answered in feigned casualness, "But when I do that, everyone says I'm hot-dogging."

Brandon unsettled by his growing uncertainty shouted, "I said to a certain degree. Don't you think that stunt you pulled yesterday was beyond the scope of your orders? Jumping to that cliff face then targeting multiple enemy units when all you were supposed to do was cover our withdrawal. Come on, that wasn't a minor deviation in orders!"

Alex recalled the scenario. Brandon in his *Scout*, Claudia in a *Battleaxe* and Court Rook in a 32 ton *Roadrunner* were supposed to advance on a fortified position and take out the enemy units, estimated to be a pair of *Stingers*, a 48 ton *Firedrake* with a 60 ton *Mandrake* in reserve. Alex's *Warlock* and Chet Rook's *Scout* were to work their way up a ridge and flank the fortifications after Brandon had engaged the enemy. Things started to go wrong right away. A lucky shot with an NPC damaged the a leg actuator on Claudia's *Battleaxe*, their biggest unit. The main strike force found itself trapped and out gunned with the *Battleaxe* neutralized. Brandon had given orders for a withdrawal, and ordered Alex and Chet to take positions on the right flank to support the retreat of the damaged *Battleaxe* and the other lighter units.

Alex had already moved into position on the ridge above the fort when the new orders came through and seen the simulated enemy Droids advancing from their fortifications to destroy the retreating strike force. Quickly evaluating the situation, he decided he'd never get back in time to properly cover the retreat. Instead he jumped the *Warlock* down onto a tiny shelf behind the advancing enemy and poured a devastating fire into their rear ark. The *Mandrake* had left the fortified hill and targeted his *Warlock*. He managed to twist and dodge his way to safety, only to discover that Chet had followed him down in his *Scout*. Unfortunately he missed the rock shelf and fell to his destruction.

Alex knew his actions had been the right ones. There was no way the main body of the lance could have successfully retreated without his diversion. The fact that Chet had disobeyed his orders and irrationally followed was not Alex's fault. It didn't make sense for Chet to follow. The younger Rook had admitted that after the debriefing. After a thoughtful pause he spoke, "Brandon, I don't mean to sound conceited but I know my actions yesterday were the only way to salvage the mission. Had I followed your orders to the letter and tried to cover your withdrawal the whole unit would have been wiped out! I was just using my initiative"

Brandon had been starring without expression at Alex the whole time, finally he exploded, "You dumb jock, you couldn't possibly know that, nobody could there were too many variables, too many different ways the scenario could have run its course. No one can trust a lance mate who decides he can do as he pleases, and I can prove it to you."

"How?"

Thoughtfully the big cadet replied, "We can run the probable outcomes of the simulation on the AI. In fact lets test it now. If I can prove to you you're over extending yourself maybe you will learn to be a team player Alex." As they headed back to the sim room Alex thought that was his longest conversation with Brandon. It was also the angriest he had ever seen him. The big man was going out of his way to help, as he did with all the other trainees. That was one of the reasons he had become the natural leader of their small class. Alex knew he was right and was pleased at the opportunity to prove it. He was surprised at how important it was to him to get the respect of his roommate. They arrived at the main terminal for the shuttle's sophisticated AI. Brandon sat at the console and quickly called up yesterday's simulation. Alex watched as Brandon programmed the computer to determine the probabilities of a successful withdrawal if Alex had followed orders.

Alex interrupted just before Brandon hit the run key. "Hey can you also program an evaluation of a successful retreat assuming I conduct my diversion?"

Brandon didn't even respond, he just began programming the second evaluation. Finally he hit the run key swiveled the chair around and said, "it should take about thirty-five minutes to iterate all the permutations. I think you will see a random distribution of probabilities of success for both sets of actions. No one could foresee all the possible outcomes of that scenario Alex. Your going to have to learn the best way to win is to work as a team. Lets shower and change while we wait"

They returned to the sim room a little later after changing into their civvies. Brandon again sat at the console and requested a printout of the results. He starred at the print out and frowned. Finally he handed the results to Alex without comment. Alex looked at the numbers without surprise. There had been only a thirteen percent chance for a successful withdrawal had Alex obeyed his orders, and that assumed the opposing commander was excessively cautious. Almost every iteration showed the destruction of the *Battleaxe* and most showed the whole strike force destroyed. When Alex's diversion was factored in the odds of success went to sixty-eight percent. The results would have been higher except the computer assumed a high probability of the *Warlock* missing the shelf and falling to destruction on the jump he had easily made.

Brandon, looked up at Alex with consternation, and then spoke, "I knew we were in trouble when the *Battleaxe* was hit. I just didn't think the situation was that bad... How the hell could you know? Humans, even aided by AI's can only juggle seven variables at a time in combat. It would be impossible for you to evaluate the situation in the split second you had and conclude that this was the better course of action.... impossible!"

Alex answered, "Brandon, I knew there was a higher probability of a trap being sprung from the arroyo today then from the right flank. Had I followed my own initiative I would have joined Claudia in the valley as soon as the arroyo was reconnoitered, because that would have given us the best chance to win. Would that have been the wrong move?"

"Off course it would have been the wrong move. It would have been a direct violation of your orders."

Alex honing in on the point he needed to make asked, "But violating my orders to come to her support after the enemy attack is acceptable?"

Brandon thoughtfully replied, "Yes at that point you would have been responding to an obvious change in the situation. That's when you need to use initiative!"

It was a revelation to Alex. No wonder he couldn't seem to coordinate with the other trainees.

"That's it!" Hesitating while he collected his thoughts, he finally began to explain his discover to his room mate, "Brandon, that's the problem I am having. I'm perceiving the changes in the situation earlier then the rest of you. It's like a chess game, you expect me to maneuver independently when I perceive a threat one move ahead, while I am responding to a move three or four moves out. Hell, I can't even conceive what looking one move ahead would be like."

Brandon responded disapprovingly, "Your jumping to the conclusion that your tactical skills are superior awful quickly, aren't you Ace?"

Alex hated being called Ace by the other trainees. He knew it was a derogatory name. He had admired Brandon's restraint in not using it before. He answered in kind, knowing Brandon didn't like being called anything other then his name, "Look Big Guy, your saying I'm letting a big head lead me to some false conclusions. Well I'm telling you your letting your ego interfere with the facts, and I can prove it.

"How?"

Alex calmly replied, "Let's you and I run some simulated combat scenarios together, with you in command of a two man lance, and then evaluate the outcomes of your orders versus my initiative. We can do it right now. We can skip lunch, I'll buy you something later."

Brandon reluctantly agreed. They quickly changed into their combat gear and entered the combat simulators for some unauthorized practice runs. Both men were tired when they finished. Alex to his surprise was only partially vindicated. Clearly he was able to out anticipate Brandon in tactical situations. He was much better at responding to a given combat scenario. What also became quite clear, was that Flanders was the better strategist, with a better understanding of how to achieve the overall goals of the mission. Alex's partial failure in the end turned into an advantage. For in the crucible of the simulators the two men measured each others capabilities, gaining renewed respect for one another as they vied to out think the virtual enemy.

Alex was relieved as they headed to the Droid bay for another round with Fuller on CombatDroid maintenance. He had solved the problem with the simulations to his own satisfaction and convinced Flanders as well. It was just a matter of time until he convinced the others.

Brandon who had been unnaturally quiet even for him finally spoke, "you know you won't be able to convince the others of this talent of yours Alex."

Alex in surprise asked, "why not?"

Brandon replied, "Look you've already proved your better then everyone else at nearly everything. If you come out now and say your a tactical genius, how do you think they're going to react?"

Alex hadn't thought about it that much. In the mines you dealt with reality or you died. Out here people ignored facts if it interfered with their ego's. He was used to dealing with Nats, who had little or no ego, or with the megalomaniac inmates of the mines, who didn't perceive any reality that wasn't of their own making. Brandon was right. The rest of the Brigadoon's wouldn't take his vindication very well when put that way. He answered, "Okay you're right. I can't come out and say I'm a tactical genius. What do I do then. I can't function in combat the way the Major and the others want me to. I just don't think that way."

Brandon after a thoughtful silence answered, "I know. Lets both think about it some." Then he looked over at Alex with a grin, "Between the two of us we ought to figure some way out of almost anything."

Brandon proved to be right again, the solution was simple once they put their heads together. They rigged a private frequency in the sims to communicate to each other. Brandon explained to Alex the appropriate response during a scenario, and Alex fed him tactical intelligence. The results were spectacular. Both of them scored higher than any trainees in Brigadoon history. They began to make deliberate errors to bring their scores down and prevent the growing attention of the senior staff.

The little conspiracy between the two young trainees brought them much closer together and slowly gained acceptance for Alex from the Rook brothers. It had the undesired result of distancing both Brandon and Alex from the only woman in the training lance, the diminutive Claudia Bovary, daughter of a famous Vegan surgeon, aristocrat and congressman. Wealthy suitors had vied for her attention due to her Nordic good looks and family connections. Claudia had been studiously polite to Alex until his operations scores went from dismal to exceptional. For some reason she took it as a personal affront that the no birth, no account could now beat her at every aspect of being a CombatJack. She believed in the nobility of fighting for truth and justice.

Their arguments over the purposes of war were a source of amusement for the others, even the Major. He often paired them in the simulators just to test their reactions to working together. Alex couldn't help feeling her idealism misplaced. War to him was just an ugly way to protect yourself and your property. Not the proving ground for noble causes. They recognized in each other totally different perspectives and the weight of their different backgrounds. It was a barrier neither of them cared to breach even though at least on Alex's part there was a physical attraction.

Chapter 9

Court and Chet had their heads together conspiratorially discussing another one of their endless pranks in the auxiliary lounge, while they drank their favorite concoction, a WitchesBrew. They were the worst or best pranksters in the Brigadoons depending on whether you were on the receiving end of their jokes or an amused observer. Universally well liked, they were skilled at breaking the tensions that could arise on a crowded shuttle. Both brothers were short, dark, very broad and hirsute. They claimed to descend from some extinct class of earth primates called gorillas, while flexing their remarkably long muscular arms. To their credit, they both were quite competent and serious during training.

Alex sat between Chet and Brandon at their favorite table nursing a carbonated water. Claudia had just arrived and sat down in her regular spot across from Alex. It was only a few hours before the next transit. They had all been given a day off because of preparations by the Brigadoon staff for the new system, a world called Fairhaven. There were a lot of rumors about possible trouble at their next destination.

Fairhaven intrigued Alex as he reviewing the files on the system. Fairhaven was a water world only eight percent of its surface was land. Amazing he thought, a world with oceans of water and not molten rock. Two small narrow equatorial continents divided by a narrow strait dominated the planet. The capital of the world New Constantine straddled the narrowest portion of the strait, connecting the two continents with a series of spectacular suspension bridges. Unlike many of the human inhabited star systems, Fairhaven lived up to its name. The two main land masses had a climate and terrain similar to Earth's Mediterranean littoral without the over development and environmental degradation of the home planet. Its surface gravity was a comfortable 89% of earth normal. Its forty-eight million inhabitants maintained a very high living standard for a planet near the edge of human inhabited space, funded by the export of Chateau Bruton Fairhaven wines and Blue Salmon stocks. Two of the most expensive luxury items in known space.

The planet had remained politically stable for centuries under the benevolent rule of the Counts of Monteverde, one of the most ancient lineage's in the Vegan Republic. The Counts were traditionally absentee landholders, supplying their highly valued services to the Republic, While a loose federation of free city states and their elected council ran the day to day affairs of the planet. Alex thought the system worked well because no matter how rancorous the disputes between the city states, the Counts military control prevented wars.

Alex looked up from his viewer as he noticed the volume of the conversation rising. The excited voice of Chet Rook was relaying the latest rumor about their next transit. ".... Scuttlebutt says we're definitely going to make landfall near New Constantine. There's been a lot of unrest along the Frontier, since The Republic began stripping these borders to reinforce the front against the GenClones. Fairhaven is the richest prize in the whole sector and we're going to make a show of force to insure no one tries anything. Landfall on a planet with some of the best food and wine in known space, great stuff bro!"

Court in a wistful voice said, "Ah, New Constantine, they say the women are more stimulating then the wines. A little shore leave would go a long way to making this old gorilla happy. What do you think Brandon. Are we going to land?"

Brandon just shrugged and continued sipping a glass of burgundy.

Claudia in one of her huffs spoke up, "You two cretins can't think about anything except your physical pleasures. Can't you see the wider implications. Fairhaven is one of the most important bastions of technology and civilization in this sector of the Vegan Republic. Why they even manufacture Droid components in New Constantine. If we land it's because Vega needs to ward off its enemies, not for the personal gratification of the two of you."

Court with a big grin replied, "you mean you won't join us on the white sand beeches along the south shore? Damn, what a shame Chet has been looking forward to seeing you in something other then a uniform."

Chet blushed. The remark had hit closer to home then his brother had anticipated.

As usual Brandon saved the situation by calmly commenting, "we might need to do more than just show ourselves."

The little bombshell caught their attention.

Claudia was the first to respond, "now what is that supposed to mean, and where did you get the scut. No holding out now."

Brandon shrugged and leaned back in his seat quietly stating, "Haven't you all noticed the absence of the Stingers. Both Captain Bouchard and Bridgette Bayonne haven't been seen in their usual haunts for the last twenty-four hours because they're making preparations."

Court in an excited voice asked, "Preparations for what?"

Brandon answered deliberately, "You were just repeating the rumor about an unidentified StarShip transiting out system when the *Hokaido* arrived. It looks like it might be heading for Fairhaven."

Chet in bafflement asked, "So what does that have to do with the Stingers?"

Alex interrupted before Brandon could answer, "Their prepping their thrust equipped Droids for a combat drop. Why do you think they're relocating them to the exit bays and fabricating ablative shielding."

Brandon looking over at Alex speculatively, "I hadn't heard about the shielding. That means they must be planning a high altitude drop"

Alex replied casually, "They only have six thrust equipped Droids in the Stingers. If they're using a high altitude drop, they must be planning to secure a landing zone for the *Bayonne*."

Brandon suddenly got the biggest grin, Alex had ever seen on his face as he hurriedly rose from his chair and grabbed Alex, "Let's go see the Captain."

Everyone started asking Brandon what was going on, but he just rushed out without comment.

Alex had kept quiet during their departure from the lounge, but finally he spoke, "Are you planning to get us in some trouble Brandon?"

Brandon replied excitedly, "Nope, you and I are going to join a combat drop to secure a DZ for this baby we're on."

Alex trying to cool his friends excitement said, "I'm not real hot on the idea of volunteering for risky missions, I here Jacks who do that don't live until retirement. Besides if Fairhaven is over run by renegades we'll have plenty of opportunities for action after we land so why rush it."

"Have you ever landed in a shuttle in an DZ that wasn't secured?" Alex shook his head, "I have.... Trust me you would rather be on the ground."

Alex thoughtfully answered, "I hadn't thought about it, but once you put it that way." As they hurried down to the Droid storage bay Alex realized that sitting in a shuttle making a landing in an unsecured DZ would be about as much fun as chewing glass. If the Captain would permit the two of them to join the planetary drop with their two thrust equipped Droids, the whole force would have a better chance of success. Once again Brandon had shown a flair for the strategic needs of the situation. It would be interesting to see if they could sell having a couple of trainees join a combat drop to the Captain.

They arrived at the outer hold where techs swarmed over six light and medium Droids. Brandon spotted Bouchard down by an enhanced *Renegade* and the Captain's own ultramodern *Ghostrunner*. They traversed the bay floor and saluted him smartly. Brandon snapped, "Cadets Flanders and Kane volunteering for special duty, Sir."

Bouchard replied laconically while checking out his Droids right leg actuators, "Cut that official frakke Brandon, what do you turkeys think you're doing down here?"

Brandon ramrod straight and looking straight ahead at empty air replied, "Sir, it has come to our attention that a couple of additional thrust equipped Droids could be of use to the Stingers in your next deployment."

Bouchard sarcastically commented, "Great, the two of you figured this out. The Colonel is going to love that."

Bridgette walking from behind her *Renegade* asked, "What did our star cadets figure out?"

Alex relaxing from his formal stance answered, "We thought since you're making ablative shielding and relocating your thrust equipped Droids to the outer bay, that two more Droids might come in handy on your mission, Sir."

Bouchard getting serious said, "You two think to much. Now why don't you cut the hero frakke and leave the thinking to your officers, before I assign you some additional duties appropriate to your skills. Like cleaning latrines."

Bridgette in a surprisingly serious tone interceded in their behalf, "Sting, you might want to give them a chance, from what I've heard they both have combat experience, so they may not be totally worthless. Why don't we ask the Colonel?"

Bouchard mulled it over for a moment, then said, "You're right two extra Droids even in the hands of mediocre pilots could make a difference. Come on let's go see the Colonel."

Bouchard gave some instructions to Lieutenant Hazard, commander of Beta lance and lead the foursome silently to Battalion HQ right below the bridge. A Brigadoon commando in dress greens ushered them into the Colonel's presence.

The Ambassador, Major Decampe and Major Henri Duvalsaint looked up from a topological display of the smaller continent on Fairhaven upon their entrance.

The Colonel spoke with creased brow, "What is it Bouchard more problems?"

Bouchard replied, "No sir, we have a proposal to improve our chances in case we face opposition in securing a DZ."

Decampe sarcastically interrupted, "It wouldn't have anything to do with the two half trained Cadets you have with you?"

Bouchard with the beginnings of a smile answered, "As a matter of fact it does sir. Cadets Flanders and Kane have figured out the reason for our activities. They come to me to offer their services and those of their Droids. I believe even with their limited experience they could make a difference if we face opposition."

The Colonel interrupted Decampe before he went into one of his diatribes on the uselessness of rookies in combat. "I know both of you think you have combat experience. But what you have done in no way prepares you for a combat drop into hostile territory; and don't get me wrong gentleman that is exactly what the Stingers are going to do. This is not some joy ride or an easy path to glory."

Brandon very seriously replied, "Colonel, you're right Kane and I haven't made a combat drop. But I suspect neither have the majority of the Stingers. While I at least have had the experience of fighting my way out of a shuttle in an unsecured DZ. Sir all I can say is if our presence can in any way prevent that from happening to this ship it is worth the risk."

Alex jibbing in, "And don't forget sir that my *Warlock* is specifically designed for just that kind if insertion. Its aerodynamic profile and advanced electronic counter measures substantially reduces the risk of detection and landing accidents. While my specialized sensors could be invaluable to the Captain during scouting patrols."

It was the tall Neuvo Jamaican, Major Duvalsaint, who broke the ensuing silence, "They're right. Their presence alone could prevent some force from engaging the drop team. I think we should let them go."

The Colonel hesitated a moment longer. Possibly he was considering whether some might perceive this as a way of reducing the risk to his daughter by placing some very green cadets at risk. "All right get them prepped for a high atmosphere insertion. We will evaluate the situation when we get there and determine whether their presence would be of value to you at that point Captain. Dismissed."

Both Alex and Brandon left the cabin without any display of emotion until they were well clear of the senior staff. Then they both broke out into wide grins. Bouchard interrupted their momentary display of pleasure by giving them a series of orders to prepare for the drop. They weren't going to have much time to enjoy the moment. They had two days to get their Droids ready, then another day to familiarize themselves with the mission.

Alex and Brandon were so busy the next three days they barely noticed the transit into Fairhaven space. After completing their preparations on the third day, they and the Stinger Jacks were called in for a briefing by Bouchard. The news was bad.

Alex and Brandon were comfortably seated when the last of the Stinger drop team arrived, Ensign Miagi. When Miagi sat down, Captain Bouchard walked to the front of the room with a pointer, and activated an electronic display of a portion of the planetary surface on an overhead screen. Bridgette as his exec was sitting to his left with some folders. Alex couldn't help noting how serious and professional she looked. He had radically changed his opinion of her as an officer in the last few days. When it came to combat she was all business and remarkably concise and competent.

Bouchard started the briefing, "Well boys and girls you've all been hearing the rumors, now you're going to get the facts as far as intel has been able to decipher them. If you haven't heard it yet," He snorted knowingly. "It's true, a well armed and well equipped mixed Droid and infantry force has invaded the planet." There was a stirring in the room as the rumors were finally confirmed. The captain continued uninterrupted. "Estimates range between 60 and 90 Droids are in the attacking force so far, and more are suspected on the way, with at least two companies of infantry in support and some StarFighter cover."

Brandon whistled. This meant that this wasn't some hit and run bandit force but a force of conquest and occupation. Alex looked around the room. No one seemed particularly concerned that the Brigadoons would be taking on a force nearly twice their strength.

Bouchard continued, "It gets worse. We haven't identified the invaders yet. They appear to be a mixture of renegades and renegade GenClone units. Initial contacts with enemy forces indicates the majority of their Droids are either enhanced or of GenClone design. Their pilots appear to be experienced. We have some footage of the fighting that took place at Karga pass two days ago. The planetary militia is in the green and black of the Count of Monteverde. The enemy Droids have no designations we recognize, but at least one SuperDroid has been identified.

The room went dark and the screen lit up with a wavering picture of a green valley surrounded by tall rocky hills. Across a hillock a line of heavy and medium Droids marched nearly abreast. Alex recognized some of the older designs, anchoring the left side of the line. Lighter Droids maneuvered through the tree line on the far side of the valley.

A line of green and black Droids advanced to meet the threat. Footage of the fighting that ensued, showed the invaders to be formidable opponents. The Fairhaven forces were out-gunned. They had approximately the same number of Droids, but only a pair of heavies, an enhanced *Warlord* and a *Mace*. The two sides started exchanging long range missile fire when they were in range.

Then they closed, with both sides trying to encircle one another. As best as Alex could tell, the results were a series of one on one actions between Droids. The camera angles weren't very helpful. Alex saw a *Gunner* fire all four of its paired 88 MM phased array lasers into an onrushing *Katana*, completely shearing off its right arm and stripping away much of the chest armor. The EMD shield shimmered green under the intense fire, very good shooting. The *Gunner* was clearly GenClone enhanced. The trivid film showed that the militia was outclassed. Within minutes the surviving Fairhavenites were fleeing the field in total disarray. The courageous stand of the *Warlord* pilot saved the militia. The 64 ton assault Droid stood besides the smoking ruin of the *Mace* and continued to pore deadly accurate Electron Projection cannon bolts and laser fire into the invaders. A pair of laser bursts sliced through the damaged cockpit of a light SuperDroid, destroying both machine and pilot. It proved to be the last hurrah for the *Warlord* as a massed barrage of high explosive armor piercing HEAP missiles crashed into its right flank. Its EMD shield blazed blue as it staggered. The Droid managed to right itself and twisted its torso to launch its own attack, when a raider *Apollo* fired its massive 120 micrometer sliver cannon directly into the *Warlord*'s humanoid torso. The hypervelocity collapsed carbon tipped slivers sliced into the armor beneath the depleted shields. For a moment the assault Droid stood apparently unscathed, then a great explosion shattered the war machine and scattered pieces of it over much of the battlefield. The camera's angle wavered then the screen went dark and the lights came back on.

Bouchard waited a moment for everyone to absorb what the film showed, then said, "That's what we're going up against once we land the *Bayonne*. We have contacted the militia forces planet side and they cannot guarantee a safe landing zone anywhere on the eastern continent even in the capitol. So we're going to go through with the backup plan and launch the thrust equipped members of the Stingers from the upper atmosphere, to secure a DZ for the *Bayonne* here." As he pointed to a spot on the map southeast of New Constantine. "Once we secure the drop zone, the *Bayonne* and the rest of the Brigadoons will join us, and we will march due north and try to flank the main invader force five hundred kilometers north of the DZ. They now control almost the entire Eastern half of the main continent. Though we believe they're spread thin suppressing the locals."

Bouchard continued with the briefing. Giving out specific assignments and mission details. Numerous questions were asked and answered. Brandon asked only one question of Bouchard, "Why don't we coordinate securing a DZ for the *Bayonne* with the militia?"

Bouchard replied, "There are some indications the raiders have infiltrated the command and communications structure of the militia. We can't afford to give away the location of the drop zone until the *Bayonne* is down. Once that happens we will contact the locals to coordinate our activities. Until then all they'll know is we're on the way."

Lieutenant Hazard, sarcastically whispered a little to loudly to his neighbor, "Great we're out numbered two to one, the local militia forces can't be trusted, and we're going to make a high atmospheric insertion with a couple of rookies to baby sit along the way."

Bouchard over hearing replied with a tight smile, "As I remember Hazard, you were looking forward to some action."

Hazard a little chagrined at being over heard put up a bold front, "I'm always interested in action, I just don't relish fighting with rookies covering my butt."

Bouchard snapped back, "That's enough Lieutenant, we are all members of the team and we will work together to insure the success of this mission, is that understood?"

The little exchange ended the briefing on a slightly sour note. Afterwards everyone rushed off to make last minute preparations. It was sixteen hours until the drop.

Chapter 10

The hive of activity subsided in the last few minutes before the bay doors opened. The eight Droids, cocooned inside their ablative shield casings looked like deadly Mechanical insects ready to hatch on the blue and green world below. All the pilots were in their cockpits busily going through their pre-launch checklists. The giant Droid storage bay was silent and completely empty, in preparation for the near vacuum when the outer bay doors opened.

The egg shaped Leviathan class shuttle began skimming the planetary atmosphere, sending giant contrails of super heated gas deflecting off the heat shields, engulfing the plasma flame of the enormous thrusters. The great ship was decelerating at nearly the maximum thrust of 2.5 g's. The leviathan slowed relative to the planetary surface as she prepared to release her cargo. As the speed subsided, the contrail faded away and four openings appeared at the base of the ship. Eight relatively small pods, in staggered sets of four, fell into the microbar pressured atmosphere, 330 kilometers above the surface of Fairhaven. The *Bayonne* turned and began thrusting to gain altitude, while the encased Droids plummeted to the planet below.

Alex sat in the shuddering cockpit of the *Warlock* watching his display for possible malfunctions caused either by the heat or the intense vibrations. The ablative shielding was already at 1600 degrees, as the thin atmosphere super heated the outer edges of the protective armor. Every centimeter of the CombatDroid shook from the vibrations caused by the 8000 kph passage through the minute pressure variations of the troposphere. The communications blackout made him feel absolutely alone during the drop. He couldn't even pick up readings on the other Droids with his passive sensors because of the cocoon surrounding the *Warlock*. The heat in his cockpit continued to rise slowly as the ablative shields slowly eroded away. They were supposed to completely disintegrate at five kilometers leaving him free to complete the final deployment with the thrusters. A drop like this should last about twenty-four minutes, assuming nothing went wrong. His biggest concern was the small disposable acetylene rocket pack attached to the casing. It was supposed to kick in at forty kilometers and slow him down to terminal velocity. If it didn't function as designed, he'd fry.

The rocket pack kicked in smoothly, right on time, Alex let out a sigh of relief. Falling for another seventy-three seconds, he fired the small demolition charge, blowing the last remnant of the casing just five kilometers above the surface. Unencumbered, he continued to plummet at the velocity of 405 meters per second. His streamlined Droid, with its small airfoils, was better suited for this kind of mission than most thrust equipped Droids. The displays became functional, showing the other seven pods still in formation. Brandon had fired his thrusters early to stabilize a spin causing him to fall slightly behind the rest of the formation. Alex sympathized with his friend. Brandon really wasn't one of the better pilots in the Brigadoons and this kind of planetary landing was difficult for even experienced pilots. Unlike his *Warlock*, most thrust equipped Droids had the aerodynamics of a meteor with a rocket engine attached. Though agile in combat, Brandon's *Scout* was no exception.

Ignoring the blue Friend or Foe ID'ed indicators on his main screen, he began scanning the green surface for potential threats. Nothing much except for some small heat sources that could either be large animals or humans. Their distribution was random, indicating it wasn't an enemy platoon preparing a warm welcome he hoped. It looked as if the drop zone was free and clear of mechanized units. That didn't mean it would stay that way, but it was a relief to know he'd have breathing space after landing. The chances of the detected heat sources being dug in enemy infantry was unlikely. There was no way that the raiders could have pinpointed the drop zone that accurately.

He fired the thrusters and landed the *Warlock* smoothly on a grassy knoll just below the tree line, overlooking the smooth flat valley. The Brigadoons were planning to use the valley to land the *Bayonne*. Alex looked around at the scenery through the visual sensors. Evergreens covered the surrounding hills, a small burbling brook flowed down the opposite side of the wild flower covered valley. Willows fluttered in a gentle breeze along the banks of the brook. A small, symmetrical, wooden chalet with intricately carved trim around the doors and windows, stood in a clearing near the stream. A herd of large herbivores grazed in its small abandoned garden, completely oblivious to the roar of Droids landing on the hills. The herbivores were the source of his thermal readings.

Free running water on the surface of a planet! He'd known it existed intellectually, but that didn't overcome the visceral reaction he felt at the sight of such a wonder. A planetary surface that wasn't immediately lethal to life was hardly imaginable to a Banshee born miner. To one who embraced living things, this was a miracle. Alex was at once both pleased and saddened by the sight. He imagined the pleasure Kyla and the other Nats would have felt if they were here. Here he was far away from the harsh realities of his home planet on a habitable world, yet there was no one to share the experience.

Alex snapped out of his reverie as an authoritative voice came over the intercom.

"Move it Kane, You're out of position." The Captain sounded tense.

Alex dismayed by his inattention, began moving to the start of his patrol area. He noticed Brandon had landed well outside the DZ and was rushing to join Bouchard, his partner for the mission. Alex also hurried to join Bridgette, in her enhanced *Renegade*, at the starting point of their recon sweep. Alex and Bridgette joined up and worked their way west to a jagged arroyo. It seemed the ideal hiding place for an enemy strike force because the high content of iron could confound a Droid's scanners. The other Droid pairs were also doing their recon sweeps at roughly the cardinal points of the compass. If all went well, the *Bayonne* would land within the hour.

Alex and Brandon paired with the two senior officers to make up for their lack of experience. Alex thought it a stupid idea. Basically they had destroyed the cohesiveness of both pairs. Now the four pilots weren't sure of the reaction of their new partners. He hoped they didn't run into trouble.

After the completion of the sweeps, all the recon units reported back no activity on any of the fronts. The lack of response to the combat drop was disconcerting. The DZ was only five hundred kilometers southwest of the capital and just four hundred kilometers due south of an area of heavy enemy activity. An over flight by one of the raiders StarFighters should have occurred by now. The raiders must have detected the approach of the *Bayonne* and the drop. Yet all fronts remained quiet. Captain Bouchard sent the all clear to the *Bayonne*. The great shuttle had nearly made one complete orbit around the planet. The landing window for the DZ was only three minutes long. Once the shuttle entered the atmosphere they had to hold the DZ against any odds for at least two hours. There was no turning back for the *Bayonne* and her crew once they started the approach.

Forty-five minutes after the all clear, Bouchard and Brandon detected Droids moving in from the Northwest. Alex picked up readings from the same direction moments later and reported four thermal readings. There was at least one heavy based on the mag readings. The *Warlock's* sophisticated full spectrum scanners, FSS, was able to pick out more detail. The worst scenario possible was happening. The *Bayonne* was committed to this DZ, and the Stingers found themselves facing a large enemy force with no possibility of withdrawal.

The Captain ordered Bridgette and Alex to flank the advancing force. The two other recon units were ordered to protect the DZ in case any of the enemy units broke through the Captain's lance. Bouchard's plan was simple enough; his command lance, composed of Alex, Brandon and Bridgette, would delay the advance of the enemy force with harassing fire. A fire lance composed of the remaining Droids under Lieutenant Hazard in his *Mandrake*, would stay in reserve to protect the DZ. If the enemy proved too powerful, the fire lance could move up in support.

Alex and Bridgette accelerated to full speed in an attempt to hide behind an iron impregnated hillock to the right of the advancing Droids. Bouchard and Brandon were moving deliberately to a better defensive position behind a seep eroded stream bank right below the same hillock. Alex activated his Stealth Counter Measures, SCM, as he reached his position. He figured the attackers would need better coordination than the defenders and asked permission to try to circle behind the enemy.

Bouchard's response was a curt "No!" With the admonition to maintain Comlink silence. By this time they had detected five enemy units, a *Kingfisher*, a *Nimrod*, and a *Mandrake*. The *Kingfisher* gave away the fact that this wasn't a militia force. The 48 ton SuperDroid clearly belonged to the invaders. The command lance was in for a fight.

Alex was slightly ahead of Bridgette's *Renegade* when he detected a flickering signal to the left. Soon there were two thermal readings. He analyzed the readout trying to determine the nature of this new threat. The less efficient detection equipment of Bridgette's Droid had apparently not sensed the two additional units and Bouchard was too far to the East. Alex opened up the command channel, "I have two more thermal readings approximately five kilometers southwest of our present position, Captain. They look like tanks."

Bouchard swore, "Frakke. Okay, I'm splitting you two up. Command four, go find out what's to the Southwest and get back ASAP. Command two, continue per the plan."

Alex wasn't happy with the orders. The two tanks were the least of their problems. Leaving the rest of his lance facing a nearly overwhelming force was a bad move, he didn't argue though. That's one thing he had learned during training. Leaning the Droid into a high speed turn, he accelerated to his flank speed of 120 kph. He quickly identified the two icons on his heads up display as *Pantheon* Light hover tanks. Alex was surprised to find himself un-intimidated by his first real Droid combat. He suspected his lack of command responsibility was lulling his usual pre-combat jitters. The two tanks moved to intercept him, their speeds nearly matching his own.

Alex and the tanks would come within long weapons range in just under a minute. Alex sent out the Friend Or Foe (FOF) identification signal without expecting a response. The tanks weren't moving like friendlies. Without hesitation he crossed a small ridge line and made visual contact. Quickly he locked his NPC at the lead vehicle and fired. Even the deadly accuracy of his modified GenClone tech NPC couldn't account for the remarkably lucky shot. The violet beam smashed into one of the two HEAP armed three ton pods, peeling away the 4 CM Durasheath armor and igniting the high explosive missiles. The resulting explosion rocked the light tank, knocking it out of control. Tanks didn't mount EMD shields and Cubed armor making them easy prey for a CombatDroid. The fast moving tank crashed into some small trees instantly destroyed. Surprisingly, it did not explode.

The second tank fired both its laser directed Thermal missile launchers at extreme range in retaliation. Alex didn't waste time dodging the DFM's. He charged head on and triggered both his left and right HEAP missile launchers in response. Bouchard had chosen that particular weapons configuration for all the weapons pods. HEAP was the most versatile pod weapon. The missiles headed for the tank with deadly accuracy, directed by the sophisticated targeting electronics of the SuperDroid. The Pantheon slued around in a desperate attempt to avoid the missile barrage. While Alex watched his APDS engage a dozen incoming missiles destroying four out of the five that posed a threat. The fifth one detonated on his EMD shield harmlessly. Alex, didn't wait to determine damage. He spun the *Warlock* around and headed back to the command lance, while his generator quickly recharged the shield. Through his rear view screen he watched as four of the HEAP rounds struck the Pantheon. Smoke and debris littered the area around the crippled tank. Neither tank would pose a threat.

Crossing back over the ridge, Alex heard and saw the distant battle. Bouchard had withdrawn the rest of the lance from their original position after nearly being overrun. He ordered Alex to join them when Alex made his report. Alex took one look at the situation and saw disaster. The enemy lance had formed a crescent and was advancing steadily on the command lance. The lighter Stingers would soon be forced into a slugging match with the heavier raiders.

Disobeying orders, he activated his FSS and ODC, then shut down all his active sensors. He then changed his line of advance to intercept the enemy lance from the rear arc. To him the choice was clear, either break the invader formation or watch the command lance disintegrate under their massed firepower.

Screaming through the wooded savanna at 250 kph, the *Warlock* was on the verge of instantaneous destruction from the slightest misstep. Only a lunatic or a desperate man would pilot a Droid at these speeds over this kind of rugged terrain. Alex hoped his suicide attack would surprise the raiders. Speeding past a small clump of trees, he spotted an enemy *Renegade* firing at an object outside his visual range. Alex shut down the ODC and slowed slightly while he lined up all his weapons on the lightly armored back of the *Renegade's* already damaged left leg. He had target lock, but wanted to make sure he was within range of both his NPC and 44 MM lasers. He only had one free shot and he better make it good.

The *Renegade's* pilot must have finally detected his presence because the humanoid Droid started to turn. This was Alex's signal. Slowly and methodically he fired first the NPC then the lasers at the exposed leg. His first shot connected above the knee, the NPC punched right through the shields. The second shot missed, vaporizing the shrubs at the feet of the Droid. With the shield down the third laser shot smashed into the damaged knee joint, destroying exposed fiberoptic circuits. The *Renegade* stumbled then regained its balance long enough to hastily fire two poorly aimed shots from its 60 MM lasers. Both missed.

He responded by triggering both pod launchers. The missiles exploded all over the enemy Droid, one of them further damaging its left leg. The 40 ton humanoid Droid crumpled to the ground, its leg twisted at a bizarre angle.

Their battle hadn't gone unnoticed. Two raider Droids turned away from the retreating command lance to face this new threat. A *Mandrake* and a *Kingfisher*. Surprise was no longer an issue so Alex deactivated the SCM gear. Bouchard immediately came on line. "Command Four, Command Four,... Alex get your butt over here, now!"

Alex dryly answered," I'm trying to comply sir, however I'm having a little difficulty disengaging from the enemy. Request fire support, if possible. Command Four out."

The staccato fire of the *Mandrake's* 50 MM sliver cannon accentuated his response. Alex was now madly twisting back and forth to avoid the combined fire of the two powerful Droids. The *Mandrake* was closer and had the better angle. Soon it would be able to bring its powerful short range weapons to bare.

Alex was in trouble. The armor and shields of the *Warlock* couldn't long stand the fire power once he cleared the copse of trees. The rest of the command lance was too busy to provide support. He was on his own, but that was the way he liked it. This would be a test of his belief that speed and maneuverability could overcome shear firepower.

Activating his ODC again, the *Warlock's* heat spiked into the red. The *Kingfisher* fired a spread of HEAP missiles at the position he had just vacated with his burst of speed. He knew the SuperDroid would be waiting for him with its heavy lasers when he cleared the trees. Alex charged just to the right of a big trunk at the edge of the clearing. As he passed it, he reached out with his left arm, grabbed the trunk and swung 90 degrees, like a child around a maypole. The bark shredded and the tree splintered under the tremendous force of the Droid's pivot. Alex scrambled to stay upright while maintaining his speed. Accomplishing the impossible, he found himself between the two enemy Droids, charging the *Mandrake*.

The *Kingfisher's* pilot again misjudged the *Warlock*, firing his heavy lasers at the position Alex had just vacated, then he found himself unable to fire again for fear of hitting the *Mandrake*. Alex grinned at the enemy pilots dilemma, as he triggered all his weapons, first the lasers then the NPC then the HEAP missiles, at the surprised *Mandrake*. He hit the heat overload bypass as alarms screamed in the cockpit. He targeted the DFM launcher hoping for an internal explosion. His deadly shots destroyed the launcher unfortunately it didn't explode. He found himself closing on the *Mandrake*, as it retaliated with a hasty shot from its sliver cannon. A stream of hyper velocity slivers traversed from right to left across Alex's path. Slivers overwhelmed his EMD shield smashing into the *Warlocks* Right pod, and knocking it of service. The *Mandrake* then fired its phased array laser dissipating his shield 50 percent.

Ignoring the heat alarms, Alex responded with his NPC and lasers stripping the torso and head of his opponent as they converged on one another. The heavier, better armored *Mandrake* had the advantage in a close in duel. Alex had no intention of slugging it out with the humanoid Droid. He surprised his opponent again by firing his thrusters and leaping directly over him. There wasn't much clearance. The apparently suicidal maneuver exposing his back to both enemy Droids was based on speed, surprise and Alex's unbounded confidence in his piloting skills.

As his leap carried him above the *Mandrake*, Alex cut his thrusters falling towards his opponent. Within reach of the enemy cockpit, Alex lashed out with his left leg, shattering the Duraplast. Not even EMD shields could repel 40 tons of kinetic energy. With sparks flying out of the cockpit, the *Mandrake* tumbled to the ground out of control. At this point Alex wasn't paying attention to anything but the controls of his unbalanced Droid. He tried desperately to stabilize the *Warlock's* landing using both the delicate touch of the CyberLink and the manual controls. The kick had destabilized the *Warlock's* flight, sending it tumbling to join its fallen opponent. For all his skill, even Alex was only able to position his Droid to partially cushion the fall.

Crashing to the ground, Alex was hurled around in the cockpit suspended by his harness. He heard the screech of shredding metal as the *Warlock's* right arm shattered on impact. The articulated legs splayed out at an unnatural angle, as they exceeded their tolerances.

Moments passed as Alex regained his orientation and then managed to bring his Droid back upright and start a limping jog back to the rest of the lance. As the old cliché went, "Discretion was now the better part of valor." He did the little he could do to avoid the long range fire from the *Kingfisher*. Bridgette came to his rescue by opening a wicked laser barrage to distract his remaining opponent. Alex had succeeded in taking down two enemy Droids. The enemy's ferocious assault started to wither with two of their units down and out. For a moment it looked as if the Stingers had won. Then both Alex and Bouchard detected more thermal readings approaching from the North.

The three surviving raider Droids withdrew to a defensive position, to await the arrival of reinforcements. Alex finally reached the lance, what he found wasn't good. Brandon's *Scout* was a battered wreck with all its weapons destroyed and much of its armor gone. It was too crippled to return to the DZ without support. If the raiders renewed their attack, Bouchard had ordered Brandon to punch out and escape on foot, rather then try to fight the helpless machine. Bridgette's *Renegade* was in only slightly better shape, with its left arm completely sheared off and both arm mounted lasers destroyed. It had become a giant metallic, one armed warrior. Alex and the Captain were both still battle ready. The *Warlock* had lost one of its launcher and damaged an arm and leg actuator.

For thirty minutes the two forces waited eight hundred meters apart. Bouchard had ordered Lieutenant Hazard to reinforce the command lance with two of the units from the fire lance. They arrived, two enhanced 32 ton *Saber*s, just before the raider reinforcements; a five Droid lance. The now reinforced enemy had eight Droids to Bouchard's five. The raiders renewed their attack. Alex and the two *Saber*s rained barrages of HEAP missiles on the attackers, inflicting some minor damage. Bouchard ordered another retreat. Brandon disobeyed the Captain's original orders, and tried to limp his crippled *Scout* to safety. Instead, he stumbled while climbing up the steep bank and fell into the open. The raiders finally had a clear target. They shredded the *Scout* with massed fire in seconds. Brandon just managed to eject before the old Droid's fusion bottle blew.

Fire, hit, dodge, retreat, fire; fire, jump, dodge, twist, retreat. The Stingers had to slowly withdraw to keep from being flanked. The trouble was they were getting closer and closer to the DZ, where they would have to make a stand. The Captain ordered Hazard and the last two Droids to join the fray. For a moment it looked like they might hold the line. Suddenly a deadly missile barrage, from a pair of *Firedrakes*, killed Ensign Miagi in his *Saber*, in a massive fireball. Bridgette's *Renegade* also took a hit, losing her remaining arm, leaving nothing but one operational machine gun. The Stingers their backs to the DZ heard the roar of the *Bayonne*'s landing in the distance. The Raiders knowing they had to break through, before the giant shuttle could disembark the rest of the Brigadoons, pressed their attack.

Alex found himself dueling the same *Kingfisher* and one of the *Firedrakes*. He was just barely surviving the multiple missiles barrages and laser fire. He felt the bitter taste of failure in his mouth. The DZ was on the verge of being overrun. Bouchard in his *Ghostrunner* had stopped giving orders, simply firing his last few remaining pod missiles quickly at some unseen opponents. It didn't matter anymore, the once organized fight had turned into a random series of individual duels. The Stinger CombatDroids were slowly being decimated.

Alex had just fired his NPC at the *Firedrake*, only to find the *Kingfisher* at his rear, lining him up for a kill shot. There was no way to avoid the shot with his shields depleted and his rear armor now paper thin, but he wouldn't abandon his Droid. Not yet anyway as he twisted desperately. The unmistakable staccato roar of a 100 MM sliver cannon drowned out the other sounds of combat. He watched the *Kingfisher* crumple under the impact of the devastating stream. A massive, red and gold *Warlord* HK walked out of the woods. 64 tons of avenging fury, firing at the surprised Raiders. Colonel Bayard came on line, "All seriously damaged Stingers withdraw to defensive positions at coordinates 28DB. All combat capable Droids charge! Let's show these raiders what Brigadoons can do!"

The Colonel's *Raptor* stormed out of the tree line, firing its devastating 120 MM sliver cannon and massed energy weapons at the already battered, bandit *Mandrake*. The 56 ton machine exploded. The Raiders had enough. Two of their more powerful units had been destroyed. They fled from the field in disarray. The battered Brigadoons did not pursue. The remaining Stingers were too damaged to give chase and the two thrust equipped heavies took defensive positions to secure the DZ. Alex was chagrined that he hadn't detected the arrival of the two heavies before they made their presence known. He'd been too preoccupied with the fire fight. Had they been enemy units... Well he didn't want to think about it. It didn't cost him this time, but he would remember the lesson, always monitor your surroundings.

Bouchard's voice came over the Brigadoon's general frequency, "Glad to have you join us Colonel, you saved our tails. Mon dieu, how did you disembark so fast? You arrived almost before the *Bayonne!*"

Bayard answered calmly, "You're right Captain, we did arrive before the shuttle. Major Duvalsaint and I did a low atmosphere jump with our Droids, when we heard you were in trouble."

Alex whistled to himself. To jump from a descending shuttle with one of those giant CombatDroids would require split second precision, and superior coordination between the CombatJack and the shuttle's crew. Not to mention all the pre-jump preparations. The techs must have worked right through the drop. It hit Alex for the first time how really good the Brigadoons were. Top to bottom, this was one of the best mercenary units in known space.

They stood guard until relieved by fresh Droids disembarking from the *Bayonne*. The four surviving Stingers and the six remaining pilots, returned to the shuttle for rest and repair. Alex was relieved just to be alive. He'd even distinguished himself in his first combat mission. Noticing Brandon limping back to the *Bayonne* despondently, Alex felt remorse at forgetting his friend. Brandon had lost both his Droid and some of his pride, at what he perceived was a poor contribution during the fight. Well Alex could deal with it later, he just didn't have the energy to reassure his friend, now.

Chapter 11

Next day at the debriefing, a depressed Bouchard reviewed the tally of their losses. Two Stinger Jacks dead; Miagi, in his *Saber*, died when his engine blew and Peter Swain had lost his life, ejecting from his *Roadrunner*, when his Pod launcher detonated. There had been hopes Peter had survived, until they found his charred body still strapped in the ejection seat. Brandon, in a subdued voice, described the Raiders firing at the ejecting CombatJack. Gasps and hisses were heard around the room. Shooting at an ejecting pilot was a serious violation of even the GenClone conventions of war.

Brandon's *Scout* and Bridgette's *Renegade* were also destroyed. The *Renegade*'s WFB was so damaged, they couldn't risk it aboard ship until it was deactivated. Fuller was now dismantling the Droid for spare parts. Alex was the only member of the drop team that was uninjured and only the *Warlock* and Bouchard's *Ghostrunner* would be ready for combat in less then one hundred hours. Bouchard's litany of failure and loss had the room quiet until Major Decampe and the Colonel walked in. Every one stood up and gave a sharp salute.

The Colonel walked to the front of the conference table and interrupted Bouchard, "The Brigadoons wish to pass our condolences and gratitude to the Stingers for the sacrifices made here on Fairhaven to secure a safe DZ. This mission will be entered into the history of the regiment as one of the outstanding achievements of our CombatJacks. You held back a force nearly twice your strength to secure a safe landing for the shuttle, suffering fifty percent casualties in the process. I consider your actions to be in the finest tradition of the Brigadoons."

Turning to Bouchard he snapped, "Damn it Captain, you need to start holding your head up. If anybody is at fault for the losses, it's me. I sent you on a nearly impossible mission and you succeeded. You and your team couldn't have done any better and that includes the trainees. Why you were responsible for the capture of a *Kingfisher* and a *Mandrake* and the destruction of three other Droids, and a pair of tank. Not to mention disabling at least two other units while being seriously out numbered and out gunned."

Bouchard answered dejectedly, "Sir, we were about to be completely destroyed until you showed up, and you were responsible for the destruction of the *Mandrake*."

Bayard placing his hand on Sting's shoulder in a fatherly gesture softly replied, "It doesn't matter Captain, you did what you had to do, you held the line. That's all I, or anyone else could have asked of you."

Alex noticed the renewed pride of the CombatJacks around the table. Bouchard looked as if the weight of the world was lifted off his shoulders. Only Brandon and Alex seemed unaffected by the heartfelt praise of the Colonel. Alex because he knew he had done the best he could by his own standards, discounted the praise. Brandon was unaffected because he was his own worst critic. No amount of praise could overcome his own performance evaluation.

The meeting broke up. The survivors of the raid were given the day off to recover while the rest of the Brigadoons consolidated their position and began coordinating activities with the militia.

Alex would normally have spent his free time overseeing the repair of the *Warlock*. He did stop at the Droid bay to make sure the repairs were progressing satisfactorily. With Fuller in charge everything was fine. For once he deferred his duty to fulfill his uncontrollable desire to see the planetary surface unencumbered. He and Mamba left the *Bayonne* and headed for the stream. The Brigadoons had moved their operations closer to the enemy lines leaving the area quiet. Wearing sandals and overalls, carrying a small lunch, he meandered down to the water. Stopping continuously to investigate the many wonders of the valley, leaves, grasshoppers, the small birds that fluttered overhead, the giant black and white bovines chewing their cud in the distance. Even the moist black earth beneath his feet transfixed him. He would stop and take deep breaths of the first un-filtered air he had ever inhaled. Redolent with the smell of plant life, wet earth and free standing water. Aromas that aroused long atrophied, ancestral memories. He'd never thought the act of breathing could be a pleasurable experience.

Finally he reached the stream near the chalet, bypassing the giant willows, with their long branches caressing the ground in the light breeze. To his surprised he discovered the structure was completely made of wood. It seemed so extravagant, until he viewed the seemingly endless forest that covered the surrounding hills. The stream itself was still the greatest wonder. Squatting on the bank, he watched hypnotically as it rippled over some rocks. Occasionally fish would leap, scales sparkling in the golden sunlight. A small, four legged creature with a marbled, hard shell swam across then dived beneath the surface. A pair of white birds with incredibly long, slender legs stalked the far rim of the stream, poking the water with their pointy beaks, sometimes catching tiny fish. Frogs whistling in the distance and hundreds of birds with their myriad songs filled the little hollow with strange and wondrous sounds.

Alex was happy. He felt contentment radiating from his surroundings into him. Whether it was the warmth of the sun on his face or the cold moisture seeping between his toes, everything just felt right. Mamba wandering back from her own excursion, dive bombed him playfully. Alex swatted at her, lost his balance, as the loosely packed bank gave way, and fell into the pool below. He hit the water unconcerned. But as he tried to stand up, he found he couldn't touch the bottom. Holding his breath, he struggled to reach the surface and air. The more he struggled the less progress he seemed to make. Starting to get desperate, he felt tiny Mamba grab his outstretched hand, and try to haul him to safety. Her ridiculous attempt seemed to bring reason back to Alex. He relaxed his oxygen starved body, then he pushed off against the bottom towards the vague shadow of the nearby bank. He knew people could float, but it didn't seem to be working for him. It was a race to see if his pathetic attempt to swim would get him to land, before he became unconscious. A controlled rage at the possibility of dying like this after all he had survived, kept him moving as he began to blackout. His arms cart wheeled through the air, something grabbed them and hauled him up and out of the water into the light of day. Coughing and choking, he found himself on the muddy bank.

Looking up through the haze of returning consciousness, he saw Brandon standing over him. Brandon, half concerned and half amused, was trying to repress the urge to laugh, as he said, "Hey Kane, don't you think you should learn to swim before going into the water? For a hotshot CombatJack you sure looked silly."

Alex, retching out the last of the water he had swallowed spluttered, "Good idea, thanks pal." Taking a breath and spitting up more water, "How did you spot me?"

Brandon amusedly replied, "Why that little flying snake flew right into my face and started chirping so frantically, I just followed him. Figured you'd be in trouble."

Mamba was hovering contritely right in front of Alex's face. Alex began a choking laugh, "Not your fault, Chirps. Thanks for getting help." His laughter turned into a mirthful howl as he rolled onto his back. Brandon, looking more concerned asked, "Are you OK Roomy? You didn't hit your head or something?"

Alex was laughing so hard he could hardly catch his breath, finally shaking his head and sucking in some air, he began to talk, "What a stupid way to die. To survive Banshee, only to die here, in a stream of water! Frakking water, of all things!"

Brandon looking puzzled said, "You know Alex, we don't know much about you, but you must come from one strange place. I saw you walking down here from the ship, looking like you were stoned on Dreamweed. Buddy, Fairhaven is a nice place, but I've never seen anyone so besotted by some grass and trees."

Alex, finally regaining control of himself, decided it was best to change the subject, "Hey Brandon, show me how to swim. Now that I'm going to be around open water all the time, I'd better learn."

They both stripped down to their briefs and entered the water. The lesson that ensued would have been a source of endless amusement for an observer. Alex succeeded in swimming only by paddling frantically to keep his head above water. His dense muscles gave him the buoyancy of a rock.

Brandon alternated between trying to improve Alex's technique and yanking him out of the water before he drowned. Mamba also joined into the spirit of things. Plunging in and out of the water, imitating Alex's clumsy attempts to swim. The clear shades of the stream completely confounded her color mutability. Every time she burst out of an underwater dive, she would be a dozen, splotchy shades of gray and green.

As Alex improved, he and Brandon explored the underwater environment. They found a natural chute upstream next to a waterfall. Using it as a slide, Brandon completed a spectacular double somersault, just as Claudia appeared on the bank in a lime green bikini and asked coyly, "Can I join in the fun?"

Both young men looked up from the water, gaping. Alex had stopped in mid-stroke, and immediately started sinking. Drinking more water he frantically started for shore. Claudia laughed, then gracefully dived in, right over his head, slicing the water almost without a splash. Alex reached the bank as Claudia's glistening blond hair broke the surface. The sight transfixed both men. Neither one of them had ever fully appreciated how beautiful their fellow trainee was. Alex sat in the shallows, unable to control his arousal. Brandon joined Claudia in a playful round of splashing and tag. They were both excellent swimmers.

The usually prim Claudia was totally out of character, free and high spirited as she played around with a flustered Brandon. All three of them finally climbed out onto the bank to dry off in the sun. By then Alex managed to control the effect on him of the half naked Amazon.

Claudia lay down between them, asking Brandon to rub some suntan lotion on her back. Brandon nervously complied. Alex began to laugh again while the others stared at him.

Finally Claudia said, "Why don't you share the joke with us, Alex?"

Alex mockingly replied, "Oh, it's this CombatJack playgirl routine you're putting on. You must think we're controlled by raging hormones. The funny thing is the big guy is falling for it."

Brandon, angrily snapped, "That's not fair, Roomy. Claudia just wanted to enjoy a swim. You're reading something into this that isn't there." Alex for the first time became aware of his friends suppressed infatuation with Claudia.

Claudia brushed herself off, wrapped her towel around herself, then sat up with a serious look on her face. "Alex is a little right Brandon." She looked enigmatically at the two of them for a moment, "When we first started training, all of us were a team. Now you and Alex have paired up and left the rest of us behind. Its OK for Chet and Court, they have each other, but its not for me. I need to be part of a team, again. I'm nearly as good as Alex and I'm better than you. I deserve better then to be left behind while you become full fledged CombatJacks."

Brandon's face fell. They all knew that Claudia was a better pilot than Brandon. Her comments reminded the Big Guy about his feelings of inadequacy. Claudia had hurt him, unintentionally.

White faced and tight lipped, Brandon replied, "You're right, I should have let you pilot my *Scout*. You would have done a better job and probably saved my Droid."

Claudia apologetically answered, "That's not what I meant, Brandon! The Colonel himself said you were both good CombatJacks. I just don't want to be left behind. I've worked most of my life, against the wishes of my family, to become a CombatJack. You two come out of no where and make me look second rate."

Brandon with a pained expression said, "The Colonel was talking about Alex. Roomy, over here, was unbelievable during that fire fight. He took out two Droids and two tanks, without breaking a sweat. Then during the retreat he was everywhere. Every time it looked like the raiders were going to break through, he was there, turning them back. I swear, at times it looked like we had two or three *Warlocks* on our side."

It was the most emotion Brandon had ever expressed. Alex broke the ensuing silence, "You two are ridiculous. You're both right and wrong. Brandon will never be a great Jack, he doesn't have the reflexes." Pausing for effect, "So what! You're good enough and you're strategic abilities are worth a couple of Droids in combat. You're an asset to any unit, and Claudia, nobody is leaving you behind. You're already as good as most of the CombatJacks in the Brigadoons. You'll get your chance. We're all going to have our fill of war before this campaign is over. Stop dwelling on your insecurities. Your strengths far out weigh your weaknesses."

Claudia sarcastically said, "That's easy for you to say, no insecurities, no fears and no frakking imperfections for the mysterious Mr. Kane. Everything comes easy to the man without a past, no emotions, no ideals. What are you fighting for Alex? Maybe you just like all the killing. We have a name for people like you where I come from; sociopath!"

Her outburst caught Alex off guard. He hadn't recognized

The depth of anger the other trainees felt towards his emotional detachment. He could see in Brandon's eyes he shared many of Claudia's feelings. Alex felt a dreadful need to respond. He couldn't stand the thought of losing these potential friends. With perfect control he replied, "I'm sorry you feel that way. I am not demonstrative even to those I care about."

The three of them went dead silent. None of them able to break the barriers created between them by Claudia's accusation. Alex desperately tried to think of the right thing to say. Staring out across the stream he finally spoke, "My history is something I don't care to share. I don't want to be condemned or pitied for my actions or my upbringing, so I keep it to myself. I am neither ashamed nor proud of it, I just accept it.

Alex took a deep almost desperate breath before he continued, "I was born in the Banshee mines for the criminally insane. My grandmother was a mass murderer, and one of your sociopaths Claudia, I loved her any way. One of my grandfathers was a professional assassin. My mother survived by selling her services to men in the mines, and I don't know who my father was. The few of us born in the Banshee mines survived by becoming ruthless.

I've personally killed, maimed and injured more people than I can count. I'd like to believe it was all in self-defense, but now that I've spent some time among civilized people, I recognize that I have been quick to use force when other options were possible. Either you were tough and unfeeling in the mines or you were dead. I can't just change the behavior that kept me alive because they don't fit in your civilized universe."

To his own horrified amazement he continued his confession, "All of those I cared about are dead now. I tried to save some of them when the mines were destroyed, but I wasn't good enough."

Alex held his head high without looking at either of his companions as he stopped speaking unable to go on any longer. For a moment there was silence and then Brandon pushed him into the water and yelled, "Hey Roomy, you still need to improve your swimming skills." Brandon jumped in afterwards with a whoop. Claudia hesitated on the bank a moment, then joined them with another perfect dive.

Hours later, as they were walking back to the ship, Claudia said, "I'm sorry about what I said earlier, Alex."

Alex responded quietly, "What you said was partially true. I can't change what I am. I'm afraid that I'll unintentionally hurt my friends, so I keep my distance." Brandon and Claudia didn't reply. They entered the *Bayonne* in silence.

Chapter 12

Alex proved to be right in his assessment of the fighting on Fairhaven. For weeks the Brigadoons and the Fairhaven militia fought a series of indecisive battles against the raiders. Slowly, from captured prisoners and intelligence sources, the identity of the raiders became clear. They were outwardly a renegade band of second line GenClone CombatJack. Intel believed they were getting covert support from their Genetic Purity League. The GPL wanted to divert Vegan forces from the GenClone border.

The GPL had bypassed half known space to open up a second front on the frontier border of the Vegan Republic. It was a testament to their technological superiority that they could maintain any kind of supply line over such a distance. They had bought the services of local Renegade Worlds with upgraded equipment and the opportunity to plunder a rich world like Fairhaven. This was critical to their plans, otherwise the costs would be too exorbitant even for them. These mostly unsavory renegades now filled out half the raider ranks. They were less formidable than the GenClones. However they were easily replaced by eager volunteers.

The possibility of the GenClones organizing the local Renegade Worlds on the Vegan border was a dangerous threat. However The Republic could not divert too many of its forces away from other contested borders without falling into the GPL trap.

The Brigadoons did receive some reinforcements and more supplies. The 2nd Brigadoon battalion was recalled, as well as a reinforced company of the Whitehaven Rangers, a Vegan long term contract mercenary force. Colonel Bayard took overall command of the forces on the planet to the dismay of the local militia officers. Count Monteverde was tied down on a critical mission for the Vegan Republic, and could not be freed to return and defend his home world. He had sent a holo tape, personally charging the Colonel with the defense of Fairhaven and ordering his key subordinates, General Brasshide and his nephew, Major Lord Philippe Demalle, to obey the Colonel as they would the Count.

The Colonel found himself with nearly a hundred and twenty Droids and six thousand support personnel at his command. They were up against a hundred and forty Droids, nearly three full regiments, and over a thousand support troops, including two companies of CyberLinked Armored

Troopers. The deadly CLATs, in their powered body suits, had proved devastatingly effective against the unprepared local militia CombatJacks. They did not fair as well against the Brigadoons or the Rangers, both groups being well versed in anti-CLAT tactics. Fortunately for Fairhaven's defenders, the invaders proved to be even less coordinated than the Colonel's fragmented command.

Alex did not envy the Colonel. The mixed forces, under his authority, proved nearly unmanageable. Particularly the militia CombatJacks. Brasshide was an incompetent, indecisive and insubordinate prima donna. His aide, Major Lord Demalle, on the other hand, developed a reputation as a ruthless and cunning CombatJack, if a little too brutal. Unfortunately, he spent most of his talents trying to undermine the Colonel and the Brigadoons, while aggrandizing himself. He had become the hero of Fairhaven after a successful defense of a border fortification during the early fighting. The handsome nephew of the Count was one of the few militia warriors to distinguish himself. Even the Brigadoon officers admitted he was as good as advertised, at least in a fight.

Alex's reputation also grew as the weeks passed. His *Warlock* was unique. He became known as the *Warlock* pilot, then just *Warlock*. At first his commanders found him to be insubordinate. Called before the Colonel for the third time, for disobeying orders and grand standing, Alex's career with the Brigadoons looked like it was over. Luckily, Captain Bouchard interceded on his behalf. The Captain convinced Bayard that Alex's talents were wasted in a rigid command structure.

Alex was reassigned to scout and disrupt enemy supply lines as a *lone wolf* Droid. The speed and sophisticated electronics of the *Warlock* plus Alex's free wheeling style made him an ideal candidate for these missions. Alex proved to be a terror in his new assignment. He uncovered and disrupted a covert assault directed at the city of Navarre, in the South. He destroyed two lightly guarded supply convoys, forcing the raiders to divert forces from the front, to protect their supply lines.

His activities became such a hindrance to the GenClones, that they assigned a Droid scout lance to hunt him down. After weeks of playing a deadly game of hide and seek, they succeeded in trapping him well behind enemy lines. Incredibly, in a running three hour battle, he destroyed two of the Droids and disabled a third, using his speed to isolate each Droid and fight them individually. This battle made his reputation. He suddenly went from troublemaker to ace warrior, as usual Alex was unaffected by his change in status.

Because of his success Colonel Bayard assigned a Ranger hunter killer lance to launch a large scale raid at a major supply depot along the Blackeel River well behind the enemy lines. Alex scouted for the lance.

Moving ahead of the Ranger lance, through the thick, temperate forest of giant cedars, Alex reviewed the assignment. He was not happy with this raid. The Ranger Droids, two fire support *Battleaxe*s, an enhanced *Katana* and a 36 ton *Lancer*, lacked stealth capabilities. They were just too slow to make a clean escape. The two APC's, carrying the infantry platoon, were also a drag on the mission.

His sophisticated sensors kept indicating activity at extreme detection range. He didn't want to think about the consequences of losing the element of surprise. They approached Lake Blackeel from the South. The lake was really nothing more than a deep reservoir in the river formed by a natural barrage. He sent a laser line of site message, reporting unidentified activity to Captain Gupta, as his *Katana* broke the tree line. Again he requested permission to go investigate the readings, and again he was denied. Alex swore to himself, growing angry at the restrictions on his movements.

Deciding to disobey orders, he powered up his FSS. Multiple Droid icons appeared on his display. Pivoting to the South to get better readings, while accelerating, he sent another laser message to the *Katana*, "Captain, it's a trap! I have eight, no nine hostile units approaching from the Southwest, the South and the East at extreme detection range. At least three of them look to be heavy Droids. It appears they're trying to herd us into the lake."

Gupta swore, then ordered his unit to retreat at full speed to the Northeast, hoping to squeeze his force between the lake and the enemy units to the East before the rest of the raider force closed the trap.

Something was wrong, the enemy stronghold was to the North. Why would their forces only be between them and safety to the South. Alex scanned the lake and detected large metal deposits on his mag scanners. Reviewing the computer's up loaded geological data, he discovered that the Blackeel area was poor in metals. He broadcast a warning to all the units, "I've got large magnetic anomalies in the lake. I think we're surrounded."

Alex contacted the lead APC, "*Warlock* to Grounder1. Do you have two satchel charges I can borrow?" Then to the Captain, "*Warlock* to Command1, I advise you to continue on present course. It looks to be the safest route. If Grounder1 can loan me those satchel charges, maybe I can clear a path."

"Grounder1 to *Warlock*, satchel charges are ready and waiting, anything you can do to get us out of this mess would be highly appreciated."

Gupta interrupting commanded, "Command1 to all units, cut the chatter and continue per last orders. *Warlock*, pull a rabbit out of your hat, if you can. Over."

Alex accelerated to flank speed as he turned to intercept the lead APC. He matched speeds with the six-wheeled vehicle and delicately picked up the two satchel charges from a foot soldier, desperately hanging on to the roof of the careening vehicle. Alex then pivoted again and headed past the Ranger Droids, right for the largest mag reading at the southern edge of the lake. He was hoping the underwater Droids didn't spring their trap early, or his plan would fail. As he reached the lake, he fired his Thrusters and launched himself into the lake.

CombatJacks didn't like operating in water because their weapons and EMD shields became useless. Alex planned to use this to his advantage as his Droid hit the water, with a massive splash. He misjudged the bottom slightly and hit with a jolt. His visual scanners picked up two indistinct humanoid shapes, facing away from him. As they turned to face him, Alex reached forward and wrapped the satchel charges around the head of one and the arm of the other. Activating both charges, he took a step backwards as the *Renegade* and the *Battleaxe* used their Thrusters. Alex followed suit. The three Droids rose on plumes of super heated vapor almost in tandem. Then the distinctive crack of satchel charges detonating, was heard over the roar of multiple Thrusters. The *Renegade* tumbled back to a watery grave its cockpit destroyed, while the *Battleaxe*, knocked off balance by the damage to its arm, managed to land awkwardly on the shore. Its right arm EPC hung uselessly at its side. Alex twisted around in mid air and managed to fire his NPC and lasers at the unbalanced *Battleaxe*, stripping the armor off the enemy Droid's legs before its shields activated.

He spotted two other Droids jumping from the lake, firing on the command lance. He had at least cut down the odds. The *Warlock* landed on the bank right behind the *Battleaxe*. The *Battleaxe* recovering from its awkward landing, exposed its damaged legs. Carefully lining up his targeting cross hairs, Alex fired the NPC at the unprotected knee at point blank range. The knee joint vaporized as did the underlying fiberoptic circuits and Crystalline internal structure. The *Battleaxe* collapsed, down and out for the rest of this battle.

Alex shifted targets to the nearest enemy Droid, an enhanced *Mandrake* with its back to him. It was standing between him and the Rangers firing its sliver cannon at Lydia Langdon's retreating *Battleaxe*. The *Mandrake* ignored the *Warlock* until Alex fired his HEAP launchers, sending eight missiles screaming towards its exposed back. The Humanoid Droid staggered under the impact of six direct hits.

An NPC melted the armor off Alex's rear carapace, as a raider *Renegade* closed in on him. Swearing to himself, Alex activated his ODC, charging away from the chasing raider force while his radiators redlined. He twisted the *Warlock*'s torso around, as he passed the *Mandrake*, and triggered his lasers ignoring the screaming alarms. Globs of armor melted from the Droid's left arm and cockpit, knocking out the phased array laser mounted in its upper torso. Alex was disappointed the shots hadn't critically damaged the *Mandrake*. Now, the *Mandrake*'s would fire its 60 MM sliver cannon into his exposed back as he fled. But Langdon's enhanced *Battleaxe* was not out of the fight. She launched a withering missile barrage. The HEAP rounds rained down on the already battered *Mandrake*. Knocked off balance, it fell to its armored knees giving Alex the opening he needed.

Alex opened a comlink to Linda, "Thanks Command2. You just saved my butt both figuratively and literally."

The feisty, brunette, chatter box, replied, "Just returning the favor, *Warlock*. You're not the only one who can dish it out."

Gupta came on line, "Command1 to all units, our way is clear. Grounder Leader, head east southeast at flank speed. Command lance, commence leapfrog retreat to cover withdrawal of APC's. *Warlock*, attach yourself to Command2 in support of leapfrog."

Alex knew a leapfrog retreat was a difficult operation to coordinate. It divided a lance into two pairs. One of the pairs would take a defensive fire suppression position, while the other pair retreated at full speed. Then they would switch, the engaging Droids withdrawing under the protective fire of the disengaged pair. Presumably, the second pair could suppress the enemy long enough for the first to disengage. It was problematic whether the allied force could slow the advance enough, outnumbered better than two to one.

Alex was supposed to coordinate with Sergeant Langdon and Corporal "Mad Jack" Jenner. He didn't think the leapfrog would work because the recon lance could swing around and flank them. He also didn't like the idea of trying to coordinate with Langdon and Mad Jack. Two of the most hard headed warriors ever to pilot CombatDroids. He spoke, "*Warlock* to Command1, high speed enemy recon lance is advancing from the south. I can cover the southern flank and prevent them from disrupting the withdrawal, if you want, sir."

There was no response for a moment, then Gupta replied, "Command1 to *Warlock*, I don't detect any force to the south." After a pause he continued, "Frankie, do it. Cover the southern flank, but your report better be right, *Warlock*. Command1, out."

Lydia snapped back on a private channel, "Command2 to *Warlock*, I don't detect anything, either. This is just another one of you ploys to avoid combined operations and I'm sick of you getting away with it, you... you insubordinate lout!"

Alex had not yet detected the advance of the raider recon lance, but he knew they were coming. He changed direction and headed south. Five minutes later he resignedly smiled, as he detected five thermal readings, closing fast from the South. Sometimes he wished his tactical judgments were wrong.

Lydia came on line, "*Warlock*, you idiotic fool, get back here before your position is overrun. For once, be a team player. You're throwing your life away, pointlessly. We have a better chance if we fight as a unit." The whine and static of EPC fire echoed in the background as the transmission ended. Alex ignored the message. She was wrong and he didn't want to betray his position to the enemy, by responding.

He found a small deep pool of water and decided to duplicate the raider trap. He jumped in, crouched down on the bottom and shut down all of his systems except his seismic detectors. The *Warlock*'s heat levels returned to green as the heat dissipated into the surrounding water. If the recon lance paid attention, they would detect the temperature rise of the pool and the mag readings from the *Warlock*. He expected they would be in too big a hurry to notice. He was right. As he detected their passage, he fired his Thrusters and exploded out of the water.

Immediately he homed in on the nearest enemy Droid, a 16 ton *Roadrunner*, and fired all of his weapons. The lightly armored Droid crashed to the ground as a lucky shot, from his NPC, sheared off a poorly armored leg. Alex then quickly dispatched the next nearest target, a tiny *Scout*, before the remaining Droids could effectively react to his attack. It got harder after that.

A GenClone 24 ton *Python* was the deadliest of his opponents. Every time he tried to take it down, the surviving pair of *Roadrunners* distracted him, making it impossible to finish the job. They continued back and forth in the deadly game of tag for ten minutes. Red alarm lights flashed all over the *Warlock*'s display board, as multiple laser hits penetrated his shields and decompressed his cubed armor. His right missile launcher went off line. His armor was taking a beating. It was time to retreat. Alex activated the ODC and began a frantic jitterbug through the forest, back to the rest of the Allied force. He had delayed the raider Droids long enough to prevent a flanking maneuver. They tried following through the dense forest, but could not match Alex's uncanny, high speed piloting skills.

Minutes later, he broke from the forest into the savanna. The four Ranger Droids were still standing, smoothly carrying out the leapfrog retreat. Both *Battleaxes* and the *Katana* were noticeably battered, while seven, nearly pristine, raider Droids were still in hot pursuit. Alex triggered his surviving HEAP launcher, firing his last volley at a nearby enemy *Katana* and followed up with the NPC as he sped past the surprised Droid.

Opening a private channel to Lydia, Alex laconically said, "Glad to see you were able to survive until I got back, Command2." Then on the command channel, "*Warlock* to Command1, raider recon lance successfully delayed, sir. Two units downed, one out of action. The others are still in hot pursuit. Requesting new instructions, over."

Gupta desperately maneuvering his Droid to avoid a missile barrage gasped out a response, "Command One, *Ahh*, to *Warlock*, support Command Two in operation leapfrog, over."

The retreat continued. The humanoid *Python* joined the fray, quickly becoming the most effective enemy Droid, despite its small size. Clearly a crack pilot was operating the SuperDroid. Using his speed to circle and attack the disengaged Ranger Droids, the enemy pilot was disrupting the retreat. Alex was too busy engaging the heavier pursuit units to deal with the darting threat. Things got progressively worse when the Ranger *Lancer* exploded from a lucky missile hit, followed quickly by the destruction of Mad Jack's *Battleaxe*. They all heard Mad Jack screaming epitaphs at the Raider Droids as he toppled over. Jack Jenner never could accept things not going exactly the way he wanted right up until the end. The Captain ordered a general retreat. Forced to keep pace with the surviving slow moving Rangers, Alex missed the freedom to just flee.

The retreat became a mad dash for survival. Energy and projectile weapons rained destruction on the fleeing Droids. Then when things appeared bleakest, two of the Brigadoon's precious Epsilon Anti-Droid StarFighters, roared over the field, blasting the pursuing raiders. On the second pass, the raiders lost heart and turned back. The StarFighter had approached undetected by using stealth technology and tree top flying. There strike had been too fast for the Renegade Droids to react.

Gupta, speaking over the open channel, "Captain Jopa Gupta of the Rangers to flight leader, your arrival was most timely. We express our thanks for your support."

An accented voice replied, "Saving trapped CombatDroids is all in a day's work for us tireless AeroJacks. Big Ben here glad to oblige, Captain."

It wasn't exactly a standard response but Gupta chose to ignore it instead he relayed additional orders, "Command1 to all units, break off engagement and form on me.", As he slowed his limping *Katana* to a walk.

Alex had spotted the *Python* fleeing alone into the southern part of the forest. The SuperDroid pilot had circled to block the retreat of the Rangers, and now found himself trapped. Alex ignored orders, and went in after the enemy Droid. The *Warlock* soon overtook the *Python*. A savage duel ensued. Both Droids were down to their NPC's with all other weapons systems destroyed or out of ammo. The *Warlock* out massed the *Python* by 16 tons, but with much of his armor decompressed and the secondary weapons destroyed, it was an equal match.

Alex mumbled to himself, "Frakke, this guy is going to be tough." As another NPC hit stripped him of more armor. The *Warlock* staggered, unbalanced by the decompression of hundreds of kilo's of compressed carbon armor. Alex carefully aimed his own NPC at the dodging *Python*'s damaged right leg and fired just as the raider pilot stepped forward. A direct hit. The leg gave way and the *Python* collapsed. Alex walked over to point blank range, targeted his NPC at the cockpit and opened a channel, "This is Brigadoon CombatJack Kane to *Python* pilot. You fought bravely, now surrender or die."

There was an inarticulate gasp, then the cockpit opened, a small fox faced wiry man walked out, coughing at the escaping tendrils of smoke from the Droid's interior. A short while later a Brigadoon rescue team came and collected the prisoner and the downed Droid. Alex, completely worn out, began the long walk back to the new regimental base in New Constantine.

Chapter 13

Alex and Brandon were helping repair the *Warlock* the next day, discussing the previous day's action, when Alex received a summons from the Colonel. He said, "Now I'm in for it. Gupta didn't say anything to me yesterday about disobeying his last order, but..."

Brandon interrupted, "You better go Alex. Whatever you're in trouble for this time, being late won't help. Besides, you may have disobeyed orders, but you're a hero. Two more confirmed Droid kills and one capture. You're practically an ace."

Alex rushed to the Colonel's ready room and was ushered in when he arrived. Alex was not surprised to see Captain Gupta and Major Decampe there. He came to attention and saluted. It was then that he noticed he still had grease on his hands.

Major Decampe disapprovingly commented, "Mr. Kane, don't you know enough to make yourself presentable before your commanding officers?"

Alex in his most martial voice replied, "Yes sir. I was working on my Droid and was told my presence was urgently requested, Sir."

The Colonel spoke, "Mr. Kane, why are you constantly being called before me for serious infractions, and why do I put up with it?" The Colonel sighed, "Do you know why you're here this time?"

Alex did not know how to answer the question. Finally, he decided the safest course was to express ignorance, "No sir."

The Colonel with an inscrutable expression commented, "Captain Gupta has described the failed raid yesterday, and your part in it. Do you want to change your answer, now?"

Perplexed and as always cautious, Alex responded, "Is there something in particular that you have in mind, Colonel? You know how confusing fire fights can be, sometimes things aren't as you recall them."

Bayard stared at Alex for an interminable time then finally spoke, "Alex, it never ceases to amaze me how you can finagle the truth to get yourself out of trouble. I had chief tech Fuller download the *Warlock*'s BlackBox. You didn't detect any scout lance when you reported their presence to Captain Gupta. What's more, you disobeyed a direct order and went off to pursue the *Python*. Now! what do you have to say for yourself?"

Alex had not expected them to check the BlackBox. He tried to recall everything that may have been recorded, so he wouldn't have to contradict the objective evidence. Thinking fast, he decided that there was no way to cover up, so he spoke an edited version of the truth, "Colonel, I don't believe I told the Captain I had detected the scout lance. I just told him they were there. It was a judgment on my part. I must not have made that clear. As for pursuing the *Python*, well I don't recall the whole event, but I had just taken a missile hit and my ears were ringing, so maybe that's why I didn't catch the order to withdraw."

To everyone's surprise, the Colonel roared in laughter. Finally he regained control of himself and spoke, "Alex, you're not a very good liar. We reviewed your recorder at the Captain's request, because he wants to award you the Ranger Silver Cluster Medallion for service beyond the call of duty. It was during that review that we came upon the discrepancies between your account and the BlackBox's." More seriously, "I am not going to press the point this time, Cadet."

Decampe, grimly interjected, "This is not a laughing matter, Colonel. If our CombatJack can't obey orders, soon we will become a rabble. This trainee is incorrigible. I don't care how good a Jack he is, he needs to be disciplined." Decampe lately was beginning to express an open dislike for both Alex and his free wheeling style.

Bayard responded seriously, "We can't punish a CombatJack just awarded the Ranger Silver Cluster, can we now Major. I believe this time you will get away with disobeying orders, Cadet. But don't make a habit of it."

Chapter 14

Back in their room he reviewed his problems with Brandon. The big guy alternated between laughing and sympathizing.

Brandon trying to encourage Alex commented, "Forget it Roomy. Try to learn from your mistakes for once. Come on, let's get ready for a night out on the town. Claudia will chew our ears off if we're late."

Alex gloomily replied, "I don't feel much like going Brandon. Besides lately I've become the third wheel. You and Claudia seem to be getting along well." The budding love affair between his two best friends was a sensitive subject. He was happy for them and tried to stay out of their way, but because of their misplaced loyalty they wouldn't let him.

Brandon answered, "Alex, I'd take you up on that offer except Chet and Court will be there as well. So Claudia and I won't be by ourselves anyway."

Alex with a knowing smile replied, "Great the two of you have finally admitted you're more than friends. I thought you would never get their."

Brandon blushed, "OK, so we haven't done a very good job of hiding our relationship."

Alex asked, "Why did you feel the need to keep it a secret? You two are a great pair, everyone admits it. You're not only compatible, but you make a great team."

Brandon hesitated before commenting, "I don't know, somehow it seems if we admit we're happy together we could lose it all. I think we both worry that this war is bringing us together. We're so incompatible in terms of our backgrounds. After all she is a member of the aristocracy, and I'm just an upstart Jack from a GenClone occupied world. Frakke, I used to look down on people like her. In my book they were a bunch of leaches living off the blood of working people like my parents. Look at me now, I'm in love with a blue blood. did you know she's distantly related to the duchess of Vega III!"

Alex laughed, "So what Brandon! You're being ridiculous. Just try telling Claudia she's a member of the idle rich and see what happens." He hesitated as a big, humorous smile plastered his face. "Knowing Claudia, she'd take a swipe at you and then challenge you to a duel. Like you and me, she's managed to overcome her birthright. So stop fretting about her ancestors and pay attention to her. We live in an age of opportunity, the old class barriers are collapsing with the GenClone invasion. It's no longer who your parents are, it's who you are that counts. Claudia recognizes what kind of man you are and she's right Buddy, you're one of the best."

Brandon, sitting on the edge of his cot, looking down at his clenched hands, replied, "I know you're right Alex, but it's hard overcoming all the baggage from my youth."

Alex reached over and slapped the gentle giant on the shoulder and offered, "That's the difference between being a man and a boy, Brandon. The man makes his own decisions, rather then letting his past make them for him. I know you're a man and so does Claudia. You'll work it out... Hey we're going to be late if we don't move it."

They rushed out of the cubicle a broad giant with a shock of dirty blond hair and a slender swarthy man, his snow white locks tied back in a pony tail with a serpent clasp, accentuating his sinister scared face. They strode with unfettered pride across the quadrangle. Both young men radiated a confidence and bravado that was half facade and half the swagger of youth.

Chapter 15

The five trainees walked into the spaceport bar laughing at one of Court's amusing anecdotes. They casually grabbed a table in the far corner overlooking the small stage and the trivid monitor, and ordered some drinks. Local militia Jacks sat at a table on the other side of the stage. One very big graceful man dominated the small party, and the bar. The blond giant was immediately recognizable as Major Lord Demalle, nephew of the Count of Monteverde and hero of Fairhaven. The man reputed to be the best CombatJack on the planet, and a Grand Master of TripleNull, the ultimate unarmed martial art.

Spacers from various ships were scattered throughout the room, as well as a strange looking troop of infantry. A dozen frail dark skinned men barely 160 cm tall wearing khaki uniforms with mini-chameleon insignias embossed on their collars. The insignia surprised Alex.

Turning to Brandon and pointing discretely at the little men, he asked, "Do you know who those troopers are?"

Brandon answered, "No, but I think I've heard of them."

Court to everyone's surprise spoke up loudly, "They're Gurkhas from the planet Himalaya." Rambling on, he continued, "They're stranded here. Philippe Demalle brought them here as part of his private army. Apparently they had some kind of falling out, so he fired them. Lowering his voice slightly, "They say their commander died under mysterious circumstances when he went to collect their pay. Nobody will hire them now that Demalle has rejected them, and they don't have enough money to leave. Poor buggers."

Alex thoughtfully said, "That explains the insignia, they come from the same planet as Mamba." He excused himself and walked over to the half starved Gurkhas, introducing himself, he offered to share a meal with them.

Their commander, a ramrod strait man with a brown wrinkled face of indeterminate age stood up and formally replied, "You are welcome at our table Ensign Kane. I am acting Jamadar Hakan Kaseem of the sixth Gurkha light infantry regiment, 2nd battalion, first company, the newly formed fighting Chameleon Corps. We are honored to break bread with the renowned pilot of the *Warlock* Droid. He then introduced The half dozen Gurkha officers and NCO's at the table.

The food and drinks arrived and the animated conversation abated as the famished soldiers ate. Alex learned that the rank of Jamadar was roughly equivalent to Captain. Kaseem had been the senior warrant officer in the half company of forty men, and had taken the field promotion needed to represent his mercenary unit in negotiations for a new contract. The Jamadar was very reticent about the death of his commanding officer and the events leading to the company's dismissal without pay by Lord Demalle.

Alex learned that the Gurkha homeland was in the high north polar mountain country of Himalaya overlooking the rich plains north of the Great Sea. They eked out a living mostly through low technology subsistence agriculture. Their only sources of foreign exchange were the credits returned to their homeland by mercenary units like the Chameleons, much as their ancient Earth ancestors had done serving the British empire 600 years earlier. Mostly these units sold their services to the wealthy plains dwelling religious pacifists. But in recent years increasing population pressures had forced some units to seek assignments off world. The Jamadar described the terror most Gurkhas felt at the thought of leaving their home world and entering, what to them, was the nearly magical, high tech, wider universe. Himalaya had been one of the earliest fringe worlds settled and had lost space faring technology during the first interregnum in 2168.

Alex was amazed to learn that the Gurkha regiments had successfully thwarted every attempt to invade Himalaya with their low tech weaponry and shear numbers. Fortunately for them Himalaya, until recently, was too backwater a world to attract the attention of its more powerful neighbors. The techniques developed by these little men, and the casualties they considered acceptable to destroy raider mechanized units impressed Alex.

The Gurkhas depended on their reputation of scrupulous honesty, and unfailing loyalty and sacrifice to make their living. It was unspoken, but became quite clear to Alex, that Demalle was threatening to compromise the Gurkha reputation if they pressed their claims on him. Kaseem was in a real bind. His people had mortgaged their nearly worthless farms, to an interplanetary corporation, to purchase their meager equipment. They had believed the contract with Demalle would easily permit them to repay their loans. Now they found themselves with a sixty thousand credit debt and no source of income. The conversation confirmed Alex's suspicions that Demalle was an unsavory lout. The poor soldiers just didn't have the sophistication to deal with the innuendo war being waged on them by their powerful former patron.

Mamba's association with Alex intrigued the Gurkhas. Mini-chameleons were legendary, rarely seen creatures even on Himalaya. The Gurkhas believed they were harbingers of good luck. The Jamadar confirmed that minichams lived in a symbiotic relationship with the giant Landwhales, that roamed the world encompassing uninhabited desert south of the Great Sea. The Gurkhas, to Alex's disappointment, knew little else of interest about minichams. He already knew that minichams didn't normally cohabitate with man. Alex was still unique in this regard, which added to his stature with the Gurkhas. Alex felt an immediate empathy with these simple but brave men.

Feeling guilty about leaving his fellow trainees for so long, he excused himself with an exchange of pleasantries and some heartfelt expressions of mutual admiration and returned to the now boisterous table of his friends. As Alex sat, he listened to Court describe loudly his version, of his one fire fight, "... Then we closed the trap and had those raiders dead to rights, except the frakking Militia ran out, leaving the back door open and most of them got away." Proudly he continued, "Bouchard and I did manage to take down a *Saber*. If it wasn't for those worthless militia cowards we would have bagged them all."

Court had been too loud during his exposition. Demalle and the other militia warriors overhearing the conversation, walked over and challenged Court. Demalle with a dangerous glint in his eyes spoke deliberately, "We couldn't help overhearing your conversation lout, your implications can only be responded to in the combat circle; unless you retract that statement now and *beg* for our pardon!"

Before Court could speak, Chet snapped, "Hey pal, I don't care who you or your uncle are, this is a private conversation. We don't need the local kingpin coming over here and threatening Brigadoons."

Brandon trying to control the damage done by the brother's ill advised remarks stood up, while placing a firm hand on Chet's shoulder, "Excuse my companions Lord Demalle, they meant no harm. They are just trainees and cannot speak for the rest of the Brigadoons. The Brigadoon's hold the Fairhaven militia, and you personally in the highest esteem."

Alex felt an immediate antipathy towards the big militia Major. His eyes reminded him of someone, he just couldn't place that look. Alex continued to sip his soda nonchalantly, while watching the half dozen other CombatJacks. Underneath his calm exterior Alex's body coiled like a spring. He regretted not bringing Mamba. But on second thought maybe it was for the best.

It was one of the Major's companions who spoke next, "A very pretty speech ensign, but I have not heard your boorish little friends apologize for their gross stupidity."

Things went downhill from there. Even Brandon's diplomacy was useless. Chet and Court both were up and ready to fight the whole bar if need be. Surprisingly it was the Major who prevented a free for all. He challenged both the brothers together to settle their differences in a duel. The brothers offered to fight him individually. Demalle declined, noting that with his training it wouldn't be fair. They argued back and forth for a while longer. Finally they agreed to the duel and a space was cleared for them. People started betting on the outcome. Most favored Demalle. His reputation was formidable.

Both Chet and Court were big men with massive arms and shoulders, and both had excelled at the Brigadoon hand to hand combat training. Alex watched Demalle as he prepared and knew they didn't have a chance. Mercury had gone through the same flexing exercises during Alex's martial arts training. Mercury could have destroyed the brothers, and he had only been a Master of TripleNull. Alex wasn't happy with the situation at all, for he had finally recognized whom Demalle resembled; *Violet Blossom!*

The fight started out well enough. Chet and Court tried grappling with the Major only to be battered nearly unconscious by a series of incredibly fast blows. They were game and kept coming back for more. The fight looked to be over when Court's leg snapped audibly and he fell to the floor in agony. Chet in a rage charged Demalle and managed to strike the first blow on the surprised Major. What happened next felt like a slow motion tragedy.

Demalle ducked underneath the next of Chet's wildly thrown fists and then threw a lightning spin kick to the head of his opponent. Alex wanted to scream, duck, as the blow connected! The head twisted at an unnatural angle as blood and tissue splattered the onlookers.

Chet was dead before he hit the floor. Court tried to stand up while screaming, "Chet!" But fell back to the floor in agony from his broken leg. Brandon and Claudia rushed over to help their surviving fallen friend.

Demalle, leaning over Chet's body said, "Mon Dieu! I didn't mean to kill the fool. He surprised me with that last blow. I must have hit him harder then I expected."

Alex knew better. A TripleNull master, let alone a grand master knew exactly where his blow was going to land and what damage it would do. Alex knew Demalle could have pulled his kick. Against a minimally trained opponent like Chet, it was nothing short of murder. He felt a cold rage simmering.

Alex walked over to a stunned bartender and said, "call in a medical evac." Then he joined the other trainees, who were trying to make the incoherent Court comfortable. Demalle walked over and apologized for the death of their friend, paying particular attention to Claudia, while ignoring Court.

Claudia turned away from ministering Court, and replied coldly, "I think it would be best if you left Major. I don't think any of us are ready to acknowledge, let alone accept your apologies."

Demalle with a half smile answered, "I sympathize, and will comply with your desires Mademoiselle. We have all lost friends in this conflict, se la guerre. I hope that you and I can renew our acquaintance at a more auspicious time."

Claudia didn't reply, but Brandon and Alex both saw the fury in her eyes at the blatant attempt to flirt with her by the killer of her friend. It was one of Demalle's militia companions who spoke next, "Come Philippe, let us leave these Brigadoon capons. I grow bored with all this forced somberness.

Brandon to Alex's surprise, responded by rising up and throwing a powerful right to the militiaman's head knocking him flat on his back. Alex and the Major interceded to prevent further fighting.

Brandon held back by Alex, roared, "You spoiled worthless aristocratic pig, don't you dare insult that dead warrior, with your oh so sophisticated barbs. Chet was worth ten of you as a human being!"

Demalle sarcastically replied, "It is hard to judge the value of a dead man. But I think it is best we left, mes amis. As he turned away. "We would not want to further deplete the forces of our allies."

Alex, coolly spoke for the first time, "You make a good point Demalle. Each Brigadoon CombatJack is an irreplaceable asset to this war. The loss of half a dozen or so of the Fairhaven militia on the other hand would be of little significance."

Demalle sneered, "Ah, I recognize you, the *Warlock* pilot. They say you are good almost as good as me, though disobedient. You would learn to keep your foolish mouth shut and obey your orders in my command. But I will assume your foolishness is caused by the loss of your friend, and not respond to your provocative remarks... This time."

Alex coolly replied, "I see, if an untrained youth provokes you, he dies, while you find excuses to avoid the provocation's of your superiors."

Demalle spoke with just a hint of anger, "You want to share the fate of your stupid friends. Well far be it for me to prevent a fool from committing suicide," Then he began to remove his tunic.

Claudia shouted, "Alex no! Enough harm has been done here tonight. Major please let the matter rest."

Demalle replied coldly, "I will defer to your wishes lovely lady, when this cadet apologizes."

Alex did not reply, he took two steps back and quickly removed his own tunic and vest. He noted the calculation in the Major's eyes at the site of all his scars. Demalle moved to face Alex and crouched in an odd combat pose, then he spoke, "I will let you choose the rules capon."

Alex crouched in the third katana of TripleNull. Standing on the balls of his feet with his arms upraised and replied, "Free for all, to the death."

People around the room gasped at his challenge. Everyone backed off to give the two of them room. The bystanders all thought he was committing suicide. Only Alex, and possibly Demalle knew otherwise. Alex understood the militia Major was the better trained fighter. He was counting on his Banshee strength, reflexes and combat experience to compensate for the Major's edge.

The two men circled each other silently for moments. Each of them adjusting their movements slightly to maintain their defensive postures. They moved in perfect unison resembling a pair of ballroom dancers, more than combatants in a death duel. Then like a cobra Demalle struck, lashing out at Alex's head with his left foot. Alex knew it was a feint, and moved to avoid the blow while waiting for the real attack. He never detected the second blow. It was his fighting instincts that made him leap sideways, and bring his right arm up en guard as Demalle's fist grazed his face. Had the blow connected it could have easily killed Alex. An incredible series of feints and blows rained down on him. He went into his best defensive shell and responded reflexively to the devastating onslaught.

The whole flurry only lasted a few seconds. But by the time it was over Alex was cut, bruised and bleeding, while Demalle still looked pristine. Alex for the first time, since Mercury had trained him in TripleNull, knew he was outclassed, and fighting for his life. He had been here before and his mind raced to find the edge he needed to even the odds, as they continued circling one another.

Demalle launched a second attack with even more fury. Alex patiently took the punishment until he saw the opening he needed; ducking underneath a head kick and rolling beneath a table, he lashed out at the opposite table leg, unobserved by his opponent, then rolled clear. It worked, the big man incredibly jumped onto the table from a flat footed stance to close with Alex. The table leg weakened by Alex's powerful kick gave way, causing Demalle to momentarily lose his balance. The Major recovered with remarkable speed and skill somersaulting sideways off the tabletop. It wasn't quite enough. Alex using his uncanny foresight had anticipated Demalle's reaction and drove a lightning drop-kick with all of his Banshee developed musculature at the Major's head. Demalle managed to deflect some of the blow with his arm or he would have died then and there. Even so he was seriously hurt. Alex could see Demalle's wrist was jammed and blood was pouring out of his ruptured ear. Alex had just landed his first blow, but it was a telling one.

They separated and went back to their circling death dance. A new expression was on Demalle's face. Alex recognized it, a mixture of fear and rage. Demalle shook his head and sub-vocalized, "I was going to let you live, but now I've changed my mind pig. That's the last time you hit me."

Alex knew he had been lucky, it was unlikely he would be able to maneuver a TripleNull grand master into another mistake. He was already battered and bruised to the point where his fighting effectiveness was declining. He knew what he had to do as Demalle struck again. Alex exposed his torso. He saw the gleam in the Major's eyes, as he launched a crippling blow at Alex's unprotected chest. Alex slid sideways and leaned into the blow. He felt his ribs crack, from a blow that would have crushed a normal mans chest, as he hurled himself at Demalle. Two devastating punches landed on Alex's head before he finally closed. Alex was sick and dizzy, he felt blood welling out of his mouth, his eye's were nearly swollen shut, and he suspected his arm was broken. He ignored all this, for now he was close enough to use the wicked infighting techniques of the Banshee miners. First he head butted the blond giant in the face, he felt satisfaction, as blood exploded out of Demalle's broken nose. He buried his teeth into his opponents neck while using his elbows, knees and head to fend off the desperate blows of Demalle. They rolled on the floor, with Alex's dirty tactics and greater strength neutralizing Demalle's skill, battering each other into pulp. Finally the two men smashed head's together, nearly knocking each other out. They both collapsed to their hands and knees. Alex recovered first. Demalle raised his hand apparently in a gesture of surrender. Alex ignored it, and drove his right leg from his kneeling position into Demalle's head in an act of poetic revenge. With an audible snap Demalle's neck twisted at an impossible angle. He tried to mouth something like a fish out of water then his eyes glazed over and with a final twitch he died. Alex collapsed. His last strike had ripped open one of his internal wounds. He looked up to see Colonel Bayard and General Brasshide enter the bar through a blurred haze just before he fainted.

Chapter 16

Alex awoke in a dark room. He tried to evaluate his surroundings, while slowly moving his appendages to ascertain the extent of his injuries. Broken ribs, fractured fibia, a concussion, cracked cheekbone and assorted sprains and bruises. His extensive experience with injuries, told him he was getting excellent medical attention, and would suffer no permanent damage. Though it would be awhile before he could fight again. Mamba fluttered down from a ceiling fixture and gently chirped in his face. He gently caressed her soft scales with his uninjured arm, comforted by her presence. They stayed together like that, with Alex dozing for an indeterminate period of time. The overhead neon lights suddenly flared. Mamba flew back to her perch awaiting his orders. Alex carefully turned his head and opened his bruised and watering eyes. He saw an unknown doctor, Major Decampe, and the Colonel walk through the port. He recognized his surroundings in the bright lights. He was in the medical cubicle of a shuttle. It did not look to be the well-equipped *Bayonne* Medical facility.

The Colonel looked at him, then turned to the doctor and said, "I thought you said he would be unconscious for days." Before the doctor could speak he interrupted, "Never mind, I, of all people should know this patient doesn't abide by medical norms. How is he doctor?"

The unknown physician rushed over and checked various pieces of medical equipment. Mumbling to himself, "Remarkable, he looks to be at least a week into his recovery."

Bayard asked quietly, "Is it possible to speak with him?"

Alex in a harsh barely audible whisper answered, "I can speak", Then louder, "I can speak."

The doctor commented to no one in particular, "Incredible, he's awake and coherent."

Bayard replied, "Then could you excuse us doctor, I need to speak to the patient in private."

The doctor sounding relieved answered, "Yes of course, please don't keep the patient too long Colonel. He may be better, but he needs his rest." Then he left the room while Bouchard and Decampe approached Alex's bed.

Alex, unable to completely move his damaged mouth continued to speak in whispers, "Greetings sir, what's the weather like out there today Major?"

The Major suppressing his anger, replied, "This is no time for your morbid humor Kane, you are in serious trouble."

Bouchard snapped back, "That's enough Major." Turning to Alex, "The Major is right, a lot of the locals want your head, over the death of Major Demalle. Do you recall what happened?"

Decampe petulantly interposed, "If it wasn't for the Colonel's intercession you would be languishing in a prison right now waiting to be tried for murder."

Alex, raising an eyebrow said, "Murder? I remember what happened Colonel, and I don't see how anyone could consider me guilty of murder. Demalle and I entered an honor duel to the death, perfectly legal on this world, and there were dozens of witnesses."

The Colonel replied thoughtfully, "You're legally correct. You didn't commit a crime, however that won't keep the locals from lynching you. They're ready to march on this shuttle and take you by force if need be. The Brigadoon's aren't very happy with you either, you may not have broken the law; but the possibility that you deliberately killed a man in cold blood, as he tried to surrender, does not sit well with them. However you may have done me, and Count Monteverde a favor. I can't go into the details, but Lord Demalle was definitely a perverted scoundrel, and more then likely a traitor. Unfortunately for you we have to suppress this information to protect our sources, and prevent a further breech with our Fairhaven allies. If the local militia finds out the truth about their hero they could become completely demoralized."

Alex noted the surprise on the Major's face. This was news to him as well. He chose not to reply to the implied question concerning his intent at the end of the fight. Alex had never killed anyone unintentionally, but that really wasn't anybody's business. "So what does this all mean Colonel. Do you intend to turn me over to the locals?"

The Colonel replied with a concerned look, "No, you will be dismissed from the Brigadoon's and provided passage off world. I am, to my own surprise unhappy to lose you. You have managed to substantially disrupt the enemy supply lines, and tie down a significant percentage of their Droids. I don't have any easy way to replace you, and your *Warlock*. Your free wheeling style has also inspired many of our light Droid pilots to greater feats of daring do."

Alex, had expected the dismissal, but was surprised at the sense of loss he felt at the thought of leaving the Brigadoons. His disappointment must have shown.

Bouchard apologetically said, "I am sorry Alex, but if I tried to keep you, I would have a revolt on my hands."

Alex suppressing a choke answered, "Colonel, I understand your position, and I am sorry to have failed you, sir. You have always been fair and honorable in your dealings with me, and given me more chances then I deserved. I wish there was some way I could repay you, and the rest of the Brigadoons. I feel like I am abandoning the regiment, just when it is most in need."

Bayard with a pained expression replied, "Alex you don't owe me or the regiment anything. As I already said, your combat skills have immeasurable contributed to the fight here. Pausing and looking at the Major a moment, "However, as a matter of fact there is something you can do to help us."

Decampe gritting his teeth interrupted, "You don't intend to keep this no account trouble making murderer in your service, do you Colonel? You promised General Brasshide that he would be dismissed without honor or preference."

Bouchard replied stiffly, "Have you ever known me to break my word Major?" The Major flinched. Bouchard stared at him a moment longer then turned to Alex, "The Major is right Alex, I have given my word. I can have nothing further to do with you officially or covertly. What I am asking you to do, will have to be done on your own, without help or acknowledgment from me. It could be critical to the survival of Fairhaven, and the Brigadoon's. Are you interested?"

Alex wasn't one to jump into some unknown adventure. It was contrary to his nature to take unnecessary risks. Those who did died young on Banshee. He responded cautiously, "I might be if it isn't to risky."

Decampe responded in disgust, "Do you see why I can't abide this lout. You give him an opportunity to redeem his honor, and he tries to bargain like a Fairhaven fisher women."

The Colonel smiled, "I am not looking for a hero who looks before he leaps Major. Your answer pleases me Alex, and I believe the opportunity I present may interest you. Have you heard of the world, Himalaya?"

Alex suppressed his surprise, apparently the Colonel wasn't aware of the origins of Mamba or of his conversation with the Gurkhas. Laconically he replied "That world does seem to keep coming up in conversations. At the look of bafflement on the Colonel's face he continued, "I was speaking to some mercenaries, native to Himalaya just before the fight."

Bayard explained, "Alex we believe that Himalaya may be a re-supply point for the GenClone raiders. Worse they may be receiving Vegan and Imperial equipment from traitors in both governments. Some of the equipment we have captured has brand new Vegan serial numbers."

Alex asked, "Why not send in Special Ops if the Vegan Republic suspects this Colonel. After all Himalaya is a Vegan world. Certainly they would be better suited to uncover a conspiracy then I am."

Bayard frowning replied, "Normally I would agree. Unfortunately the situation on Himalaya is unique. Though it exists in the Vegan sphere of influence it remains essentially independent. Both Imperial and Vegan companies maintain harvesting and processing facilities for the natural longevity drug, SymXtend, on a large island in the Great Sea. The rest of the northern hemisphere is controlled by Unity Faith Pacifists. The UFP will have nothing to do with off worlders. SymXtend has become important in recent years because it has proven to be more effective then its synthetic analogs."

Alex questioned with a raised eyebrow, "Pacifists are preventing Special Ops from uncovering a GenClone re-supply base?"

The Colonel with a quirky smile replied, "Not exactly.... Himalaya is in a strategically insignificant sector near the Fringe border. However the recent discovery of the value of SymXtend derivatives, has made the planet economically important to both the Empire and us. Also valuable deposits of minerals are now being discovered. If either side tries to take control of the world it could destroy the delicate peace we now have with the Coalition and threaten our alliance against the GPL. Both sides give lip service to the independence of the UFP for that reason."

Alex still didn't have a clear understanding of the political ramifications and further questioned,

"Why don't the Empire and the Vegan Republic cooperate. It can't be in either sides interests to have GenClones running a covert op from Himalaya."

The Colonel clarified, "You're right, but their are other forces at work. The corporations, with the licenses to produce SymXtend, would reap enormous profits, if they eliminated their rivals. The General Biogentics conglomerate has been lobbying very hard in Congress, for The Republic to take control of the world. I suspect Matsui Mining and Manufacturing is doing the same at the Bukharan court. There are strong anti-peace forces on both sides of the border supporting these companies, and blocking any cooperation on Himalaya. Both companies, may in fact see the GenClones on Himalaya, as an excuse for government intervention."

Alex smiled derisively, "Loyalty isn't important for giant conglomerates, is it, or they wouldn't be trying to undermine their government's policies for a few extra credits. So the Coalition and Vega have their hands tied, if they want to maintain their uneasy peace. How can I help?"

Bayard answered, "The UFP is opposed to the use of their world for military activity. They also suspect someone is transshipping war materials through Himalaya. They are interested in hiring a mercenary unit to track down and eliminate this threat, before we or the Coalition do it for them."

Alex ironically commented, "Not total pacifists are they?"

Bayard paused while he thought out a response then said, "As a matter of fact, they have died by the thousands rather then use arms during various raids on their world. They started using some local mountain people to defend themselves hundreds of years ago rather then face extermination. They changed their doctrine to permit the use of mercenaries only when threatened with genocide. I see your skepticism, but I believe they aren't hypocrites. They have only used force when faced with extermination so far."

Alex asked, "I don't see how these circumstances qualify?"

Bayard answered, "You of all people must have some idea what a three way struggle between us, the Coalition, and the GenClones would do to any world."

Alex commented, "I am not exactly a mercenary unit, why would they want to hire me?"

Bayard replied, "Basically they can't afford anyone else. In fact their representative on this world barely has enough credits to pay for you and your Droid's passage. They were hoping to hire a unit by giving them 100 percent of any salvage."

Alex interrupted, "...And they can't find any self respecting mercenary unit to accept a deal like that. Where are their profits from the SymXtend licenses?"

The Major interjected, a grim smile on his face, "Apparently the cost of operations have eaten up all the profits."

Bayard spoke in defense of the big interplanetary conglomerates, "I don't believe the corporations are doctoring their books significantly. Both Matsui and GB have poured enormous amounts of capital into their respective manufacturing installations, trying to out do one another. Their installations are now small high tech cities on the opposite ends of the Crescent Isle." He paused then continued, "All I am asking you to do is meet with the representative of the planetary council and listen to her proposal."

Fate was playing tricks on Alex. Matsui on Mamba's home world. The only opportunity for employment on the same world. The Gurkha's indebted to a large conglomerate from that same world, and wanting to return home. There were unanswered questions. Why would either company want to foreclose on worthless mountain real-estate? Why would a world with apparently great natural resources remain poor and nearly undefended? It didn't make sense. Wealth did not tolerate a vacuum. Someone would end up in control of the riches generated by Himalaya. There were opportunities for an ambitious CombatJack. Fate seemed to be deciding his life for him again. Sometimes it was best to go with the flow. "Colonel, it isn't necessary, I will accept the contract as outlined by you."

Decampe responded with a look of triumph in his eyes, "It isn't that easy, you aren't licensed as a mercenary. If you're hired without a license, you're nothing more then a bandit."

From the expression on his face, this barrier obviously hadn't occurred to the Colonel. Alex smiled, "I wouldn't worry about it too much Major, I have the means to accept the commission legally. Colonel I will need to start making preparations. Could you invite the Himalayan Ambassador to see me tomorrow? Also I would request that you release the GenClone CombatJack I captured into my care." Alex had learned enough about the captured GenClone Jack, Jaimee Khorsa, to believe he might be willing to join Alex's new venture.

The Colonel looked surprised at the speed with which Alex had adjusted to the idea, then turned to Decampe and said "Arrange the Ambassadors visit Major." Hesitating a moment, "and arrange for the transfer of Khorsa to this shuttle as well.

Major Decampe in surprise asked, "Colonel, you don't seriously plan to release a GenClone prisoner into his care", as he pointed vehemently at Alex.

"Yes I am", then turning back to Alex he continued, "He will remain under guard until this ship leaves, after that he is your responsibility. By the way, You are on the privately owned *Horatio* class shuttle, *Tiara II*, Captain Morgan commanding, which will depart in eight days on a route that will eventually take you to Himalaya. You will have to leave at that time. I will arrange the transfer of the *Warlock*. You are not to leave the shuttle under any circumstances. There are supporters of Major Demalle watching this ship and I will not have another incident.

Alex exhausted by the long conversation responded, "Yes Colonel, I will need someone familiar with this world to run errands for me. Can you recommend someone...?"

At that moment Brandon and Claudia burst into the room past a startled guard. The guard apologized, "I'm sorry Colonel, I couldn't stop them without using force."

Bayard replied, "That's all right corporal, return to your post."

Brandon acting as spokesman jumped in with, "Colonel, we're here to insure our fellow trainee and friend receives justice." Then to Alex, "Roomy if they're holding you here against your will we'll get you out."

Bayard, in a voice like winter frost, "Ensign, I hope you aren't implying that anyone under my command would not receive justice. As for your friend, he is being kept here secretly for his own protection.

Brandon taken aback replied, "I, I didn't mean to... I mean we all know you're an honorable man Colonel. We just heard rumors that Alex was being turned over to the locals and...."

Alex interrupting his floundering friend, "The Colonel has graciously arranged for my safe passage off planet against strong political pressure from the locals. He has been more then fair in his dealings with me. I do thank both of you for trying to help. I will miss you."

Claudia questioningly intervened, "You have been dismissed from the Brigadoons?"

Alex interrupting Brandon before he could protest, "The Colonel is within his rights. Killing Demalle burned my bridges on Fairhaven, and with the Brigadoon's. I know what many of our fellow warriors think of my action. My presence would be too disruptive for me to stay."

Brandon and Claudia didn't protest his remark. They looked down at the floor to avoid his eyes. Their reactions brought home to Alex the truth of his circumstances. His stomach churned as it finally hit home, he no longer was a member of the regiment. It must have shown on his face because Claudia asked, "what do you plan to do Alex."

Wanting to put his friends at ease, "I have an opportunity with another mercenary unit." With a forced smile, "Don't worry about me Claudia, I always land on my feet."

Brandon had been struggling with something during the conversation. He swallowed hard and then with a look of resolution he spoke, "Colonel, I would like to resign my commission. It has been an honor to serve with you and the Brigadoons but I will be leaving with Alex."

Alex, snapped back, "Don't be stupid you big ox, you're a Brigadoon. What makes you think I want you with me anyway. You'll just slow me down." Alex knew when Brandon got that muley look on his face, nothing short of doomsday could change his mind. "Claudia talk sense to him, he isn't doing any of us any good by resigning." Then trying another tact, "Brandon you can't abandon the Brigadoons in the middle of a war its cowardice."

Claudia spoke to the Colonel with a forced nonchalance, "Colonel, I also wish to tender my resignation. We also were involved with the brawl in the bar against your orders, and our continued presence will be divisive to the allies. Alex with our recent losses their aren't enough Droids to go around. I don't think our departure will be a significant loss to the Brigadoons."

Decampe querulously spoke, as he pointed at Alex, "Ensign, Bovary, don't be ridiculous, Don't throw away a great future and abandon your comrades in the regiment over this."

Alex with his mouth hanging open in shock, looked at the startled faces of the others. Even the Colonel was dumfounded. Claudia had wanted acceptance as a Brigadoon CombatJack more than anything in the universe. It was inconceivable she would just up and resign.

The Colonel was the first to recover, "If I thought I could change either of your minds I would. You're departure will be a loss to the Brigadoon's. Don't underestimate your contributions. You both have done well. Flanders you lost your Droid fighting for the Brigadoon's, it will be replaced. I will arrange to have the *Python* captured by Mr. Kane repaired and transferred to this ship. If you find it acceptable, the difference in value between it and your old *Scout* will be your and Miss Bovary's compensation for service.

Both Brandon and Claudia responded, thanking the Colonel and Accepting his generous offer. The Colonel and the Major excused themselves with the admonition to not tire out Alex.

The three off them looked at each other uncomfortably. Finally Alex asked the question, "Why."

Brandon spoke first hesitatingly, "Roomy, I'm a better exec then I am a commander and if I'm going to have to take orders from someone; I'd rather it was you, than most of the hide bound officers we have served."

Claudia looked up at Brandon, then reaching over and held his hand. Then she turned to Alex, "I go where Brandon goes. Besides someone has got to look out for you two big dolts. And don't listen to this big ox. He's going with you because he likes and respects you and so do I." More vehemently, "I don't care what others believe you did what had to be done by killing that monster. The son of a bitch radiated evil. I just wish we didn't have to abandon the Brigadoons in the middle of a war."

Alex replied with a smile, "Maybe we aren't." Then Alex outlined the Colonel's proposal for stopping the flow of supplies to the raiders.

Claudia and Brandon were relieved to find out they weren't really abandoning the regiment. They whole heartily entered into the preparations for the mission.

Alex instructed, "Claudia, there is a leather pouch containing some very valuable blue crystals hidden beneath my bed. If properly cut they make the finest NPC modulating crystals known. Can you arrange with Dr. Tsay and a jeweler to have them cut appropriately. Make sure we have one cut for the *Python*'s NPC and a spare. Arrange with Dr. Tsay to sell about half the cut stones. Their rarity will make them incredibly valuable.

Then turning to Brandon he continued, "I need you to recruit a tech force to maintain our equipment Brandon." Then handing him a slip of paper. "This is a numbered bank account, there are 182,126 credits in it. If you have to; spend up to 20,000 in signing bonuses. The rest of it I will need. We will need at least six good techs. Also try to hire anyone trained in anti-Droid infantry tactics. We're going to be working with some half trained infantry mercs, and I don't think we know enough to bring them up to speed. There are three other people I need to see quickly, make sure the GenClone prisoner Khorsa is allowed to see me as soon as he arrives. The Colonel has arranged for me to meet with Ambassador Doran tomorrow. I will also need to see one Jamadar Kaseem. You can track him down at that bar we were at last night. Invite him here tell him the Chameleon CombatJack thinks he can save his bond and get him home if he's interested." They discussed various other details for a while longer as Alex grew tired. Finally Claudia noticing Alex's fatigue ushered Brandon out of the room. Alex stayed awake for a short while plans and questions whirring in his mind. He fell asleep still trying to understand how he had gone from Banshee prisoner to commander of a non-existent mercenary brigade on a hair brained mission in less then a year. His last thought was he had missed his twenty-first birthday.

Chapter 17

Brandon and a short round woman of Asian Indian ancestry with an ageless face awakened him late the following morning. She bore a red dot in the middle of her forehead, and wore a red and green sari with a matching turban. A woman remarkably out of place amongst the angular somber CombatJacks. She bore an air of tranquillity and love of life that seemed to reach out and enfold everything around her. Mamba in an unprecedented show of affection flew down to her shoulder and chirped gently into her smiling face.

She spoke, "good morning Commander Kane, I am ambassador Halaya Doran. I understand from your executive officer here and the good Colonel that you are interested in accepting a contract with my government?"

Alex smiled, Brandon or the Colonel had obviously promoted him to commander, and named Brandon as his exec for the ambassadors benefit. Alex did not think it appropriate to lie to anyone that could capture the affections of Mamba so readily and replied, "I am interested in your commission Ambassador. I am not a commander and Brandon really isn't my executive officer. We are just a couple of foot loose CombatJack looking for work."

Doran smiled conspiratorially, "The Colonel has told me all about you *Commander* Kane. I believe you're entitled to a rank appropriate for both our needs, even if your mercenary unit presently consists of just two CombatDroids. Has the Colonel told you of our situation and the terms of our contract?"

Alex replied, "Briefly, can you fill out the details and terms?"

Doran responded, "I will have to tell you some of the politics of Himalaya first. My Husband, the High Priest of Mathura Mukharbindu, and hereditary ruler of all Neo-Hindu's on Himalaya sent me here to recruit a mercenary unit at the request of the religious council. My husband is one of the five members of that council which rules our world. The other four senior members are Arch Bishop Jean Paul of the Reformed Church, Ahmed III, High Imam of the Islamic revival, Patriarch Khoren of the Orthodox Church and the lay leader of the Buddhists, High Monk Michael Cockburn. Together these five religions form the UFP. A unified faith whose central thesis is that all religions contain elements of the ultimate metaphysical truth. This plus our commitment to peaceful coexistence are the defining tenants of our world. Are you familiar with the early history of man?"

Alex rolled his eyes as he replied, "Not very madam."

Doran dedicatedly continued lecturing, "Religious tolerance was a revelation back in the early Twenty-first century; when Saint Joichem Washington founded the UFP in North America. Many had claimed before him to be religiously tolerant, but they were hypocrites, because they chose to ignore or deride the tenants of other faiths. Joichem was born poor and black in an era when skin pigmentation and religious affiliation were used to separate people throughout the home world. Wars were fought over slight differences in religion or minor differences in ethnic background. We still see remnants of this spiritual decay in the policies of the GenClones. Washington was the first to recognize that all faiths are just different aspects of the ultimate truth. He founded the UFP to promote this great truth."

Alex uncomfortably interrupted, "Madame I don't mean to be rude, but I am a simple mercenary. I am more used to dealing with politics and war then the beliefs of a population. I guess what I'm saying Ambassador is I am more interested in the present."

Doran smiled and then laughed, "I guess you find my fervent love of history and my faith unsettling. I don't believe you to be a simple mercenary Commander. Some have said I have the second sight, and I believe you could be a great force for good or evil. But for now let us deal with the mundane practical issues at hand. She looked at Alex almost avariciously for a moment. Alex had a suspicion that the Ambassador was not through with proselytizing. It made him uncomfortable, but their was nothing he could do about it so he chose to ignore it.

She continued, "The council is divided on my mission. All of us recognize the growing threat of the covert war being waged on our world. We don't even know who all the players are. Our Vegan Attaché has notified us of possible GenClone involvement, and we suspect that both Matsui and the General Biogenetic's subsidiary Symcorp are up to no good. The two SymXtend licensed companies are not supposed to operate outside the Crescent Isle, but we detected some activities that almost certainly tie back to them. I will provide you with a copy of our intelligence files on the various participants and activities. Don't look so surprised Commander, knowledge in whatever form has always been more powerful then the sword. The fact that we choose not to fight does not mean we do not track and evaluate threats to us."

Alex nodded in response, astounded that she had read his thoughts. He did not think he had given away anything in his expression.

Doran after a pause continued, "We will have plenty of opportunity to discuss the situation on our flight home. If you will excuse me, I will leave you to rest now Commander."

Alex had definitely detected a hint of amusement in the way Doran emphasized *Commander*. He smiled in response as he replied, "I look forward to it Madame."

An hour after the ambassador left Jamadar Kaseem walked into his sick bay cubicle 'come office. After the formal introductions Alex went right to the point, "Jamadar, I have a proposal for you that may resolve your present difficulties, but I need some information first."

"You are an honorable man Ensign Kane, I will try to answer your questions if it is possible and does not violate my honor or responsibilities. I could better judge what I can or cannot tell you if I understood your offer better sir."

The little officer wasn't going to take Alex's offer on faith. Well that was all right. Alex preferred dealing with realists, "Jamadar, I have been offered a commission to form a mercenary unit to help in a covert operation. The UFP council and Vega are sponsoring this mission indirectly. I can't give you any more details without your cooperation. Are you interested?"

The Jamadar standing at ease but still looking ramrod straight replied, "What exactly is your offer ensign?"

Alex recognized the subtle unstated question, how did a Brigadoon cadet get such an assignment. He chose to ignore it, "I would like to attach my Droid units to your mercenary company, purchase the equipment to bring you up to fighting form and pay the down payment on your loan. In exchange for this I want you and your men to elect me your commander during this mission."

The Jamadar quietly mulled the idea over for a few moments and then asked, "You need us for our mercenary license and manpower. You ask me to place the safety of my man in the hands of an untrained youth for some money. This is the same mistake we made when we entered into a contract with the late Major Demalle. What guarantees do we have that you will not lead us into a worse situation?"

Alex had thought the Gurkha officer would jump at the opportunity to rearm and pay off their debt. He understood why a capable man like Kaseem would not want to subordinate himself to a youth like Alex. With a sinking feeling he responded, "I can give you no assurances, other then I will do my best to look out for the best interests of those in my command, and will never ask anyone to do something I would not do myself. I will also listen to the council of my senior officers including you, though I will be ultimately responsible for any command decisions." It sounded pompous even to him, but he meant it, "I know this isn't much but its all I can commit to."

The Jamadar saluted crisply then, "Our total debt is 200 thousand C-notes. The first installment of 50 thousand is due in two weeks. Otherwise it is a standard five year note. Can we cover the debt Commander?"

It took Alex a moment to recognize that the Gurkha officer had just accepted his offer, then he responded in kind, "Yes we can cover it, though it will strain our finances a little bit. We may not be able to purchase all the equipment we need." Hesitating a moment Alex decided to ask the question, "Off the record Jamadar, what made you accept?"

The Jamadar formally replied, "I had no choice sir. Yours was the only offer available. My man and I would rather forfeit our lives then fail our families back home. However I am pleased by your response Sir. I believe if you listen to the advise of your subordinates, you could become a very successful commanding officer, Sir."

It took Alex a moment to note the very subtle warning in the response. Alex smiled, "I will endeavor to become a good officer in your eyes Jamadar." Alex thought he noticed a quirk in the lips on Kaseem's usually immobile face. "At ease Jamadar, we need to review the mission details and plans."

The Jamadar stayed an exhausting three hours, signing contracts, disposing of funds, agreeing on equipment requirements for their limited cash, and planning training. It was just the beginning of the frantic preparations during the ensuing days.

Alex established a staff group initially consisting of himself Brandon, Claudia, Kaseem and their new chief tech Jaimie Fuller. Occasionally Ambassador Doran joined them for updates on the political situation.

Jaimie Fuller was a fortuitous addition to their group. The nephew of Robart Fuller had arrived with the Brigadoon and Ranger reinforcements. He had developed a friendship with Brandon and Claudia. An excellent Tech in his own right, Jaimie had grown weary of being compared to his brilliant uncle, and decided to break out on his own. He had joined them with the consent of his uncle, and thrown himself into the new job with gusto. Jaimie was a nondescript slovenly man in his mid thirties, however his reputation as a top flight tech had made it easier to recruit the rest of their technical team. It was doubtful they would have been able to recruit the minimum six techs they needed for their equipment, without his silent presence. Unlike his voluble uncle the younger Fuller was nearly mute. Mumbling an occasional pearl of technical minutia only to those who shared his love of the great war machines. Alex liked the man's silent competence if not his appearance.

Staff met every day in the sick bay to review their plans. Slowly things began to fall in place. Their Droids were stowed away aboard the *Tiara II*, spare parts were purchased, the installment on the Gurkha loan was paid, and the Gurkhas boarded the ship with newly purchased small arms, including a great number of shoulder launched HEAP anti-Droid missiles and two newly purchased hover APC's. Claudia had succeeded in selling the blue crystals. They received an impressive 300,000 C-bills for the cut crystals Tsay sold. They needed every note. Fuller and his tech team familiarized themselves with their new charges and upgraded their laser weapons by installing some of the blue crystals.

After every staff, Alex would sit with his Liegeman Khorsa and try to familiarize himself with GenClone culture. Even the strange concept of liege/lord relationships was daunting. Clones raised in crèches would become lieges of a senior member of their Clone gene sept once they left the crèche. Totally submitting to the will of their seniors until they demonstrated their value to GenClone society. Cloning had been necessary during mans early colonization of space with sub light Scoop RamJet drives. The early colonist separated by light years from Earth's influence and under the tremendous stress of acclimating to worlds inhospitable to humans had evolved many bizarre cultures. The advent of the CM drive in 2210 had reintegrated many of these societies back into the mainstream of humanity with a few exceptions. The GenClone ruled GPL being the most powerful and radical of these.

Khorsa would talk endlessly about technical details and combat but rarely spoke of his society. Over time they developed a mutual respect for one another. Alex began to trust the rodent faced man to run critical errands for him. He decided to release Khorsa from his bond as soon as it was technically and socially feasible. He wanted the CombatJack as an ally not a servant.

Two days before departure Alex had recovered enough to move from the sick bay to surprisingly comfortable quarters between the Ambassador's and Captain Tomas Morgan's suites. It reflected his new status as a mercenary commander. While reviewing the final preparations, Alex continued to worry about his new command's short comings. They had tried to recruit either some air support or additional CombatJacks, without much luck. Two mercenary fighter pilots disgruntled at the loss of their StarFighters had joined, including Big Ben Richtover. But without their rides they were nothing more then glorified tech assistants.

Alex was racking his brain trying to find solutions to their remaining problems, when Khorsa walked in silent as always and said, "Commander, Colonel Bayard is outside and would like to see you."

"Well don't keep him waiting let him in." What now, the Colonel wouldn't have arrived unannounced unless it was something urgent or covert.

Bayard and Khorsa entered the room. Alex was dismissing his Liegeman, when the Colonel interrupted. "I think it would be better if he stayed. He may have a part in what I want to discuss."

Alex ordered, "Mr. Khorsa join us. Well Colonel to what do I owe the pleasure."

The Colonel chose to ignore the question, "I am impressed with your preparations. You have managed to recruit and equip a small but capable force in an astonishingly short time. You have some interesting sources of funds. Is there anything else that you need?"

Alex wasn't surprised the Colonel had kept tabs on him. It would have been difficult to keep his preparations a secret even if he wanted to. "As you probably know Colonel we could use a few more techs and are still looking for some Anti-Droid trained troopers. Is there any particular reason you should ask?"

The Colonel seemed uneasy as he spoke, "We may be able to help one another."

Alex with growing interest, "Oh?"

"I have two captured raider CyberLinked Assault Troopers and their CLAT suits imprisoned aboard the *Bayonne*. I need to get them off planet before they're lynched, and the *Tiara II* is the only ship leaving soon. Captain Morgan won't take responsibility for them and I can't spare personnel to guard them. You must have heard of the massacre at Bolden's Creek? These CLATs weren't involved but...."

Alex interrupted "If they volunteer to join us, they're welcome." Alex with a grin, "I'm glad I could be of service again Colonel."

The Colonel sighed in relief. They finalized the details of the transfer shook hands and wished each other luck. As the Colonel left, Alex thought regretfully this is probably the last time I will ever see the man.

Chapter 17

Alex, Claudia, Kaseem and Brandon watched silently through a view port as Fairhaven receded to a small, blue sphere. Each occupied with their own thoughts. Alex reviewed his new command. For the first time since his childhood, he wondered if he was in over his head. He inventoried the small force: two SuperDroids, his *Warlock* and Brandon's lighter *Python*; four CombatJacks, if he counted Khorsa; two StarFighter pilots, without their StarFighters; six techs to maintain their equipment; a half trained anti-Droid Gurkha company made up of thirty-six men and two officers; Sergeant Bolithio and her three man anti-Droid squad, two untrustworthy CLATs and their infantry armor, two APC's, three ancient Pantheon light tanks and one light hover transport, all armed with 10 MM sliver cannons; miscellaneous small arms, including a variety of Pod weapons and infantry shoulder mounted launchers. It was a motley complement of fifty-seven men and women. This was all he had to find and destroy a potentially well organized GenClone resupply station.

He smiled ironically as he considered how different his new responsibilities were, versus commanding the Nats in a rumble back on Banshee. There was one big similarity; if he made a mistake, people who relied on him would die!

Turning to the others, "OK, we're on our own now, no more Colonel Bayard and the Brigadoons to back us up. Claudia, can you put a training schedule for the Droid simulator together. Keep my schedule light for the next few weeks, I'll be busy."

Claudia, to his surprise, replied formally, "Yes sir."

Alex continued, "Brandon, you, Jamadar Kaseem and Sergeant Bolithio need to develop an integrated operations plan and assignments for our infantry. Also set up a joint ops training schedule. We're fortunate that Captain Morgan has agreed to pressurize the empty, main storage bay for us. When we get to Himalaya, we need to be one fighting force if we're to have any chance of success."

Kaseem ever formal spoke, "Commander, it will be difficult for my men to work with a female. More so if she is placed in a position of authority. Our traditions have never permitted the use of women in combat."

Pausing a moment to collect his thoughts, the formal intent looks of the others unnerved Alex. It brought home to Alex the loneliness of command. He was now the commanding officer with all the expectations and responsibilities that went with it. His inner resolve helped him in his first, major command decision, "I've decided to place you , Jamadar Kaseem, in overall command of the infantry. Sergeant Bolithio will be your executive officer. I want our two infantry forces integrated. The Gurkhas will just have to get used to working with female soldiers. They'll have to face reality head on."

Brandon brought up the next concern, "What about the issue of rank commander. I believe a Sub-Jamadar outranks a Sergeant. It is somewhat equivalent to second lieutenant. There will be some resentment."

Alex replied, "I've been thinking about our rankings. I'm going to have to hand out some promotions if we're going to become a Mercenary unit. Brandon, as my exec, I'm promoting you to First Lieutenant, Claudia, you and Bolithio will become Second Lieutenants and Jaimie Fuller will become our Chief Tech. Those promoted to officer rank and the Jamadar will become the staff. Brandon, or I should say Lieutenant, please arrange our first staff meeting for 0400 hours. Please notify the others and arrange for their participation."

Claudia interjected, "If we're going to become a mercenary unit, you also will need a formal rank, commander is too vague sir. We'll also need a new name." With a nod towards Kaseem, "The fighting Fifth Gurkhas is no longer appropriate. If I could make a suggestion, how about Major Kane's Chameleons. It sounds good and we don't have to change any of our logos."

Alex was surprised when the Jamadar agreed. "I agree with Lieutenant Bovary, Sir. The rank of Major is appropriate for a command of this size and Kane's Chameleons is a unit designation that will be most well received by my men. I would also recommend that we have a formal commissioning ceremony for the new officers. It is important to establish formal procedures in a new military unit, Sir. We need to start developing our own traditions and esprit de corps."

Alex had been about to deny Claudia's recommendations, except he recalled Kaseem's admonitions about not listening to his officers, "Excellent suggestions even if I'm a bit leery about my new rank. Jamadar can you get together with Sar..., I mean Lieutenant Bolithio and arrange the ceremony. You are the two most experienced officers concerning ceremonial procedures. Brandon, as we establish practices, let's document them into our own operations manual. As you say Jamadar, if this unit is to last, we need to establish traditions."

Brandon replied, "Alex, I mean Major, I still have most of my notes from the Brigadoon's ops manual. I think I can use them as a starting point."

Alex looked at the intent faces of his officers. It was a start.

Chapter 18

aptain Morgan walked into Alex's small office two days out from Fairhaven and said, "We have a problem, Commander."

Alex thought *we* usually translated into *you* with the Captain. The competent but lazy Captain Morgan was trying to dump more of his work onto Alex. Alex politely replied, with a raised eyebrow, "What would that be, Captain?"

"We just found a stowaway in one of our storage lockers."

Alex, calmly replied, "Captain, I agree you have a problem, but I fail to see how I'm concerned."

Morgan answered, "She claims to be a member of your mercenary outfit and asked to meet with you, even though she doesn't know you by name."

A stowaway breaking into Morgan's comfortable routine and making demands would normally warrant a stay in the brig. Alex replied, emphatically, "I know we didn't leave anyone behind, so whoever she is, she's not my responsibility."

Morgan looking at his feet uncertainly mumbled, "Uhm, I know her story doesn't make sense, but I think you ought to join me and meet her. She certainly isn't, uhm, typical."

Alex looked at the usually unflappable Captain in disbelief. He wanted to send the man packing, but he was curious as to the cause of the Captain's discomfort. Rising from his chair, "All right, let's go."

They headed for the sick bay with Morgan reluctantly providing some more nearly incoherent details about their unwanted guest. Alex interrupted the Captain rumblings, "Get a grip Captain, this should be straight forward. Dealing with the occasional stowaway is well within your capabilities."

Morgan finally went quiet. Even he recognized he wasn't acting rationally. Alex began to worry about the health and competence of the shuttle skipper. This is all I need, a Captain going over the edge.

Things became clearer when they arrived at sick bay. The obviously fatigued, young woman sitting on the edge of the medical bed was stunning. The Captain was so besotted with her he could barely make the introductions.

Morgan stuttered, "Uhm, Miss Roxanne Rudnauman, uhm this is Commander Kane of the, ah," then turning to Alex while adjusting his collar, "Ah, Commander, what are you calling your mercenary company, again?"

Alex looked on with amusement at the sixty year old shuttle Captain, then hesitated before turning to the woman and replying, with a slight bow, "Alex Kane, commander of the newly organized Chameleon Corps, Miss Rudnauman. I understand you claim to be a member of the Chameleons?"

Rudnauman fluttered her long eyelashes at him and shyly looked down. Alex noted she was wearing a very short, sheer smock with very little underneath. As his eyes traveled down a long length of exposed leg, he thought of one of Court's typically crude remarks, "Legs that go all the way up and make a complete ass of themselves."

She looked up at him. Her eyes were huge, brilliant, violet pools of lambent fire. Her perfect lips cried out to be kissed, dusky skin, the texture of Sveltan lace, begged to be caressed. Waist length, midnight black hair draped across an exposed, perfect shoulder down to the rounded curve of her...

Forgotten on his shoulder, Mamba suddenly lashed out with claw and fang, ripping his ear lobe and breaking his nearly hypnotic fixation. He was irrationally enraged at the mini-chameleon for the distraction. It was the unprecedented anger at Mamba that indicated he was overreacting. Surreptitiously he looked at the Captain. The man was still looking at Rudnauman like an adoring puppy.

She spoke, "Commander, I hope you will forgive my little white lie. I needed to speak to you about my circumstances."

Alex broke out in a sweat at the dulcet tones. The effect the young woman was having on him and the Captain was inexplicable. If it hadn't been for Mamba, he would probably be standing there with the same idiotic look on his face as Morgan. Regaining his composure he answered rigidly, "I am here now Miss Rudnauman, please speak."

She replied, "Please call me Roxanne, Commander." Pausing a moment, "I would like to ask you and your command for political asylum."

Her request caught Alex off guard. Political asylum was a rarely used section of the Universal Articles of War. He better be careful or he might find himself obligated to protect this woman against his wishes. Responding sharply he asked, "Why and from whom?"

Roxanne, hesitatingly, "I am a member of the Asturian nobility related to King Ludvig the Fourth." With a sob she continued, "The King was just killed in the fighting on Fairhaven and my position is now untenable."

Alex decided this was getting too complicated. King Ludvig the Fourth was the leader of the largest mercenary force supporting the GenClones on Fairhaven. His death and the presence of a relation on board the *Tiara II* would require a finesse he didn't possess. He decided to get some help. "Miss Rudnauman please hold off on the rest of your story until I have some of my staff officers join us." Using the intercom, he requested Brandon and Claudia join him in the sick bay. He excused himself and the Captain and left, while asking Morgan to keep the conversation with their unwanted guest private, until they evaluated the validity of her claims. Morgan agreed, relieved that Alex would take responsibility for the stowaway. He knew he wasn't acting rationally in the presence of Miss Rudnauman.

Brandon and Claudia arrived together in a rush. Apparently they had heard a tone of urgency in his voice. Alex explained the situation, stumbling over Miss Rudnauman's strange effect on Morgan and himself.

Claudia sarcastically, "Alex, do you really think this girl is a high born Asturian noble? This supposedly, remarkably attractive woman seems to be affecting your judgment. Men! Thousands of years of civilization and a pretty face can still turn them into brainless, rutting machines!"

Brandon grinning at Alex's obvious discomfort, "I have to see this siren that can turn our fearless leader and the sage Captain into drooling idiots."

Getting a hold of himself, Alex answered amusingly, "Good suggestion, but I want Claudia and I to go in there with you to observe your reaction." With both anticipation and reluctance, Alex opened the door. Roxanne was standing at the entrance just as enticing as ever. Mamba bit deep into Alex's neck. He felt the familiar chemical rush all the way down to his toes. It felt as if a haze lifted and he looked at the woman with renewed objectivity.

She was unquestionably an exotic beauty, but in and of itself, it didn't explain her initial effect on him. Roxanne rested her eyes on Brandon and Alex like a contented cat. Then in a very innocent voice, she purred, "I am sorry if I displeased you in some way, Commander. I was just trying..."

Claudia shoved Roxanne back and snapped, "I don't know how you're doing it witch, but I'm not going to let you undermine the crew on this ship." She sealed the lock then turned to Brandon and slapped him hard across the face, "Get that look off your homely face, you big dope."

It was Alex's turn to sardonically grin, "Well that's the siren, Brandon. It would appear you also aren't immune to her spell."

Brandon, "What happened, it felt like somebody plugged into my head and turned off everything except...." Pausing as he looked sideways at a grim Claudia, he decided, wisely, to change the subject. "Wow Claudia, can you hit!" As he rubbed his cheek.

Claudia possessively grabbed his arm then, in a saccharine sweet voice, replied, "I was just trying to break you out of the trance that Amazon had placed on you. I hope I didn't hurt you *much*."

Brandon started to say, "She didn't look like an Amazon to..." The look on Claudia's face changed his mind.

Alex came to his friend's rescue after an uncomfortable silence, "Claudia, whatever she's doing to us it doesn't seem to affect you."

"Oh, I know what she's doing to you. Men!"

Alex answered firmly, "No, I don't think you do. It has to be something chemical or maybe empathic. Pheromones or some kind of inhaled drug. I believe Mamba may have neutralized the effect on me. That very enigmatic woman is playing a very dangerous game and she apparently wants to involve the Chameleons."

Claudia calming down asked, "You think she's some kind of spy or saboteur?"

Alex thoughtfully answered, "I don't know, but you and I need to find out. Brandon, I think it best if you returned to your previous duties."

A grateful and relieved Claudia agreed, "He's right Brandon. You have no protection against this effect. Alex, are you sure it's safe for you?"

"I believe so." Then to a departing Brandon he shouted, "We'll review our findings with you later." Turning back to Claudia he continued, "Let's meet with our guest, again." Stepping into the room, they found Roxanne crumpled in the corner, weeping. If it was an act, it was a very good one. Claudia, without sympathy, snapped, "Get up, we need to talk to you."

As Roxanne climbed off the floor and turned to face them, Alex noted she was younger than he'd first thought. He continued to admire her scantily clad beauty with a more objective eye. His initial perception of slender perfection was incorrect but not by much. Her forehead was broader and her tear stained cheekbones were higher than the standard aesthetic norms. She was also more muscular. The overall impression was of aristocracy, intelligence and strength. Alex still liked what he saw.

Claudia snapped again, "Well, who the frakke are you and what the Hell are you doing to the men?"

Roxanne, trying to stifle a sob, replied, "I'm sorry. I didn't think it would happen to me. I don't understand. This is awful. Please, I don't want to cause any more problems. You have to keep men away from men. Please." Then she looked up at Alex, her face cleared up a little as she wiped away her tears with a bare arm, "How come you're not affected?"

Alex in a neutral voice, "Affected by what, Miss Rudnauman?"

Roxanne paused then looked up hopefully, "You really aren't affected." She pulled herself together and looked with interest at the two of them. "I think there has been a misunderstanding, that kooky Captain was just infatuated with me, he made me think I was doing something to him." Emphatically, "And I wasn't, otherwise you'd be affected also. But..."

Alex interrupted, "Excuse me Miss Rudnauman, your analysis is inaccurate. Whatever you did to the Captain you also did to Brandon and me. I have an antidote to this effect you keep referencing. So I think you better explain it, right now."

In indignation she replied, "That's ridiculous. You're clearly in complete control of yourself, which would be impossible if..., there are no antidotes. Even a homosexual male couldn't resist."

Claudia interrupted, with a quirky smile, "Major Kane has very normal sexual inclinations. Whatever this affect is, you had better start explaining before I start tearing out your fingernails, one at a time!"

Roxanne slumped down into the bunk, whispering to herself, "So it is happening."

In frustration, Claudia yelled, "What is happening?"

A clearly distraught Roxanne responded, "I'm becoming a Triarch."

Claudia barely controlling her temper asked through gritted teeth, "Woman, what are you talking about?"

Alex interceded, "What exactly do you mean by Triarch, Miss Rudnauman?"

Shrugging her elegant shoulders, she answered, "You might as well know. I'm the daughter of King-Consort Ludvig the Fourth and Queen Lydia Rudnauman."

Detecting some hesitation he suspected she was telling half truths.

Looking down, she continued, "I am, no, was a member of my father's invasion force on Fairhaven. It probably won't matter to you, but I did not support the alliance of my home world with the GenClones. Once my father signed the treaty, I had to support his position, at least publicly."

Alex knew Ludvig ruled the mysterious 'lost' world of Asturia one of the more powerful Fringe worlds. The king was the most important ally of the GenClones on Fairhaven because he had the most CombatDroids and the highest tech world on the Vegan Republic's Fringe border. He spoke, "Recent reports indicate Ludvig may have been mortally wounded at Seagrun Pass. Are you now telling us he is definitely dead?"

Roxanne whispered in sorrow, "Yes, he's dead. He was a good man and a good father until Mother died. He never really recovered. He just lost perspective and I couldn't help him."

Claudia and Alex looked at each other in surprise. Could this really be the daughter of the Asturian King?

Claudia disgustedly asked, "And you decided to abandon your people after your father's death?"

Roxanne emphatically shouted, "No! I had to leave. I would have been a source of dissension and discord."

Claudia sarcastically asked, "You mean this effect thing?"

Roxanne replied, "No the change hadn't started yet." She wailed, "It wasn't supposed to happen at all."

Alex pacified the agitated princess as best he could, "Remain calm Miss Rudnauman. Please try to explain this change rationally. Take your time." Looking pointedly at Claudia, "We won't interrupt."

Roxanne discoursed distractedly, "On my world, certain genetically predisposed women develop a peculiar power over men, usually a few years after puberty. Those who develop this power are referred to as Triarches, in the rare cases where the effect is very strong they are called Truzen Triarches." Pausing, then evasively "Among other things the power enables a woman to speed life's natural healing process and makes her more attractive to men. A Truzen Triarch can also increase the longevity and strength of herself and those around her." She gulped desperately for air. The thought of transforming into a Triarch obviously terrified her.

She continued, "Triarches suffer profound manic depression during this transition. During Melanjou, as it is called, a Triarch becomes emotionally unstable and extremely disruptive to the men around her."

Alex interrupted, "Do you know what causes this effect?"

Oblivious to the question, Roxanne droned on, "There are so many legends amongst my people about Triarches. They believe Triarches are angels of mercy, bringing joy and healing into the world. A community with a Triarch is considered blessed, as is her mate. But a Triarch going through Melanjou is always sent to the cloister in the Barque Mountains, otherwise she can destroy the cohesion of a community. Setting brother against brother, enraging the wives and sweethearts of the communities men."

Alex intervened again, "That still doesn't explain why you are asking for asylum. You just told us you didn't expect this transformation to occur."

Roxanne, looking up, "The change is upon me, please you must shelter me from men or I'll be an endless source of strife."

Claudia in disgust snapped, "Do you believe this? She has to be insane."

Alex explained, "Claudia, I've read a little about Asturia. There is a well defined legend about women with the powers she describes. When we first met, my perception of her was distorted. It must be some kind of pheromone she is exuding. Airborne chemical mood stimulants are not unknown. A mutation that could enable women to produce such a chemical is quite possible. Especially on a world with strong myogenetic organics like Asturia. How else do you explain the effect she has over the men on this ship. Razor's Axiom applies, her explanation makes the only sense given the evidence." Turning back to Roxanne, "When you left Fairhaven you didn't believe you were becoming a Triarch. Is that correct?"

She nodded in reply.

Alex continuing, "Then why did you leave? And why are you asking us for asylum? I would think you would want to go into one of your cloisters until this change is complete, not stay with a bunch of surly mercenaries."

Alex noted the look of hopeless pride as Roxanne looked up and spoke, "I am the only daughter of Ludvig the Fourth and Lydia Rudnauman. The Asturian monarchy is matrilineal, making me the Princess Heir to the Dragon Throne. I am the greatest marital prize of my warrior people. With the unexpected death of my father, an orderly process for choosing my mate, the future king of Asturia is no longer possible. If I had stayed on Fairhaven, civil war would have ensued between my father's commanders to gain possession of me. If I go to Asturia the same thing will happen there, amongst the great counts. If I can stay clear of the feuding factions and contact my Uncle Bonaduce, Count of Hildebrandt, he may be able to prevent the civil war by calling a meeting of the Grand Council."

Claudia, snorting, "Barbaric, you're just some kind of prize in a colossal power grab amongst your world's nobles."

Roxanne emphatically, "No! Our matrilineal system has prevented civil war on Asturia for nearly three hundred years. Can you say the same of any other independent Fringe world?"

Claudia responded, "Well it sounds to me like you should have a civil war every time a king dies."

Roxanne desperately trying to justify her society answered, "No, typically either the king or the High Council, in his absence, would call all potential suitors to the Capitol. The High Council, then selects a variety of trials to determine the best candidates. The princess chooses the future king from the winners. The system has almost always given us competent rulers, and since everyone from yeomen to great count is eligible, all the people have a stake in the system."

Alex again trying to understand what this young women was doing on the shuttle asked, "So why don't you get the protection of this High Council of yours? Why this sudden untraditional power grab by your father's commanders?"

"My father foolishly divided the High Council. Half of them are now fighting to get a piece of

Fairhaven. So there is no quorum either here or at home. Worse, the presence of the GenClones and GenClone technology has corrupted many of our leaders. Many would forcibly marry me and present the Council with a 'fait accompli' against all our traditions. It is appalling. I knew we shouldn't have dealt with the GenClones. Already, it is destroying our way of life."

Alex contemplatively asked, "Roxanne, what will your father's commanders do, once they find out you're gone?"

She replied, "They will assume I have either fled to my uncle, or that I have run off with a potential suitor. So they'll need to return to Asturia to protect their holdings against a vengeful, new king." Pausing, "Or they will try to beat me home and kidnap me before my uncle can convene the High Council. In either case most of them will almost certainly abandon Fairhaven for home."

Alex began to laugh. Both women looked at him strangely as his rumbling chuckle grew louder.

Claudia piqued by his reaction asked, "What does your peculiar sense of humor find amusing in this situation?"

Alex, controlling his mirth, replied, "Two things. First the Asturian contingent comprises nearly a full regiment of the raider force. Miss or should I say Princess Rudnauman's departure from Fairhaven will cause nearly a quarter of the invasion force to abandon the campaign. Our stowaway has indirectly done more for the Vegan forces than all our fighting to date. Second, we have to give her asylum and not tell anyone because if word slips out that she's here, we'll have every Asturian combat shuttle charging towards this old cow. Even if we manage to rendezvous with the StarShip and Transit ahead of them, we will be hounded by Asturian warlords, no matter where we go."

Claudia asked, "You're not going to notify Colonel Bayard?"

"This ship doesn't have any secured communications. If we try to notify him, the news will probably be intercepted. I believe we are stuck with you, Princess. Now what do we do about it?"

Roxanne looked down and said, "You will have to keep me apart from men for three to five months, until I regain control of my body and emotions. It will be extremely difficult, since I will be suffering through a Melanjou induced emotional roller coaster, and I may find the isolation objectionable." Roxanne looked away from them in embarrassment, "A Triarch in Melanjou is capable of deliberately causing havoc among men."

Alex thought a moment, "Well we can't let everyone know who you are. So let's try this; you're a relative of one of Claudia's old family friends that ran away from home to become a CombatJack, against your family's wishes. You were traveling under an assumed name. Your real name will be..., any suggestions?"

Claudia offered, "Roxy Trevoren would be a good choice. The Trevorens are a large hidebound family on Vega. Our families used to ski together."

Happy that Claudia was contributing Alex said, "Good, so you're now Roxy Trevoren, CombatJack trainee in the Chameleons. By the way, do you have any training on Droids?"

Roxanne answered petulantly, "I truly hate being called Roxy I would prefer Roxanne. As for your question Major, yes I am capable of operating a full spectrum CyberLink and have piloted my cousin's *Renegade*. My father would have flayed the both of us had he found out. It isn't exactly appropriate for the Princess Heir to risk her life in combat."

Claudia, tartly replied, "I think we should stick with Roxy, we want to obscure any reference to your real origins. It's unfortunate that you gave your real name to Captain Morgan or we could modify it completely."

Roxanne queried, "What about my isolation. How are you going to explain that?"

Alex, with a wicked smile directed at Claudia answered, "You are now afflicted with Tukarian fever and will have to be kept in quarantine. Claudia, your records show you have already had Tukarian fever, so you can share quarters with your long, lost friend, Miss Trevoran. That particular disease, though rarely fatal, does cause bizarre behavior. That should help explain anything odd you might do."

Claudia in outrage swore, "Damn you Alex. You're going to afflict me with this", pointing at Roxanne, "for the rest of this trip!"

Alex trying not to laugh at Claudia's chagrin offered, "Unless you come up with a better cover story, yes."

Claudia stood there, ready to explode, but couldn't think of anything appropriate to say.

They reviewed the details of the plan a few more times before implementing it. To his surprise the crew readily accepted the story. Claudia explained to him that runaway aristocrats were more common than one would expect.

The rest of the two month roundabout voyage to Himalaya was productive but mostly uneventful. The multiple transits and various stops went by almost unnoticed as Alex and Brandon instituted a rigorous training program for the Chameleons, keeping them too busy for trouble making. Alex was pleased with the caliber of the men and women in his new command.

Fuller turned out to be nearly as good a chief tech as his famous uncle. In his own quiet way, he turned the technical staff into an efficient team. The results showed in their equipment. Even the second rate weapons used by the Gurkhas were performing at peak capabilities. As Fuller occasionally mumbled, "If you're going to fix it, fix it right."

The Gurkhas were a bigger surprise. At first they were very resistant to taking orders from the newly promoted Lieutenant Bolithio. A week into the voyage, two of them made some discourteous noises in her direction. She responded by putting both of them in sick bay with multiple injuries. Alex was concerned by the use of force by an officer to maintain order. His concern proved unfounded. The Gurkhas began to obey Bolithio's commands with alacrity, rather than risk the ignominy of being beaten by a woman. Remarkably once they accepted the Lieutenant's authority, they absorbed her advanced anti-Droid infantry training like sponges. As Bolithio was heard to say, in her colorful way, "These little buggers learn faster than any troops I've ever had. Give me an army of them and I could take Terra!"

The Princess proved to be a better Droid pilot then expected, at least on the simulators. Except for her inability to fire at even a simulated opponent. It became apparent that violence of any kind was an ordeal for the transforming Triarch. Alex believed she would have made a good addition to the Chameleons, except for her condition. Claudia, Brandon and Khorsa were already highly skilled veteran warriors. They had proved their abilities conclusively on Fairhaven and were coming together as a team. Khorsa to Alex's relief finally agreed to join the Chameleons as a CombatJack half way through their voyage. His belief in GenClone superiority had been shattered after his defeat on Fairhaven. Always mocked for his imperfect heredity by higher class GenClones, the transition was easier for him then anticipated.

Alex unexpectedly found himself spending a great deal of time with the Princess. Claudia could barely tolerate Roxanne's mood swings, and spent most of her time away from their quarters. With no other female officers entrusted with their secret, Alex became the only regular contact for the lonely woman. They found out a great deal about one another in long rambling conversations.

Roxanne's unveiling of the many mysteries and social curiosities of Asturia fascinated Alex. Living in the Asturian cut throat court with a degenerating father, while the social contract that protected the royal line collapsed, sounded almost as bad as growing up on Banshee.

Alex found himself relating some stories of his violent past to the sympathetic Princess. As different as their backgrounds were, they found a great deal of commonality in their lives. Alex knew he was falling hard for the Princess. He kept telling himself it was just the close confinement or some Triarch induced effect but didn't really believe it. Suffering through Melanjou, Roxanne alternated between trying to seduce him and hating him. Luckily the interludes of rationality were getting longer as the transition progressed. As he caught glimpses of the real woman behind the emotional roller coaster, his attraction grew stronger. What was a mine rat from Banshee doing falling in love with a Princess? It was a dilemma he struggled with during the last leg of the voyage.

Jumping into the Himalayan system quickly distracted him from his emotional entanglements. Decisions had to be made and fast.

Chapter 19

He looked around the cramped, nondescript conference room with pride. The senior Chameleon officers had evolved into a well-honed team during their long voyage and they looked the part. They stood out in their newly designed half-dress uniforms; flared, navy blue pantaloons and sky blue tunics with gold and black piping. The contrast against the dull gray metal walls and dingy, ancient furniture was startling. Alex had at first thought the uniforms garish, when Claudia proposed the color scheme. He had to admit they looked sharp and martial at the same time. The whole unit was happy with the results. But Alex knew it would be their training and skills tested on the battlefields not their uniforms.

Sitting in his usual position at the center of the drab, oval table, with Brandon and Claudia sitting comfortably to his right and Jamadar Kaseem and Lieutenant Bolithio in their usual places to his left. He almost smiled at the incongruous pair. The powerfully built, nearly two meters tall blond Valkyrie and the slight, dark skinned Gurkha had become a mutual admiration committee. They worked together like a pair of hunting Dovarian Hellcats. The pairing, which had been his biggest concern, was turning into the heart of the Corps. There was even some speculation they might be intimate. Alex had his doubts.

Fuller, as always, stood near the exit at the back of the small room fumbling half heartily with a small servo mechanism. He always looked like he was ready to bolt from the room. It was rare to see the Chief without some mechanical device in his hands. Tinkering with machines seemed to ease his discomfort in the company of so many people. Lieutenant "Big Ben" Richtover sat disconsolately at the base of the table. Ben was rarely good company lately. These conferences seemed to further remind him of the loss of his StarFighter. Their lack of space and air assets seemed to always be a discussion point. Alex sometimes regretted recruiting him. But he felt he owed the man who had saved their tails at the Blackeel river raid. Besides Captain Bouchard highly recommended him and he was a capable tech. Richtover took great pride in his descent from some legendary pre-space atmospheric craft pilot. Neither Alex nor any of the other Chameleons had ever heard of this supposedly famous Red Baron.

Ambassador Doran and Captain Morgan arrived late and sat down at the other side of the conference table. They had become a regular part of the Chameleon staff meetings since the Transit to Himalaya. Their presence was Alex's signal to start the session. He stood up next to the wall map and reviewed the situation, "Well it's confirmed. We detected an unidentified StarShip of GenClone design exiting from a pirate jump point just as we arrived. An unknown and unauthorized shuttle landed on Himalaya, somewhere in the Northern Arctic zone two days later. Its cargo and exact location are unknown. It would appear that Colonel Bayard's speculation about the GenClones using Himalaya as a staging area was correct. We believe the GenClones have located their operations somewhere in Kaolyn Province due north of the capital. The area is under populated, and the terrain is rugged enough to hide a shuttle base."

Jamadar Kaseem asked, "There are many places in the Great Arctic Range that fulfill this criteria, Major. Why is Kaolyn suspected?"

Alex replied, "Two reasons, first the area is close enough to the coastal region, that supplies could be hauled overland to a secret base. As Colonel Bayard noted, Vegan and Imperial equipment is getting into the hands of the GenClones." Turning to Doran, "Ambassador."

Doran added, "We have had reports of unexplained *fires in the sky* by shepherds in Kaolyn Province. Also there have been unexplained disappearances of local peasants." She hesitated a moment and looked at Alex. Alex nodded in response, "I have just received a coded report from my husband that a ring of smugglers was intercepted, hauling equipment into the area."

Bolithio in excitement said, "If they've been interrogated then we should know exactly where the GenClone base is!"

Doran softly replied, "I'm afraid not. Our security forces are not permitted to use force, or to carry arms. They confiscated the equipment and released the smugglers into the custody of their religious councilors."

Bolithio in disbelief asked, "What if the smugglers had put up a fight. Would you just have let them go?"

Doran, aghast answered, "Our people would never resort to violence Sergeant! Smuggling is one thing, using force on a fellow human is quite another!"

Bolithio responded, "But the equipment could be used against your own people by the GenClones."

Doran, defensively answered, "The supplies did not include weapons. No Himalayan would commerce in tools of destruction. The acquisition of wealth is frowned upon but not forbidden by our beliefs. These smugglers were just misguided in their actions."

Alex interrupted an open mouthed Bolithio. "I don't think a discussion of Himalayan social norms is of value right now. If I may summarize Ambassador. The smugglers were interviewed and were quite cooperative. Surprisingly, they were not aware who was purchasing the supplies. Furthermore the threat of excommunication is more powerful than torture for most Himalayan citizens. The smugglers and their mule train apparently are contacted in the foothills by a guide, then escorted to a prearranged point, where the supplies are transferred to hover transports. The meeting and contact locations are varied with each shipment, but they are all located in the Kaolyn foothills, here." As he pointed at the map, "Credits show up in a numbered bank account in Matsuisan a day later, in payment."

Brandon speculated, "Do you think Matsui is involved Alex? It's hard to believe the GenClones could establish credit and a banking system in a corporate city, without the knowledge and cooperation of the parent corporation."

Alex answered, "We don't have enough evidence to make that call. The GenClones have to be getting some support from traitors or double agents. Matsui would be first on my list, but there are others including Symcorp that are suspect. I would think Matsui would be careful to avoid any hint of collaboration with the GenClones. Emperor Bukhara IX doesn't treat traitors kindly."

The Jamadar focused the meeting by interjecting, "Excuse me Sir, it is my humble opinion that the Chameleons were hired to capture and destroy a GenClone base, not to investigate GenClone financial dealings."

Alex was chagrined that he had let the meeting ramble. Another reminder that he might be in over his head, even commanding this small mercenary outfit. Colonel Bayard or Captain Bouchard always were in control of their briefings. Humbly he replied, "Jamadar you are correct. We are here to develop a plan for dealing with the suspected GenClone base and idle speculation won't help us towards that goal. The key point is we are now confident that the base is somewhere in this part of Kaolyn Province. It's still a very large area to scout. Our mission is to locate the base and take it out covertly." Looking at the tight lipped Ambassador, "With minimal casualties."

Doran uncomfortably added, "Commander, if it looks like there may be heavy casualties, the Council would prefer to negotiate a settlement with the GenClones."

Alex, Brandon and Claudia had already anticipated this discussion with Doran. The thought of violence truly upset her. Alex attempted to appease her, "Of course Ambassador. It would not be in the best interest of the Chameleons to fight a battle with heavy casualties." He was only partially lying. He didn't care about the loses of the GenClones, as long as his own troops were unscathed. But it wasn't worth further argument with his employer to clarify that point. Alex knew negotiating with the GenClones would probably be fruitless. GPL GenClones were single minded in their goal to conquer known space. The other officers did not comment. He suspected they understood his real position and liked the Ambassador enough not to make it an issue.

Richtover resignedly commented, "Too bad we don't have any StarFighters. Armstrong and I could just fly over the area until we spotted them. I suppose you're going to land in the target zone and blunder around in your slow footed Droids until you trip over the GenClones, Major?"

Alex emphatically replied, "No Lieutenant! We don't plan to give up our only advantage that easily. The government on Himalaya and probably the GenClones know the Ambassador has been successful in hiring a mercenary outfit. But they don't know the composition or the mission. Lieutenant Flanders has developed a strategy to use this to our advantage. Jamadar Kaseem and most of our infantry and armor will land in the Capitol, and make a lot of noise about investigating strange activities in Kaolyn Province while doing nothing. Captain Morgan if you can make an elliptic approach over Kaolyn Province on your way to the capitol, the CombatDroid lance, Sergeant Bolithio and C and E platoons will do a low altitude drop here." As he pointed to a high plateau in the center of the province. "From there we will covertly scout the region until we find the base. Then we'll either capture it, if it's not heavily protected, or report its location to the government, if it's beyond our capabilities. Ambassador Doran has kindly agreed not to disclose our true force strength, or this plan, even to the High Council until the base is located. Comments?"

Alex had spent the morning with Brandon and Claudia working out the broad outline of the plan, it was the only one that made sense given their lack of information. The other officers in the room proposed various alternatives and upgrades. Alex let Brandon field most of the questions. He was better at explaining than Alex. Two upgrades to the plan were added. Kaseem proposed they bring additional small arms for the decommissioned 22nd Gurkha Brigade. They lived near the DZ and would probably volunteer to join in tracking down and expelling intruders from their home territory.

Kaseem seemed upset about something, though if was difficult to tell with the taciturn officer. Fuller surprisingly proposed leading a tech team to evaluate the GenClone technology. Alex suspected Fuller was more interested in analyzing GenClone Droids then in the mission itself, but the idea made sense. Everyone volunteered for the drop. Alex had already chosen who would go, but kept it to himself. Brandon wasn't on the list and Alex didn't want the anticipated confrontation with his exec aired publicly.

Hours of haranguing later, they completed the final details of the plan. Everyone left to make preparations except for Alex, Brandon and Claudia. Lieutenant Bolithio and Jamadar Kaseem went to gather C and E company for a mission briefing with Alex. Back in the conference room he broached the most controversial aspect of the plan, "We have a few minutes before the foot sloggers arrive. Claudia, I'm assigning you to the *Python* for the drop."

Brandon opened his mouth to speak, then shut up. His objections went unsaid. He recognized that she was the better CombatJack.

Alex uncomfortably continued, "Brandon, you will take command of the infantry forces in Asmara. I'm counting..."

Brandon exploded out of his seat shouting, "No way Alex! I'm not going to play at being a merc while you and Claudia risk your lives. I can fight with the anti-Droid infantry. I'm as good or better than anyone with a rocket launcher."

Alex his face an unreadable mask answered, "I know Brandon, but I need someone in charge at the capitol capable of dealing with the religious rulers of Himalaya, and of carrying off the bluff we're running. Kaseem isn't qualified and that leaves you. Besides once we find the base we can recombine our forces before we engage."

Brandon, clearly enraged swore, "Don't BS me Alex! If you find that base you're going to take it out if you can. You forget, I know your style. I'm not going to Asmara!"

Claudia with a pained expression tried to intervene, "Brandon..."

Alex grimly interrupted, "You're my friend Brandon, but I have a responsibility to everyone in the Chameleons to do everything in my power to maximize our chances of success. I need you in the Capitol. You are the only one that can do the job. So I'm giving you a direct order Lieutenant. If you can't follow orders you can resign your commission."

The two stared at one another for what felt like an eternity. Claudia sat quietly looking at her hands. Alex felt terrible, he knew he had created a barrier between him and his best friend that might be insurmountable.

Finally Brandon saluted rigidly and answered sarcastically, "Yes sir, Major, I won't abandon my unit in combat. So until this assignment is over I'll take your orders, Sir." Then he turned and left the room. Claudia got up, looked at Alex enigmatically and followed Brandon out.

Alex sat at the table feeling miserable until Bolithio and Kaseem returned with a score of troopers. They crammed into the conference room. Alex stood up next to Bolithio and asked her to review the mission.

She briefed the group with their assignments and reviewed the drop itself. "The *Tiara II* will close to within eight hundred meters of the DZ and slow to a speed of four hundred kph. The Droids will jump first then the APC's will be dropped, unmanned using equipment chutes, and finally the rest of us will follow in pairs at two second intervals. We will be over the DZ for only thirty-eight seconds so there will be no room for error."

The Gurkha troopers erupted into a babble of noise at this announcement. Whispering to each other and waving their arms.

Leutenant Bolithio snapped, "Attention!" As the room quieted she asked, "What is the matter with you all?"

Sub Jamadar Javreel asked, "Leutenant, can we get closer to the ground before we make the jump?"

Bolithio, her face turning red at the unexpected opposition to the plan by the usually stolid Gurkha troopers, "Yes we can, but the optimum distance for the drop is eight hundred meters. It minimizes the risk of detection and accident. Do you have a problem with that Javreel?"

There was some more whispering in their foreign tongue before Javreel replied, "Leutenant we would still prefer a lower drop point. Respectfully Leutenant, we think we would have a better chance if we jumped below two hundred meters."

Alex couldn't comprehend the request. Two person parasailers would be too risky to operate at such a low level. The wings might not fully deploy before the troopers grounded.

Bolithio had heard enough and exploded all over the hapless Gurkhas in an ear blistering tirade about their ancestral and anatomical deficiencies. Kaseem interrupted her quietly but forcibly. "Leutenant, the plan has been established, our honor demands that we do as we are ordered, individual lives are not important."

The Gurkhas stood and saluted grimly. Their silence and rigid stances were not reassuring. It suddenly dawned on Alex that there must be a misunderstanding.

Alex insightfully asked, "Lieutenant, have you trained the new troops on parasail insertions yet?"

Bolithio quizzically replied, "No, we'll have time to run some simulations before the drop, Sir. I planned to put out a training schedule after this meeting, Major." She saluted stiffly, a further sign of her outrage at the trooper's behavior. Bolithio fell back on military etiquette when she was unsure.

Alex turned to Kaseem and asked, "Jamadar are you and your troopers familiar with parasails?"

The Jamadar looking baffled answered, "Sir?"

Alex grinned sardonically, "I believe the Gurkha troopers will be less resistant to the mission once they familiarize themselves with the use of parasails, Lieutenant."

Bolithio red faced yelled at the Gurkhas, "Well how in frakke did you all expect to get down? With nothing but your equipment?"

Javreel hesitantly replied, "Yes Mam."

Bolithio shouted, "That's insane, you would all die on impact!"

Kaseem deliberately replied, "We knew that Lieutenant, that is why we preferred a lower drop. We thought the chances of survival would be higher. It would be wasteful to die before meeting the enemy."

The usually irrepressible Bolithio was speechless for the second time that day. She probably felt like Alex. Unable to decide whether to laugh or scream at the Gurkha troopers. A culture that was familiar with interstellar travel, and yet had such huge holes in their understanding of more conventional technologies. Another example of humanity's decline since the Second Great Interstellar War. Alex wondered what other pieces of critical knowledge his Gurkha soldiers lacked that could lead to disaster. "Jamadar, I admire the courage and commitment of your men, but I think it would be a shame to suffer casualties due to a lack of understanding."

With a crisp salute Kaseem replied, "Yes sir."

Alex added to Bolithio, "And Lieutenant in future I think the less we assume and the better we question the understanding of our subordinates, the better off we will all be."

Bolithio clearly embarrassed replied stiffly, "Understood Major."

Alex dismissed them and went to check on the *Warlock*. He wanted to call on Roxanne, but he didn't have the energy to deal with the still moody princess after his mentally grueling day. He almost wished he was back on Banshee, with nothing to worry about except his own survival. Life had been harsh but simple back then.

Chapter 20

The drop had gone smoothly. Alex scanned the surrounding ice covered terrain with his passive sensors only. He watched as the troopers folded up their parasails and buried them in the deep snow. The DZ would be marked and the equipment recovered later if they were successful. The infantrymen then climbed aboard and fired up their two hover APC's. Claudia was already moving her *Python* up the southern ridge to check the next valley. Snow flakes gusted across the stark white landscape swirling around the surrounding peaks.

Alex walked the *Warlock* up another ridge compensating slightly for the blast of wind as he cleared the valley rim. Temperatures were below minus 40 degrees and the gale force winds above the valley made the wind chill lethal. The Gurkhas had laughed when Bolithio had warned them of the dangers of hypothermia and frostbite at these altitudes. As Sub-Jamadar Kaseem noted, his troopers had been herding yaks and neuvo-llamas under these conditions long before they had learned to read and write. Javreel had even made some recommendations to Bolithio on the cold weather gear used by the non-Himalayans. Alex was pleased to see that she was open to suggestions from her subordinates.

Hand signal and laser light transmissions flew across the clearing as the small force sorted itself. 24 anti-Droid troopers and their APC's, a Pantheon light tank armed with a 16 shot quad HEAP launcher, two CLAT's, four techs and two SuperDroids formed the strike team. Not much of a force to take on a covert GenClone base of unknown size. There was a communication and active sensor blackout for the entire mission. Alex wanted to keep their presence here, near the roof of this world, a secret. His worst nightmare was for a superior GenClone force to detect them first. A single GenClone Droid lance could destroy them in minutes if they were caught off guard.

Over the next few hours the strike force secured the DZ undetected. A slowly spreading circle of land was explored. The lead APC, commanded by Javreel, found an ideal base camp in an area of hot springs with a heavy iron content. The iron and heat would make their equipment difficult to detect. The site was also well protected from the wind and relatively free of ice. The smooth teamwork of the motley strike force was impressive. Brandon was not only a brilliant strategist but a first rate executive officer. He had coordinated the training of their diverse little company, until they functioned like a well-oiled machine. Even the unusual requirements of this mission didn't phase the soldiers.

That evening Alex, Claudia, Bolithio and Javreel reviewed the mission status over a dinner consisting of some unappealing field rations, as flakes of snow lazily drifted around their tent. The snow, the cold bite of the air in his lungs were wonderful new experiences for Alex. Only the awful food reminded him of the real reason for their presence amongst the ice bound spires.

Alex idly wondered why field rations tasted so bad. Modern food storage techniques should have permitted a much higher quality meal. He decided it must have something to do with the military psyche. Maybe bad food gave the troops something to complain about other then their officers. He noticed the Gurkhas in his command gobbling the rations down with pleasure. A smile quirked his face. It hadn't been all that long ago when the half eaten, reconstituted chicken in its microwave tray would have been a gourmet meal for him. He had seen convicts kill one another over less appetizing meals. It occurred to him, again, that he'd come a long way in the past year. Looking at the Gurkhas uncomplaining acceptance of their lives, he decided maybe the changes weren't all for the best. Then looking again at the snow covered peaks, he decided things could be much worse.

Claudia broke his reverie, "What are you smiling about Alex?"

Alex answered, "Nothing important." Then deciding a little more explanation was in order, he swept his hand around, "It's just fantastic. Life is harsh here, but I can understand why the Gurkhas always return. It's sometimes hard to take in all the things I've seen and done in the past year."

She smiled back conspiratorially, "I know. Why anybody would spend their time simpering in a court when this wonderful universe is out here waiting to be explored is beyond me."

After a few moments of silently enjoying the splendid surroundings, they got back down to business. Alex had decided to modify the recon pattern based on their base camp. If the Chameleons recognized the advantage of locating in an area with a high metal content and a thermal background, the same would almost certainly have occurred to the GenClones. They all agreed that locations with these characteristics should be investigated first, and a new recon pattern was developed.

For four days teams of Gurkha troopers in native costume roamed Kaolyn Province looking for traces of a GenClone base. Over eighty members of the 22nd Gurkha Brigade had joined in the effort. The supply of small arms, provided by the Chameleons, helped to cement a good working relationship with the 22nd.

Alex and Javreel had met with the 22nd's commanding officer, a Subhadar Chondra. Alex discovered that Subhadar was a rank equivalent to Colonel. the willingness of the ram rod straight Chondra to follow orders from a junior mercenary officer like Alex was a surprise. The senior officer impressed even Bolithio with his professionalism.

While scaling a small outcropping Javreel finally explained the anomaly to Alex in his broken Terrananglo, "The Subhadar is shamed most deeply at foreigners operating in his homelands without his forces knowing, sir. Even more shameful, without your help he is most helpless to remove these accursed GenClonesmen, Commander. You have seen the poorness of their equipment." With great pride, the Sub-Jamadar continued, "Our infantry is trained and armed most exceedingly better than any Gurkha Brigade."

So the Subhadar needed the Chameleons to regain his pride and lost authority. He was letting the foreign mercenaries take the lead because he couldn't deal with GenClone technology. The more surprising insight, was Javreel's obvious pride at being a Chameleon. It was increasingly clear to Alex, that the Gurkha's in his command had gained a great deal of status, by being accepted as equals by the rest of the Chameleons. Alex hadn't recognized the depth of prejudice the little warriors must face, when they tried marketing themselves as mercenaries. The few off world contracts the Gurkha's had negotiated, had been low paying, high risk military drudge work. Alex found himself agreeing with Bolithio, given proper equipment and training, Gurkha infantry could be the best in known space. He just hoped that Javreel and his platoon understood the limitations of even good infantry against CombatDroids. Only under very special circumstances could good anti-Droid infantry be effective against the armored shielded monsters of modern warfare.

Those circumstances might soon be tested, as they reached the ridge line, and looked down on a cleverly hidden GenClone base. The base was discovered accidentally that morning by a scout from the 22nd. Fortunately he wasn't detected. Javreel and Alex, in their very expensive nearly invisible Chameleon suits, were conducting the first in depth recon. Thermal suppressers nearly eliminated their heat signature, while the color mutable suit coatings mimicked the surrounding snow covered terrain. They had moved slowly and silently the last hundred meters to prevent activating any potential motion detectors, communicating in whispers and rudimentary Banshee hand speak. Alex had introduced hand speak to the Chameleons with great success. It enabled the unit to communicate effectively during covert ops like this. Sound could travel a long way at these altitudes.

Javreel began snapping pictures with a high resolution Sony K45 Camera, while Alex scanned the scene with a Bausch-Lambert Model 8 binocular. Stretched out below them in the volcanic crater was a picturesque frozen lake, surrounded by deciduous forest, with a small clearing at the base of the opposite ridge. In the clearing, nearly indiscernible under camouflage netting was a *Horatio* class shuttle. A stream of activity flowed back and forth from a cave in the cliff wall and the shuttle. Javreel whispered angrily, as he recognized chained Gurkhas being forced to carry heavy loads from the cave to the ship. "This is were all my missing people have gone!"

Alex spotted only two Droids, a 32 ton *Bounder* and a *Kingfisher*. Both were medium thrust equipped SuperDroids, either one could match firepower with both the Chameleon Droids. Conventional infantry, and at least two of the GenClones giant CLATs were also present. Alex thought, this isn't going to be easy, but it could be worse.

Chapter 21

Alex sat fidgeting in his *Warlock* behind the ridge line two kilometers from the GenClone base. Claudia in her powered down *Python* was fifty meters to his left. They had been waiting in their assigned position for two hours, while Bolithio and her anti-Droid infantry implemented the first part of the assault. The Gurkhas planted radio detonated anti-Droid mines along the standard patrol routes of the GenClone Droids. Reconnaissance had detected only the two Droids. In addition there was a CLAT platoon, and a score of conventional non GenClone infantry in the valley; as well as a variety of Techs and the crew of the well-armed shuttle. Alex had decided that they needed to reduce the odds before they hit the base.

The heart of the Chameleon attack plan was surprise, and the use of their superior infantry numbers to advantage. Alex knew they had to take control of the shuttle before it could bring its devastating weapons into play. Phase two of the plan was responsible for accomplishing this critical part of the mission. The majority of the Gurkha infantry, nearly one-hundred men should now be repelling their way down the ice bound cliff right above the shuttle. Chondra and Javreel were pleased to command this assault. They both down played the risks of the terrifying climb down the sheer cliff face, and the attack on the heavily armed shuttle; because it relied on the traditionally Gurkha skills of mountain climbing and stealthy attacks with small arms. Alex wasn't so sanguine.

Timing was absolutely critical. The Gurkha's had to hit the shuttle at dawn, when its bay doors were opened for unloading. That meant Bolithio had to detonate the mines when any pre dawn patrol approached the minefield. Alex kept worrying about a change in the GenClone routine or some unexpected event. The limitations of their intelligence also concerned him. They had only scouted the camp for two days from a long distance for fear of detection. He wished Brandon had reviewed the plan. Alex trusted him to recognize flaws.

The reliance on others for critical parts of the plan had Alex ready to scream. Sometimes he wondered if he had the right temperament for command. He hated relying on subordinates. People were going to die today. The idea that friends of his were at risk because of his plan was unnerving. Mamba agitated at Alex's uncharacteristic behavior nipped him twice to calm him.

The pre-dawn light of the red sun began to illuminate the stark surrounding cliffs, when multiple explosions shattered the snowbound silence. Alex powered up the *Warlock* then activated his ODC and thrusters, jumping up and over the ridge, down into the GenClone valley with Claudia's *Python* close behind. Finally action to relieve the interminable wait. As he landed on the valley floor he used his passive sensors to scan the terrain. A grim smile came to his face as he spotted a downed Droid. The *Kingfisher* looked to have lost a foot sheared off by a powerful explosion. Bolithio's anti-Droid troops were swarming all over the prone machine. The mines had worked even better than expected. The other GenClone Droid, the *Bounder* was leaving the cave entrance, charging towards its downed companion. Alex changed course to intercept. Claudia followed, both still maintaining Communication silence.

The *Bounder* pilot was distracted so he didn't spot them until they were in long firing range. Even the SCM and surrounding forest shouldn't have prevented earlier detection. Alex and Claudia quickly moved into range, and triggered their HEAP batteries almost simultaneously. He was relieved to launch the first wave of missiles. He had risked using inferno warheads on the first volley, counting on surprise, to allow his *Warlock* the first shot in any exchange. Claudia had been appalled at the risk, but Alex wanted every possible edge. Multiple warheads arrowed into the advancing *Bounder*. Its APDS went into action engaging and destroying half of the eight missiles. The surviving Missiles hit, their detonations staggering the Droid, and depleting its EMD shields. Plasma gel from the infernos spread across the cubed armor causing serious decompression. The Bounder blazed white hot on Alex's thermal sensors, as it pivoted to challenge the advancing Chameleon Droids and fired one of its paired EPC's. Alex dodged left, as the hasty shot just missed him. GenClone technology again impressed him. Conventional Droids would have shut down from heat overload after taking four inferno rounds. The SuperDroid was still moving and still combat capable. At least for the moment.

Claudia triggered her NPC just missing the dodging Bounder. Alex broke Communications silence, "Command1 to Command2 commence phase three." Claudia broke off her attack on the SuperDroid and went to support the infantry attack on the shuttle. Her fire power was needed against the GenClone CLATs. Alex spotted the savage fire fight taking place at the bay doors of the shuttle. Taking the ship was the most critical part of the raid.

Alex fired his NPC, the violet beam slashed into the torso of the unshielded Bounder. The deadly hit was too much for the 32 ton Droid's radiators, with a shudder it shutdown. He watched the pilot eject. Alex thought as he turned towards the cave entrance to start phase four, "this raid is going like clockwork." He changed his mind a moment later, as a humanoid shaped 48 ton *Stormwarden* marched out of the cave. The *Stormwarden* was almost universally considered the deadliest all purpose medium SuperDroid. The most maneuverable in its weight class it still carried a terrifying modular arsenal. Paired heavy EPC's and 44 MM Phased Array laser bolts streaked from the monster into the mass of soldiers at the base of the shuttle instantly incinerating every unarmored thing the lethal beams touched. The *Stormwarden* pilot didn't seem to care which troops he killed. Alex howled in rage, activating his ODC again, he charged the unexpected intruder. He lined up all his long range weapons triggering them in quick succession. The *Stormwarden* turned to face its new challenger, its powerful 10 MM shield blazing blue under the impact of a HEAP missile and NPC and laser hits, it remained unscathed. Even at 250 KPH, Alex knew he wouldn't be able to reach the awesome war machine, before its massed weaponry slagged the *Warlock*. And his usual hit and run tactics wouldn't work, because it would leave the infantry and Claudia helpless every time he withdrew. The *Warlock* was a superb machine, but it sacrificed fire power for speed and wasn't designed for slugging duels with a front line fighter like the *Stormwarden*. The only chance for his command was to charge the enemy Droid and hopefully manage a crippling shot before he was destroyed.

As the massed weapons of the *Stormwarden* stabbed into the *Warlock* he doubted the sanity of his attack. Each volley sliced through his shield and destroyed large chunks of armor and equipment on his steadily disintegrating Droid. His limited ability to dodge was the only thing keeping him alive. Warning lights lit up all over his board as the left Pod launcher and medium laser went off line. He replied again with all of the *Warlock*'s remaining weapons, calmly and with pinpoint accuracy. The NPC and his remaining 44 MM laser scored hits on the *Stormwarden*'s left leg for the second time. A HEAP round exploded along the enemy Droid's left shoulder joint shredding more armor. He was hurting the big machine as he closed, but not enough. Claudia also fired a HEAP volley with limited effect. Alex spotted her *Python* battling a swarm of CLATs at the foot of the shuttle. She wouldn't be much help now, and the *Warlock* couldn't survive much longer.

Alex wouldn't break off the attack and leave his troops exposed. He felt sick, as he charged into the gaping maws of the *Stormwarden*'s twin EPC barrels and its massed Pod launchers. He twisted the Droid torso aside as he spotted the EPC coils charging, managing to avoid one of the deadly bolts of man made lightning. It wasn't enough, the other bolt overwhelmed his shield and vaporized his remaining right side armor. The missiles that followed irrevocably crippled the *Warlock*, damaging the engine, the shield generator and the stabilizers. Smoke billowed out of the *Warlock* as parts sloughed off. Alarms indicated imminent engine failure. Alex overrode them. His left leg actuator failed with his next stride and the *Warlock* began to topple. Alex deftly used his momentum to fall towards the GenClone Droid then fired his remaining undamaged thrusters, hurling the *Warlock* in a flat trajectory directly at the nearby GenClone machine. The *Stormwarden* Jack recognized his danger, and chose to try to avoid the hurtling Droid rather then finishing its pilot. It was too late. Alex triggered his ejection seat as he watched the struggling pilot desperately shift his Droid aside only meters away. They were so close the ejection seat caromed off the *Stormwarden* only a fraction of a second before the *Warlock* crashed into it. 40 tons of Droid traveling at 250 KPH was an unstoppable force. The last thing Alex remembered was spinning out of control, and a massive explosion lighting up the whole universe.

Chapter 22

Alex opened his eyes slowly. The room seemed to spin around before his unfocused eyes. He kept blinking away the tears trying to see where he was. A scratchy voice whispered "Where am I?" He recognized it as his own. From a remote distance, he heard a voice sounding like someone yelling down an echo chamber, "Alex, Alexx, Alexxss."

The room finally stopped spinning as he focused on the tear blurred face of Brandon Flanders. "Brandon what are you doing here?" Recalling the fire fight, Alex suddenly jerked up causing his dizziness to return. He croaked, "The *Stormwarden*, did I get it? The shuttle?"

Brandon calmly replied, "Easy Alex, everything is going to be all right buddy. You took out the *Stormwarden*, and we captured the GenClone base."

Alex took a moment to assimilate the news as the rest of the room came slowly into focus. He was in a medical bay, Claudia, and Ambassador Doran were standing behind Brandon. He asked, "How did you get here so fast?"

"Alex I've been here a week, you've been unconscious nearly two weeks now. It was touch and go for a while buddy, but you're going to make it. Rest now. The Medic says we can speak longer tomorrow."

He felt a pinprick in his arm and looked sideways spotting a previously unseen Medic sticking a hypodermic in his arm. Mamba licked his nose and purred contentedly as his eyes closed.

The next time he awoke he was more lucid. He began doing the mental portion of his I Ching exercises to clear the cobwebs. He recalled the end of his duel with the *Stormwarden*, and hazily remembered a conversation with Brandon. "Had he really been out for two weeks? What was happening to the Chameleons?" After a short time a Medic walked in and said in surprise, "Sir, you're awake."

Alex whispered in a bone dry voice, "Yes, I would like to see my Exec now if he's available."

The medic hurrying out of the room answered, "Of course sir, please remain still, you are seriously hurt and we wouldn't want you to re-injure yourself."

Alex with a pained shrug, "I wouldn't worry too much, with all this medical tape and all these splints there isn't much I can move."

The Medic ignored the comment as he left. Soon he returned with Brandon and Claudia in tow. Brandon with a broad smile spoke, "Our fearless commander finally awakes from his beauty sleep. It looks like you'll need another hundred years or so of rest to make that ugly puss fit for company, Alex."

Alex with a smile, "Did you get the name of that runaway monorail?"

Claudia was the only person Alex knew who could express concern and sarcasm simultaneously, "A monorail couldn't have come close to doing the damage you did to yourself Alex. Using your Droid as a missile is one of the best methods I've ever seen for committing suicide. Why you're still alive is beyond me." She picked up a chart at the base of the bed, "Nine broken bones, thirty-five percent of your body burned, massive internal bleeding, punctured lung, bruised liver, concussion, and assorted lesser injuries."

Alex in feigned surprise asked, "What no hangnails?" His attempt at humor elicited a grim silence in response. His friends were really concerned. "OK, lets get down to business, what's our status?"

Claudia and Brandon looked at one another, finally Claudia spoke, "It's going to take a while to explain, things have gotten complicated. Maybe we should wait."

Alex wanted to groan, he thought with the capture of the GenClone base their mission was finished. "I'm feeling OK right now and I'll tell you if I get tired. Go ahead."

Brandon turned to Claudia, "Go ahead babe, tell him the good news first."

Claudia, "After you took out the *Stormwarden*, it was just a mop up operation. Javreel's troops secured the shuttle while Chondra took the survivors of the 22nd and captured the Cave. Bolithio's platoon secured all three enemy SuperDroids and the parameter soon after. This base is an unbelievable find, it was a secret refit and supply point for the Terran Colonial Administration Army before their withdrawal in the 1st Interstellar War. The GenClones have been methodically dismantling and moving the facility, but there are still thousands of tons of supplies and we still haven't inventoried all of it. It includes a couple of StarFighters captured on the shuttle, dozens of infantry vehicles including hover tanks. As well as GenClone and Terran CLAT suits."

Claudia interrupted, "There are also large quantities of GenClone Tech enhancement kits, that were being transshipped to their allies on Fairhaven. We are fabulously rich, if what's left of the Himalayan government abides by the salvage portion of our contract. That is assuming we can get it all off planet."

Brandon added, "Don't forget the three SuperDroids you captured, they're fully repaired and ready to go. That *Stormwarden* you took down was piloted by the mission commander, a Colonel Hanson Pryde, a famous genengineered Jack. The GenClone pilots we captured can't believe you defeated him in single combat with a lighter Droid. He was supposed to be the best. You've added another notch to your rep."

Alex thoughtfully, "He was good, nearly too good." Pausing a moment, "I was lucky, it could have gone either way. Besides as I recall, we took each other out. At best it was a tie." Alex suppressed a shudder as he recalled the fight. He had never faced an opponent as deadly. It had been a very close call. He changed the subject to avoid thinking about those last few moments, "How's the *Warlock*?"

Brandon cautiously replied, "I am sorry Alex it was a total loss. The only thing we salvaged from it was the ODC system and some leg actuators."

Alex kept thinking to himself it was just a machine, but in his heart he knew better. The *Warlock* was the closest thing to a home he had.

Claudia, sensitive to Alex's attachment to his old Droid, changed the subject, "We were also lucky with the prisoners we freed. A lot of both the Techs and some of the freed soldiers have volunteered to join the Chameleons, and are now helping to repair and organize our equipment. They're the real reason we have the SuperDroids ready to go. We also have some unusual company that you will want to interview when you're up to it."

Brandon filled in more details, "This base explains why the GPL were able to launch this campaign. There were enough supplies here to support a couple of regiments for years. There are extensive repair and medical facilities and a power plant. Not to mention a fully operational mining complex. All of it shielded and underground."

Alex asked, "Where did they move all those supplies?"

Brandon pulled up a stool and sat down as he replied, "As Claudia noted, some were shipped to their allies on Fairhaven as payment, and the rest was sent to a mothballed mining complex on Nemesis. Nemesis is a moon circling the nearly uninhabited world of Tortuga Prime. The mine is on the dark side of the moon so the GenClones can operate out of it covertly. Like Earth's moon, Nemesis had a rotation synchronized with its orbit so the same side of the moon always faces away from Tortuga."

Alex always interested in the wider universe asked, "Tortuga, isn't that one of the Anarchist Schism worlds? Its not too far from here is it?"

Brandon leaning forward responded, "Yes and no. The Tortuga system is an anarchist stronghold. Dozens of pirate groups operate out of its large asteroid belt. Every attempt to root them out has failed because they simply pack up and move their mobile bases to another asteroid any time somebody gets angry enough to attack. You're right about them being close, Tortuga is only four light years from here. Tortuga Prime is surface habitable, but lacks certain critical trace elements necessary for earth normal life."

Claudia interrupted, "We've seen some pictures. It's an interesting place. The oceans have a spectacularly colorful, fully developed local ecosystem, with a nearly intelligent cephalopod at the top of the food chain. While the two main continents are covered with a monotonously uniform poisonous moss. The few humans live on a small island in the south sea, where the critical trace elements have been shipped in to support what's supposed to be a small farming and mining community. Mostly the locals survive by selling supplies and alcohol to the pirates. The pirates treat the island as neutral territory for their internal conflicts. The pirates and Tortuga Primes still rely on imported and pirated food supplements to survive. The intriguing thing about the local fauna..."

Brandon cut her off, "Claudia you're rambling. We know you were top of your class in the Vega IV University Exobiology program. But this really isn't the time."

Claudia went quiet with an inscrutable expression on her face as she glanced at Alex.

Alex hadn't known of Claudia's scientific background, he thought for a moment how little he really knew her. "So there is still an operational GenClone base near this part of the border, and they must be working with the pirates of Tortuga?"

Claudia sitting down on the adjacent bed answered, "We don't know. They may have pulled out. The GenClones were salvaging what they could here, and leaving when we hit. The prisoners we interviewed indicated this whole campaign has failed. It appears that the coalition of Fringe Worlds, GenClones and pirates that attacked Fairhaven collapsed and was defeated by the Brigadoons. The death of the Asturian king and the disappearance of his daughter destroyed them as a cohesive fighting force. You were right Alex, we won this war when you gave asylum to Roxanne. The GenClones are cutting their losses for now. And it looks like they're abandoning their allies in the process."

Brandon continued, "The Vegan Republic has probably had enough of Tortugan pirates and Asturian warlords. My guess is they will hire a big expeditionary force to clean both places out, and make sure the GenClones are gone permanently. The pirates may have cut their own throats throwing in their lot with the GenClones."

Alex thoughtfully commented, "I wouldn't count on Vegan retaliation. They don't have the resources right now. It would take a massive force just to locate the pirates in an asteroid belt. There may be a way…" Alex stopped as he found himself meandering out loud. He didn't like it, though he knew it was just avoidance, so he finally got around to asking the questions he was afraid to ask. He looked up at Brandon and Claudia, "What kind of casualties did we take?"

Claudia hesitated glancing at Brandon, then grimly she replied, "Twelve dead, twenty-two injured, nine of them permanently disabled in the fighting for the base. Mostly from the 22nd Gurkha regiment. Of the officers, only you and Bolithio were injured. She took a laser hit but she is recovering nicely and is back on the job. There were also sixteen prisoners killed when they revolted in the mine complex. The GenClones took three times that number of casualties." With a lot of distaste on her face, "The slave laborers killed a lot of them out of hand, before we secured the base. It was a real mess for a while down there. We had GenClone CLATs, and conventional troops, hundreds of vengeful prisoners and frightened GenClone Techs running around loose in those tunnels shooting at each other. Bolithio and Javreel sealed up the mine, then took two bloody days to secure it. Frakke, those Gurkhas are tough. It was door to door fighting all the way."

Brandon added, "If it wasn't for your Princess, the casualties would have been worse. Now that she's become a Triarch she really does have amazing healing powers. The officers all know who she is now and I don't know how much longer we can keep up the deception. Without her there would have been at least a dozen more deaths. She worked everyday until she collapsed from exhaustion. The troops adore her."

Claudia caustically snapped, "She worked on everyone except you Alex. She claimed she couldn't help you, without even coming to see you. After all you've done for her she didn't even come to see you, not once! She would have let you die, when she could have helped! I am sick of hearing about how wonderful she is. The ingrate."

Alex defended Roxanne, "I'm sure she had her reasons. My physiology is strange enough that maybe she couldn't help." But Claudia's words kept echoing in his mind like a dirge, "She didn't even come to see you." For two frakking weeks she hadn't come to see him! The terrible anguish he felt at this revelation surprised him. It overwhelmed his sense of loss at the high casualties, and the destruction of the *Warlock*. He didn't have any intentions towards Roxanne, did he?

Brandon standing up said, "She's also been helpful in weeding out spies and saboteurs from those volunteering to join the Chameleons. She is some kind of phenomenal living lie detector. She was able to identify a couple of Matsui spies for us. It's nearly impossible to tell her a lie. Unnerving really." Brandon stopped his monologue for a moment, and looked at Alex with concern, "Alex are you all right?"

Alex answered in a subdued voice, "I'm tired Brandon, leave the bad news for tomorrow if it can wait."

Brandon softly, " There isn't anything we can do about it right now anyway."

The next day Alex sat at the edge of the bed while a Medic removed his splints. The young woman mumbled a soothing meaningless chatter, as she ministered Alex, "...Well, amazing how fast your bones have knit, and the skin grafts are taking real well, except for the one on your left cheek. You've still got a ways to go, but your twice as far along in your recovery as I would have expected when you got here."

Alex ignored the chatter. He knew his condition better than the Medic. He had lived with injuries, many of them serious, all his life. He would need to take it easy for a couple of days. After that his amazing recuperative powers would have repaired most of the damage.

Brandon walked in and was startled to see him sitting up, "Nurse are you sure he should be up yet?"

The Medic responded, "It's amazing his condition has really improved since yesterday Lieutenant. His broken arms are knitting together faster than anything I've ever seen and..."

Alex not wanting to hear the same thing again interrupted, "I'm OK medic, can you leave us, I need to talk to the Exec."

"Yes, but don't overexert yourself," She gave a poorly disguised meaningful look to Brandon as she left.

Alex asked, "Ignore that look she gave you, I'm in better shape than she believes possible. I'm ready for that bad news now."

Brandon looking at his hands thoughtfully for a moment, "You were right you know."

"About what?"

Brandon looking up continued, "About sending me to the Capitol. I'm not saying I did a great job when things began coming apart, but Kaseem couldn't have handled it."

Alex suddenly very worried asked, "Handled what?"

Brandon pulled up a stool and sat down as he started relating his story, "It's a long story and I better start at the beginning. You know how mad I was about being part of the diversion in Asmara. I guess I was in a sulk, so I let Kaseem handle everything the first couple of days."

Brandon continued, "We disembarked from the shuttle and set up camp at a villa across the Styx River from Asmara. Kaseem did his usual excellent job deploying the troops and tanks and setting up a perimeter. You know how Kaseem is. He didn't say anything but still managed to communicate his disapproval of my lack of interest in commanding the unit." Brandon paused for a moment, "Truly a professional soldier. In his own quite way he exudes devotion to honor and duty better then anyone I've ever met.

I'm rambling again. Two days after we set up camp, the muckety muck High Council, The Magliss, called me and Kaseem to testify. It was appalling. Half of them were ready to breach our contract on the spot. One of them went so far as to claim, hiring mercenaries was worse than drinking the blood of children. It's the first time I've ever seen Kaseem upset. The other half was complaining we weren't strong enough to deal with the GenClones.

"They really tore into Kaseem about leaving Himalaya and joining an "Alien" mercenary outfit. They called him traitor and worse. Then they ripped into me about the worthlessness of my command. They wanted to hire off planet mercs not their local Gurkhas. This went on for hours. I finally told them if they breached contract I'd bring them up before the International Court of Justice at the Haag, then we got up and left. Doran and her husband, the High Priest, came by later that afternoon and told us to ignore the Magliss. They explained everyone is scared both for their lives and their peaceful way of life, and they were acting foolishly. I guess I can't blame them."

"It all became moot the next couple of days. Two companies of Matsui CombatDroids hit the Symcorp enclave and captured it, claiming Symcorp was in league with the GenClones. Apparently the mercenary company, Garrison's Guards, hired by Symcorp to protect their facilities betrayed their employer. Garrison and his senior officers killed or imprisoned all of the Guards opposed to breaching contract. Then they took their Droids over to Matsui in the middle of the fight. It was a massacre after that. The remaining Symcorp forces were wiped out."

Brandon paused for a moment to capture his breath, "Then things got really interesting for the Chameleons. Kaseem and I had met with a Subhadar Joichem, Commander of the 12th Gurkha Regiment, stationed in Asmara. Their equipment was awful. Half the troops had homemade shotguns if you can believe that! Kaseem convinced me to pay them with some small arms and hire them to do some long range patrols. It ended up saving our butts.

"A GenClone Droid lance, *Renegades* and *Superscouts*, nearly caught us with our pants down. Joichem's troops warned us just in time and we pulled out minutes before they overran our camp. They didn't even pause, heading right into Asmara, and started destroying the city. It was pointless the natives didn't have any weapons and wouldn't fight even if they did. The whole dockside region along the river was burning within minutes."

Brandon looking down at his hands again, twisting his fingers brutally and then continued in a horrified whisper, "There are tens of thousands of people living in poverty in the walled wooden shanty's along the docks. Many of them Gurkha laborers. They were trapped, the only exits out of that warren were jammed with refugees. It was frakking genocide. Kaseem was grimly stolid, he said there was nothing we could do except die uselessly.

But I couldn't watch it happen, I ordered the Chameleons into combat. I stationed the first anti-Droid squad outside the city walls down by the river, and the second and third squads on the camp side across the river from the city. Some of the 16th regiment volunteered to join us, and I split them between the two infantry groups. Then we charged the Droids with the two Pantheon hover tanks and the APC. We stayed at long range and used our HEAP missiles. We finally got their attention and they sent a pair of *Superscout*s after us. I withdrew across the river. It was the only advantage we had. We could move and fire across water a lot better then the Droids.

"They fell into the trap. One *Superscout* stayed on the Asmara side of the river and provided covering fire while the other one jumped over in pursuit. Kaseem had the first anti-Droid squad all over the covering *Superscout* as soon as it took position. He lost 6 troopers to cap a knee and take it down. Those Gurkhas are the bravest men I've ever seen, unarmored foot sloggers attacking a Droid! The second *Superscout* was out in the open without cover and we poured it on. It landed awkwardly. The second and third squads jumped it. They took out the cockpit and captured the pilot with a lucky DFM hit. I ordered one of our Droid transports to collect the second *Superscout* and sent an APC over to pick up the first squad."

The three remaining GenClone Droids came in pursuit. It's what we wanted. They left the city which gave the civilians a chance to escape. I used the two tanks to provide covering fire while the APC's and transports got away. Blumy delayed too long and his APC caught a round and blew up. I didn't even check for survivors. We just ran for it." Brandon again looked down at his hands.

Alex interrupted, "There's nothing you could have done, two light hover tanks against three medium Droids is hopeless. You had a responsibility to your command."

Brandon ignoring the remark continued, "The Droids kept pressing us as we retreated. Which was fine by me, since we kept leading them away from the city, until we spotted two more Droids blocking our retreat. I thought we'd bought it. Then I recognized them as Terran designs, a *Battleaxe* and a *NightHawk*. I thought Matsui might be sending help at the time. A good thing I was wrong. The Droids charged right by us and attacked the *Renegades*. I joined the attack with my tank. The GenClones had enough and pulled back to the city.

Later I met with the two pilots and found out how really crazy the situation was. They were recently recruited members of Garrison's Guards. They had been on patrol during the Matsui attack on Symcorp and were warned of Garrison's betrayal by an escaped Tech. They decided to unilaterally resign from the Guards because of Garrison's betrayal, and were heading for Asmara hoping to find a shuttle going off world. I convinced them to join up with us instead. I thought we could use a few more CombatJacks. It may not have been the brightest move in hind sight."

Brandon took a deep breath and paused as he looked at Alex before continuing his recital, "Things kept getting worse. Lieutenant Converse, the *NightHawk* pilot, recognized the pilot of the *Superscout* as a Matsui CombatJack, with all that implies. It didn't surprise any of us, when Matsui Droids showed up in the Capitol that evening ostensibly to protect Asmara from the GenClones. When the Magliss complained, the Matsui commander declared martial law and arrested many of the leaders for cooperating with the GenClones. Some of them including Ambassador Doran escaped and joined us.

When my shot up troop got here, Claudia and I pooled our intelligence and pieced together the Matsui plan. It's clear that Matsui's running a very risky game to gain total control of this world. They covertly supported the GenClone invasion of Fairhaven and Himalaya. Then they accuse Symcorp of the dastardly deed and attack them, followed by the attack on Asmara by false Matsui covert operatives disguised as GenClones. Then they used that as an excuse to intercede and take over the local government. Pretty slick, but it's hard for any of us to believe they'll get away with it. Vega can't let an Empire corporation take over an allied world."

Alex contemplatively commented, "No reason why they shouldn't. Both The Republic and the Coalition desperately want to maintain their uneasy alliance. They both know the GenClone threat has to be stopped first. The old saying that *possession is nine tenths of the law* may apply here, as long as Matsui agrees to continue supplying SymXtend to the Vegan Republic. And I'm sure they'll be more than happy to do so at a substantial profit." Alex paused a moment while he thought through all the implications, "Matsui will probably have to compensate Symcorp stockholders for their facilities, but only at a fraction of their actual value. You can bet their lawyers have all those angles covered. Their justification may be paper thin but if there's no one around to contradict their lies when Vega and the Empire investigate, it may not matter."

Alex was chagrined at the thought of Matsui getting away with this scam. He started to think about ways to interfere, but decided his responsibilities to the Chameleons overrode any personal vendetta he might have with Matsui. "It doesn't matter to us anyway. We've completed our assignment and can pull out of here now."

Brandon hesitatingly replied, "I'm afraid we remain involved. If they get away with it, we're dead."

Alex with a raised eyebrow asked, "How are the Chameleons involved?"

Brandon answered, "Matsui's puppet government in Asmara is accusing the Chameleons of breaching contract. They claim we presented only token resistance to the attack on the Capitol. Matsui claims to have evidence that we were in league with the GenClones all along. While Major Garrison is accusing Lieutenant Converse of treason and has declared anyone associated with him renegade. I'm sorry Alex," as he hung his head, "I guess I messed up recruiting Converse and his troop."

Alex contemplated the situation for a moment and then a feral grin began to spread across his face, turning into a gleam of demonic glee. "Nothing to apologize for Brandon, everything you did was honorable and correct. Matsui is the criminal here not you or me. I was going to let them get away with this land grab against my better judgment." He chuckled wickedly, "But now we're going to turn the tables on them. There is one hole in their plan big enough to ride a Droid through, and we're going to do just that."

Brandon surprised by Alex's sudden enthusiasm offered, "It's going to mean a fight, they have six times the Droids we do."

Alex answered, "All the better. The only thing I really need before we get started is a new employer. Brandon can you find me a high level official for the Symcorp conglomerate?"

Brandon grinned, both relieved at the ease of the request, and that Alex had a plan, "No problem boss, the director of Symcorp operations is hiding out with us. Matsui has issued a warrant for his arrest for treason. Can you believe the gall? He isn't exactly decisive. You may have trouble getting him to go along."

"Let me worry about that, just set up a meeting with him for later this afternoon. Right now you and I have to evaluate our assets and flesh out our options."

Chapter 23

Alex sat comfortably in the *Stormwarden* cockpit and watched the majority of his command as they executed another in the series of exercises designed by the twistedly shrewd mind of Brandon Flanders. Lieutenant Converse in his *NightHawk* entered the valley with Sergeant Grease Kearney in his enhanced *Battleaxe* right behind him. Laura Wu, assigned to the newly captured and repaired *Superscout,* joined them as she left her position in the eastern forest with a rush. The three Droid fire lance charged across the open field. Suddenly conventional armored infantry sprouted from the ground pouring DFM's and 4 MM laser fire into the Droids. The Droids formed a tight, fast moving circle and responded with their short range weapons and APDS. The encounter didn't last long. Alex's computer simulator showed the infantry platoon wiped out with only minor damage to the Droids.

Converse led his lance across the rest of the valley in obvious pride. He had demonstrated his contention again that infantry was useless against Droids. But Brandon wasn't done yet. Suddenly a mock charge exploded at the feet of the *Battleaxe.* Alex's display indicated a crippling wound. Droid EMD shields did not protect ground contact surfaces and even the 4.8 CM of Cubed armor covering the *Battleaxes* feet would decompress with a large enough charge. Before the other Droids could respond a deadly barrage of HEAP missiles shot across the peaks and rained down on the two remaining Droids. Alex watched pleased with the simulated damage caused by the impacts. Four Pantheon medium hover tanks burst out of a cleft in the cliff and charged the Droids concentrating fire on the *Superscout.* The massed missile barrage overwhelmed the Droid's point defense system and overloaded its shields.

The Droids returned fire. It looked like a stand off, when more armored infantry opened fire from hidden positions at the cliff base into the flank of the Droids. The *Superscout* was destroyed within moments as its shields failed. One of the Pantheons was also destroyed. It was too little too late and Co... ... ... later. The newly promoted Captain Belishi ... over the intercom, "Well Lieutenant Converse, do you still think infantry and tanks are helpless against Droids?"

Converse replied tersely, "Fire1 to Frog1, well done Captain." The lieutenant couldn't hide his chagrin at the defeat.

Brandon in his newly assigned *Kingfisher* and Claudia in her *Bounder* strode out of their lake side hideout. Brandon declared, "Command2 to all units, a well executed trial. The cloud cover is starting to break, so lets get all traces of our presence under cover. Their will be a debriefing at 1400 hours for all officers and NCO's.

Alex turned The *Stormwarden* around and headed for the cavern. Khorsa in the *Python* followed suite. The week of grueling exercises was beginning to have an effect. The Chameleons were simulating aspects of the plan Brandon and he had developed to challenge Matsui. He would have liked more Droids, but what he really needed was more and better anti-Droid infantry. Bolithio's newly formed company had done well, but even against the fire lance under ideal conditions they had suffered forty percent casualties. Well he knew what he had to do. He just didn't look forward to it.

After the debriefing Alex and Brandon toured the lower portion of the mining complex. It was Alex's first detailed tour of the mines. The medical staff was awed by the speed of his recovery, but had still placed restrictions on his movements. The difficult to traverse lower portions of the mines had been off limits for him until today.

The medics had removed his remaining casts only that morning, surprised again to find the broken bones knit in half the normal time. The cuts, burns and internal injuries were also almost completely healed. Alex was still not one hundred percent but his ninety percent was robust health for most people.

The first place he wanted to see was the secret data storage center they had discovered yesterday in the lower tunnels. The place had remained untouched for eighty years, even the GenClones hadn't stumbled across it during their occupation. Alex crawled up the final narrow tunnel through the blasted false rock wall into the small cavern riddled with electrical cables and sophisticated hardware. A couple of Chameleon techs were working to power up some of the systems. Alex asked Brandon, "Did we find out anything valuable yet?"

Brandon shrugged, "Not really. We've concluded this was a regional data center for the TCA. Fuller tells me that the data base is huge. He believes a great deal of knowledge is in those files if we can ever break those codes."

Alex excited at the possibility of new knowledge, went over an accessed a live 3C terminal. "Brandon I have some expertise at breaking codes why don't you leave me here for a few hours and finish up your other duties before we continue the tour."

Brandon replied, "Alex, operating a 3C terminal is not something any novice can do. I have some training and I wouldn't risk frying my brain on one of those things."

Alex grinned, "I know all about 3C's Brandon. I am somewhat of an expert," as he sat down and pulled out his old 3C interface gear from his duffel bag.

Brandon commented, "Alex you're a never ending source of surprises. I'll see you at 1500 hours. Don't get your brain cooked buddy."

Alex only half heard his friend leave, as he carefully began to interface with the virtual reality world in the ancient Artificial Limited Intelligence. Within an hour he had cracked the not so impregnable code. Alex was surprised to find that the systems he had used on Banshee were more sophisticated. At least in one field the colonies had made some advances in the last 80 years.

The information in the system was fascinating and exciting. Alex skimmed through barely understood technical data banks that reviewed what was still state of the art weapons systems and manufacturing techniques. He skipped through reams of long outdated political data, troop movements, and the personality profiles of long dead movers and shakers. Alex didn't have time to garner any particular piece of information. It would take hundreds of trained man hours to decipher the huge data base, but he did fortuitously find one spectacular piece of knowledge.

His prize find was a data log from an ancient Seeker class exploration vessel. The StarShip had surveyed dozens of nearby stars for usable planets it had discovered the locations of three surface habitable worlds on the outskirts of the Fringe only a few transits from Himalaya. Surface habitable worlds were still rare and with virtually no exploration taking place anymore the locations of such worlds were extremely valuable. The ship had made a number of covert return voyages to the most promising worlds to seed them with Terra based genengineered life forms and transport terraforming automated equipment. Interesting, Alex thought, the TCA military had been making secret preparations fearing the loss of its authority over 80 years ago. Immersed in the virtual reality world it took him a moment to recognize an outside stimulant. He quickly down loaded the data into a hard disk and powered down the system. Looking up from his terminal, he saw a concerned Brandon.

His exec said, "Alex are you all right. I've been trying to get your attention for 15 minutes now."

Alex apologized as he wiped the perspiration off his face. He reviewed his discoveries with Brandon. They agreed to keep the information to themselves for now. Brandon would arrange to down load the data disk into the *Salamander's* AI in a security file. The *Salamander* was the captured GenClone combat shuttle newly commissioned into the Chameleon's service. The two of them continued their tour, with Alex returning to the more immediate concerns about the up coming conflict with Matsui.

Alex had spent the last four days developing the tactical assault plan on Matsui and evaluating the growing forces under his command. He was impressed by the speedy integration of the new recruits. Brandon had again done a remarkable job turning a rabble into a semblance of a mixed forces battalion. With seven Droids, two 40 ton *Foxbat* StarFighters, a *Horatio* class combat shuttle, multiple tanks and other assorted support vehicles the Chameleons had acquired an enormous amount of material assets and recruits.

Two dozen veteran tech volunteers, many of them experts at maintaining GenClone technology, including a senior design engineer Yolanda Newton had joined the Chameleons. She was the tech leading the effort to power up the data center, as well as helping Fuller complete the modification to the *Stormwarden*. The two skilled technicians were constantly coming up with new ways to customize Droids. Yolanda fortunately seemed willing to defer to Fuller's leadership, even though she had better qualifications. At Fuller's request she was promoted to second in command of the techs.

Unfortunately only one of the GenClone CombatJack had accepted a post in the Chameleons.

Alex had met Commander Sam Martin at the officer's mess on his first day out of sick bay. One of the rare GenClones opposed to the League's genetic purity tenants, Martin had gladly joined the Chameleons after the brutal treatment he had suffered as a Liegeman of a GPL supporter. The remaining GPL Jacks chose imprisonment rather then allegiance to a mercenary regiment. Alex didn't have a Droid for Martin. But he expected that to change soon.

As Alex followed Brandon into another large cavern Chosa Yoshi Nobunaga saluted him. The commanding officer of the eight surviving Imperial Covert Operatives. ICO's were the best special forces in the galaxy. Trained in almost every form of combat, they were often sent on covert, nearly impossible missions. Chosa Nobunaga, the squad commander was unwilling to return to the Imperial military after his capture by the GenClones on his last mission. He had chosen the Chameleons over suicide for his own inscrutable reasons. Alex didn't believe fear had entered that decision after meeting the man. Of pure Japanese ancestry, the slender officer was very proud of his family's long, proud tradition of service to the Imperial Coalition and its pre-space flight predecessor Japan. He had agreed to join the Chameleons as long as he did not have to betray his nation. Fortunately, after learning of Matsui's plot, he had agreed that a campaign against the corporation was in the best interests of the Empire. Alex was glad to have the ICO team on his side.

Other freed soldiers had joined the growing number of Gurkha recruits to form two full 120 man companies of infantry. Brandon had organized them into the 1st armored infantry company under the command of the newly promoted Captain Bolithio; and the 2nd mechanized urban warfare company under Jamadar Kaseem. The ICO team reported directly to the command lance and Alex.

Alex's biggest surprise, was seeing Captain Morgan while touring the captured shuttle. Morgan had turned up like a bad credit. When Matsui captured Symcorp City they confiscated his shuttle. The good captain had responded by sabotaging one of the nacelles on the *Tiara II* and fleeing with his crew. Morgan had gladly joined the Chameleons when Brandon had given him command of the newly christened *Horatio* class shuttle, *Salamander*. Alex wasn't sure who was happier, Morgan now that he had a bridge to command, or Richtover and his new StarFighter.

For all the pluses of the new recruits one freed prisoner soured the whole thing for Alex. Tomas Bonaduce, son of Count Bonaduce and Roxanne's second cousin. Though a CombatJack he chose to remain independent of the Chameleons. He claimed he could not make any allegiances that could interfere with his obligations to protect the Princess. Alex wasn't sure he believed the charming noble, but there wasn't much he could do about it. Bonaduce spent almost all off his time accompanying Roxanne. The two of them had studiously avoided Alex since his release. Alex hadn't liked Tomas on sight. He suspected he was jealous of the handsome and debonair noble. He would have been jealous of any man who spent time with Roxanne. Alex kept trying to convince himself that it didn't matter and he would get over the Princess. But he was too honest with himself. He distracted himself by paying attention to the caverns as Brandon escorted Alex into its lower portion.

Alex commented, "This is just as impressive as you claimed Brandon. You and Claudia have done a terrific job organizing this place and integrating the new recruits into the Chameleons."

Brandon leaned down to work his way through another narrow opening in the tunnel and answered, "Thanks boss, we were lucky in the quality of the new recruits." They passed a couple of techs still in their green GPL fatigues. They stared at Alex a moment then averted their eyes. "Take those two, they have fifteen years experience maintaining GenClone equipment. They're pleased to be part of the Chameleons because we don't treat our techs as second class citizens. They've done terrific work on the SuperDroids we captured."

Alex asked, "How come everybody stares or looks away when we pass?"

Brandon laughed, "Alex you've already got one of the biggest reps around. These guys have all heard about the *Warlock* Jack. Now you show up here and take out Colonel Hanson Pryde in single combat. Its too bad your rep doesn't sway the CLATs we captured. We could use them in your mad scheme."

Alex replied, "We not only could use them Brandon, they're critical to success."

Brandon commented, "Commander Vicegrip and his CLAT platoon could care less about what you want Alex. They fought valiantly and wouldn't surrender, preferring death to defeat at the hands of mercenaries. We finally trapped them in one of the lower mines and gassed them out. The rumor is the GenClones sent him out here to prevent his killing anymore of their elite Jacks in duels. I can believe it, he even dwarfs the other giants that operate GPL CyberLinked Armor and he acts like everyone in the universe is scum. Wouldn't even talk to me."

Alex mused, "Unusual name. Where is he now?"

Brandon answered, "It's the only name he uses. They say he earned it. Supposedly once he gets his hands on you, you're dead. Once you see him you'll believe it. He'll be in the prisoners mess for lunch just down a few corridors."

Alex had worked his way down here primarily to investigate the data base and meet the GenClone CLATs. The GPL had modified the genes of their CyberLinked troopers increasing their size and strength by over 50 percent. These *supermen* operated specially enlarged CyberLinked 2.4 ton armored suits that carried almost twice the fire power of their conventional counterparts. GenClone CLAT's were far and away the deadliest infantry in human history. "We're going to need him on our side, so lets go recruit him."

Brandon tried to argue Alex out of the idea the rest of the way there. Two Gurkha guards saluted smartly as they approached the prison doors. They opened the prison mess lock at Alex's orders without question. Alex noticed one of them speaking quietly into his headphone. Shortly afterwards four more heavily armed troopers showed up to escort them.

Alex inwardly smiled at their efficiency. The Gurkhas were prepared for any contingency. Alex ordered them to stay at the entrance as he walked into the large room carved out of the rock. The prisoners lined up to receive food concentrates from an automated dispenser at the far corner of the room were the first to note the recent arrivals. the angry babble quieted into uneasy whispers except from one table, where nine huge men and women sat by themselves. Even in the company of the genengineered giants, Visegrip stood out. The broad coal black Trooper could stare Alex in the face sitting down. Muscles rippled upon muscles, their perfection marred only by an incredible number of scars. Vicegrip and his command conspicuously ignored Alex and Brandon. Alex walked over to the table and spoke quietly to the giant, "I understand you command the CLATs. I would like to speak to you privately for a moment Commander."

Visegrip pointedly ignored him. "Pass that swill Marsha."

Alex undaunted, "I'm here to recruit you into the Chameleons Visegrip. We usually don't take on second rate losers, but I thought it would be a shame to waste a dozen perfectly good CLAT suits for lack of oxen big enough to operate them. So I'm willing to take on a few of you as trainees."

The silence in the room was deafening. The big CLAT looked up with a nasty sneer on his face. "Easy to talk big, little man, with all those guards at your back. I don't serve with mercenary weaklings and scum. Better to die a prisoner."

Alex smiled, he knew he had him now. He leaned over the table, his face only inches from the massive broken and pockmarked nose. Alex incongruously thought, this is the ugliest collection of human features I have ever seen. He makes Marco look good. No wonder this guy is so mean. Then he shouted into Visegrip's face so all could here "They say you're tough. You're not tough, you're just so ugly your opponents puked themselves to death looking at you." Lowering his voice to a whisper only the giant could hear, he continued, "I was born in the Banshee penal sanitarium. My ancestors were the most degenerate scum of this degenerate universe and I'm smarter, tougher and meaner then anything the GenClones have ever bred in their idiot generating vats, not to mention a hell of a lot better looking. Remember who I am when I tear you apart, you big ugly ox."

A twitch appeared in Visegrip's cheek as he slowly stood up and up and up. Alex began to wonder if he had bit off more then he could chew.

Visegrip barely suppressing incredible rage, "Are you just a big mouth, or are you going to back that up shrimp, in a duel?"

Alex smiling, used the GenClone negotiating procedure to get what he wanted, "You want to fight me? What do you bid?"

Visegrip taken aback hesitated, "I don't have anything to bid."

Alex ignored Brandon's frantic efforts to stop what was happening "Yes you do, you can bid service to me and the Chameleons. You and all of your command."

"And if you lose."

"You are free to leave this prison, I will even arrange passage for you to Asturia where you can hook up with your GPL."

Visegrip, with a feral grin, "Dead men can't arrange anything."

Alex pointed at Brandon, then with a smile replied, "Captain Flanders, my exec will abide by my agreement. Oh and I want the rest of your command to take the same oath just in case I can't resist killing you."

After further bantering and some preliminaries, Alex and Visegrip faced off in a hastily sketched battle circle. Alex wasn't worried about his opponent's size. In his youth he had fought men that were proportionally bigger to him then Visegrip. Skill and speed would overcome size. Visegrip's professional fighters crouch did concern him. It wasn't just size the big man had going for him. Alex suddenly wished he was at one hundred percent. This wasn't going to be easy.

They circled for a moment. Visegrip trying to corner him. Alex feinted right then lashed out with his left foot at a knee. Visegrip twisted out of the way amazingly fast for a man of his size.

Even so Alex's edged foot smashed hard into the muscle right above the joint. The blow would have knocked most men down. Visegrip didn't even stagger.

Alex recognized this was going to take a while and he could not afford the mistake that let those huge hands get to him. He went into the triple null fighting void. The universe slowed down as his concentration totally focused on the dance of death with the big trooper. Like a wraith, Alex rained down a deadly series of kicks punches and chops on his opponent, who appeared hopelessly immobile under the lightning assault. Alex darted in and out like a wolf tackling an injured boar. In his trance like state he didn't even notice the horror he was committing on the helpless Vicegrip. The man's face was pulp, welts and bruises covered his entire body and still he wouldn't go down.

Alex began to tire. The blows he inflicted on the big man swelled his hands and feet. It was like hitting hull metal, the giant was invulnerable. He darted in trying to inflict a crippling kick to the already damaged left knee, when Alex's partially healed broken leg gave a little. Like a drowning man reaching desperately for a lifeline, Vicegrip reached out grabbing Alex's shoulder in his infamous grasp. Alex went ballistic, lashing out with every trick he knew to break the hold. Nothing worked. Slowly, Alex was drawn into the enveloping grasp of his massive opponent. Visegrip got his second hand on him. Alex felt his bones beginning to creek under the enormous pressure. His spine was slowly bent backwards as the giant grappled him face to hideous face. Visegrip looked ecstatic, as he inexorably crushed Alex. One of his injured ribs cracked, air was squeezed out of his lungs and his vision began to blur then go black. Blood trickled out of his nose. A mental scream exploded in his mind. No! Mindless animal rage coursed through his body. Like a coiled spring every Banshee developed muscle in Alex seemed to contract simultaneously. He snapped forward and crashed his forehead into the grotesque nose. The impact knocked both men nearly unconscious. Visegrip dazed, loosened his hold. Alex with the last of his strength spun out of the hold and smashed his fist into his opponent's windpipe.

Alex fell to his knees only half conscience and disgorged blood, mucous and bile. As his vision slowly cleared he looked up and saw Visegrip twitching on the floor. As his eyes traversed slowly higher he saw the horrified, stunned faces of prisoners and guards. He staggered to his feet. Fortunately Brandon stepped forward to give him a hand or he would have fallen again. He managed to get a couple of breaths in and spoke with only a slight waver in his voice. "Is he alive?"

One of the CLATs bent over and checked, "Yes but he needs a doctor."

"Guards, get a medic, quickly" Then catching his breath, "Brandon arrange new quarters for our newest recruits and issue them their armored suits."

Brandon asked, "Alex are you sure that's a good idea."

Alex replied loudly enough for everyone to hear, "They will abide by the outcome. Nobody has ever accused GenClones of violating an agreement." Then in a whisper "Get me out of here."

Alex awoke the next morning with a groan. He looked around and spoke out-loud to himself at the sight of the sick bay, "Not again." He sat up with a wince as he felt the pain in his chest. Not too bad, he thought, but I better take it easy for a few days this time. He started some I Ching exercises to relax his stiffened muscles with some success. After a while Brandon walked in with Claudia. They both looked at him reproachfully.

Brandon finally spoke, "We've found an ideal base camp within striking distance of the Crescent Isle. I can have the forces we've selected moved there covertly within four days. The Gurkha regiments already have the area blanketed with recon teams. We've had some excellent news while you were a sleep. The senior officers of all thirty-two Gurkha regiments have agreed to support us if we agree to help oust Matsui. They're already providing us with valuable intelligence and are infiltrating more and more troops onto the Crescent Isle in anticipation of your actions."

Alex with a half smile ordered, "Then commence plan Crescent Storm, and Claudia stop giving me that look, we need the GenClone CLATs if we are to succeed. By the way how is Visegrip?"

Claudia nagged, "He's in better shape then you. God that man is a brute. His face looks like someone took a vibroblade to it, and yet he's back commanding his CLATs with only a limp to give away he's hurting."

Alex got up with a wince, "Well I better emulate his example and join my command. Let's get this plan into motion."

Chapter 24

At dusk Alex wandered away from the temporary camp through the sparse pine forest. He felt the need to get away from the constant demands on his time, just for an evening. Mamba flew away into the trees as he left the camouflaged clearing. She continued to happily spend much of her time alone exploring her home world. Alex did not begrudge her the freedom. She always managed to find her way back to him when she was done with her mysterious expeditions.

The meandering path he followed was nearly undetectable, with only the sounds of pine needles crunching beneath his boots, the distant call of Whippoorwills and the buzzing of insects to disrupt his troubled thoughts. He stepped abruptly out of the woods onto the high bank above pristine Lake Lapis Lazuli. The setting sun blazed a path of wavering light down the middle of the lake as the shadows from the distant mountains slowly engulfed the landscape. He stood transfixed as the world slowly transformed from bright sunlight to the soft dark of dusk. Alex never tired of the constantly changing beauty of this world. He crouched down with a slight wince, and picked up smooth stones and skipped them across the water. He counted the number of skips by the noise unable to see the individual splashes in the expanding dark.

Brandon had shown him how to flick the stones to get multiple skips back on Fairhaven. It felt like ages ago since they had splashed around in the waters of that distant world without a care, without responsibilities, secure in their invulnerability and confident in the skills of their officers. He doubted his man had the same confidence in him.

The doubts about his abilities to command this scale an operation gnawed at him whenever he slowed down. Worse there was no one with whom he could share his insecurities. Alex didn't need to add to Brandon's own worries and Roxanne, well he had only seen her in passing since leaving the sick bay. Why was she avoiding him? What had he done? Was she too good to talk with a Banshee brat now that she was a full blown Triarch? The questions ate at him, as did the fear of what he was capable of doing to get back in her graces. He hurled a large stone as hard as he could into the lake to release the suppressed emotions he felt. The noise silenced the forest denizens for a moment. He rose silently and turned back towards the camp. The little interlude hadn't helped much. Sleep would remain an elusive goal for him, so he might as well bury himself in work instead of brooding. A rustling in the underbrush caught his attention as he neared the tree line. He placed his hand on the butt of his holstered laser pistol and silently flanked the position where the noise had originated.

Like a cobra, he struck at a human shadow, knocking down the unseen intruder. Alex felt pain in his chest from his still injured ribs on impact. He pinned the intruder to the ground, laser pistol squarely pointed at the midsection.

Roxanne's out of breath voice spoke, "I was hoping I could speak to you privately, it would be easier if you got off my chest."

Alex climbed up reluctantly and leaned against the bowl of a giant pine to ease the ache in his ribs. He had to overcome an overwhelming desire to make love to this woman. He was shocked and weakened by the strength of the urge. The effort to resist was so overpowering that it made him dizzy. He recovered slowly. What was wrong with him? In a slurred voice he spoke, "You should know better than to sneak up on someone in a war zone. It's a good way to get killed." He shook his head to clear away the haze, "How did you find me anyway?"

Roxanne dusting herself off replied, "Oh, I can generally sense where you are most of the time, and the splash of the rock directed me right to you."

Alex sarcastically asked, "Another one of your unique Triarch talents. Maybe now we can use you to hunt down escaped prisoners and lost children as well as heal people." The bitterness in his voice surprised him.

"Don't be silly, it only works with..., Anyway, that's not why I came out here to see you."

Formally Alex asked, "You have business to discuss with me Princess Rudnauman?"

Chagrined she replied, "Oh Alex, I know you're mad at me, and I don't blame you, but you don't understand. I had very good reasons for avoiding you. I just can't explain them yet."

Alex answered in a voice as cold as the snow on the surrounding peaks, "There is nothing to explain Princess. You have no obligations to me."

Roxanne choked back a sob, "Will you stop it? Please believe me, I wanted to visit you and treat your injuries more than anything in the universe. I couldn't, the consequences would have been disastrous for both of us. Please Alex, forgive me." Her pleading tailed off and she whispered, "I did it for you." Wheedling, "Please Alex, It was for you."

Roxanne's anguish was like a knife in his heart. He desperately wanted to reach out and comfort her. But Alex knew instinctively that if he relented, this woman would own him body and soul. He wouldn't succumb. "Princess, you have business to discuss?"

They stood there in silence avoiding looking at each other's shadowed faces, as the moon Everest like a glittering opal rose above distant Kaytoo. Roxanne was half illuminated by the new risen moon but Alex couldn't read her expression as she turned away and looked out across the now silvered surface of Lapis Lazuli. Roxanne spoke dreamily, "It's perfect isn't it? A full moon, a warm breeze rustling the trees above an idyllic lake, soft pine needles densely scattered across the ground just like a blanket. Here we are all alone, in our own little valley surrounded by endless forests and majestic peaks, and all we can do is hurt one another." She looked up at him, "Silly isn't it. You would think we could find something better to do."

The surrounding temperature seemed to rise as Alex suddenly realized Mamba wasn't around to protect him from the Triarch effect. No wonder he was reacting so strangely to Roxanne's presence. In a voice he barely recognized as his own, he replied, "Ah, if I didn't know better Rox..., Princess, I would say you're trying to seduce me again. I thought you were now a full Triarch and could control yourself."

She leaned closer to him, the breath of her voice caressing his cheek as she whispered, "I *am* in control of my desires Alex. Would it be so horrible if I was seducing you?"

Panic surged through Alex. Roxanne was acting as if she was still suffering through Melanjou. No he mustn't let her control him like this. It wouldn't be right for either of them if he took advantage of her lack of control. He stepped away and strode to the edge of the bank, like a man fleeing demons. He half shouted, "No! I mean yes, I will not be manipulated by you or my desires." Under his breath, "Not even by the woman I love." His unheard declaration shocked him out of the trance. He loved Roxanne the person, not the lust inducing Triarch. What was he going to do with this enigmatic woman, who went from completely ignoring him to using all her skills to seduce him.

She followed him and sat down at his feet and began to cry in relief, "Thank God" she kept whispering to herself.

Alex feeling he was back in control of himself and sensing he had passed through some terrible ordeal, knelt down besides her and gently spoke, "I love you Roxanne Rudnauman, I would do anything to protect and comfort you. But I will not become your lackey."

Through her tears she spoke firmly, "I don't want you for a lackey Alex Kane. I want you as my lover and my friend. I never wanted to fall in love with you. I just couldn't help it." She looked up at him with joy in her violet eyes, "Love is very dangerous for a Triarch and for the one she loves. If a Triarch's lover succumbs to her instinctive desire for control, they will end up destroying each other in mutual revulsion. I have learned to control my emotions around others. Now you and I have learned to control ourselves around one another. Had I come and healed you when you were injured and weak, I would have gained power over you and made you my puppet, against my own wishes and your own nature. It was agony staying away! But I had to. Forgive me Alex." She looked out across the lake, "I love you Alex and I don't care about the consequences."

Her explanation was implausible, but somehow he knew it was the truth. He had felt the power she could exert over men and instinctively knew, that like a flame to a moth, any lover unable to resist would be destroyed. He leaned over and kissed her for the first time. First he kissed her salty tears away, then her sweet lips. Slowly they removed their clothes and wrapped themselves in each other's arms, unwilling to separate for even a moment. Alex winced as Roxanne's weight pressed up against an injured rib.

"You're hurt! Maybe we should wait Alex."

Alex grimaced and adjusted his position for more comfort. Then he laughed gently, "I may be hurt, but I'm not dead," and pulled her closer to him.

The following morning they awakened to the rising sun and languidly made love again on the pine leave strewn earth at the edge of the lake. They moved slowly, much of their fire cooled by their frantic activities of the night before. Alex suspected that Roxanne's first time hadn't been much fun for her. He had probably been too rough given his prolonged abstinence. He hoped he had made up for it later. He rolled onto his back with a sigh and with a mischievous smile that made him look his real age said, "I don't know which is better, the first good nights sleep I've had in weeks or making love to the most beautiful woman in the universe."

Roxanne stretched sensuously, rubbing her thigh up against Alex. He was struck dumb again. Roxanne giggled, suddenly jumped up and ran past the startled Alex, diving gracefully into the lake and howling like a little girl. "Well while you're trying to figure that out, I'll just go for a swim." Her raven locks exploded out of the water as she surged to the surface with a broad smile and yelled, "Come in silly, it's perfect."

He plunged in after her, feet first. He never could get use to the thought of hurtling head first towards any surface even water. The air exploded out of his lungs as he hit the cold mountain fed lake. He spluttered back to the surface where Roxanne engulfed him in her arms and her laughter. She pulled him beneath the water again before he could catch his breath while asking him with her arms firmly wrapped around his shoulders, "Now which did you conclude was better, me or sleep?"

Alex in response grabbed her around the waist and plunged them both beneath the water. They came up laughing and kissing. He finally answered her question seriously, "You my love, always you." They played in the lake as long as they could bare the cold. Finally they climbed back up onto a big rock, to dry in the sun stark naked. Alex stared at Roxanne in unabashed appreciation. "I can't get used to the idea. Why in the world would a wonderful person like you have anything to do with a patchwork Banshee mine rat like me?"

Roxanne climbed up on her elbows and traced one of the many scars on his chest with a gentle touch. She whispered, "so many scars Alex. I don't know how you survived so many fights." Then shaking her head, and starring at him seriously, "You completely underestimate yourself Alex. I am a Triarch. It is our nature to be attracted to the dominant male. It may be primitive, but in this way we keep our communities stable. Our mates have always been among the most influential men on Asturia and we have always channeled their efforts into directions that benefited the community. Ultimately that and not our healing powers, has kept the peace and prosperity on our world. The matrilineal dragon throne was just an outgrowth of this. Whatever else you may be Alex, you are clearly a man who commands others."

Alex frowning, "Do you plan to channel my energies into constructive paths?"

She paused then answered, "I didn't want to get into this now. If you were Asturian you would understand the unwritten bargain we have just made." She turned to him, "Please don't get upset about what I'm about to explain. It is a Triarch's nature to influence her mate towards positive goals. I won't lie about it to you Alex. Try to keep an open mind. All a Triarch really does is channel her mates more destructive urges into positive channels. It's not a matter of control. Triarches have ultimately always set the boundaries within which the men of our world operate. Had Tamerlane or Napoleon or Cherenko been mated to a Triarch they would have still become great conquerors. They just wouldn't have committed the atrocities along the way that they did." She looked at Alex with concern unable to gauge his response. "Alex I would have explained earlier except well..." She looked down, her sentence unfinished.

Surprisingly Alex accepted her explanation without concern, to a very large extent it reminded him of the role Kyla had played in his life. He was used to the idea of a woman he loved setting the boundaries of acceptable behavior for him. "It's OK Roxanne, I trust your instincts to do what's right more than my own. As long as you don't ask me to break my word, I can happily live within this contract."

Alex could have spent the rest of his life in the idyllic spot. But the serious discussion and his recollection of Kyla saddened him and reminded him of his responsibilities. They worked their way back to the beach in silence and put on their clothes. Roxanne kissed him, "We need to keep our romance a secret for a while, otherwise we will become targets for Asturian assassins." She walked back into the forest by herself. He watched until she disappeared, then turned and memorized every aspect of the spot. A smile crossed his face. All kinds of emotions stirred in him. He felt renewed, no matter what the universe threw at him, now he could face it with equanimity.

Chapter 25

Alex's absence from camp had not gone unnoticed. Captain Bolithio and Visegrip were waiting for him at his tent. Bolithio paced nervously while Visegrip stood like a statue. Bolithio tight-lipped spoke, "Major I am placing Commander Visegrip under disciplinary review. His attitude and actions are disrupting the cohesiveness of my command. He continues to refer to the Gurkha troopers, including Jamadar Kaseem, as turds expressly against my orders. He ignores commands as he pleases and his actions are no longer acceptable."

Alex knew it was serious if the indomitable Bolithio decided she needed his help with Visegrip. Typically the Captain handled transgressions summarily and immediately. Alex had hoped that the two senior infantry commanders would come to an accommodation.

It wasn't working. They had developed an instantaneous antipathy for each other since their first meeting, and it had degenerated since then. Alex knew Visegrip was making unflattering noises about Bolithio. So just when he needed them all working together, the situation had come to a head.

Alex walked in and sat on the edge of his field desk, buying time while he decided what to do. "You present me with a problem Captain. I need both of you if our plans are to succeed." He thought he detected a glint of malice in Visegrip's eyes. It angered Alex that the giant CLAT thought he could get away with his behavior.

Bolithio stiffly replied, "Sir his constant insults and insinuations about the first infantry company are destroying the morale of my troops. I won't tolerate his actions any longer!"

Alex came to a decision, "You won't have to. Commander, you and your CLATs will report directly to me from now on. We will be engaging a superior force within the next few days and I expect you to coordinate your efforts with all the other units in this command." Alex stood up and walked over to the giant, drawing his laser pistol and pointing it at Visegrip; his voice becoming harsh as he continued, "And let me make myself perfectly clear commander. The next time I find out you are disrupting the efficiency of this unit in any way, I will blow your brains out and ask questions later." They stared at each other a moment, neither one giving a centimeter. "Do I make myself clear Commander?"

Visegrip gave an insulting salute and replied sarcastically, "Yes," pause, "Sir."

Alex holstered his pistol and then brutally kicked the CLAT in the groin. Visegrip fell to his knees. "I don't recall giving you permission to stand down Commander. Attention."

The big CLAT wobbled to his feet. Alex, his voice laced with fury, "You will salute me properly and respond to my instructions in a proper manner from now on Commander. This is your last chance." Alex placed his hand on the grip of the laser pistol again, "Now. Do you understand?"

At rigid attention the big CLAT saluted and replied rigidly, "Yes Sir."

Brandon walked in at that moment and paused. Alex returned the Commanders salute nonchalantly, "Dismissed."

Both Bolithio and Visegrip left grimly.

Brandon turned to Alex after watching the set shoulders of the two senior officers march away in different directions. "Trouble?"

Alex let the fury he felt dissipate, "I had to resort to violence to get Visegrip to obey orders. The CLATs are now reporting directly to me. Bolithio couldn't manage them and I'm not sure I can. I came this close to killing Visegrip. This close."

Brandon grinned, "I'm sorry I missed it. Visegrip is a pain in the butt all right, but if anyone can handle him, you can Alex. Claudia thinks you insulted him when you placed him under Bolithio's command. I think you did the right thing by having him report to you directly. You may not know it, but he insults everything about the Chameleons except you. You're the only one he respects. By the way, where were you last night?"

Alex looked down at his field desk and replied in feigned nonchalance, "I went for a walk."

Brandon said questioningly, "A long walk?" and then waited for Alex to comment, when Alex didn't respond he continued. "I just thought I'd come and tell you the hover tanks arrived last night. Everything is set to go and it's time to tell everyone the next step." They both turned as Director McCloud popped his bald head into the tent uncertainly. Alex began to wonder if he shouldn't post guards at his tent to prevent these random intrusions.

Turning to Brandon Alex agreed, "OK, set up a staff meeting this afternoon. Make sure that you invite the Princess."

Brandon raised an eyebrow but made no comment. Alex turned to the Director and asked, "You wished to see me Sir?"

The diminutive Director said, "Ah yes you too Lieutenant Flanders. Ah, I don't know quite how to say this Commander, but I've been hearing things."

Brandon asked, "What kind of things Director?"

"Well a lot of the personnel seem to think attacking Symcorp City is suicide. I just wanted to make it clear Major that I don't expect you to sacrifice lives pointlessly to fulfill your contract."

Alex smiled. He liked the bespectacled Director. The nondescript man looked better suited teaching at a University, then managing one of the biggest Symcorp installations. McCloud's apparent indecision was really just a by-product of a powerful intelligence seeing to many aspects of a problem. His razor sharp analytical mind, and his ability to juggle multiple tasks effectively, had made him one of the most sought after managers in the Vegan Republic. "Director, first of all, I would not needlessly sacrifice my command for any contract; and second, who said anything about attacking Symcorp City?"

McCloud in surprise asked, "But isn't that what you contracted with me to do?"

Alex explained, "The contract specifies I can conduct any actions that returns the control of the Symcorp facilities to it's legitimate owners. An assault against Matsui's massed forces in Symcorp is not the way to do that."

McCloud perplexed asked, "Then what do you plan to do? If you don't mind my asking Major?"

With a smile Brandon replied, "We're going to capture Matsuisan."

Alex added, "Matsuisan is the more valuable installation and is less well defended. We are going to exploit the basic flaw in the Matsui plan. They don't have the forces to defend Matsuisan, Symcorp City and the mainland cities against a determined resistance. Once we control Matsuisan, you can negotiate a return of assets to their rightful owners."

McCloud commented, "Matsui's Superintendent Hojo cannot negotiate in good faith. The Coalition will have his head for actions threatening the Empire-Vegan Alliance if the details of his mad scheme are revealed. I guarantee you Major that both the empire and Vega will be sending their best investigators here soon to unravel this mess and Hojo cannot afford to have any of us testify if his plan is to succeed. They will have to attack us. Major I am not a military man, but if you capture Matsuisan won't they be able to bring overwhelming force to bare? After all, they do out number you six to one."

Alex smiled grimly and looked at Brandon as if to say I told you so. "Your analysis of the situation is the same as mine Director. We have one military edge that we will exploit to neutralize their numerical superiority. You will have to have faith in our military expertise for now sir, since I will not reveal all the details of the plan yet."

Brandon to McCloud, "Sir, you are invited to the staff review this afternoon of course. We will finalize the details of the raid to capture Matsuisan then."

McCloud shaking his head answered, "I don't know why I have faith in you two young men, but I do. Somehow I almost feel sorry for Superintendent Hojo. He has no idea what he's up against, does he. Oh and Major you will need my skills to manage Matsuisan once you capture it. I will have my most trusted senior staff start preparations. If you will excuse me gentlemen." As he stepped out of the tent with new purpose in his stride.

Brandon commented, "Surprising little man isn't he?" Brandon like most soldiers discounted non martial skills.

Alex replied, "That man in his field is as skilled as General Deip is a mercenary commander. He has managed some of the most complex projects in known space. A good deal of our plan depends on him maintaining control of any civilian installations we capture. Now lets get back to our jobs."

Chapter 26

Alex repelled up and over the cliff face, just below the looming fortress that dominated Matsuisan. The other members of the sabotage team spread out along the cliff edge right above the calm moonlit sea. There were no signs of detection. Two ICO members crawled forward smoothly detecting and deactivating some of the remote sensors that guarded the fort. They waved the rest of the team forward. Alex moved as quickly as he could with forty kilos of plastique in his backpack. Mamba fully alert glided overhead looking for threats. In fifteen minutes they reached the base of the massively armed fort without setting off any of the alarms. Four members of the squad used their cowled drilling lasers to drill demolition holes, according to Alex's instructions. Newly promoted Captain Nobunaga and the remaining trooper stood sentry duty after unpacking their explosives.

Alex leaned against the wall and caressed a silent watchful Mamba, as he waited for the holes to be drilled. The Chameleons had force marched across the mainland all day along a route scouted by the 22nd Gurkha. They had reached the eastern straight separating the mainland from the Crescent Isle and Matsuisan at dusk undetected. Then the hover tanks and manned hover APC's skimmed across the calm sea in a roundabout path scouted by local fishing boats bringing them into their assigned positions for this assault. The Droids had made the crossing underwater across the narrowest portion of the shallow strait, reaching the base of the cliff undetected. The whole plan had been contingent upon hundreds of Gurkha scouts and fisher folk establishing a secure route for his forces. Matsui had so alienated the locals, that support for the Chameleons was nearly universal. So far everything had gone according to plan. Alex hoped to continue using the locals to keep tabs on Matsui and its forces long after this mission. The support of the locals was one of the Chameleon's biggest advantages.

Alex set about preparing the charges. To his surprise he had turned out to be the closest thing to an explosives expert in the Chameleons. Belichic and her old squad were supposed to carry out this part of the attack, but they weren't familiar with shaped charges. Alex had modified the plan at the last minute to permit him to be here. He wasn't happy being away from his Droid and out of touch with the rest of the command while they worked themselves into their planned positions. So he worked quickly to prep the plastique and set the detonators. The fortress had a sturdy Durasheath shell with multiple laser, EPC and sliver cannon turrets. The charges he was setting should destroy the entire east wall, enabling the Chameleons to attack from the sea without facing the withering fire of the forts massed weapons. Properly placed the two hundred kilo's of plastique should be enough for the job, and Alex fervently hoped his knowledge of mining charges was applicable to fortresses.

In ten minutes the holes were drilled, the charges were placed and the detonators activated. The team hurriedly headed back towards the relative safety of the sea cliff with a collective sigh of relief. The demolition team had just completed the trickiest part of the mission, and the most critical. But as they moved along the east wall, one of the forts giant bay doors suddenly opened, the light from the interior illuminating the area. The squad quickly went to ground, as two *Roadrunners* and two infantry carrying ground cars left the installation. The lead Droid walked by not ten meters from Alex and Mamba. He felt completely exposed as he hugged the ground out in the open. He had never really considered before how terrifying an enemy Droid would appear to a human on foot. His respect for the CLATs and Anti-Droid infantry went up as he swallowed the coppery taste of fear. The Matsui force was heading for the town, when the lead APC spotted an ICO member in its headlights, as he tried to crawl out of the way. All hell broke loose. The ground cars disgorged their soldiers. All of them firing into the dark at once. The strike squad only had light weapons, but they returned fire as best they could. Alex fired his laser pistol at a charging Matsui trooper and watched him collapse either injured or dead. He yelled out, "Retreat to the south wall, we'll get massacred if we try to get back to the cliffs."

Then he fired again and turned to flee, only to find himself face to face with two armored security guards, carrying machine pistols. They pointed their guns at him and opened fire while he desperately dived at the feet of the one to the left. A bullet creased his shoulder as he slid his foot into the guard's knee with a resounding snap. The soldier collapsed in agony, while Alex desperately twisted to face his second opponent. The second guard was down twitching, Mamba hissing angrily was still lashing his face with her poisoned barb. Alex grabbed the two machine pistols called Mamba to him and continued to flee.

The surviving members of the squad beat a hasty retreat to the south wall, firing to slow down the pursuit. The Droids had initially been slow to react, but that changed suddenly as they turned to pursue Alex and his squad. Unfortunately the demolition team had nothing to use against a Droid. Alex grimaced from the painful bullet hole in his shoulder, as he jumped into an old shell crater. He thought, "Why is it that the best laid plans can go awry so fast? Why did this patrol appear just now? His squad had almost been clear. Now there was no chance for relief until the demolition charges detonated, worse the fort would be alerted to the upcoming attack." All he, Captain Nobunaga and the three other survivors could do was crouch down in the old shell crater, firing sporadically and awaiting their fate.

The two *Roadrunners* were closing on the squad passing near the fort, when the series of shaped charges detonated. For a moment the fort seemed undamaged except for a shroud of dust rising from its base, then the entire forty-five meter high east wall began to topple ponderously. The lead *Roadrunner* suddenly recognized its danger and began to back pedal. The wall fell faster and faster.

The *Roadrunner* managed to avoid most of the tumbling wall, but one huge chunk of Durasheath shattered the left leg of the Droid sending it tumbling to earth. Alex and his squad burrowed into the dirt, as debris and chunks of the east wall filled the air. Secondary explosions reverberated throughout the fort as ammunition bins detonated. Alex used the ensuing confusion and the clouds of dust, to lead his squad back towards the cliff. They reached it just as more CombatDroids disgorged from the northern side of the fort.

Alex reached his repelling line and slid down into his waiting camouflaged Droid. He scrambled into the cockpit and kick started the giant machine, simultaneously activating his CyberLink Relay. Then he slapped a field dressing on his wounded shoulder while speeding through his start-up check list. Alex sensed more than saw the rest of the Chameleon Droids hurtling up the cliff face. Fortunately all his Droids mounted thrusters or this plan wouldn't have worked he thought, as he activated his own thrusters and roared up the cliff. He was only a few minutes behind the rest of the already engaged Chameleons.

Two heavy Droids, an enhanced 64 ton *Mastiff* and a 60 ton *Crossbow*, supported by the surviving *Roadrunner* and a *Renegade* were holding their own against the Chameleons. Alex knew more Droids would be working their way around the fort soon, and the odds would then favor the defenders. He had to change the odds quickly. He charged the *Crossbow*, locked his newly installed twin 80 MM NPC's onto the right arm mounted twin 60 MM sliver cannons, and fired. With the superior GenClone ALI targeting system both shots went home right through the shields coring the arm actuator. The arm fell uselessly to the Droid's side. He switched targets to the partially damaged left leg and launched a quad HEAP barrage . With its main armaments down the *Crossbow* was no match for his *Stormwarden*, but he needed to finish it fast. Multiple impacts from the HEAP missiles shredded armor on the already damaged leg and the left torso, twisting the heavy Droid sideways. Alex continued to close as the enemy pilot regained control of his machine and turned targeting the *Crossbow*'s left arm EPC at the *Stormwarden*. Alex waited until the last possible moment and then twisted aside, while activating the newly installed ODC system. The EPC bolt shot harmlessly past. The *Crossbow*'s single 50 MM laser was more effective draining his shields 50 percent, but the submunitions volley that followed was intercepted by Alex's APDS. Alex had closed into effective range for his intermediate weapons. His twin 40 MM lasers lashed the already savaged left leg of the *Crossbow* overwhelming the Droids shields, then at point blank range he fired a second Heap volley at the exact same spot. From the knee down the leg sheared completely off as three of the missiles went home. The heavy Droid fell backwards, down and out of the fight.

Alex had been watching the progress of the rest of the fight with a part of his mind. The devastating assault of the *Mastiff* destroyed Sergeant Gonzales' *Battleaxe* in an engine explosion. But the rest of the Chameleons had quickly dispatched the remaining *Roadrunner* and the *Renegade*. Claudia had circled to the right of the *Mastiff* and was slowly carving her opponent up with deadly accurate EPC fire. The *Mastiff* was retreating slowly while laying down a terrifying barrage of its own. Alex spotted Chameleon CLATs swarming from the cliff, over the downed *Crossbow*, and bouncing their way towards the surviving enemy *Mastiff*. Alex continued his rush towards the fort but twisted his torso sideways to attack the rear arc of the *Mastiff*, and screen the attack of the CLATs. He triggered all his long range weapons. Lasers and HEAP missiles explosively decompressed Cubed armor across the massive war machine but it kept moving.

Alex whispered half to Mamba and half to himself, "We can't waste much more time finishing off that heavy Droid." Then he opened a line, "*Warlock* to Fire1, Converse take the rest of your lance and finish off that *Mastiff*. Command2, and Command3 form on me. Command4, start phase two."

Claudia and Brandon disengaged and sped past the *Mastiff* to join Alex. Converse's *NightHawk* closed to melee range on the enemy heavy and smashed a powerful blow with his armored fist, shearing off the left vambrace. CLATs were scurrying over the *Mastiff* like tsetse flies on a bull, sucking the lifeblood out of the crippled giant.

Alex spotted the second infantry company's hover APC's racing for the breech in the east wall. Khorsa with his *Python* was already closing on the infantry to provide fire support for the main assault on the fort. Two more Matsui Droids suddenly walked around the north east corner of the fort. Alex identified them as another *Mastiff* and the second largest Droid in existence the 72 ton *Warlord* . A shiver went through Alex at the sight. Their intel had indicated two under manned Droid lances were all that guarded Matsuisan. What they hadn't known was they included heavies and a *Warlord* assault Droid. The second *Mastiff* shrugged off the impacts from SCRAM missiles fired by Bolithio's anti-Droid infantry hidden in the foliage down by the stream northeast of the fort. The HEAP barrages from the Pantheon hover tanks hidden beneath the stream embankment were more effective. Bolithio's anti-Droid troopers were using laser targeting gear to direct the HEAP missiles to their targets, vastly improving the accuracy of the indirect fire from the fire support tanks.

The *Mastiff* was complete shrouded by the multiple explosions of over sixty HEAP missiles, damaged, it strode through the fireball still functional. Claudia and Brandon opened fire at long range. The *Mastiff* retaliated with its own devastating long range missile barrage. Brandon's *Kingfisher* took the brunt of the attack and staggered nearly collapsing under the massed HEAP missiles. Alex yelled out and beat his fist on the Duraplast canopy, "We can't win like this, we'll be destroyed as an effective fighting force if this continues. "*Warlock* to Command2 break left at flank speed. *Warlock* to Bullfrog1, Bolithio concentrate your fire on the *Warlord* , now. Command3 break right and support Bullfrog." Responses came in quickly as the units moved to follow his orders.

Good, the *Mastiff* was swinging around to track the *Kingfisher* for a kill shot, exposing its paired 8 shot HEAP launchers to his weapons, just as he had expected. He had one chance and he better make it work if he wanted to save his best friend. He locked both NPC'S on the right missile launcher while slowing his charge to increase his accuracy. The armored covers on the 8 shots opened before his targeting crosshairs. His nervousness was transmitted to Mamba. The minicham nipped him on the neck calming Alex down almost immediately. He gently squeezed the trigger on his main weapons praying for them to hit home. Both violet NPC beams slashed into the launcher detonating the missiles as they left their launch tubes. The resulting fireball blew the right launcher and the right arm right off the Droid and shorted the shield generator of the humanoid machine. It staggered backwards, firing its left side 8 shot uselessly into the sky.

The *Mastiff* was seriously crippled. Alex triggered his quad rack at the big Droid's damaged head stripping away all the remaining armor and staggering the *Mastiff* again. Then he followed up with his lasers. One of the lasers penetrated the damaged cockpit probably killing the pilot. The Droid froze in place with tendrils of smoke rising from the shattered cockpit. Alex didn't savor his victory, but pivoted slightly to engage the oncoming *Warlord* . Another Matsui Droid, an enhanced *Katana* had joined the fray from the city to the south. "Frakke how many Droids are there!"

The Pantheon HEAP barrage and Claudia had kept the assault Droid occupied for the time he had needed to finish off the *Mastiff*. Converse and the Fire Lance had finally finished off the first *Mastiff* but from his read-outs they were in no condition to continue fighting. Claudia's *Bounder* had taken a beating from the *Warlord* and was also on the verge of shutdown. Fortunately the second company and Khorsa had reached the fort safely, due to the covering fire from the battered Chameleon Droids. Alex issued a new series of orders "*Warlock* to all units, Toad Star1 secure downed Droids. Toad Star2 support the second company assault on the fort. Frog5 and Frog6 disengage from Droid assault and support the second company." Bolithio's heavy Anti-Droid infantry would join the attack on the fort, their SCRAM missiles depleted they were no longer effective against the giant war machines. He gave one final order, "All remaining units concentrate fire on enemy *Katana*." On his private line he contacted Brandon, "*Warlock* to Command2 take command, I'm going to be busy for a while."

Visegrip replied tersely, "Toad1 to *Warlock*, we will comply." The other members of the Chameleons acknowledged his orders one after another.

Alex now found himself engaging the *Warlord* alone. The assault Droid out weighed him by half. The multiple missile and EPC hits had damaged the massive machine but nowhere near enough to even the odds. Again Alex would test speed and maneuverability against raw fire power. He continued his charge right at the assault Droid, firing his weapons carefully not to overload his already over stressed systems. The *Warlord* lined up its left and right arm 105 MM gauss cannons. The gaping maws of death pointed right at Alex. He waited until the last moment then broke left while activating his ODC. The twin shots missed due to the *Warlock*'s sudden maneuver and burst of speed to 160 KPH. Alex cut back towards the enemy Droid as the gauss shells exploded harmlessly to his right, and retaliated with his 4 shot. The fight went on like this, with Alex using his speed to avoid the gauss cannons and slowly cutting up the *Warlord* with his long range weapons. Able to maneuver at will he pirouetted and hopped the *Stormwarden* around like a speedy scout Droid, avoiding the desperate volleys of the cumbersome assault Droid with relative ease. Alex had detected a slight hesitation before firing from the enemy pilot, once he acquired a target lock. Alex took advantage of this pattern, to neutralize the fire power advantage of the bigger opponent.

The rest of his command took down the *Katana* quickly.

The *Warlord* pilot with his Droid slowly disintegrating underneath him, and now faced with a whole company of Droids and tanks, surrendered soon after. The fighting for the fort, which Alex found out later had been vicious, also subsided as the Chameleon tanks and Droids closed on the breached wall.

Alex scanned the six surviving Chameleon Droids as he strode to the fort. Battered as they were, they were still a cohesive fighting force. They had won, and with the captured Droids and a little time they would be ready for the next phase better and stronger. All he had to do now was give them that time.

Chapter 27

Controlled chaos reigned over the fort for the next twenty-four hours. They all feared that Garrison's Guards and Matsui could attack with their forces from Symcorp City in less then forty-eight hours, with nearly two full Droid companies. Alex was everywhere trying to get everything done at the same time. A defensive parameter was established scouts were dispatched, prisoners interviewed, new recruits enlisted, care for the dead and wounded organized, equipment repaired and new assignments given to the survivors. All the Chameleon officers and men worked together with volunteers from the 22nd and 24th Gurkha regiments to get the seemingly endless work done.

Director McCloud was invaluable in reorganizing the Matsui civilian personnel and maintaining order in Matsuisan proper. He persuaded the senior managers to continue in their present jobs until the military issues were resolved, one way or the other. Then he contacted the civilian authorities in the city and gained their support. Even more important to the Chameleons, he quickly arranged to have all the Droid repair facilities manned with Chameleon techs and local volunteers. The four Droid bays were fully operational three hours after the fort was captured. Fuller took advantage of the state of the art facilities to frantically try to bring their damaged and captured Droids back on line for the next anticipated confrontation with Matsui.

Two more Guard CombatJack were found imprisoned in the fort. Both had opposed Garrison's breech of contract and had suffered the consequences. Vowing revenge on their former commander, they immediately signed on with the Chameleons and were assigned to Lieutenant Converse's lance. Alex hoped to have the captured *Katana* and *Roadrunner* operational, now that he had pilots for them. It would bring the fire lance up to full strength after the loss of Sergeant Gonzales', and his *Battleaxe*, the fire lance was down to two damaged Droids.

The three heavy Droids and the assault Droid were all salvageable. The *Warlord* had suffered very little damage other then major loss of armor. Alex had set getting it back in service as Fuller's number one priority. All he needed now was a pilot checked out on the powerful assault Droid. He was reviewing the new duty restore with Brandon, Claudia and Javreel in the Matsui administrative office complex when McCloud brought him the solution.

A Gurkha guard saluted sharply at the entrance to the Chameleon's new HQ, "Sir! Director McCloud and Lady Yamamoto to see you."

Alex like most Jacks, knew of Lady Yamamoto and her role in the defense of Terranova against the GenClones, "Let them in private." The Director and a tall middle aged oriental woman entered She had perfect military bearing and was graceful and feminine at the same time. She was as formidable in person as her reputation.

McCloud looking around commented, "Very plush, real teak and mahogany furniture, and Archanian spiders silk carpets." He whistled in appreciation, "Matsui's senior personnel have much nicer facilities, but a little on the garish side. Would you mind if we tasted the wine Major?"

Alex hid a smile. McCloud was full of good cheer and bravado now that he was back in his element. The man was invaluable, so Alex ignored his supercilious attitude. The twinkle in the Director's eyes indicated that he was just play acting anyway. Alex replied with an arched brow, "Certainly Director, please pour yourself and your guest a glass and have a seat." Alex stood up and bowed, "The noble Lady Elandra Yamamoto Chosa of The Fifth Terranova Rangers I presume. I am honored to meet so renowned a warrior, from so illustrious a family."

Yamamoto responded with a graceful bow, "I am honored to meet the famous Major Kane."

Alex using his grandmother's training went through the series of genuflections required by Bukharan nobility, to the surprise of everyone including Brandon. Yamamoto responded in kind, showing no overt surprise, except for a slight hesitation at the response to the "First ceremonial greeting to an esteemed peer." The surprised hesitation, unnoticeable to anyone but Alex and Elandra, gave him a distinct advantage in any negotiations, since he was within his rights to treat it as an insult.

After the formal greeting they all sat around a small delicately carved conference table in plush dark green arm chairs. Alex politely said, "I wish to extend my appreciation to you Director for your efforts here. I hope my troops have been cooperating in every way possible?"

McCloud swirling the wine in a cut crystal goblet, answered, "Oh your troops have helped me immeasurably Major, and things are going as smoothly as can be expected. We do have a legal concern that needs to be resolved, if we don't want to be declared outlaws though."

Claudia looked at Yamamoto and spoke in outrage, "You can't mean we violated any rules capturing this place, given what Matsui has done on Himalaya!"

Alex interrupted, "Maybe we should let the Director explain before we jump to conclusions Claudia. Director?"

McCloud continued, "I will defer the explanation to Lady Yamamoto. I believe she can explain it better than I."

Yamamoto spoke, "I am a minor stockholder in Matsui Mining and Manufacturing's operations here in Himalaya, so I am familiar with some things that affect this situation, that are not yet common knowledge. You are probably not aware of this but Emperor Bukhara IX is also a significant stockholder in Matsui and its operations here. In retrospect it was probably not a good idea for the head of the Coalition to invest in a corporation operating in nominally Vegan space." Alex suddenly had a sinking feeling in his stomach, he guessed what was coming as Yamamoto paused and looked directly at Alex. "You must see Major, how the capture of an Imperial corporate facility, operating in Vegan space, by a mercenary force working for a Vegan corporation, would cause a great loss of face for the Emperor, especially since he is a major stockholder. All the atavistic feelings the citizens of the Empire feel towards the Vegan Republic will be reinforced."

Claudia interrupted, "That's ridiculous, Matsui clearly provoked this whole mess. They attacked Symcorp City on an absurd pretext. Off course the Vegan Coalition would retaliate."

Alex stared at Claudia warningly, then spoke to Elandra, "Lady Yamamoto, I thank you for clarifying the situation, and please excuse my over zealous subordinate. She speaks hastily sometimes, even though she is an excellent warrior." Claudia was open-mouthed at the admonition. Brandon hid a smile from his lover. He knew as well as Alex that Claudia was three years older than Alex, and treated him like a younger brother.

Elandra gracefully replied, "No apologies necessary Major. I believe all young warriors must have fire in their veins when it comes to upholding the honor of their nation. I find your honesty refreshing Lieutenant Bovary."

Alex graciously asked, "If I may further enlighten my staff about your warning Lady Yamamoto?" He turned to face his officers after a nearly imperceptible nod of consent from Elandra he continued, "Matsui went into this elaborate scheme knowing they had Theodore Bukhara as a stockholder. The Emperor has to defend the interests of Matsui against any retaliation from Vega, or lose status among his own people. In effect we have attacked The property of the ruler of the Empire. Don't give me that look Claudia because it gets worse. Vega's Congress understands this as well as we do, and is not going to undermine the authority of its Coalition allies for Symcorp, or an unknown mercenary outfit. Vega will disown us, and discredit our actions to save the Emperor's face."

Claudia chagrined snapped, "They wouldn't. The citizens of the Republic would never accept such an act of cowardice."

McCloud interceded, "You have just stated the dilemma perfectly. Both nations are constrained by the expectations of their people. Yet both Vega and the Empire could fall to the GenClones if they renew their old feud now. Himalaya may be the tinderbox to ignite another border war." The room went quiet. For the first time they all understood how really critical were the events on Himalaya.

Alex chose to change the subject a moment, while he worked on a glimmer of an idea to resolve the present situation. He turned to Lady Yamamoto, "Lady, I understand you were being held under house arrest until our arrival?"

Yamamoto answered, "Please call me Elandra. I have forsworn all of the trappings of Bukharan nobility and military rank since the death of my regiment on Terranova." She frowned regretfully, "Though I am not without some undeserved and unwanted influence at court. I suspect I would have suffered worse then house arrest were I a less public figure."

Alex knew her story, as commander of the 5th Terranova Rangers assault company, the fabled *Doomslayers*, she had watched her entire command destroyed guarding the Emperor's flank at the battle of Terranova. She had been the only survivor of the courageous stand against the multiple assaults of GenClone SuperDroids. Alex understood her better than she knew. He had watched all the Nats die fleeing Banshee and shared the same mixed emotions about being the only survivor. She had fled to Himalaya and a religious commune, away from all she had been and known just like he had buried himself in a new life to try to forget the accusing faces of dead comrades. "Elandra, I have heard of your pledge never to command CombatJacks again, but does your honor forbid you to serve under the command of another?"

Elandra looked at him quizzically as she answered, "You would trust an ex-Bukharan officer to pilot one of your Droids against an Imperial corporation?"

Alex answered with a wry smile, "I would trust you with anything once you gave me your pledge Great Lady," Alex deliberately used the formal title to emphasize the point, "However I would not ask you to betray your nation Elandra. I believe that I may have a way to resolve the present dilemma. Defeating the Matsui forces on this planet would be required."

Elandra replied, "As we already noted, right or wrong the Empire cannot let Matsui fail. I don't see how defeating Matsui will resolve the potential conflict between the Empire and Vega. In fact it would make matters worse."

Brandon glumly asked, "The Republic will almost certainly agree to whatever the Empire demands to maintain the peace. What do you think the Emperor will demand?"

Yamamoto thoughtfully answered after a slight pause, "At the least he will ask for the return of all Matsui assets, and that those involved be punished or outlawed."

There was silence around the room as everyone digested the news, finally Claudia spoke, "There has to be a way out. I cannot believe that Matsui can use the politics of the great nations to their advantage so irrevocably. The Chameleons are trying to look out for the interests of both the Empire and Vega. How can our good intentions result in our destruction?"

McCloud leaning back in his chair commented, "History is paved with good intentions resulting in disaster."

Alex, thoughtfully interjected, "You may have hit on the solution Claudia."

Brandon grunted, "Oh?"

Alex continued, "Its quite simple really, we need to represent both Empire and Republic interests equally."

McCloud with a sudden glimmer in his eyes said, "An elegant solution, but how do we achieve it Major?"

Alex stood up from behind the desk and started pacing as he said, "Simple enough, we will need an employer who represents Imperial interests on Himalaya."

Brandon interrupted, "We can't hire out to two sides of a conflict!"

Alex frowning replied, "I don't believe we would be. Both the Empire and the Vegan Republic want a return to the status quo on this world. Each side wants their corporate assets returned to their rightful owners. This would remove the source of friction between the two great powers. We are presently employed by Symcorp, and theoretically do not represent the interests of either Vega or the Empire. Alex stopped pacing then with a raised eyebrow he asked McCloud, "Isn't that so Director?"

McCloud, with growing understanding replied with a mischievous smile, "You have expressed the interests of the great powers exceedingly well Major. The more I deal with you the more impressed I become. Those also happen to be the interests of General Biogenetics, Symcorp's parent corporation. You are probably unaware of the fact that The Republic is the major stockholder in the GB conglomerate. GB takes its orders from Congress."

Claudia expressed her major concern, "OK we have one half of the equation. How do we get an Imperial employer?"

Yamamoto frowning said, "I believe Major Kane and Director McCloud are hoping I may be of help."

McCloud seriously replied, "Whatever else you may think of us, we are trying to look out for the best interests of humanity." Fervently, "We must not let the alliance between Empire and Republic fail lady, or we shall all find ourselves under the GenClone yoke."

McCloud's vehemence surprised Alex. It seemed that anti GenClone feelings were not just prevalent amongst the ruling classes.

Elandra sighed a response, "I suspected you knew Director, though I am surprised the Major understood.

Alex looked confused. "Understood what Lady?"

Elandra in surprise, "You really don't know. Maybe I should explain. I am still a noble of the Empire and a Matsui stockholder, even though I have informally renounced these positions. To make a long explanation short, under certain circumstances, I have the authority to act in Matsui's and the Empire's interests. So I could theoretically hire you to stop a criminal rogue operation, such as the one being conducted by Superintendent Hojo. By defining it as a rogue operation, violating the Matsui corporate charter and Imperial law, I make this an internal matter, removing the onus for action from the Emperor. I will off course be at fault if I should be shown to have misjudged the situation. My family could suffer great dishonor, so I would not do this lightly." She paused looking down at her hands, then firmly looked up, "But you are right Director, honor demands I take action to prevent a breech between our nations."

Alex, "I was born in the Empire Elandra. I understand and admire you for the risk you take."

McCloud added with an expression of complete honesty, "You do a great deed today Lady!"

Alex smiled, at the Director's exuberance and winked at Elandra, "Are you checked out on a *Warlord*, Elandra?"

She replied, "I am, and I will join the Chameleons provisionally but only at the rank of CombatJack. I will abide by my vow never again to command."

For much of the rest of the meeting details were worked out about the nature of the Chameleon's new contract. They needed to insure it would be legally binding in a Bukharan court. Alex took both of his employers into his confidence and reviewed the details of Hopscotch with them. Elandra was enamored with the boldness of the plan, while Director McCloud began to get that nervous look again. They were finalizing the changes needed when word came that a Matsui representative was on the line. They transferred the inbound call to the monitor in the conference room, after agreeing on a response.

Superintendent Hojo's face flashed on the screen. Alex sucked in his breath as he recognized one of the many former managers of the Banshee mines. It was a small universe he thought. Here he was hundreds of light years from Banshee only to meet one of his corporate jailers. After his unnoticed initial surprise he remained impassive. Hojo could not possibly remember one of the nameless faces from his stay on Banshee. They had all agreed to let the Director and Elandra do the speaking.

Hojo brusquely said, "Ah, traitor McCloud, I should have expected to find you behind this criminal act. Are they holding you hostage Lady Yamamoto? If so they will pay." The Superintendent was playing the concerned executive for the recordings.

Elandra rudely replied, "No Hojo, the only person who has held me against my wishes lately has been you." Then formally, "as a minority stockholder in Matsui Mining and Manufacturing Incorporated, and a noblewomen of the realm, I formally relieve you of all your present responsibilities for breaching the Matsui charter, and for acts of treason committed against the Empire."

Hojo his face suffused with shock and rage screamed, "Insanity, you cannot do this!" Then regaining control of himself a shrewd look crossed his face, "Of course, the Vegan criminals are making you do this. You must have suffered greatly to commit this act of treason. Do not worry Lady you will be freed soon."

Elandra stood up smiling rapaciously, "I will see you hang traitor if I don't get you in my Droid sites first. The game is over Hojo, we have already transmitted compelling evidence of your crimes to Imperial Security Police. Surrender now!"

Hojo smirked, "You have chosen the wrong side Yamamoto, evidence can be fraudulent as the ISP surely know, and Major Garrison, the new commander of Matsui forces on Himalaya, will retake Matsuisan soon."

Elandra gracefully answered, "Win or lose, I have chosen the right side Hojosan. The side of honor and duty. A warrior only chooses the wrong side when she doesn't follow the tenets of Bushido. An honorless money grubber like you would not understand that. Bring on your Major Garrison, we are ready for him, and I will lead the way in the captured *Warlord*. She switched off the transmission with a feral grin on her face.

Brandon like the others hadn't spoken during the entire transmission said, "Well lets hope they delay their attack. Because we sure aren't ready yet."

McCloud commented, "Hojo has to delay until he develops a comprehensive plan to explain away our transmission to the ISP. That will take some time."

Claudia added, "No doubt Garrison will also want to recall his forces from the mainland. Lady Yamamoto must have placed some doubts into his mind as to our strength. We shall see."

The frantic pace of preparations continued for five more days, everyone expecting a Matsui assault at any time. But nothing materialized. The only activity their scouts observed was Garrison's forces converging on Symcorp City. It looked like Matsui was going to throw their entire military force at them and that's exactly what they did. Garrison's delay had been a tactical error. It had given the Chameleon's the time they needed to prepare and they used it well, as Garrison and Hojo would soon find out.

Chapter 28

The *Stormwarden* strode quickly into the repair bay. Everything had checked out fine, during the tests on the Droid's new configuration in the morning trial. Alex shutdown the giant machine, popped the canopy, and rushed down the gantry heading for the Command Center. Finally news of a move by Matsui.

Alex worked his way through the fort, past madly rushing techs and soldiers responding to the red alert he had issued. Word had arrived moments earlier that two reinforced companies of Matsui Droids were departing Symcorp City and heading this way. Alex caught up with Brandon in the lift, also just returning from the Droid test course.

Alex pushed the Command Center floor button and turned to Brandon, "How does your new Droid handle?"

Brandon excitedly, "Great! I've fully checked her out. The *Crossbow* is the ideal Droid for the way I fight. She's fast for a heavy Droid and has tremendous long range firepower."

Alex, "No problem with the customized GenClone 60 MM sliver cannons?"

"No, I adjusted the targeting system to compensate for the lower recoil, if anything she shoots better. The additional ammo and the addition of the 3C ALI really improves the capabilities of the Droid and my ability to coordinate our forces."

Alex reinforced his execs enthusiasm, "It shows, you looked sharp out there today." Alex paused uncertain how Brandon would react to the changes he was going to announce, "I've come to a decision, I'm promoting you to captain and giving you command of the Chameleon's first CombatDroid company. I'm going to spend most of my time coordinating the combined operations we're going to need to win the upcoming campaign. So I need you to take on more responsibility." He looked at Brandon speculatively, "What do you think?"

Brandon was thoughtful for a moment, then answered, "It makes sense. You can't keep doing everything yourself as much as you would like to. Who else do you plan to assign to the command lance?"

"Elandra in the *Warlord* and Petrov in the *Mastiff*. Your lance will be short a Droid for awhile."

"Strange isn't it. Six months ago I was worried about making the cut as a Droid pilot in an ancient broken down *Scout*. Now I find myself in a state of the art heavy Droid commanding a full Droid company." A big grin spread across his face, "I guess I'd be crazy if I wasn't a little bit scared, but you know after all we've been through I feel I can handle it."

Alex grinned back sardonically, "Good! I'm nervous too Brandon, I've been in over my head so long, it's beginning to feel normal to me."

Brandon asked, "Do you think Lady Yamamoto would agree to be my exec, or would that violate her vow?"

Alex answered, "I think if you offer it to her in a way that keeps her out of the chain of command she may accept.

Brandon asked, "Who's going to take command of the Beta lance?"

"Claudia. I plan to reassign the *Superscout* to her lance to round it out. Lieutenant Converse will remain in charge of the Fire lance, with the addition of the captured *Katana*, *Renegade* and *Roadrunner* to bring him up to full complement. Fuller informed me this morning that the *Roadrunner* will be ready by eighteen hundred hours. I'm assigning Gizzard to the Droid. He's checked out on *Roadrunners*."

Brandon nodded as the lift door opened on the Command Center. A Gurkha guard saluted as they entered. They saluted back as Brandon spotted Elandra across the room, "There she is, if you'll excuse me Major, I'll go ask her."

Alex joined the senior Chameleon command group clustered around the communication and satellite observation centers. Claudia, Bolithio, McCloud, and Kaseem were all there, as was Subhadar Chondra, their liaison to the Gurkha regiments. Alex listened for a moment, pleased with the teamwork, the relaxed by-play and mutual respect he observed. Alex interrupted by asking Claudia, the senior Chameleon officer present for an update, "Ahm, any change in the status since the last report Lieutenant?"

Claudia with an exaggerated salute, she never could get used to the idea that Alex was her commanding officer, "We have just received confirmation from Jamadar Javreel and his forward deployment group sir. Two companies of Droids, a company of light tanks, mostly 25 ton tracked *Corsairs*, and a variety of support vehicles, left Symcorp City at 0730 hours. As of 1100 hours, they are still marching towards the great gap in our general direction. They are not making very good time. The main force is moving at approximately forty-five KPH, a rather leisurely pace. If you consider the terrain they will have to traverse, and the surprises we have in store for them along the way, they won't be here in less then 60 hours, more likely 72 hours."

Brandon and Elandra joined them at that point. Brandon, "Lady Yamamoto has updated me on the situation Sir. She has also agreed to become the executive officer of the first company."

Claudia startled by the announcement asked, "I thought you were the exec?"

Alex jumped in to explain the modified command structure before Claudia got the wrong idea. Her first command nonplused Claudia. Though she didn't react other then giving Brandon a thoughtful look. The others congratulated Brandon and Claudia on their promotions. Alex interrupted the small but heartfelt celebration, and began to make final preparations for operation Hopscotch by commenting, "We may have more time but I want Captain Morgan and Lieutenant

Richtover in position by 1830 hours tomorrow. Javreel and Visegrip should be ready to initiate a diversion no later then 1900 hours."

Kaseem added, "The soldiers will be hiding for many hours, before Matsui reaches the halfway point. This will be most difficult for them Major."

Alex answered, "Agreed Kaseem, but better for then to wait then for the diversion to be delayed. We don't know that Garrison does not plan to accelerate his pace once he leaves the environs of Symcorp City. He's not a fool, and must be aware we have scouts in the area. The last thing we can afford to do is underestimate our enemies."

Kaseem nodded in reply. "Most assuredly Sir."

Brandon offered, "The *Mastiff* is the only Droid we won't have ready in time Sir. Fuller reports another 60 hours of repairs will be required even at double time. I'm not sure it matters we don't have a qualified pilot anyway."

Alex answered, "That's no longer true. I have spoken to Princess Rudnauman, she has ordered Lord Bonaduce to help us in anyway possible. He has agreed to man the *Mastiff* for the Chameleons, as long as we don't do anything contrary to the interests of the Princess or Asturia."

Alex couldn't help noting the uneasy looks and averted eyes of some of his officers at his declaration. Maybe his interludes with Roxanne were not the big secret he thought.

Claudia commented sarcastically, "And if he or the Princess decides in the middle of a fire fight that we are no longer serving her interests what does he do? March off and leave us in the lurch."

Alex firmly replied, "I am comfortable that the Princess and Lord Bonaduce will meet their commitments to us."

Claudia dripping Vitriol snapped, "I'm sure you are Sir."

Alex falling back on military etiquette in response asked, "Do you have a problem Lieutenant?"

Claudia answered firmly, "No, but I'm beginning to wonder if you have one Major. You can't have two masters in the middle of a campaign, Sir."

Alex was ready to snap Claudia's head off, but the uncertain looks of the other officers, told him this wasn't just her opinion. So he tempered his reply. Looking at Elandra and then McCloud he replied with a smile, "We already have two employers and that seems to be manageable." No one laughed, "OK lets get it out in the open. What's your concern Claudia?"

"Look Alex, none of us wants to get into your personal life, but Roxanne is the Princess Heir to the Asturian throne and a Triarch. Which means she sleeps with men for political reasons. We have already seen how she can manipulate a man to her own ends. Now the question in all of our minds, if I may speak for the rest of us, is why is she sleeping with the commander of the Chameleons?"

Claudia's blunt question appalled Alex. Worse at the back of his mind he had a niggling doubt about the answer to the same question. The whole group was dead silent waiting for the response. None of them returned his looks. Keeping his churning emotions firmly under control he finally spoke, "All right, lets assume you're right, and Roxanne is sleeping with me for political motives." He almost choked on the words, "It doesn't change anything. We're going to need the *Mastiff*, and Bonaduce is the only available pilot. The Chameleons are of no use to the Princess unless we survive the upcoming fight. Her interests and ours are aligned at least for the moment."

Claudia answered hesitantly, "Maybe, but what about your judgment Alex, how do we know you are looking out for the Chameleon's best interests?"

There was no answer he could give. What could he say to convince these people, his people, that he wouldn't betray them for a woman, even one he loved. Alex wasn't even sure how he would choose between Roxanne and the Chameleons?

Elandra interceded in his defense, "I have given my oath to Major Kane. I trust in his honor and," as she looked pointedly at Claudia, "He has done nothing to make me regret my decision."

There was silence after Elandra's declaration of faith. Alex decided there wasn't anything more to say, "All right lets get back to work, we have a battle to plan."

Chapter 29

Twelve Droids formed up on the tarmac at the Matsuisan space port at parade rest, while the dawn sun rose above the western ocean reflected off their burnished surfaces. Four Pantheon hover tanks and two hover APC's formed up on the right flank, as the roar of a landing shuttle drowned out all other noise. The *Horatio* class shuttle, with *Salamander* newly embossed on her sides landed smoothly. The vapor fumes cleared the air quickly and the massive Droid bay doors lowered soon afterwards.

Alex ordered the first company to board and the tanks and APC's to follow. Captain Morgan came on-line and began to direct the various machines to their prearranged storage locations. It was critical that the weight distribution be stabilized for the flight and during the upcoming atmospheric drop.

Alex picked up some chatter as junior CombatJacks began to speculate about the meaning of the sudden change of plans. Only the senior officers knew all the details of Hopscotch. Everyone else believed this was just a parade drill. Alex spoke firmly on a secured line. "This is *Warlock* to all units, *All units maintain Communication silence*. We are going into combat soon. Details of the plan will be communicated to all of you after we launch." That should perk them up he thought with a smile.

Their three heaviest Droids had boarded first. They weren't equipped with thrusters so they would have to wait until the Salamander landed before they could disembark. Alex watched as the initial confusion subsided and the Droids and tanks boarded in orderly fashion. He was the last one up.

Three hours after the start of loading, the spherical shuttle was airborne on a tail of fire. Its deadly cargo safely cacooned in the hold. The sixteen hundred kilometer flight to Symcorp City would take the Chameleons just over two hours. Alex gave the orders to Javreel and his forward deployed saboteurs to begin the first phase of the attack. Javreel and half his Anti-Droid company, Visegrip and his CLATs and some Gurkha militiamen were to launch a diversionary raid on the weak gun emplacements in the western suburbs of Symcorp City.

Alex was nervous. The plan made sense and had progressed well so far, but it would become more difficult to execute from here on out. Garrison and his main force had taken nearly two days to reach the halfway point between Symcorp City and Matsuisan, located at opposite ends of the Crescent Isle. Garrison was now a thousand difficult overland kilometers away from either city. The series of Anti-Droid traps, that the Chameleons and their Gurkha militia allies had thrown at the guards had done very little damage, but it had slowed the guard's progress down to a crawl.

The overall plan was based on a simple premise; use the Chameleon's air lift generated mobility and air superiority to control both ends of the Isle. Fortify both corporate installations and wait for Garrison to make a move. Alex could then deploy his mobile Droid force at either end of the Isle ahead of the guards, using the *Salamander* for transport. Isolated in the middle of the island without repair facilities and supplies, the Guards could fall apart. He worried about all the things that could go wrong, the rest of the trip to the DZ. They were to drop on the plateau just east of Symcorp City and south of the small landing field and the grounded *Tiara II*. The air drop would be risky if the small Matsui force defending the city was ready for them. Javreel's and Visegrip's diversion was supposed to draw the defenders to the western suburbs, to protect the power generating station located there.

Morgan suddenly spoke to Alex over the private line. "We're three minutes from the DZ Major. Everything looks clear so far. I just received a message from Jamadar Javreel, quote, "Am engaged with ground forces, plus one medium and one light Droid in western suburbs. No sign of the other three Droids we have previously scouted."

Morgan paused then interrupted himself, "Major, our radar has just scanned two low flying StarFighters approaching from the north."

There was some static on the line for a moment.

"Sorry Major, I just identified the craft, it's Richtover and the *Foxbats* he's five minutes from the DZ. He's still maintaining Communication silence."

Alex answered, "Thank you Captain. Make preparations for the drop." Alex then changed to the general frequency, "All units the mission is on, Alpha and Beta Lances make final preparation for drop. ETD in two minutes twelve seconds and counting."

The last few moments flew by. The outer bay doors opened and eight Droids started the short drop to earth. Alex didn't think he would ever get used to the exhilaration of free falling in 48 tons of war machine, not knowing what you would face when you landed. Mamba held onto his shoulder firmly to keep from floating away. At two hundred meters he fired his thrusters, crushing him down into the seat at the massive deceleration. Thump, he hit the earth, all his GenClone quality scanners probing the surroundings for threats. Nothing! Claudia's voice crackled over his speaker. "Beta1 to Beta Lance, sound off." Her lance mates called in their positions and status, they were all down safely and converging on their pre-assigned positions.

Converse spoke, "I've got trouble here Major, three Droids approaching me and Fire4. I've identified two of them as heavies."

Alex answered, "I'm on my way. Beta1 continue per the mission briefing."

Claudia, acknowledged. "Lets go people."

Alex picked up the three red icons identifying the enemy Droids, as he cleared the trees, "*Warlock* to Raptor1, attack enemy units at coordinate DD23."

Richtover broke his comlink silence, "Raptor1 to *Warlock*, with pleasure Major. Damn these *Foxbats* fly like silk, and wait 'til those Matsui Droid jocks feel the punch we're going to deliver."

Alex considered reprimanding Richtover, but decided against it. The poor space pilot had been grounded for months and couldn't contain his enthusiasm. Alex was running at flank speed to join Converse's *NightHawk* before the Matsui Droids overran him. A second blue icon identified as Grizzard's *Roadrunner* was even more exposed then the *NightHawk*. The rest of the fire lance had scattered during the drop and were too far away to be of help. The *NightHawk* was retreating and exchanging fire at long range with the Matsui Droids, when the two *Foxbats* roared over the tree tops, followed by their sonic shock waves. They strafed the startled Matsui Droids, disabling a *Grim Reaper* with multiple missile hits. The confusion, the arrival of the *Foxbats* caused, gave Alex time to link up with Converse. They tried to provide supporting fire for the *Roadrunner*, but the massed assault of the two heavies soon slagged the light Droid. Grizzard fought valiantly but it wasn't enough.

Alex, "*Warlock* to Fire4, Grizzard punch out now!" Alex watched as an escape pod hurled skyward, just before the *Roadrunner*'s engine exploded in a nuclear fireball. Alex couldn't tell if Grizzard had cleared the blast zone in time.

The rest of the fight was anti-climatic. The Chameleon forces outnumbered and out gunned the unprepared defenders of Symcorp City. When Beta Lance joined the Fire Lance the two shot up Matsui Droids, a *Mace* and an *Firedrake*, surrendered. The Chameleons overran the weak fortifications of the city and joined up with Javreel and his team soon after. One of the Droids engaged with Javreel's force, a *Roadrunner* XL fled the city. The other Droid a *Lancer* was crippled by the CLATs and surrendered to the fire lance. In all they had captured four Droids, two of them with only minor damage, a pair of light tanks and over 120 prisoners. They also recaptured the shuttle *Tiara II* with its nacelles still damaged, and freed two dozen members of Symcorp's house mercenaries, including Five CombatJacks. Three of them joined the Chameleons.

The other CombatJacks had been tortured and broken at the whim of Major Garrison. Apparently their resistance had annoyed him. The physically and psychically scarred men wanted to join the Chameleons and get revenge, but the declining quality of recruits was already a concern. Of the three warriors he recruited only one of them met the minimum standard he wanted to set for the Chameleons. Unfortunately he didn't have a choice if he wanted to man all his captured Droids, not with Garrison 32 hours quick march away.

Reorganizing Symcorp City proved a much easier task then organizing Matsuisan. Director McCloud took complete charge of the facility he had run for the past two years. With most of his old staff freed and happy to be working with the likable McCloud again, things went smoothly. Alex focused his attention organizing the campaign against Garrison, now isolated in the center of the island.

He ordered Richtover to continuously strafe the Matsui Droids to the AeroJacks satisfaction, and dispatched more anti-Droid infantry to the combat theater. Symcorp had only two inadequate Droid repair platforms, so Alex shipped the three most severely damaged Droids back to Matsuisan. For the third time in as many weeks he shuffled assignments, trying to assign the best Droids to the most experienced pilots. Lieutenant Converse was qualified on a *Firedrake*, and was ecstatic when Alex Assigned him the captured 48 ton Droid. The Lieutenant recommended Gizzard be reassigned to the *NightHawk*. Gizzard had fortuitously survived the destruction of the *Roadrunner* with only minor burns. The *Mace* reassigned to its original Symcorp pilot was also sent back to Matsuisan aboard the Salamander for repair.

Converse took command of these three Droids and the *Mastiff* stationed in Matsuisan, in a newly formed heavy close assault lance. The second *Mace* and the Lancer were assigned to Brandon's Command lance with the recently freed Symcorp CombatJack as pilots. The *Katana* and *Renegade* went to Claudia's lance. Her lance was humorously christened Claudia's Clods, after two of her Droids stumbled over the same drainage ditch entering the city. Claudia to everyone's surprise responded by officially renaming her lance the Clods, turning the tables on her subordinates, who were aware of her usually prickly sense of propriety.

The final change Alex made was to form a combined forces strike force under his command. It consisted of the *Python*, two CLAT squads with their hover APC, and the four Pantheon light tanks. Alex also ordered repairing the *Tiara II* as the top priority for his Techs. They were now totally dependent on the *Salamander* for their air transport. If anything were to happen to the shuttle the Chameleons would be split between the two cities, easy prey for Garrison's Guards.

After another chaotic day of preparations, Alex finally collapsed totally fatigued, in a borrowed bunk. He thought as he closed his eyes, everything will be ready in time, now its Matsui's move. Mamba fluttered up to a perch on a hanging overhead light fixture, and chirped playfully, happy that her symbiot had finally settled down from the hyperactive levels he had maintained since recovering from his injuries, back at the GenClone base. Mamba intuitively recognized that even with her help Alex could not maintain his frantic pace for much longer. Mamba dimly wished her companion's mate was here to comfort him.

Chapter 30

Alex paced up and down in front of the marble topped table in the spacious oak paneled conference room. All the Chameleon officers stationed in Symcorp City were there. They were awaiting the arrival of the contingent from Matsuisan. The door opened and in walked Roxanne, Lord Bonaduce, Kaseem, Converse and Fuller. The four of them had made the trip from Matsuisan on one of the Chameleon's VTOL aircraft. Alex had convinced himself that their communications weren't secure enough to risk teleconferencing this staff meeting. He and probably everyone else suspected that this was just an excuse to see Roxanne again.

He stopped pacing as Roxanne took a seat. For a moment, he really didn't care what everyone thought, he was just glad to see her again. Lately she had been deliberately keeping her distance from him. Nothing he did seemed to please her anymore as she spent more and more of her time cloistered with Bonaduce. He wanted to go over and just hold her, but he couldn't help noting the averted eyes and the subdued tones of his officers. They weren't overtly looking, but they would be judging his response closely.

For the first time ever he felt nervous in front of this group. McCloud and Elandra were sitting at the base of the table with their heads together sharing an amusing anecdote. To the left Chondra, Javreel and the just seated Kaseem exchanged greetings in their native tongue, and then were quiet, as was their norm in the company of non-Gurkhas. Bolithio and Visegrip had apparently buried the hatchet, fortunately not in each other after their last mission. They sat on the right discussing tactics in the closest thing to a whisper either of them could manage. Claudia, Brandon, Morgan, and Converse sat quietly at the head of the table to his right. While Ambassador Doran, Lord Bonaduce, Richtover and Roxanne sat to his left. Roxanne and Claudia directly across from each other silently starred daggers at one another.

Alex decided to start before words were exchanged. "All right lets get right down to business." The room went quiet, "It's been two days since we captured Symcorp City and we still haven't seen any response from the Matsui forces. Garrison is sitting in his temporary camp slowly letting his forces deteriorate under our constant hit and run tactics. Lieutenant Richtover's constant strafing, and the attacks of Subhadar Chondra's ground forces in coordination with Jamadar Kaseem's command have inflicted significant damage. The questions before us, is why hasn't Garrison made a move against either city, and what do we do about it, if anything?"

There was no response for awhile, then Converse broke the seemingly interminable silence, "I don't understand it Major. Garrison is not stupid. He has to know that sitting still is the worst thing he can do. More importantly, inactivity is contrary to his nature. I would have bet you a years pay that he would be attacking one of the cities by now. He may be a traitor but he's got guts."

Elandra added, "I agree with the Lieutenant's assessment, but I believe we are discounting a critical factor. Garrison may be in overall command of the Matsui forces but he still takes his orders from superintendent Hojo."

Converse replied, "I don't believe anybody could stop Garrison from coming after us. We've defeated him soundly twice and made him look the fool. He has to want revenge!"

Elandra commented, "True, but we cannot forget that half of his command consists of Matsui corporate warriors, loyal to the superintendent. We should not ignore the most obvious reason for their lack of action. It is quite possible that their leaders cannot agree on what to do, and by default they end up doing nothing."

To everyone's surprise Javreel ventured a rare opinion, "There is another factor we must consider. The Matsui forces probably have an exaggerated opinion of our strength."

Claudia disagreed, "Jamadar, they must have some pretty decent intel on our force strength by now. Frakke, half the planet knows how many Droids we have!"

Javreel undaunted answered, "In all deference Lieutenant, you are looking at the situation from our perspective. Look at it from Matsui's view. An unknown force appears out of thin air and captures the most powerful stronghold on the planet with apparent ease. Maybe the Matsui forces in Matsuisan were incompetent and caught by surprise, so you discount some of this success. But then within days, this same force launches a successful raid nearly two-thousand kilometers away using space and shuttle assets again of unknown origin. They may have intelligence showing our existing strength, but they have to be concerned about what additional resources we have at our disposal. All of you tend to underestimate your accomplishments. To an outsider you must appear to be a crack mercenary force with powerful resources and backers. From Matsui's perspective, we must appear formidable and mysterious."

The Jamadar paused with one of his rare smiles then added with a slight nod to Alex, "No doubt this is the reason the Major held our space assets in reserve during the attack on Matsuisan."

It was the longest speech any of them had heard from the usually terse Jamadar. The group was silent as they mulled the point over. The Jamadar's rarely expressed views were respect by everyone there. Alex noted the nods as people found themselves agreeing with his position.

Brandon asked, "Is that why you wanted to keep our space assets a secret at Matsuisan?"

Alex replied, "Not really. I wanted Garrison to come at us with everything he could and leave Symcorp City defenseless. He wouldn't have done that had he known we had a shuttle available. Keeping our true resources a mystery was a secondary factor. If it has had anything to do with Garrison's immobility great. Its given us time to ready our forces while his deteriorate. But the question before us is still what will Garrison do, and what do we want to do different?"

McCloud offered, "Do not underestimate the superintendent. I believe your analysis is correct

Jamadar. But Hojo and Garrison now have their backs up against the wall. Desperate man are unpredictable, they could do anything."

McCloud had hit on the point that most concerned Alex. It crystallized in his mind the reason for this meeting. "You're all right. And I've come to a decision. We will not give up the initiative. We must keep the pressure on Hojo and Garrison and force them into more bad judgments."

Richtover commented, "We're already keeping the pressure on Major. I'm pounding them every day and the Gurkha eighteenth infantry regiment is also doing its part. What more do you want?"

Alex started counting off his plans on his fingers as he said, "First, I want security around all our installations doubled particularly around the shuttles. If the Salamander is crippled we're in serious trouble. We have to be prepared for a covert attack. Subhadar Chondra, I will need the support of the Gurkha regiments to do this."

Chondra formally replied, "We are at your disposal Major."

"Thank you Subhadar. Second I will be leading strike force Alpha against the Guards. With hover transports we can be in position to attack them in sixteen hours. We need to keep up the pressure, and frankly based on the satellite surveillance neither the air strikes or the eighteenth regiment are doing much damage now that we've lost the element of surprise. I want to keep Garrison and Hojo off balance."

Visegrip asked respectfully in his gravely voice, "If you don't object Major, I would like to take command of your CLAT forces. This security duty is beneath a true warrior."

Alex with amused sarcasm, "Always the diplomat aren't we Visegrip? I guess I'd better bring you along just to keep you out of trouble."

Claudia added, "Major, I would recommend that Lieutenant Khorsa be reassigned to the *Python* for this operation. When it comes to hit and run tactics he is second only to you."

Alex agreed, other details were worked out quickly. The group soon broke up to make the preparations. Only Roxanne and Lord Bonaduce remained.

Roxanne spoke, "Would you mind leaving us Lord Bonaduce?"

He replied with a formal bow and an ingratiating smile that made Alex's back teeth itch, "Of course your highness," as he got up and left.

Roxanne asked, "Is something wrong?"

Alex as he shuffled his briefing papers, "You do know that just about everybody on this planet knows who you are now, and about our relationship. Your friend Lord Bonaduce has not been discreet."

Roxanne frowned, "He's very young. He could not help letting slip who I really am to some of his companions. Besides he didn't know we were trying to keep my identity secret. If you hadn't opened access to the WH transmit station, we wouldn't be worried about word of my presence leaking out to Asturia, and to my enemies there."

Alex controlling his outrage, "Bonaduce is older then you and for that matter me. Youth is no excuse for the way he has endangered your life." Sarcastically, "He had to guess you were traveling under an alias for some reason. As for the WH transmit facility, you forget I am an employee of Symcorp and Lady Yamamoto. Any action I took to restrict access to a WH transmit would have violated our contract. I am not a Garrison, and I won't risk outlawry for my people! Not even for you."

Roxanne stormed into Alex's space. Her face only centimeters away from his, violet fire reflected from her eyes as she rigidly replied, "I did not mean to criticize you, Major. I may be under Chameleon protection, but you had best understand that Lord Bonaduce is my one loyal and trusted vassal and subject to royal protection. I will not tolerate your continued verbal assaults on him. Do I make myself clear."

Alex unable to control the urge, leaned over and kissed her. Roxanne slapped him hard across the cheek leaving her hand print on his face, and bringing tears to his eyes with the strength of the blow. They stood for a moment staring at each other. Roxanne's nostrils flared as she sucked in deep breaths to keep her anger in control. Alex just stood there stunned.

Roxanne in a cold rage, "Who do you think you are? You think because you've slept with me a few times, and helped me out of a dilemma, I'm your plaything on demand! I am the Princess Heir of Asturia, and I will accept nothing less then the respect I am due, not even from you!"

Alex rubbed his burning cheek as he recovered from his surprise. Very formally he replied, "I didn't mean any disrespect Princess. I may be a nobody mercenary but I just happen to be in love with you, and I thought you felt the same about me. I am not by nature a spontaneous or overtly affectionate person." Then more formally, "I apologize for offending you with my behavior your Highness, raised as I was, I sometimes don't act appropriately." He bowed and turned to leave.

Roxanne watched as he started to walk away, "Wait!"

Alex turned.

Roxanne, "Your actions weren't inappropriate, my behavior was." She hesitated for a moment, then spoke regally, "I apologize." In a gentler voice she continued, "I need to distance myself from you Alex for both our sakes. I just want you to understand that I wasn't using you when...," Pausing, "When we were together. I love you, and a part of me will always love you. But I am a Triarch, and the Princess Heir, and I must do what's best for my people, not what I want." She looked away, took a deep breath, "And that means I was wrong, you can't be in my future. My people could never except you as Prince Consort. I'm sorry if I led you on."

Alex bowed again. He felt an incredible feeling of loss, and a terrible need to lash out against a universe that continued to take away the things he loved. Much of his rage was directed against Bonaduce. The man had deliberately undercut Alex at every opportunity. Alex knew Roxanne had been swayed by the elegant Count's constant warnings of civil war, if she took up with a foreigner.

Alex replied rigidly, "Of course Princess, I would not force myself upon you against your wishes. There is no need for you to feel guilt. Your *services* paid for any assistance I may have provided. Consider us quits." He turned and walked away quickly, without looking at her. He didn't want to know if he had hurt her or not. As he passed the trooper guarding the door he knew it was good that he had forgotten how to cry a long, long time ago.

Chapter 31

The *Stormwarden* moved delicately up the tree shrouded ridge. A *Python* moved just as quietly a hundred meters to the left. Somewhere far ahead there were two Matsui Droids providing air cover for the bulk of the Matsui forces snaking their way through the Elk River canyon. High above, the Chameleon's two StarFighters circled like vultures, waiting for an opening in the anti-aircraft screen thrown up by Garrison's Droids.

Things had been going smoothly until four hours ago. Alex had led Alpha force within striking distance of the still encamped Matsui position without a hitch. They had quickly hooked up with the soldiers from the 18th and 24th Gurkha regiments surrounding the encampment. Then scouts reported Garrison had broken camp and was on the move towards Matsuisan. Fifteen minutes later Brandon had sent an urgent message via secured satellite relay; the *Salamander* had been sabotaged by one of their newly hired techs. All of Alex's efforts to protect the shuttle had failed to take into consideration the possibility of a mole being planted in the Chameleon's ranks. He had made a horrible mistake and unless a miracle happened the few defenders in Matsuisan would pay the ultimate price. All he could do was hit the Matsui forces as hard as he could, as long as he could.

Brandon's static filled voice came over the scrambled line, intruding on Alex's grim thoughts. "Major, we've completed the damage assessment on the *Salamander*."

Alex flicked on his communicator, "How bad is it?"

With only a slight pause Brandon replied, "It's bad, it will take at least 100 hours of work to make her air-worthy again."

Bile rose in Alex's throat at the dreadful news, "All right, lets start planning the evacuation of Matsuisan."

Brandon answered, "Alex, Fuller has an alternative plan. He thinks we can use one of the Nacelles from the *Salamander* to repair the *Tiara II* in under 50 hours."

Alex with a glimmer of hope in his voice, "That's too long, Garrison will be at Matsuisan by tomorrow afternoon at his present pace."

Brandon was off line for many moments as he talked over options with the staff, then he spoke, "Major, we've been reviewing our options here. Lady Yamamoto believes if the superintendent regains control of Matsuisan, he will be able to convince any Empire investigator of the validity of his actions. This would discredit her and the Chameleons and endanger an open split between the Empire and Vega.

Alex exasperated answered, "I know that already Captain. Why do you think we needed to capture both cities." Alex angry at himself for losing his temper. "Sorry Brandon, I didn't mean that the way it sounded."

Brandon with humor in his voice, "It's okay Alex." There was silence over the line for a moment then Brandon spoke again, "Major, all the officers both here and in Matsuisan think we ought to try to defend Matsuisan until we can repair the *Tiara II*. We have worked out a plan. Basically we could move all our hover tanks and hover transports to Matsuisan ahead of Garrison. We can even transport some of our lighter Droids. We think properly fortified Matsuisan can hold out the 10 hours or so needed until we can transport the 1st company there."

Alex thought about the plan for a few moments, "It won't work. Your company will be landing in the middle of a battle, trapped aboard an under-armed shuttle. Worse the forces in Matsuisan will have to defend the spaceport and the fort for 15 hours, not 10. It will take you at least four hours to disembark your company, Brandon. It's far to risky."

Alex paused thoughtfully for a moment as he reviewed the option, "I need to speak to Captain Morgan and Fuller. Are they there?"

Brandon replied, "I'll fetch them."

Fuller came on-line moments later. Alex suspected all the officers were huddled around the communication center awaiting the outcome of this discussion. "You wish to speak to us, sir?"

"Two questions Mr. Fuller; First, can we fly the *Tiara II* at low altitude without pressurizing the cabin and sealing the bay doors?" Alex heard some mumbled discussion taking place on the line.

Finally Morgan replied, "It can be done Major, but we'd have to fly at very low altitudes and go slow. It would take an additional hour to make the hop."

"That's acceptable Captain, you would save three hours disembarking after you landed."

Morgan, "Well, I'll be! You're right. Properly loaded I could simulate a combat drop in the old tub."

"The second question I have concerns the repairs to the nacelles. If I recall correctly the alignment of the cells is critical for high speed accelerations in space. Can we speed up the repairs Mr. Fuller if we just complete a single stage alignment, and will that enable the *Tiara II* to make the short hop to Matsuisan?"

Fuller hesitatingly, "It would be sloppy work, sir. I wouldn't recommend it."

Alex could almost see the pained expression on Fuller's face at the thought of an incomplete repair. Sharply Alex replied, "That's not what I asked you, Chief Tech."

Brandon came on-line, "We've only got a few minutes until our satellite hook-up goes off line Mr. Fuller, so hurry."

Morgan interjected, "I can make a short atmospheric hop, with a nacelle slightly out of alignment." Pause, "Ah, I've done it before." Morgan had just admitted to an illegal maneuver that could get his license revoked. No wonder he had hesitated.

Fuller in a pained voice, "If we don't do the second stage alignment we can cut six hours off the repairs, Major."

Alex, knowing he had only moments left before the communication satellite went below the horizon, spoke quickly, "Brandon do everything you can to get The *Tiara II* ready. If you can have the 1st company in Matsuisan in less then 45 hours we go with your plan. Alpha force and the 18th and 24th are going to slow down the Guards. Work out the details then..." The up-link panel light went out. Fate and his own incompetence had dealt him this hand. As always he would play it the best he could.

So he opened the channel to the rest of Alpha force and explained the situation. "... In conclusion it's up to us to slow down Matsui enough to permit our forces to get into position."

Visegrip came on-line with a grim laugh, "I will say one thing Major, serving under your command is never dull." There was laughter in response to his comment.

Alex his mind whirling with plans gave out one final order, "All right people, we're nearly in position. Communication silence in 2 minutes. Let's earn our pay."

Alex and Khorsa worked their way down another slope paralleling the Elk River gorge. Equipped with undetectable SCM suits, the Droids moved slowly to decrease their heat signature. Alex fervently hoped these precautions were enough to keep them undetected until they closed in on the two enemy icons now showing on his display.

The four *Pantheon* thrust equipped hover tanks had hopped down from the flat plateau to the west onto a small Elk River tributary, and were now moving up the stream on his flank. Hover crafts were restricted to the small open areas along the banks of the stream once they left the savanna covered plateau. Alex hoped his calculated risk in moving the Pantheons into the confining forest didn't backfire. There was only one escape route for the tanks.

The two Droids accelerated as they cleared the ridge. Alex's electronics identified a Matsui *Gunner* and a *Firedrake*, both overlooking the Elk River canyon and the advancing Matsui main force, five hundred meters below. As Alex and Khorsa cleared the forest, the *Gunner* finally detected them and began to turn. Alex carefully aligned his crosshairs on the right torso of the heavy Droid and triggered both NPC's. Mega joules of energy sliced through shields and decompressed chunks of Cubed armor off the right torso and arm of the vaguely humanoid machine. Alex then triggered his launchers. Per the prearranged plan Khorsa also targeted the same Droid. His newly installed 80 MM laser and DFM Launcher fired almost in unison with the *Stormwarden's*. The combined fire shredded armor on the right torso and disabled the right arm mount. The real devastation was yet to come. Signaled by the *Python's* almost imperceptible targeting laser beam, which directed the missile fire from the *Pantheons*, hidden along the creek.

The Gunner had completed its turn and was bringing its undamaged left arm mounted weapons to bare on Alex, when 60 Laser Directed Missiles swept over the tree line and converged on it. The roar and billowing flames of multiple explosions completely shrouded the *Gunner*. Its shield sparkled violet and failed under the massed assault. When the smoke cleared the heavy Droid was face down on the ground, with smoke and flames billowing out of multiple breaches in its shattered armor. The attack had worked to perfection. The *Gunner* had exposed its damaged right side unknowingly to the deadly missile barrage. Some of the HEAP rounds, unable to lock on the

Gunner, had hit the nearby *Firedrake*. Its pilot remained undaunted and turned to bring his own HEAP missiles to bare.

Alex smiled as he recognized a path was now clear for the circling *Foxbats* to strafe the main body of Droids strung out in the valley. "*Warlock* to Raptor1, the door is open."

"Ye haw, on our way *Warlock*," Richtover yelled.

Alex had backed hastily into some screening trees to protect himself from the *Firedrake*. He tracked the incoming Barrage of HEAP missiles. The first launch was high and to the right. Alex moved away from the explosions that shattered nearby trees. Debris rained down on his Droid with little effect. The second barrage was more accurate. Alex pivoted on his right leg as his APDS engaged a dozen incoming missiles. Four of the missiles penetrated his defensive fire and detonated on his EMD shield, temporarily depleting it and staggering the *Stormwarden*.

Khorsa was already positioning his Droid to respond to the attack, as Alex charged forward to close with the *Firedrake*. Visegrip opened a comlink, "Toad1 to *Warlock*, I've got a fast moving scout lance heading your way up the canyon wall. Commencing delaying action." Garrison was responding quickly to their raid. Visegrip's CLATs and a Gurkha anti-Droid platoon were protecting the only easy path up from the canyon floor. Their job was to delay any attack until the hover tanks escaped. But Alex had not anticipated the quick response. His hover tanks would be easy kills if caught by the stream.

"*Warlock* to Pantheon1, withdraw at maximum speed now." Alex then hastily triggered his NPC's and missiles at the now retreating *Firedrake*. The *Firedrake* pilot now facing two SuperDroids, decided retreat was in order. Alex ordered Khorsa to break off the attack. The two of them would have to screen the retreating hover tanks. As they rushed through the intervening woods, Alex fleetingly spotted the StarFighter strafing the Droids still in the canyon.

Moments later, "Raptor1 to *Warlock*, attack completed successfully. We hurt them some sir. I have minor damage to my left airfoil. Do you wish me to continue strafing?"

Alex replied firmly, "*Warlock* to Raptor1, break off attack and return to base per the plan. Repeat, return to base. We can't risk losing your fighters Lieutenant." At least not yet, thought Alex.

Richtover replied, "Understood. Good luck *Warlock*. We'll be back as soon as we repair and re-arm."

The rest of the fire fight was a confusing mess. Alex lost track of his forces, and just hoped everyone followed the withdrawal plan. Alex and Khorsa continuously attacked the scout lance and then dodged back into the woods. The scout lance, reinforced by the *Firedrake*, pressed forward knowing more reinforcements were on the way. Visegrip sprung a series of brilliant traps on the Matsui Droids doing little damage but making them cautious and slowing them down. Mostly because of his actions, the Pantheon's reached the plateau ahead of the Matsui Droids.

Alex and Khorsa continued their retreat, hotly pursued by the scout lance, until they found themselves trapped against the exposed shear cliff wall leading up to the plateau. A waterfall tumbled into a pool that formed the headwaters of the unnamed creek. They stood side by side pouring fire into the approaching Droids, planning to take out as many of them as they could before they went down. Newly promoted Jamadar Kaseem wasn't about to let his commander fall so easily. He positioned the *Pantheons* at the plateau edge and poured a devastating missile barrage into the Matsui scout lance. It was too much, they broke and fled, giving Alex and Khorsa a chance to withdraw up the low cliff. Alex led his small force back to their temporary camp and safety.

The raid was a limited success, a *Gunner* was destroyed and scouts reported the Matsui forces had stopped to reorganize. They also noted damage to at least five other Droids, including a badly limping *Renegade*. His own force was battered but all his units were still operable and to Alex's surprised relief, they hadn't lost a single soldier. Alex would now rendezvous with their VTOL aircraft to resupply and refit his small force. Alex smiled grimly as he thought about Garrison's lack of supplies. His pleasure was tempered with concern. A little slower on the retreat and Alpha force could have ceased to exist. There would be no rest for his small field command. A quick resupply and some minor repairs, then back into the fray.

The rest of the day was a continuation of the initial assault. Alpha force targeted the scout lance on its next raid. Alex feinted a repetition of the earlier assault on Garrison's screening units, but this time he kept his fighters in reserve until he retreated before the hard charging scout lance. Led away from their air defenses the scout lance was an easy target for the Chameleon StarFighters. The attack destroyed a *Superscout* as well as further damaging the limping *Renegade*. The Chameleons didn't go unscathed, they lost one of their tanks and had 5 casualties.

This was just the beginning of the ordeal for Alpha force and their Gurkha allies. Next they led the Matsui scout lance into a minefield. Trapped between the minefield, the Elk River, and the *Pantheons*, the scout lance should have been destroyed. Unfortunately a *Roadrunner XL* pilot, the same one who had escaped from Symcorp City, jumped across the field and flanked the *Pantheons*. Alex was forced to withdraw or lose his tanks to the deadly barrages of the *Roadrunner*. The Chameleons developed a grudging respect for the *Roadrunner* pilot. He continued to thwart their best laid plans. As Khorsa remarked, "That pilot is good enough to be one of us."

Alpha force then supported a series of traps already laid by the Gurkha regiments. Combinations of minefields and anti-Droid infantry assaults slowed the progress of the Matsui forces down to a crawl, as they tried to work their way out of the forested foothills that covered the central regions of the Crescent Isle. The Chameleons used their anti-Droid mines and weapons lavishly. Alex had ordered a non-stop resupply of materials used by the infantry. It was working, it seemed that every time Alex withdrew, another VTOL aircraft or hover transport would be ready to resupply his small force and the allied Gurkhas. Even the huge stockpile of weapons at the captured GenClone base began to dwindle.

Garrison continued forward relentlessly, but finally he brought his exhausted battalion to a stop as he cleared the foothills. Thank heaven, Alex thought, he was so tired he could barely crawl out of his battered Droid at their night camp. He turned over command to a fresh contingent of troopers dispatched from Symcorp City. The ability to relieve his forces via airlift was proving to be one of his biggest advantages. Garrison would have to start abandoning his damaged equipment and injured soldiers soon if he wanted to maintain his pace. Alex fervently hoped the Matsui commander chose to slow down instead.

Five hours later his hopes were turned to ash. Alex was back in his Droid running across the open plains. Matsui was on the move again hoping to out race the Chameleon screening force. They had abandoned a couple of their more seriously damaged Droids and their slower moving vehicles including their *Corsair* tanks.

Alex and Khorsa had developed a hair brained contingency plan. The closer they came to the Matsui lines the crazier it seemed. Alex believed trying to move the worn-out, un-integrated Matsui and Guard Droids quickly at night would result in a great deal of confusion. He wanted to attack while Garrison was still trying to form his line of march.

The two Alpha Droids charged unsupported right at the heart of the Matsui force. Alex had enemy icons all across his display. There were so many his computer was overloading trying to identify them. In the distance he could see spotlights from some of the nearer Droids moving in random patterns. "Good," he thought "they're still not organized!" As unobtrusively as possible, with a 48 ton war machine he charged across the open plain towards overwhelming odds partially shielded by his stealth SCM suit. He and Khorsa charged into the enemy lines undetected. Alex opened fire on a *Mace* that blocked his path, targeted a *Patriot* next, as he activated his ODC system to keep up with Khorsa's fast running, madly firing *Python*. Hundreds of intertwining energy beams lit up the night sky as the Matsui Droids returned fire. Tired warriors fired randomly or at each other, unable to identify the Chameleon Droids in their ranks. Alex did every thing he could to add to the confusion. Dodging back and forth to make it appear more Chameleon Droids were present, and firing at odd intervals to confuse target locks. Alex and Khorsa had one enormous edge, they knew that anything they detected was an enemy target. Alex used this to advantage as he fired at a hesitating *Battleaxe*. Careening from one enemy target to the next, firing his weapons as fast as they recharged, Alex yelled incoherently, half in terror and half in battle joy. The mad suicide charge, to Alex's disbelief, carried them through the entire enemy line with only minor damage.

As they fled the scene Khorsa with an exalted whoop screamed, "Incredible sir just incredible. If I hadn't participated in this, I wouldn't believe it myself. I'm not sure I believe it even now. Unbelievable! They're still shooting at each other back there! Two Droids charge a battalion and survive. The GenClones would conserve our genes for such a feat Major."

Khorsa continued his ecstatic diatribe while Alex watched through his rear display as the explosions and laser pyrotechnics slowly dissipated. He doubted Matsui would be ready to move before dawn. Another three hours gained. Would it be enough?

Alex used the time gained to set another ambush, and another one after that. All through the morning Alpha force launched a series of quick hit and run attacks against the steadily advancing Matsui juggernaut. Garrison must have suspected something because he drove his forces forward with single minded determination. Attrition began to tell on both sides. By noon Alpha force was down to two hover tanks and Eight worn out CLATs plus the two battered Droids. The Matsui forces abandoned another damaged Droid, leaving a token infantry force to protect the limping 32 ton *Catalan*. Alex suspected Garrison wanted him to attack the *Catalan* and stop harassing the main body. It was a forlorn hope.

Alex desperate to slow down the advance chose instead a risky frontal assault, with the remainder of Alpha force and every anti-Droid trooper he could get into position at the Hamurabi river crossing. They had already blown the lone bridge.

He half slept, dead tired at the controls of his Droid, until the signal came of approaching enemy forces. Gurkha skirmishers from the other side of the river swarmed into their waiting hover APC's and fled. There were fewer of them then he had sent out. The campaign was getting bloody. The APC's just cleared the river, when a lance of medium Droids strode from the forest on the opposite bank. The river was too wide to jump and too deep to cross without a Droid being submerged. Garrison could avoid the crossing by moving up river eighty kilometers. Alpha force couldn't hold them here for long. More Matsui CombatDroids cleared the forest. Two Droid lances entered the river and began the crossing, while the remainder of the Matsui forces provided suppressing fire at the tree line where the Chameleons were hidden. Garrison had anticipated part of the trap.

Alex ordered, "All units return fire and begin withdrawal." Sporadic fire broke out all along the east bank. Alex didn't join in, he had to keep his position hidden for a few moments longer. On a private channel he contacted Visegrip, "Toad1 are you ready?"

Visegrip's gravely voice replied, "A stupid way to fight Major, but we are ready."

Alex could see a few of the bent and tied down willows with their satchel charges near the water line. He waited until the line of advancing Droids entered the target area, just beyond the deepest part of the river, then gave the signal. The CLATs fired their lasers not at the water bound Droids, but at the ropes holding the willows in place, and like ancient catapults the willows sprung forward hurling their giant satchel charges towards the Matsui force. Most of the charges detonated harmlessly in the river. One charge flogged the exposed head of a *Nimrod*. EMD shields were deactivated by immersion in water, so the *Nimrod* staggered as exposed armor decompressed. The second wave of satchel charges was even less effective, but they achieved the result Alex wanted. Some of the enemy CombatJacks seeing relative safety only meters away began firing their thrusters to reach the bank. As they arced through the air, their supporting fire from the opposite bank tapered off for fear of hitting the soaring Droids. As they landed on the bank, Alpha force struck with a vengeance.

Alex targeted a *Saber*, his remaining NPC scoured armor from its head and torso. He switched targets to a *Superscout* that had landed awkwardly, savaging it with his missiles and remaining laser. He watched as a CLAT squad jumped out from behind a tree and swarmed the staggering *Superscout*. All along the line, hidden tanks and infantry poured fire into the Matsui Droids as they reached the bank. It wasn't enough. More Droids strode out of the water. Their added fire overwhelmed his command. Alex ordered a retreat. Infantry first while the two Alpha Droids and their remaining tank held the line. Alex ordered the reflective smoke bombs detonated. The billowing clouds of smoke and refractive aluminum shrapnel confused the Matsui warriors long enough for Alex and Khorsa to escape. It was too late for their remaining *Pantheon*. An enemy *Battleaxe* hit its cowling with a EPC bolt and it crashed into a tree in a mighty fireball.

The two battered Droids fled after the surviving APC's and fast fleeing VTOL aircraft, when Visegrip came on line, "Toad1 to *Warlock* I have two enemy Droids bearing down from the south. We aren't going to get by them without help."

Alex answered, "*Warlock* to all units break Northeast, we will cover you." He and Khorsa continued due East until they spotted the two Droids. It was the ubiquitous *Roadrunner* XL again and another *Renegade*. Normally they wouldn't have posed much threat to the pair of SuperDroids, except both the *Stormwarden* and *Python* were badly battered. The four Droids dueled at long range, running parallel to each other. Alex only had his left arm NPC and Khorsa was down to a couple of rounds in his missile launcher. The two of them took hit after hit from the fresher Matsui Droids. Alex began to feel despair when the *Python* lost its remaining launcher and began to limp. His *Stormwarden* had lost two more radiators slowing his rate of fire to prevent an engine overload. The *Roadrunner* pilot smelling blood closed for the kill. Alex ordered Khorsa to flee with his now unarmed Droid, as he turned to fight what looked to be his last battle. The *Stormwarden* staggered under a DFM barrage as it charged. "Damn that pilot is good," He thought. Suddenly CLATs sprung from the ground firing inferno rounds and lasers. The *Renegade* was awash in liquid fire and its pilot panicked, turned and fled. Alex and the *Roadrunner* pilot exchanged fire again. More inferno rounds struck the *Roadrunner*. It was too much, the pilot withdrew gracefully, still firing his weapons. No panic there, Alex thought as he activated his Comlink, "I thought I told you to withdraw Visegrip?"

Visegrip with his evil rumbling laugh replied, "And miss all the fun Major."

Alex answered, "If you hadn't just saved my life I might court-martial you, but thanks, thanks to all of you. Now lets get moving."

The one sided duel went on and on all through the afternoon and into the evening. With Alex's pitiful force becoming less and less effective. Khorsa and his *Python* withdrew to Matsuisan for refit, the Droid was too damaged to fight any longer. Richtover's *Foxbat* was badly raked by laser fire and barely made it back to base. With only one StarFighter left, the Chameleons chose not to risk it in combat, and used it primarily for surveillance to Richtover's chagrin. Chameleon and Gurkha VTOL fighters were destroyed. The Matsui forces suffered as well. Losing some ground vehicles and another Droid.

Two hundred kilometers outside Matsuisan a small force of hover tanks and light Droids joined Alpha force. A storm brewed, with rain and wind grounding his remaining VTOL aircraft and hampering his supply lines. Alex's reinforced command waited along the last physical barrier before the city, Gobblers pass. The pass was not much of a barrier to a Droid, but it did provide excellent cover for its defenders and its high iron content made detection of mines difficult. the Chameleon's would use this to advantage. Alex hoped to hold Garrison here for a couple of hours. Half an hour into the fight, Garrison overwhelmed his little force and forced a retreat. They had taken heavy losses. Inexplicably The Matsui advance stopped after traversing the pass. Alex was to find out later that Garrison's mighty *Warlord Prime* had stepped on a mine. The Matsui commander was too arrogant to lead his force without his Droid so the whole advance stopped for field repairs. For once the Chameleons were in luck. Alex ordered everyone back to Matsuisan to reinforce the defenses.

He stopped, not 10 kilometers from the Matsui forces while a tech team attempted hasty repairs to a damaged leg actuator on the *Stormwarden*. Alex with his Comlink on the blink, had turned over command to Converse. He stood a lonely vigil in the storm tossed night, completely out of touch with events outside his sensor range.

Chapter 32

Alex was shadowing the Matsui force as it approached the outskirts of Matsuisan. With his Comlink on the blink, he remained out of touch with the rest of the Chameleons. False dawn colored the overcast horizon red, and sent eerie shadows scurrying through the sparse forest surrounding the city. It was going to be a cold wet day for dying, he thought morbidly. Alex spotted the advancing Guards. Garrison had his depleted forces arrayed in a classic phalanx. He had less then twenty Droids left many of them damaged in some way. With his 72 ton *Warlord Prime* leading the way, he marched on undaunted. The Matsui force passed the outer city defenses unchallenged. Alex began to wonder if the defenders had abandoned the city. Then as the sun breached the clouds, it reflected off a burnished line of Droids and tanks, advancing from the fort and city in the equally classic pincer. Simultaneously the ground along the second line of defenses erupted with anti-Droid infantry, while a lone StarFighter screamed from behind the distant fort to spread fire and confusion into the enemy ranks. Alex exalted, Brandon and his company had made it!

There would be no finesse in the final fight. the Chameleon Droids and tanks poured a wall of fire into their opponents. Using ammunition profligately. The Anti-Droid infantry swarmed around the Matsui Droids seemingly uncaring about their own survival in the maelstrom of fire. VTOL aircraft and the lone StarFighter attacked the fringes of the advance compressing the Matsui force inward into the hail of fire from artillery barrages. Garrison charged his *Warlord Prime* forward bravely trying to break through the encirclement, shouting challenges over his Comlink. A *Warlord* flanked by a *Mastiff* and a *Crossbow* holding the center of the Chameleon line, poured round after round of fire into the *Warlord Prime*, nearly slicing off one leg at the knee and savaging the head and torso of the assault Droid. The one legged humanoid machine continued to fight, dragging itself forward desperately even as the last vestiges of its EMD shield failed. Alex attacked from the flank, kicking a disoriented *Battleaxe* aside, he fired his NPC into the *Warlord Prime's* damaged cockpit. He had no regrets as the cockpit exploded outward killing Garrison. Moments later a *Katana's* sliver cannon savaged his *Stormwarden* battering his damaged systems. His Droid toppled forward out of the fight jamming his cockpit hatch and trapping Alex. He sat there and watched fragments of the raging battle with his damaged sensors.

The Matsui and Guard Droids fought valiantly. They had a slight numerical superiority, but the Chameleons were fresh, and better coordinated and equipped. It was a close fight, but the death of the Guard's commander and his fearsome *Warlord Prime* took the heart out of them. Soon Matsui and Guard Jacks were either surrendering or fleeing. Alex saw the last of them limp away as he tried to extricate himself from his jammed cockpit.

They had won! Alex finally shattered the damaged Duraplast hatch with a brutal kick, and crawled out into the smoke streaming skyward from his Droid, with Mamba still perched on his shoulder unconcernedly. He coughed a couple of times before he finally reached fresh air. The bone deep weariness he felt had him stumbling across the charred earth as he headed for the fort. He passed soldiers securing surrendering Matsui soldiers, while other men and women rushed around the field salvaging equipment, tending the injured and recovering the dead. Alex didn't feel anything but a vague mind numbing relief. Relief that one more desperate gambit had worked, relief that the Chameleons could finally get some rest, but mostly relief at not having to make any more life or death decisions.

He hitched a ride to the fort on a passing jeep. The driver didn't even recognize his commander through all the grime and soot covering Alex's unadorned cooling vest. He grabbed a field ration from a food bin as he saluted a guard. Then he decided to stop by his quarters and shower and change before heading for the Command Center. The Gurkha guard outside the security area recognized him fortunately, and passed on his location to the Command Center at Alex's request. Alex was in no hurry. For once he was going to let Brandon and the other officers handle the situation while he cleaned up. He collapsed onto his bunk as he entered his cubicle, just letting the tension ease out of his body for a moment. Mamba curled up on the headboard and went to sleep unconcernedly.

Alex awoke sweating and disoriented, for a heartbeat he felt a desperate need to maneuver the *Stormwarden* away from incoming missiles. Then he came fully awake and recognized his old quarters in the Matsuisan fort. He let out a ragged sigh of relief, as he climbed out of the cot, and went to the fresher to wash-up. He looked into the mirror and saw a face he barely recognized. Sunken cheeks and his usually perfectly groomed white hair, strewn all over his face in greasy locks. He hadn't looked this bad since leaving Banshee. Washed and changed into his undress uniform he headed back to work, looking a little better even though he was still bone tired. He left the still sleeping minicham behind for once.

He entered the Command Center to find most of his officers, the senior civilians and Roxanne huddled around the Comlink. He felt a sinking feeling in his stomach. There should have been just the standard duty roster, something was happening. Bolithio spotted him first and gave a cursory salute, while nudging some of the others. They went quiet as he approached and asked. "Well, what's going on now?"

Everyone looked at Brandon and the Princess. Brandon finally spoke. His face was noticeably nervous, "We have detected a number of incoming StarShips, Sir."

Alex thought, oh no not yet, "Have we identified them Captain?"

Brandon replied, "Some of them sir. Six shuttles have separated, and are on their way here as of 2100 hours. Some old friends are aboard."

Alex questioned, "Oh?"

Brandon continued, "Ambassador Alcorn is coming as the special representative of the Vegan Republic to Himalaya. Colonel Bayard and the Stingers are her escort. Their *Horatio* class shuttle *Navarre* will arrive in three days at their present speed."

McCloud commented, "Madame Alcorn herself, a most imminent lady and a confidant of President Houston. It is good that a person of her caliber was sent."

The sinking pit in his stomach kept getting worse, not the Bayards, they'd see right through him. He asked tight lipped, "And the others?"

Brandon again as spokesman replied, "Another shuttle is carrying both a special envoy from the Empire and Matsui's senior vice president Lord Tomarawa."

"Lord Tomarawa is considered one of the most brilliant businessmen and negotiators in the Empire. He has very powerful friends throughout the government. The fact that he has been sent here is not a good omen," said Elandra.

Alex sarcastically asked, "Well do you have any other good news for me?"

Roxanne pale faced answered, "The other four shuttles are carrying Asturian factions looking for me. I have contacted a number of them and requested that they take no military actions on this world."

Brandon added, "So far two have agreed to the Princess Heir's request. Though the Princess is not convinced Count Hightower's commitment will be kept. Count Bastille has responded by threatening to remove the Princess by force, and destroying anyone who gets in his way and we have no response from the other Asturian shuttles."

Alex in a forlorn voice asked, "How did they find us so quickly, and do we have any idea as to what kind of forces they have at their disposal?"

Lord Bonaduce spoke up, as he twirled the tip of his red mustache. "The Asturians backtracked the *Tiara II*, They were only one transit away, when word leaked out of the Princess's presence here. You shouldn't have opened the WH transmit station Major. There are spies everywhere including Asturian ones."

Alex his scar turning scarlet snapped, "If you were more circumspect in your dealings with the Princess, this might not have happened."

Before Bonaduce could reply, Roxanne seeking to head off a confrontation jumped in and changed the subject, "Both Hightower and Bastille were in the invasion of Fairhaven. They both command reinforced Droid companies. They must have taken casualties, but they may have picked up allies as well. So it's hard to tell how strong they are now."

Brandon offered his analysis, "Bastille and Hightower are sharing what appears to be a *Hercules* combat shuttle. Which means combined they can't have much more then a reinforced battalion, no more than 50 Droids."

Roxanne offered a little more reassurance by saying, "They don't trust each other, so I wouldn't expect them to cooperate."

Alex went over to the spatial tracking display to evaluate the situation himself, and to give himself time to think. The rest of the room went silent again. He was angry and he really didn't care who knew it for once. He regained control of himself, "OK, lets deal with this invasion right now!" Alex turned to the nearby Communications tech, "Open a general channel to everyone up there."

He took a deep breath, "To all inbound shuttles this is Major Alex Kane, Commander of the Chameleon Corps Mercenary Battalion. The Chameleon Corps is presently employed protecting the Symcorp and Matsui facilities on Himalaya under a state of martial law. All lawful ships are welcome to land at Matsuisan space field to...," He paused, "To discuss any legal issues that need to be resolved or to conduct lawful business. Anyone taking any action deemed hostile by me or my employers will be attacked by Chameleon space assets before landing. Some actions that will be deemed hostile are; attempting to land anywhere outside of Matsuisan space port, arming weapons during planetary approach, disembarking any military assets without permission and any damn thing else I decide. Director McCloud and Lady Yamamoto our employers will act as liaison to the representatives of the Empire and the Republic. As for the forces from Asturia, Princess Rudnauman is under Chameleon protection. You can meet with her peacefully or you can fight. I would highly recommend the former course."

Alex turned away from the Comlink, and turned towards Brandon, "Captain secure the landing field here and make preparations to fend off a planetary assault. Elandra, Mr. McCloud I hope you can convince the representatives of your nations as to the rightness of our actions. Princess I hope you can keep your country men peaceful. Frankly I've had enough. I'm going hiking for a couple of days. I'll be back in time for the fireworks." Alex walked out of the room without another word leaving half his officers open mouthed at his uncharacteristic outburst.

Alex returned to his quarters to claim Mamba and the supplies Roxanne and he had gathered for a camping trip planned weeks earlier. It was a bad reminder of thoughts he was trying to suppress. He smashed Roxanne's kit across the room in a fit of rage. He knew he had to get away from people before he did something regrettable. Here he was the triumphant commander of his own mercenary company and it was nothing but ashes to him. Deep down inside he had been anticipating this time to try to reconcile with the Princess. The loss of that opportunity felt like the death of a close friend. More fawning lordlings would seek her favor, undermining Alex's only real hope of happiness. On top of the stress of the last few months it was too much even for him. The internal demon he had controlled all his adult life was almost loose. He had funneled that anger into staying alive until he met Roxanne. She had made it fade away for a while. Now the demon was back with a vengeance wanting to strike out at anything and everything in meaningless destruction. The scar bisecting his face felt hot as he rushed out of the fort and headed into the forest at a run. He ignored the startled bystanders he passed. He ran and ran until his physical exhaustion matched his mental fatigue and the demon was back in its cage.

Chapter 33

The smoke rose lazily from the small campfire through the mist shrouded overhanging branches. The dawn sunlight barely penetrated through the dense forest into the little glade overlooking the steep banked creek. A figure gracefully rose from between the giant gnarled roots of a great bole, and glided past the campfire down to the trickling stream of water, bending over to wash bare skin covered by a patch work of scars both ancient and new. The man hauled in a line with two large blue speckled fish and returned to the camp, his white pony tail bobbing to the smooth rhythm of his walk.

Alex cleaned his overnight catch while preparing the rest of his breakfast. Gathering your own food was a novelty he still enjoyed. He was still a little squeamish about eating animal flesh, even fish, but he was getting over it. Building on the rudimentary skills learned from Kaseem during the invasion of the GenClone base, he was getting good at camping. He ate and packed up his camp in preparations for another move. Then he sat down completely still on a stone outcropping and watched the sun burn off the mist and reveal the emerald forest. The cacophonous calls of dawn risen birds slowly drowned out the sound of the burbling brook.

With one exception he had buried himself in the mundane daily chores of living since leaving the fort. He broke his isolation only once, four days ago he returned to the fort to command the defenses as the inbound shuttles approached. The landings had proved anti-climatic. None of the various Asturian factions chose to violate the restrictions. His threat, and the divisiveness among the Asturian nobles resulted in everyone abiding by a fragile peace. At least when it came to open warfare.

The war of words was quite another matter. No sooner had the shuttles landed then the new arrivals started violently arguing their competing claims. Alex thought he was rested enough to deal with the situation. After listening to accusations, backbiting rumor mongering and legal diatribes for the better part of a day, he decided he needed more time alone.

A rustling broke his reverie. He placed his left hand on the butt of the laser pistol and watched something progress through the undergrowth clumsily. Moments later a disheveled Claudia and Brandon burst into the clearing covered with brambles.

Brandon on spotting Alex swore, "Frakke Alex. Where have you been?"

Alex looked at the two of them for a moment and then grinned at their ridiculous appearance, "I've been wandering around. how did you find me?"

Claudia peevishly replied, "Javreel finally agreed to get some local hunters to help us track you down. They pointed out your fire and left us up there." As she nodded up the hill while continuing to brush herself off. "Damn it Alex you can't keep abandoning your responsibilities like this. We need you back running the Chameleons before things get completely out of hand."

Alex answered, "I know."

Claudia ignoring his remark, "The UFP, Bayard, the Imperials, everyone wants to talk..., What did you say?"

Alex repeated, "I said I know. I was planning to return today. I don't have the right to dump this mess on Brandon and you any longer."

Claudia mollified added, "No one denies you needed a rest Alex. You've had a lot on your shoulders lately."

Alex ignored her remark and asked, "How is the situation with the Asturians?"

Brandon looked at Claudia for a moment before speaking, "Hard to tell. There's been a lot of fist fights and one knife fight over what to do with the Princess. Ah, your name keeps coming up."

Claudia angrily added, "Those ignorant savages still put a lot of credence in chastity. All her potential suitors are upset about her relationship with you. Somehow she's managed to keep them from killing each other, or us. Though how she puts up with those cretins I don't know."

Brandon interrupted, "Don't forget to tell him that he's public enemy number one on all their lists. Watch your back around the Asturians Alex. I don't put anything past most of them. Even though I kind of like them. Asturians are cut throat when it comes to their politics, but they're honest and friendly to a fault otherwise. By the way, Lord Bonaduce is now Count Bonaduce. We received a priority message on the WH transmit verifying the death of his father and older brother."

Claudia added, "He's taking it hard. His family was close."

"Its bad news for the Princess as well. His oath to protect her is null and void now that he's become Count. Apparently Counts are forbidden from taking personal fealty oaths to Asturian royalty. Part of their checks and balances system. She's basically without any personal supporters now. The Monarchists still want to make her queen but on their terms," Brandon said as he moved forward and crouched down next to Alex.

Mamba fluttered down from one of the trees and landed on Alex's shoulder right then. Poking her head in his pocket for some nuts. Alex absentmindedly caressed her scales as he replied, "Brandon, my back is always watched and I'm always careful." He turned to Claudia curious about her tone, "If I didn't know better Claudia, I might have detected a note of sympathy for Roxanne."

Claudia paused before replying, "I guess I have been a little hard on her. I've spent more time talking with her in the last few days then I did on the *Tiara II*. She's nice once you get to know her." She hesitated a moment longer then blurted out, "She's also still in love with you. The poor girl thinks she has to sacrifice her personal desires to fulfill her role as Princess. And it's eating her up. Hell, I wouldn't trade places with her for anything. She has all this responsibility and no authority to get anything done. A ruler's absolute nightmare."

Claudia paused a moment, "Alex, no one else will say it, so I will. She claims she pushed you out of her life to protect the integrity of the Asturian throne. I think she did it to protect you, and if you had any sense you'd know it."

There was quiet in the glade. Embarrassed by the revelation Brandon and Claudia stood around trying to avoid looking at Alex. Alex sat thoughtfully on the slab sided rock and asked, "Are you sure you're not being manipulated by her Claudia?"

"As sure as I know I'm in love with this big dope." Punching Brandon in the shoulder affectionately, "And you're a pig for asking that question about the woman you love."

Alex started chuckling, which turned into a laugh of relief and then joy while his two friends looked on in wonder. Then he jumped up and shouted "Well that changes everything. Lets go. I have a Princess to save and a kingdom to place at her feet."

He walked up to the two of them and slapped them heartily on their backs as they began climbing up the embankment. After reaching level ground they marched in single file through the forest. Alex leading the way with exuberant strides, was moving too fast for the bewildered Brandon and Claudia to do anything but follow. He stopped suddenly and turned. Brandon and Claudia collided with him, as a frown appeared on his face.

Claudia said, "I think I like the change in you. But what are you planning Alex?"

"I think I have an outline of a plan to extricate Vega, the Empire, Roxanne, and the Chameleon's out of this mess honorably." He replied then hesitated a moment before continuing more deliberately. "It just hit me that I may be committing the Chameleons to a course of action that may not be favored by its officers. And I need to be completely confident that the Chameleons will follow where I lead. Unfortunately I can't reveal the details just yet. Not even to you."

Brandon and Claudia exchanged glances and then burst into laughter. Alex looked on baffled by their amusement. Finally Claudia spluttered out an explanation, "Alex you are so dense in some ways."

"Oh."

Brandon regaining control answered the unasked question, "Alex you've become one of the most legendary mercenary commanders of our time almost overnight. A year ago you commanded one medium SuperDroid. Again and again you've overcome nearly insurmountable odds. And you've done it in a way that has brought you the absolute loyalty of the Chameleon's. We will follow you to hell and back after what you've accomplished, and that includes the two of us."

Alex replied, "You're right, we have achieved a great deal together. The two of you deserve as much credit as I."

Claudia explained, "Neither one of us destroyed a Droid lance single handed or extricated a Ranger lance from a sure fire trap on Fairhaven."

Brandon added, "Or defeated Colonel Pryde and Commander Vicegrip the ultimate GenClone super soldiers in single combat."

Claudia continued, "And we didn't kill the monstrous TripleNull grand master Major Demalle in hand to hand combat. Now that they've opened up that dungeon of horrors he called a home, and freed his pitiful prisoners, you've become a hero on Fairhaven. In fact Count Monteverde will award you the Fairhaven Legion of Honor for your deeds." Brandon gave her an exasperated look. "Damn, I was supposed to keep that a secret, I'm sorry Brandon."

Brandon exasperated, replied, "And you always complain I can't keep a secret."

Alex interrupted, "All right, so I have built a reputation as a good CombatJack, and a bad man in hand to hand combat. That still doesn't mean I have a right to lead the Chameleons. Claudia you once told me you can't run a mercenary outfit with two masters. I think you're right." Alex hesitated a moment and then spoke softly, "I need the Chameleons to save Roxanne and her kingdom, but I won't place all of you in danger for personal reasons."

Brandon offered in a serious tone, "Do what you have to Alex. We'll back you all the way."

Alex thoughtfully replied, "I can't prove to you or to myself that I'm looking out for the Chameleon's best interests? In fact I will probably favor Asturian interests over those of the Chameleons, if things work out the way I want."

Claudia embarrassed said in a subdued voice, "It doesn't matter Alex. The Chameleons will follow where you lead. Right or wrong. If you betray our trust we will deal with it when it happens."

Brandon added, "Alex why are you so worried about this plan of yours?"

Alex contemplating the risk he was asking of his friends replied distractedly, "I plan to use the Chameleons to place Roxanne on her throne. I will try to avoid it, but it will almost certainly involve heavy fighting at some point."

Brandon commented, "We're mercenaries Alex. That's what we do, fight under contract."

Alex snapped his finger, "That's it. I will have Roxanne hire the Chameleons. Brandon you're going to have to negotiate the deal. I obviously have a conflict of interest."

Brandon chuckled, "I think I'll assign Claudia that task. She'll squeeze every credit she can out of your Princess."

Claudia frowning said, "Unfortunately the Princess has no wealth until she becomes Queen." Sighing, "It looks like another salvage contract."

Alex snapped, "No, I believe I can solve Roxanne's funding problem. If you aren't too expensive Claudia. I will give you one bit of advice." With a smile like a shark, "Sacrifice as much up front payment as possible to increase your salvage percentage."

Claudia laughed, "Why do I suddenly think you're going to be on the other side of the negotiating table from me."

They all laughed at the thought of Alex and Claudia haggling. Then by unspoken consent, the three of them continued their march back to the fort, speaking only of the unimportant details of life, the inconsequential things that bond friendships. Their plans and dreams for the future were left for another time, another place.

Chapter 34

The next morning, at his request the UFP council met with Alex. The eighteen members sat in formal garb behind a temporary table mounted on a dais, whispering to one another. Alex thought the room was deliberately arranged like a judicial proceeding with him as the accused. Subhadars Chondra and Chia'll, representing the interests of the Gurkhas, sat to Alex's left denoting their lower status. Alex thought they would be the only ones sympathetic to his position.

He had been up all night preparing his presentation and evaluating the council members. He was familiar with the Dorans and their positions. Head Monk Cockburn, one of the original members of the council, and a survivor of the attack on the Capitol, was the leader of the Isolationists. He and a small vocal minority wanted to expunge all foreigners from their world. Alex wondered about Cockburn, his history was not consistent with the fanaticism of the others Isolationists. The rest of the council were new members. Most of them were Conservators, and naively wanted a return to the status quo. Their most vocal spokesman was the newly crowned Cardinal Braiden. His main opposition was the new High Imam Kareema Shah, leader of the neo-proselytizers. She and her followers believed it was time to spread their faith through the stars.

It was amazing that they were all present on such short notice. Alex filed that fact away. He might be out numbered, but all the factions wanted something from him, or they wouldn't have come out in such force. Cockburn now the head of the Council, called the meeting to order, "This meeting was called by me at the request of Major Kane. He believes he can find a solution to our present difficulties with the foreigners on Himalaya. Major I believe I need to warn you, that there is no consensus on this Council as to how we should respond to recent events, but we will listen to your proposal with interest, and may have some alternatives of our own."

Alex noticed a hasty enigmatic glance pass between Cockburn and Shah. Interesting, the two of then as allies made no sense, but something was going on. Alex stood up and bowed, carefully sucking in a deep breath before what was the most important speech of his life, "Members of the ruling council of Himalaya, Honorable Chairman and representatives of the Gurkha Nation, I am honored at the opportunity to speak before such an illustrious body. As a military man, I often find it useful to review the situation and options before discussing a course of action. I believe it may prove helpful here.

Alex noted a couple of annoyed looks directed at the Gurkha officers. Many members of the UFP still wanted to treat Gurkhas as second class citizens and did not like their inclusion in this meeting. Alex thought, that will change and soon and continued, "Let me summarize the present situation. Matsui's military adventures violated its lease agreement for the Empire portion of the Crescent Isle. Some of you also believe the military response by Symcorp and the Chameleons also constitutes a violation."

One of the new councilors jumped up waving a contract in the air and yelling, "We don't believe Symcorp and you mercenaries violated the lease contract, we have irrevocable evidence, mercenary scum!"

Cockburn interrupted the forthcoming tirade, "I believe we all agreed to hear Major Kane out! We can express our positions later. I apologize Major. Please continue."

Anxious murmurs followed the outburst, while Cockburn glared up and down the head table. The Council finally quieted and faced Alex who continued his speech. "Personally I happen to agree with the learned Councilor. This body is well within its contractual rights to declare a breach of contract by both Matsui and Symcorp, and to order them to leave this world." Alex looked all along the raised table. He had their full attention now. The Conservators were smiling or nodding, the Proselytizers, who wanted the income from the foreign corporations to fund their programs, were frowning. Others like the Dorans and Cockburn kept their thoughts to themselves.

Alex then dropped his first bombshell, "Of course that is not a viable option." Alex waited until Cockburn asked the question, "Why is that Major?"

"I think many of you already suspect the answer but I will state it openly. Both Vega and the Empire invested hundreds of millions of credits to develop the SymXtend process. Neither of them can abandon corporate assets that will provide significant taxable income, not without a fight. Of even more significance are the following facts I have extracted from Symcorp and Matsui files. As of January 1, 2459, Symcorp has become the number one rejuvenating drug in human space. It accounts for thirty-six percent of the market and is clearly superior to all other products. Most of it is going to the wealthiest elements in the Human Sphere. They will not permit this Council to cut off the flow of this critical drug. Forces far beyond your ability to control are now committed to the continued harvesting of SymXtend on Himalaya."

The stunned silence following his revelation turned into a raucous discussion. Alex doubted that any of them had understood the true extent of SymXtends importance. Alex easily detected the undertones of fear amongst the Conservators and Isolationists. The Proselytizers were also suddenly concerned. They wanted to control the wealth generated by SymXtend, not be controlled by it. Cockburn finally brought the Council back to order and asked Alex to continue.

Alex complied, "Let me tell you my military perspective on the situation. Himalaya has now become a strategically important world. Maybe as important as one of the high tech CombatDroid producing planets. That leaves you with only three options. One, continue trying to return to the status quo, which amounts to planetary suicide. You will create the exact same environment that resulted in Matsui's power grab. Except now the sharks will be the great nations, so the scale of the conflict will be larger. Himalaya will become a battleground between imperial armies." Alex paused to let them digest this. The parochial pacifists on the Council would need time to assimilate this fact, before he continued. "Ordering one or both of the enfranchised companies to leave Himalaya will have the exact same outcome.

Option two, abandon your freedom and join one of the great powers. In this case you could ask for protection from President Houston or Emperor Bukhara and become a full member planet. This off course would substantially reduce your independence. It might prevent war coming to Himalaya but that is not guaranteed. Almost certainly your way of life would slowly be compromised by the pernicious influence of your new rulers."

Again Alex stopped to let the Councilors discuss his comments. They finally quieted down.

High Priest Doran spoke dryly, "You have expressed the concerns some of us have about the present situation with great clarity Major Kane. Many of us on this Council have been thinking along the same lines, though maybe we had not admitted to ourselves the full gravity of the situation." He swept the room with a steely glance, a look that said I told you so. "As you might suspect neither of the options you have outlined is palatable. So we are now primed for you third option. Major?", as he crossed his arms and waited Alex out.

Alex smiled, "Let me respond to your unasked question with one of my own. What is the root source of the UFP's present difficulties?"

Shah, pounding the table shouted, "Matsui!"

Cockburn yelled, "All foreigners!"

Alex answered, "You are both partially correct, but you still haven't identified the root cause, why are the foreigners here?"

Ambassador Doran offered, "They are here because of SymXtend, our world has nothing else of value."

Alex knew that Himalaya had other things of value, but it didn't serve his interests to point this out, "You are correct Ambassador. If you could eliminate SymXtend, the off worlders would leave."

Cardinal Braiden thoughtfully commented, "Of course there is no way for us to destroy the source of SymXtend, and even if we could, by your own admission the great powers would try to stop us. So what is your point Major?"

"You're right Cardinal Braiden you cannot eliminate SymXtend production from Himalaya." He paused dramatically, "But you could turn over control of the producing areas to a third party not affiliated with the Empire or Vega!"

Pandemonium broke out. Cockburn, his face suffused an angry red, "So you would have us give away our only source of wealth and turn over control of our world to some unknown third party. Do you think we are mad?"

Alex, with a false mask of grim outrage, bowed formally," You seem to have rejected my proposal without choosing to hear it. I will leave you to resolve your dilemma without my help. Good day gentlemen, ladies."

High Priest Doran snapped, "Wait." Turning to Cockburn, "I have dealt with the Major before,

I believe we ought to hear him out. None of our options are acceptable, let us not reject anything out of hand."

Cockburn nodded querulously, "Go on Major."

Alex pleased with the response he had elicited continued his speech, "There are only two ways to guarantee peace on the Fringe, remain so insignificant that the avaricious don't bother with you, or become militarily and economically important enough to discourage potential invaders. This planet remained peaceful because it had nothing of value to the rest of humanity. That is no longer true. The only way you can keep your world peaceful is to become too important to be easily attacked."

High Priest Doran interrupted, "What does that have to do with turning control of SymXtend over to a third party?"

Alex answered politely, "You are unwilling and unable to defend SymXtend production on Himalaya. Whether the members of this Council like it or not, SymXtend production will need to be defended. The Republic and the Empire and humanity will accept no less. Therefore, if you are unwilling to throw in your lot with one of them, your only other option is to turn over control of SymXtend production to a third party."

Cardinal Braiden caustically snapped, "You wouldn't be volunteering your services, would you now Major?"

Alex noticed many of the Councilors were receptive. It was time for the paradigm shift. "Not directly, your Holiness, as a matter of fact I would recommend you turn over the Crescent Isle, the Moon Everest and a few other key facilities to the Asturian throne for an annual percentage of the wealth generated from SymXtend. In return Asturia would take over responsibility for defending all of Himalaya with some key provisions to insure they do not abuse their power."

Braiden screamed, "Ridiculous! You expect us to put our faith in the hands of barbarians from Asturia. Why they have been one of the greatest threats to our peace for hundreds of years!"

Alex, answered disarmingly, "You have hit on one of the advantages of using the Asturian throne. You turn a potential threat into an ally. But I think once you hear the constraints placed on the Asturians, you may see the advantages."

Ambassador Doran spoke up, "Major we are not blind to the chaotic situation on Asturia. There isn't even a monarch to negotiate such an agreement. And even if Princess Rudnauman is placed on the throne, she will not have the ability to control her recalcitrant Counts. Besides the Republic and the Empire are not going to give up their interests on Himalaya, as you yourself noted."

The Councilors were now looking at obstacles to such an agreement rather then rejecting it out of hand. Alex hid his pleasure at this change. "Let me answer your last objection first. I am convinced that once such an agreement is reached between Asturia and Himalaya, that the Asturian throne can negotiate an acceptable settlement with Vega and the Empire. I cannot reveal to you why this is so, but you can make the contract contingent on such an outcome."

Alex scanned the Councilors and saw growing interest, he was about to tell them a series of half truths. "I am negotiating this agreement for Princess designate Rudnauman." *It would have been true if he had talked to her ahead of time, he hoped.* "She will be the signatory for Asturia. Moreover she has contracted the Chameleons to defend her interests both here and on Asturia, and has received pledges of support from many of the Counts." *Support from the royalists who had their own interests in mind.* "Given this level of support, it will not be long before she is fully restored to her throne." *Long is a relative term.* "I will personally pledge to you that the resources to defend Himalaya will be available." *If I'm lucky I may be able to deliver.*

Braiden interrupted angrily, "Are we going to sit here and listen to this drivel. We will be going from the frying pan into the fire if we negotiate with the Asturians. At least Vega and the Empire are moderately civilized."

Alex used his ace card now. "I would agree with His Holiness, in general but one provision of the contract will prevent violations of any agreement and insure your continued way of life."

Shah, coyly asked, "And what would that be, Major?"

Alex turned to the Gurkha commanders. "The Queen will assign the primary defense of this planet to the Gurkha regiments with CombatDroid forces held in reserve. Funds from SymXtend profits will go to outfit the regiments with top of the line infantry gear including anti-Droid equipment, with the Chameleons assigned to train the regiments. The Gurkhas live by a code, that does not permit them to breech a contract. They will serve the Asturian throne only as long as the throne abides by its contract terms with the UFP."

Cockburn thoughtfully commented, "Why do we need the Asturian throne to use the Gurkha's to defend our world. We could employ them directly and hire a mercenary unit to train them and provide CombatDroid support ourselves."

Chondra stood up stiffly, bowed, and answered the question with heartfelt vehemence, "The Gurkha regiments will no longer serve this Council directly. Historically you have insured the death of thousands of our people, by not providing us with the equipment we needed. Worse, you have stuck your collective heads in a hole every time an external threat has appeared. It is Gurkha lives that die while you vacillate on how to respond. We will no longer take military direction from pacifists!"

Chondra then turned to Alex, "Major we mistakenly believed that we would be reporting to you. I will have to review the change in the command structure with the other Subhadars before I can commit the Gurkha nation to this plan."

The objection startled Alex. He had mistakenly assumed the Gurkha officers would understand the contract had to be with an institution and not an individual, when he had presented it to them the evening before. "Of course Subhadar, I apologize for the misunderstanding. But I hope you make it clear to your fellow officers that I am just a man. Contracts between great nations have to be transacted between institutions that outlive men, such as this Council and the Asturian throne. I also hope you can reassure them that I hold myself personally responsible for making sure this arrangement works."

Chondra nodded stiffly, saluted, and sat back down, while a rising tide of noise rose from the dais.

Cockburn shouted above everyone else, "The Council has much to discuss Major. Can you and Subhadars Chondra and Chia'll leave us to our deliberations for three hours. We will reconvene at 1300 hours."

Alex and the Gurkhas left bowing politely as they exited through the massive double doors guarded by saluting Gurkha troopers. Alex turned to Chondra as he exited, "My apologies again Subhadar, please…"

Chondra interrupted, "No Major, it is I who should apologize. I understand your position and I believe I can get the other regimental commanders consent to your proposal before the Council reconvenes. I will need but one reassurance from you."

Alex replied, "If I can do it Subhadar."

Chondra continued, "For a period of five years you personally must be in charge of Himalaya's planetary defenses. It will take us that long to become properly equipped and trained, and I trust no other with the defense of my home world in these dangerous times."

Alex hesitated then said, "I will have other responsibilities Subhadar. It is unlikely that I can command Himalaya's defenses all the time."

Chondra replied, "That is not necessary Major. What I ask is that you have overall responsibility for this world's defenses."

Alex relieved answered, "I can promise you this Subhadar, if this planet falls to an invader, I will die defending it. How I will defend it will be up to me. Is that assurance enough?"

Chondra with a slight bow replied, "That is satisfactory Major Kane. We do not commit our honor lightly and it has been our experience that neither do you. I will relay our discussion to my fellow commanders, and have a response before we reconvene."

Alex detected the veiled threat in the Subhadars words as he smiled knowingly in response. "Thank you Subhadar. If you will excuse me, I have much to do." The two men saluted and went their separate ways.

Alex charged off down the hall to Brandon's office, he needed to find McCloud quickly. Storming into Brandon's office, he shouted, "Have you found him yet?"

From behind the door a laconic voice responded, "If you're referring to me, I've been here for over an hour."

Alex spotted McCloud leaning back in a swivel chair next to Brandon. "Director McCloud, I am very anxious to talk to you."

McCloud answered, "I gathered that from the Captain's frantic efforts to keep me here. By the way I'm no longer a director. Symcorp has fired me. It seems that even my reputation couldn't prevent my becoming a scapegoat for this mess."

Alex smiled, "Good! I'm sorry for your loss Mr. McCloud, but it makes my life easier."

Wryly the diminutive man responded, "Not much of a loss really. It was about time I moved on anyway. How can I help you."

Alex emphatically answered, "I have a position for you. I desperately need a man with your managerial skills."

McCloud laughed, "Major even if I wanted to work for a mercenary unit, you couldn't afford my services."

Alex replied with his best shark like smile, "First I consider you a friend and I would prefer you call me Alex from now on."

McCloud nodded with a slight smile, "And you can call me Martin."

Alex answered, "I wasn't planning to hire you for the Chameleons."

McCloud replied with a surprised, "Oh?"

Alex continued, "I want to hire you to negotiate the new contract ceding the Crescent Isle and some other assets on Himalaya to the Asturian throne. Then I want you to negotiate new lease terms with the Republic and the Empire for the Crown. I have another proposal after that which you might find even more interesting."

McCloud popped up out of his chair, then sat back down thoughtfully while looking from Alex to Brandon.

Brandon excitedly asked, "You really pulled it off?"

Alex with a slight frown answered, "Not yet, but I think I have them hooked." He then went into the details of the negotiation with the two of them.

McCloud whistled, "Brilliant Alex, you don't need me to do your negotiating for you. Though I must say the Isolationists may still give you trouble."

Alex smiled, "I have one last gambit if they prove to be an obstacle. I can't discuss anything else with you Martin until I have your commitment. Well are you interested?"

Martin replied, "Whether I'm under contract or not, I'll hold everything said here in confidence, as I'm sure you already know." McCloud sat back in the chair, his hands clasped before his face for a moment, "You do know you're treading a very dangerous course. You're involving yourself in the great game of galactic politics."

Alex responded dead seriously, "Martin, I'm involving myself in that game more than even you suspect. I don't have much choice, it's the only way I know to save people I care about. And Brandon I'm not just referring to Roxanne. The Gurkhas need a champion and the pacifists of this world need and deserve protection. I know the risks and am walking into them with my eyes open."

McCloud smiled warmly, "I accept, I always have had a soft spot for the underdog. But it's going to cost you. I don't come cheap."

Alex reached his hand out, "Done. We can work out satisfactory terms later." The three men shook hands, all of them feeling that an important event in history had just taken place.

Alex added, "When you're negotiating the details keep in mind the following long term objectives I have in mind. First I plan to turn the Crescent Isle into the infantry mercenary capitol of known space. Not only will we train and outfit Gurkha regiments but we will be the hiring hall for infantry and Droid mercs for the entire Fringe."

Brandon startled commented, "The UFP won't like that."

McCloud replied, "It won't matter what they like, if we structure the contract right. But I don't like to cheat during negotiations Alex."

Alex explained, "It's in their long term interests. Mercenary supplying worlds are among the most peaceful. No one wants to risk attacking a world swarming with mercs and all the great powers need to maintain good relations with mercenaries they may eventually need to hire. The Himalayans may not see it now but this is in their long term best interests."

McCloud nodded agreement, "You're right, I never gave it much thought. But the mercenary recruiting worlds of Sahara and Pollyshaven have been at peace for ages."

Alex continued, "We also may have a civil war, but on Asturia not here." Alex contemplated the horrors of internecine warfare. He put the thought aside and continued explaining his overall plan, "After we have finalized all these negotiations I want you to become the Asturian Royal Chancellor For External Economic Affairs. As Chancellor I want you to develop an economic plan to integrate the abundant supply of cheap Himalayan labor with Asturian technical expertise and mineral wealth to develop a viable growing codependent economy. Keep in mind other planets may end up choosing to join us. You'll have some SymXtend generated income to finance the changes needed. Also I'm giving you a free hand to negotiate deals with outside companies, individuals, governments or anyone else. I'm counting on you expertise to keep us from getting into a compromising situation or antagonizing our neighbors as we expand into the Fringe."

McCloud replied only half jokingly, "You aren't planning to form you own empire, are you Alex?"

Alex paused before replying, "No, but I do plan to make the Asturia/Himalaya alliance big enough and strong enough to discourage external threats."

McCloud noted cautiously, "It's going to have to get a lot bigger than it is."

Alex answered wryly, "I know."

They all looked at each other in silence as they contemplated the implications of those two words.

They finalized the details over lunch and then returned to the meeting hall. Alex had swept the hall for bugs the previous night. He had Gurkhas and Nobunaga's ICO force maintaining a security blanket around the proceedings. The last thing he needed was third party interference with the Council's secret deliberations. When Alex entered the room with McCloud, they were all waiting for him.

Cockburn, taking a deep breath, snapped, "I don't recall extending an invitation to Director McCloud, Major."

Alex answered formally, "Mr. McCloud is now employed by the Asturian throne as its chief negotiator, sir. He has the complete trust of Princess Rudnauman and myself. If we come to a settlement today he will be responsible for working out the mutually satisfactory details." Alex had scored points, the Council had a high regard for McCloud.

Cockburn opened the conference with the minutes of the last session. Then the conference degenerated into a shouting match. With a vocal minority of Isolationists totally opposed to Alex's proposal arguing with the lukewarm supporters. Others wanted to add their own pet programs into the agreement. Alex listened intently. Given time he thought the Council would come around to his point of view. The trouble was he didn't have time. He decided to use his ace in the hole. Cockburn finally regained control of the meeting. "As you can see Major, we are unable to make decision at this time."

Alex replied, "Sir, I believe I may be able to resolve the present conflict with an addition to our agreement."

Cockburn ordered, "Continue."

Alex removed a data chip from his pocket and placed it into the main computer display.

A. M. Megahed

Information on one of the three forgotten habitable worlds discovered by the Seeker StarShip scrolled across the screen.

Braiden asked caustically, "What is the point of this? Why should we care about some obscure world?"

Alex unflappably answered, "This uninhabited world was discovered and seeded hundreds of years ago by a TCA Seeker class ship. The records were lost until recently. It's coordinates are only two transits away from here, and are known only to the Chameleon's senior officers. Those of you who find coexistence with outsiders intolerable could colonize this world under our agreement. Funds from SymXtend profits could subsidize the costs of colonization if the Council chooses to do so." Looking at the flushed, eager faces, he knew he had them.

Alex had deliberately selected the least appealing of the lost worlds from the TCA cache. The UFP Isolationists believed in the purifying properties of hardship and struggle. Also the less appealing the world the less likely others might covet it. Besides he had uses for the other lost worlds.

It was Cockburn who finally broke the silence, "Am I to understand you are offering us this world in exchange for the Crescent Isle, Major?"

Alex replied firmly, "I am offering you as much of this world as you choose to colonize with the understanding that it remains an Asturian protectorate. I am offering you complete control of all internal affairs within any region you colonize, including any of the islands or either of the two smaller continents. You may colonize the main continent but Asturian law will prevail there. One point I need to make clear. I don't have days to wait for you to make a decision. You have to decide now."

A tide of noise arose over the chamber as everyone stated shouting at once. Alex dozed standing up while listening to two hours of mind numbing speeches. It became apparent that there was no way the UFP could reject access to a virgin world for their crowded population. McCloud startled Alex out of his wide eyed nap with a jab. The Council was ready to really negotiate. A selected group of Councilors, Alex and McCloud adjoined to a smaller room and began the serious discussions.

Alex thanked heaven a dozen times that evening that he had recruited McCloud. No detail was too small to become an issue during the endless negotiations. Without the ever calm McCloud, Alex would have been overwhelmed and the negotiations might have failed. They signed the final agreement near dawn. Alex and McCloud left the conference room satisfied with the terms.

McCloud, gleefully whispered, "I think that's the most fun I've ever had in my life."

Alex looked at the bespectacled man in disbelief, "You must be deranged, I would rather chew glass with an acid chaser then go through that again."

McCloud laughing as he slapped Alex on the back explained, "We've just negotiated a federation of three worlds, a lucrative contract to control the most valuable drug in the Universe and military control of this region of space!" He slapped Alex again in glee and then whispered, "And most of it was a bluff. You haven't even talked to the Princess about what you're doing and she doesn't have the authority to negotiate the deal anyway. I can't wait to tell the Vegan and Imperial negotiators about this. The look on their faces. I think you better get the approval of the Princess before we meet with them tonight or this could be a disaster."

Alex, unemotionally answered, "She won't come out of seclusion until the meeting with the Asturian nobles after tomorrow. I've tried but she's being watched too carefully by them for me to see her before then."

McCloud's eyes grew big. "You're joking, the Asturians will drill her on this deal and she won't know anything about it. The whole thing will fall apart!"

Alex with a wicked grin answered, "I guess I'll have to crash the Asturian Council meeting. I'm getting tired of hearing about how those louts are pushing Roxanne around." Grimly, "It's time someone put a stop to that." Alex mulled over another scheme as they went back to the officer's suits to catch a nap and to change. He smiled inwardly as a nasty surprise for some of the most vociferous opponents of Roxanne bubbled to the surface. "Martin, can you find out for me who has legal title to the shuttles and StarShips the Asturians are using?"

McCloud answered, "I think so. I should be able to verify their registry. What mad scheme are you hatching now Alex?"

"Get me the data first then we'll see." On that note they split up and went to their separate quarters.

Chapter 35

Ambassador Doran, Martin and Alex entered the teak veneered conference room to the stares of the already seated representatives. The demarcation between Imperial and Vegan contingents was rigid. Colonel Bayard, Ambassador Alcorn, Symcorp board member Dr. Morales and their assistants sat to the left of the oval table. While Lord Tomarawa, and Baron Sanyosan, and their underlings sat on the right, with Lady Yamamoto sitting at the base of the table denoting her ambiguous status. There were three empty seats at the head of the table. Doran, Alex and Martin sat down in them.

The wealthy, well-connected Baron Sanyosan was the first to speak. An unknown commodity to both Alex and Martin, the recently retired commander of the 5th Legion was new to his diplomatic responsibilities. "High Priest Doran, what is the meaning of this? Inviting a mercenary and the discredited Mr. McCloud to these discussions!"

Doran nervously replied, "Major Kane and Mr. McCloud are here to negotiate the lease agreements around the Crescent Isle..."

Bayard in surprise interrupted, "You've designated the two of them as your negotiators?"

Doran with a twinkle in her eyes answered, "Not exactly. They are the negotiators for the Asturian Crown. Under an agreement we have just signed, we have ceded all rights to the Isle to Asturia."

McCloud nonchalantly broke the stunned silence. "Thank you Your Holiness, I think we better get started. We have a new proposal, we want to review with this..."

Dr. Morales exploded, "this is ridiculous! If you wanted to sell the Crescent Isle, you should have given us the opportunity to bid on it. How can you turn the SymXtend supply over to these, these pirates Doran!"

Alex interrupted, "Dr. Morales, there is no reason to be insulting. The UFP Council and the Asturian Throne have come to a politically negotiated settlement. It's a done deal. I think the issue before us now, is how do we manage the production and supply of SymXtend."

The inscrutable Tomarawa replied, "There is also the issue of security for Himalaya and the SymXtend producing facilities."

Alex leaned back casually before continuing, "The Asturian Throne is now the guarantor of that security, and there is no reason for either Vega or the Empire to concern themselves with that issue any longer." He noticed a light go on in the silent Alcorn's face. She began to see the outline of his plan to diffuse the situation. Alex suspected Tomarawa, his lidded eyes unreadable also understood. The others sat in disbelief.

Sanyosan shouted in outrage, "I think everything is still an issue. The Asturians can't even defend their own world, let alone Himalaya after the beating they took on Fairhaven. Besides the Crown is still in dispute."

Alex, firmly answered, "That is our concern not yours Baron. If we should fail to defend Himalaya there may be reason for outside interference. Until then as two independent worlds our internal agreements are no concern of yours."

Morales standing up indignantly snapped, "You are wrong Major. We have binding agreements with the government of Himalaya. You cannot arbitrarily abrogate them with this slight of hand! What's more you have illegally in your possession property belonging to Symcorp." Sarcastically, "You and that traitor McCloud are not going to get away with this. How long have you planned this power play Martin. First you hire the Chameleons for Symcorp, then they conveniently end up your employers."

McCloud stood up angrily and raged, "Morales you're a crook and a coward. You got your underlings to fire me without cause and now you accuse me of betraying my employer without proof."

Alex not sure whether Martin was acting or not interrupted, "Gentlemen, gentlemen let us not lose our tempers. I want to make it clear to all of you that I hired Mr. McCloud just yesterday. I did not even hint at such an opportunity until then. Primarily because it hadn't occurred to me until recently that Asturia would need his services." Alex waited until the two glowering men sat back down before continuing. "As for your agreements with Himalaya, they are still binding on Asturia as long as they are not already breached."

Alcorn politely asked, "Exactly who is it you are representing in these negotiations Major? The Asturian crown remains in dispute. You continue to claim you represent the Crown. Does that mean Princess Rudnauman?"

Alex answered, "We represent the Princes, rightful heir to the throne. Before you all object, keep in mind that the Princess and her loyalists are capable of complying with the provisions of this agreement and that is really all that should matter to you."

The discussion continued with multiple objections raised. Alex and Martin answered them patiently until the representatives exhausted all legitimate excuses not to negotiate. The contract between Himalaya and Asturia was valid and everyone there knew it.

Alex looked around the conference table. Most of the faces were noncommittal. Alcorn had just a hint of approval in her eyes while Bayard looked concerned. The only outright hostile face was Morales, who just glared at McCloud like an enraged Otcat.

Alex finally initiated the true negotiations, "My proposal is simple. The Republic and Empire should both continue to operate SymXtend extraction and distribution facilities on the Crescent Isle, with some modifications to the existing contract. The most important of these changes will be; one, Asturia will now be responsible for Crescent Isle security. This will of course result in an increase on the tariff for extraction, to pay for this protection." There was some grumbling but they let him continue, "And two, Matsui will no longer be permitted to operate on this world. Their violation of contract was willful and severe. They will have to sell their facilities to a buyer acceptable to the Empire and Asturia."

Tomarawa commented inscrutably, "I cannot speak for the Empire, but this proposal is patently not acceptable to Matsui. The issue of contract violation has not been arbitrated and you continue to hold many of our assets, including this facility and our corporate Droids illegally. Once those facilities are returned to our control we can discuss these proposals. Until then you are just another pirate." There was no heat in Tomarawa's voice. It was difficult to tell what the man was really after.

Sanyosan, looking first at Tomarawa for guidance, blustered, "The Empire will not be dictated to! This proposal is patently absurd. The false accusations of contract violations need to be arbitrated first."

Alex leaned back thoughtfully, then he leaned forward and emphatically spoke, "I am going to be brutally frank. We all know the evidence of contract breach is overwhelming and Matsui will lose any arbitration. Neither Princess Rudnauman nor the UFP have the time for a lengthy mediation. You all know this and some of you want to use this fact to coerce me into negotiating a less favorable deal." He had their attention, "But let me make my position clear. The Chameleons will continue to control the Crescent Isle and the production of SymXtend until a new agreement is reached."

Tomarawa unemotionally noted, "The Empire might consider that an act of aggression on your part."

Alex replied, "Well that would be extremely unfortunate since Asturia will fight and ask for Vegan assistance if the Empire initiates hostile actions against Himalaya. Ladies and gentlemen, we can continue posturing and risking a collapse of the Republic Coalition détente, or we can negotiate a mutually acceptable agreement along the lines I have outlined. If you think about it, it really is the best solution for everyone concerned."

Tomarawa answered wryly, "Except of course for Matsui."

Alex firmly answered, "Matsui has blatantly violated its agreements Lord Tomarawa. Your company needs to be penalized for that and the loss of life caused by its actions." Alex swept the room with a challenging stare, "Matsui's status on Himalaya is a divisive one. Let us see what we can agree to, then address the thornier issues."

His suggestion was generally accepted and serious discussion around a comprehensive settlement began. Slowly they reached agreement on all the key points except for Matsui's status. Alex and Martin agreed to reduce the tariff increase to SymXtend and the Matsuisan owners for a period of five years to pay for military equipment and facilities already in their possession. They also agreed to a number of security arrangements with Vega. The session broke up in the afternoon with all but the Matsui issue resolved. As they left the conference room, Alcorn and Bayard intercepted Alex and Martin.

Alcorn said, "Very impressive Alex. So far you've done very well. You're going to have to back down on Matsui or the agreement will fail. I have dealt with Lord Tomarawa before, he will not permit his company to lose face by admitting guilt and that is what you are forcing him to do."

Bayard with a frown added, "Debra is impressed with your negotiating skills Major. I am concerned that you may have overextended yourself. You don't have the military assets to defend Asturia and Himalaya. Someone will test you and if you falter your whole scheme falls apart like a house of cards."

Alex, fatigued by the frantic pace of the last two days, replied abruptly, "I have resources you don't know about Colonel." Referring to the Gurkhas. "As for Matsui, I won't back down because it invites future opportunism if I do, and also because it would be unprincipled."

Alcorn commented, "I understand your concerns Alex. But Tomarawa will undermine everything you've accomplished if you stand your ground."

Alex answered, "We will see."

Alcorn looking at him curiously before continuing, "You are a remarkably self confident man, Alex." Then with a smile she changed the subject, "We are having a reception tonight for my daughter, in honor of her promotion to Commander of the Stingers. I know she would like you both to attend. I hope our negotiating differences do not interfere with our personal relationships."

Martin replied sauvely, "I wouldn't miss it, Ambassador."

Alex also agreed to attend, but informed them he would be late due to a prior commitment. Surprised at Alcorn's earlier comment, he asked, "I don't consider myself especially self confident, Ambassador. You were hinting that I am arrogant. I'm curious as to why you believe this."

Alcorn laughed, "Alex I know you and I believe its just ignorance on your part. You simply do not comprehend who you are dealing with, some of the most respected and feared mediators in known space. For instance, you seem unconcerned about dealing with Lord Tomarawa, a man whose accomplishments in the corporate and diplomatic arenas are legendary."

Alex shrugged, "On Banshee I learned to do what had to be done to survive. Handling dangerous men and dangerous situations was a daily occurrence. Honestly Ambassador, I haven't met anybody outside the mines that could equal my enemies on Banshee."

Alcorn, with a raised eyebrow said, "And off course you survived?"

Alex recalling life in the mines, replied grimly, "I was the only one who survived." He turned to the Colonel and changed the subject abruptly. He didn't have time to dwell on those he'd left behind. "Sir if Bridgette is given command of the Stingers, what happens to Captain Bouchard?"

Alcorn answered with a concerned look, "Either he takes a demotion or he quits. He has many other lucrative offers. The Vegan high command offered him a Major's commission and command of an assault company. It will tare Bridgette apart if he leaves." Looking at Bayard with pierced lips, "I think you have placed both of them in an untenable situation dear."

Alex in surprise asked, "You think Bouchard might quit?"

Bayard snapped, "If she can't handle this, how can I place her in charge of hundreds of lives as commander of the Brigadoons?" Alex noted the tension between the two of them over this subject. As usual, he looked at the revelation as an opportunity. He excused himself quickly, and went on to call on Bouchard and Bridgette. There would be time for a much needed rest later.

A short while later, Bridgette and Bouchard invited him in to their sitting room. It was no great secret they were living together. He thought, that might be one of the reasons the old fashioned Colonel wanted to bring their relationship to a head. The three of them exchanged histories since their separation and laughed over some of their shared memories. Bridgette became unnaturally terse. Alex couldn't help noticing the worry lines around her eyes. Their mood grew somber as they discussed lost comrades.

Bridgette suddenly changed the subject as was her wont, "You know about my promotion, then you must also know we're not exactly thrilled about the turn of events. Father is trying to push Sting into making a decision about me. That's the only reason he didn't offer him a new command of his own. He can be so rigid about some things."

Alex asked, "What are your plans Sting?"

Bouchard with a frown replied, "Kind of a personal question isn't it Alex, or should I call you Major now?"

Alex ignored the tension and answered the question openly, "It's still Alex to you unless you want it different. I didn't mean to pry, But I have a stake in your decision,"

Bridgette said, "Oh?"

Alex continued, "I'd like to offer the Stingers a sub-contract with the Chameleons and Sting a battalion command if you're interested Sting. You get to stay together and Sting gets promoted to Major. It's better then the slap in the face your father intended. You might have guessed the Chameleons desperately need experienced officers."

Bouchard and Bridgette stared at each other and then burst into amused laughter. Bouchard finally explained, "Alex you have audacity. Even if you could afford us, why would we affiliate a crack mercenary company like the Stingers with your make shift outfit? No reflection on your abilities Alex. You have done remarkable things, but you aren't experienced enough to command that size force." Dejectedly, "Alex we just aren't willing to sacrifice the Stingers to fulfill our personal desires."

Alex wouldn't give up that easily. He explained his overall goals to them to their open mouthed astonishment. "...You're right Sting, I may be overextended and as you can see I need experienced people desperately. But I still think the Stingers can benefit by working under contract to the Chameleons and Asturia."

Bouchard looked meditative, while Bridgette commented, "Alex your crazier then me if you think you're going to pull this off. You're going to get yourself killed and your command destroyed, trying to put your Princess on her throne!" For a long moment no one spoke.

Finally Bouchard broke the silence, "Alex if you can get Tomarawa to agree to pulling Matsui off of Himalaya, I will accept your offer." He then turned to Bridgette. "I'm just an ordinary CombatJack. The Colonel is never going to welcome me as a son-in-law unless I make a reputation on my own. This could be my best shot, and if Alex gets Matsui to leave, I'm going for it."

Bridgette dazed, put her hand to her throat as if to hold back a scream and whispered, "You don't have to prove yourself to anyone Sting, not even my father." Then in a firming voice, "You know I can't go risking the Stingers on Alex's hare brained plot without making a mockery of my responsibilities. We will have to separate. What about our plans to challenge the GenClones together?"

Bouchard in torment spoke, "Bridgette, maybe I need to prove to myself I can make it on my own. I'm not asking you to sub-contract the Stingers." Looking away, "I understand you now have to look out for their best interests,"

Alex uncomfortable with the pain he had engendered, interceded, "Bridgette you do know I have a depot full of GenClone and TCA equipment. If you choose to accept a contract with the Chameleons, I will give the Stingers first shot at the enhancement kits, as well as lucrative financial terms. Enhancing the Stinger Droids is the only way you'll ever be able to challenge the GenClones. It would be a smart move for your company."

Bridgette looked contemplative before she finally replied, "All right Alex. Let me think about this while you deal with the Matsui issue. I will tell you my intentions tonight at my so called promotion celebration."

Alex departed awkwardly, feeling contemptible for taking advantage of people he liked to achieve his own ends. He wondered if that was the real cost of leadership; the constant betrayal of friendship to achieve larger goals. He felt uncharacteristically listless and needed rest before he bearded Tomarawa in his den. He whispered to himself, "Back three days and I'm already worn out and mumbling to myself."

Chapter 36

The surprisingly large office for a shuttle was tastefully furnished. The elegantly dressed oriental man leaning back in a hand crafted swivel chair ignored Alex as he was escorted into the room by an elegant receptionist. Alex looked around curiously, spotting state of the art electronics hidden behind expensive wall panels in the massive mahogany desk. Everything spoke of wealth and power including the beautiful but unobtrusive receptionist.

Tomarawa let Alex stand for a moment before looking up from his terminal, "I don't usually make appointments on such short notice Major. You have ten minutes."

Alex, without comment, walked over to the desk and placed a data disk carefully down on the polished surface, then sat, uninvited, in a plush high backed chair. Mamba slipped from beneath the collar of his uniform and faded into the hand woven silk tapestries behind the desk. Tomarawa picked up the disk and up-loaded it on his terminal. He scanned the data almost without expression. Alex, hyper-tuned to Tomarawa's reaction, did observe a very slight twitch half way through the report. the Matsui executive then sat back, clasped his hands together and looked up at Alex, commenting noncommittally, "This is interesting. Where did you get it?"

Alex responded with his own question, "Is the data interesting enough to change your position on Himalaya?"

Tomarawa's face spread into a semblance of a smile, "You think you can blackmail me with this outdated news about corruption on Banshee. I am disappointed in you Major."

Alex smiled back, "I am just a simple soldier Lord Tomarawa, and defer to your better judgment in such matters. But are you not concerned that Emperor Bukhara IX will be upset at finding Matsui has twice dealt with the GenClones, his arch enemies." With a nonchalant wave of his arm, "No doubt the tax evasion and other criminal activities outlined on that disk can be dealt with appropriately by a man in your position. After all it was probably just a couple of rogue managers exceeding their authority. I doubt anyone would consider it a pattern. Certainly not one justifying the dismantling of a great conglomerate like Matsui." Then in feigned indifference, "But that tie in with the GenClones, most disconcerting."

Both men stared at each other in complete silence for a long moment. Alex would wait Tomarawa out. If the data he had down loaded from the manager's office on Banshee didn't give him leverage over the Bukharan noble, his whole elaborate plan fell apart.

Alex was getting nervous when Tomarawa finally spoke, "You are correct. If the unproven allegations in this disk get to certain sources, it could cause Matsui harm. Unfortunately I cannot agree to pulling Matsui out of Himalaya, even if I wanted it." Tomarawa paused for a moment deep in thought, "I will be honest with you Major. Matsui can not afford either the loss of face, or the loss of the investment here. We have poured hundreds of millions of credits into this world. The whole corporation is at risk if we suffer a second disaster like Banshee."

For the first time Alex saw a crack in the impenetrable facade, but it didn't ring true. Why would Tomarawa so readily admit to his problems. It was out of character and gave Alex the advantage. Even more bothersome was his attitude. It almost seemed the Matsui executive was pleased with the information on the disk. It made no sense. Alex did a mental shrug. He didn't understand what was going on so he would stick with his original plan. Matsui was in a bind, and he could give them a way out. First a little more pressure. "Lord Tomarawa, I would like nothing better then to see the demise of Matsui." Pausing, "But I am more interested in finalizing the Himalayan/Asturian alliance. So I have a proposition for Matsui, that saves face and salvages most of your investment on this world."

Tomarawa unimpressed, "I am listening."

Alex smiled, "Gift the facilities in Matsuisan to the Emperor, as a show of support to the Empire." Tomarawa sat impassively waiting for Alex to continue. "Then get Baron Sanyosan to gift to Matsui the earnings from the extraction facilities for the next five years in a show of gratitude. I am sure the Baron will be receptive to such a proposal from you. Matsui would recover its investment and receive a moderate, if not spectacular return, as well as gain enormous prestige by this act of national fealty. You personally would gain the gratitude of the Emperor for resolving a messy issue."

Tomarawa seemingly unconcerned, "Who would run Matsuisan for the Emperor?"

Alex wryly answered, "I rather thought a management team led by Mr. McCloud could contract to run the facilities. His personal integrity is above dispute and his other responsibilities for Asturia will keep him here."

Tomarawa began a deep rumbling laugh that turned into a side splitting guffaws. Alex looked on in astonishment as the elegant executive practically fell out of his chair before regaining control of himself. Wiping tears from his eyes, Tomarawa replied, "Major, you have unbelievable gall. You just offered to take control of my assets for a pittance." A toothy grin spread across the long face giving it a devilish appearance, "What's worse, you're going to get away with it, if you agree to keep everything in this disk confidential and erase all record of it in your possession."

Alex startled, nodded agreement. Tomarawa reached across the table and offered his hand, informally sealing the arrangement. Alex shook the proffered hand and replied, "I didn't expect it to be this easy. Frankly I'm surprised."

Tomarawa replied with a raised eyebrow, "Why is that Major? You came in here expecting me to accede to you demands because of this disk. Why are you surprised I wouldn't recognize the strength of your position and capitulate immediately?"

Alex answered forthrightly, "You are not without leverage sir. It must be evident to you that I need a quick agreement."

Tomarawa smiled, "But Major I want you to succeed. The Empire also has a stake in maintaining the uneasy peace with Vega."

Alex suddenly nervous asked, "But you don't represent the Empire? Or do you?"

Tomarawa with a wave of his arm replied, "Ah, you begin to see. I think it would be best if I explain, but you must keep everything I tell you confidential." Alex nodded. "As you suspect I am not just a VIP for Matsui. I am here in many capacities. The data disk you have provided, will break open a conspiracy between traitorous elements in the Empire and the GenClones. This conspiracy threatens the very heart of the Empire. Consider my quick agreement to your offer, reward for that information. Besides it does enable Matsui to extricate itself from this untenable position. So I serve both my masters well. Something I am not always able to do."

Alex thought: I'm dealing with Imperial Security! "It seems, I gave away too much. But we shook on a deal."

Tomarawa with a raised eyebrow commented, "You negotiated very well Alex considering you didn't know the true value of the information you had. Tell me how you acquired it and maybe we could work out an appropriate enumeration."

Alex grimly answered, "I don't want spy money Lord Tomarawa, but I'll tell you anyway." Alex skipping certain details, outlined his escape from Banshee and the ransacking of the Fort's computer files."

Tomarawa commented, "A fascinating story Major. If I didn't have so much objective evidence I might not believe it." In an almost friendly tone, "Alex, if you ever get tired of playing soldier come and see me. My master can use a man with your talents."

Alex smiled, "I am content where I am Lord Tomarawa. If you will excuse me sir, I have a party to attend."

Tomarawa asked, "You are going to the Bayard affair?"

Alex replied, "Yes."

Tomarawa offered, "Then let us go together, we can finalize the details in my car, and it should be interesting to see the reaction as we enter together. I must caution you to keep our agreement to ourselves until I have had a chance to brief the Baron."

Alex, trying to cover his anxiety asked "You don't foresee any problems sir?"

Tomarawa replied with a knowing smile, "Oh, I wouldn't worry, the Baron knows his role."

Alex thought Alcorn was right, I am out of my league, as they walked to a sleek ground car. The smooth trip from the space base to the Bayard's temporary residence on the outskirts of Matsuisan was unnerving for Alex. Tomarawa was suave congeniality during the ride. Every time the two men agreed to a detail, Alex recalled the devilish grin of the little Lord. He wished he had brought Martin along. He kept worrying about what he was giving away. Alex had no doubt that Lord Tomarawa could destroy his madcap scheme easily. He was going to have to correct his statement to Lady Alcorn. There were people scarier than a Banshee gang lord.

Their arrival together at the Bayard's party did cause a stir. Baron Sanyosan came over immediately and took aside Tomarawa. Alex could follow the course of the conversation by the changing expressions on the Baron's face. The man was a fool. Everyone in the room could see his surprise, anger and then his acquiescence. Tomarawa nodded to Alex afterwards, clearing the way for him to notify others of their agreement.

Alex explained the situation first to McCloud, Claudia and Brandon, as they wandered over to join him. He overheard Tomarawa outlining the new agreement to the Bayards at the same time. It was like listening in stereo. Everyone was surprised and throughout the night both Tomarawa and Alex had to deflect probing questions about the reason for the change in the Matsui position.

An equally astounding event occurred late in the evening, when many of the celebrants had loosened up under the influence of the freely flowing liquor. Bridgette and Bouchard jumped up on a table, shortly after speaking to Alex and made an announcement.

Bouchard, happily shouted, "Ladies and gentlemen, friends and colleagues. I am pleased to say that this lovely lady," as he placed his arm around Bridgette, "has finally agreed to marry me." Cheers and friendly banter greeted the announcement. Bouchard, a big grin plastered on his face, waved his hands for silence. "On a more serious note, I am resigning my commission with the Brigadoons to accept command of the Chameleons 2nd Battalion." Silence greeted the news. "Bridge I believe you have something to announce as well?"

Bridgette answered seriously, "As the new Commander Operator of the Stinger Company, I have accepted a contract offer with the Chameleon's 2nd Droid Battalion under the command of Major Sting Bouchard. For the Stinger Jacks out there, we get first shot at the Chameleon's GenClone enhancement kits and a chance to prove ourselves defending the Himalayan/Asturian Alliance. Best of all from my perspective the Stingers get to continue serving under their old commander, Sting."

As a ragged cheer went up, Alex looked over to see Colonel Bayard looking at him enigmatically. Alex walked over to confront the Colonel. "Sir, I hope you aren't displeased by the turn of events?"

Bayard answered, "I am too surprised to have formed an opinion yet. Other then knowing you were behind this. You are an endless source of surprises Major." Sarcastically, "Or is it Colonel or your Majesty, yet?"

Alcorn overhearing the conversation walked over and tucked her arm into her husband's and said with a big smile, "Don't harass the young man dear. He just saved your daughter's happiness and restored the balance of power between Vega and the Empire, and the really nice thing about it is he did it all for the love of Princess Rudnauman. Both your motivations and your actions are noble Alex."

Alex in embarrassment replied, "I think you give me too much credit Lady Alcorn. I am not even sure of my motivations sometimes. And what I have done has placed people's lives at risk."

"No one has pristine motivations Alex. Most of us believe we try to do right and yet many times we cause great harm instead. That does not mean we ought to stop trying," Alcorn, answered seriously as she squeezed the Colonel's arm and continued with a smile. "But now I am getting too serious. This is a happy occasion. My only daughter is getting married and it's time I made my way through that mob, to tell her how pleased I am. Are you coming dear?"

Colonel Bayard looked at Alex again and shrugged as a small smile crept over his face, "I guess

211

I have to defer to your judgment Debra. I always did like Sting, I just wanted him to stop deferring to Bridge."

"Colonel, I believe this was his decision all the way, Bridgette went along when he demonstrated it would benefit the Stingers. Personally sir, I have always thought Major Bouchard to be everything I would like to be. An officer and a gentleman in the truest sense of the word. I am honored that he would agree to serve with me," Alex commented.

Alcorn, with a knowing smile offered, "Bouchard envies your hell rake, free wheeling style Alex. He wishes he could act on his decisions as quickly as you do. Though I must say I am happy he isn't like you in that way. It's hell on wives. I won't envy yours."

Bayard added, "Don't get me wrong Alex. I have the highest opinion of Bouchard. My daughter couldn't have done better." Then in a very serious tone, he added, "Try not to get them killed." The Colonel turned and walked away, not waiting for a response. Alex stood there uncertain about what to do.

Alcorn patted him on the shoulder as she walked by, "It's not you Alex. He likes you a great deal. The Colonel thinks the times are passing him by and he's not ready yet. He'll get over it."

Chapter 37

Alex left the party well after midnight. Things were going surprisingly well. Now all he had to do was bring the Asturian nobility to heel and hope Roxanne agreed to his strategy to place her on the throne. He was tired which made him careless. Halfway down the hall to his quarters a shadow slipped out of a recess and reached for him. Startled, Alex grabbed an extended arm and twisted to avoid any unseen weapons. Assailant and victim tumbled to the floor. Mamba unexpectedly fluttered away disinterestedly, rather then helping her master. Alex rose into a combat crouch and found himself looking at a disheveled Roxanne.

She smiled, "Alex we must stop meeting this way." Rubbing her sore shoulder, "The Princess Heir can't go around bruised all the time."

"What are you doing here? I thought you had to stay in seclusion until the Council meeting tomorrow. Something about having to complete your training as a Triarch," Alex answered in surprise.

Roxanne looking around furtively said, "You're right I'm not supposed to be here. Let's go to your room, and I'll explain." They hurried over to Alex's cubicle, and entered.

Alex sealed the door and asked, "Well?"

Roxanne, reached up and languorously kissed him, Alex unable to help himself responded breathlessly. They broke apart as Roxanne exhaled, "Is that anyway to meet the love of your life."

Alex in a half hearted attempt at firmness, "Roxanne don't start, we need to talk. A lot is happening."

"I know. that's why I'm here. But no matter how much our future duties intrude on our personal lives, you had better always take the time to treat me like a woman, or else." Roxanne answered seriously.

Alex didn't know what to say. Two minutes alone and she already had him on the defensive. For once he did the right thing. He leaned forward and kissed her back. Roxanne broke the lip lock this time, and sat on his bunk still holding his hand. Smiling again, she huskily purred, "That's better. Now we can get down to business."

Alex sat on the bunk next to her. It felt good to have her thigh pressed up against his. The fatigue left him, like a fog in a rising sun, replaced by arousal. Alex hoarsely, "Can business wait a while?"

Roxanne responded by stretching out on the bunk with a come hither look on her face. Alex came.

A long time later. Alex happily holding his princess said, "I guess I will never get any sleep again. But I don't seem to mind right now." As he smiled stupidly.

Roxanne extricated herself from his arms, and put her clothes back on, "I don't have much time and we have a lot to do. Merisa has kept me informed, about what's been happening, but I think I need to understand what you're up to."

"Who's Marisa and you never did explain to me what you're doing here?" Alex asked.

Roxanne replied, "All right Alex, I guess I have some explaining to do. Marisa is the senior Triarch healer with the Asturian forces. As soon as she found out I had gone Triarch, she ordered me into seclusion to receive a crash course in my new powers and duties. There was so much I didn't know and stil don't." She suddenly looked away, "I'm so sorry Alex. The way I treated you was abominable. I was so afraid of failing my duties as Princess Heir, I turned against the only man I could ever love. Worse I almost betrayed my nation and the Triarchy itself in the process."

"There is nothing to forgive. I understand better then most being overwhelmed by unwanted responsibilities. I think I always understood why you left me. I just couldn't accept it." Alex said as he hugged her closer to him.

"Alex, you don't understand. I'm a Triarch now. When I seduced you, I was a Triarch." Roxanne replied emphatically.

Alex half mockingly groaned, "I'm not going to have to listen to another convoluted explanation of what it means to be a Triarch."

Roxanne grinned and poked him in the solar plexus. "Yes you are. I told you once, a Triarch is naturally attracted to a man who is a born leader of her community. By marrying and channeling the energies of the male leaders of Asturia we have maintained peace and freedom for our people. That, more than the matriarchal throne is the key to Asturian survival and prosperity. The senior Triarches believe Asturia has reached a crossroads. They don't know what to do about it. But they believe a strong charismatic leader is needed."

"Is that supposed to be me?" Alex said as he sat up.

Roxanne frowned as she answered, "Marisa isn't sure. But she says I'm very likely a Truzen Triarch, which means my ability to select the right mate for my community is nearly infallible. She says I should follow my instincts in selecting the Prince Consort. My instincts led me to you."

Alex ruminated over the news for a moment before saying. "I'm not sure I like the idea that you love me because of some incomprehensible intuition. But I guess it's a lot better then you not loving me at all." Then he gave her another big squeeze.

Roxanne hugged him back and asked with a raised eyebrow, "You don't object to becoming Prince Consort?"

"Oh, I've resigned myself to that fact. Once Claudia told me you loved me, I knew the only way we could be together was to secure your kingdom for you and become your consort, with all that entails." Alex answered.

Alex then explained his overall plan and what had happened.

Roxanne commented, "The details are more unbelievable then the rumors I've heard. I still don't understand how you got Lord Tomarawa to agree to withdraw from Himalaya?"

"I promised him not to tell." Alex replied.

Roxanne pensively said, "Tomorrow, I plan to tell the Grand Council of my choice of you for Prince Consort. It could lead to open warfare. I have an idea to prevent that."

Alex skeptically said, "I don't think there is any way to prevent a civil war on Asturia, Roxanne. There are just too many intractable differences among the nobles. The best we can do is to make it short and minimize casualties."

"No Alex you're wrong! I've already set in motion powerful forces to head off any rebellion." Evasively she continued, "You don't need to know the details, but many of the leaders of Asturia given incentives will support me and my claim to the throne."

After a long thoughtful pause Alex commented, "Your Triarchy again."

Breaking away from Alex Roxanne turned, faced him and said, "Don't underestimate its influence. Your actions in forming the Himalayan Asturian alliance have already gained you and me great status amongst my people. Your military prowess is unquestioned. If we handle ourselves well in the council meeting tomorrow, and can neutralize Count Hightower, opposition to my ascent to the throne could collapse."

"That's a big 'if' Roxanne. Hightower wants to rule Asturia and from what I understand, he has enormous support amongst the northern barons," said Alex.

Roxanne smiled, "If we can weaken him and make him look the fool, that support could wither away. Especially if the Triarchy opposes him back home."

Alex thoughtfully answered, "You know your people better then I do. How do we neutralize him?"

"The *Hercules* combat shuttle, *Astor Queen*, is the property of the Crown. Hightower is in possession of it right now. Captain Prebble has always been a strong supporter of the Rudnauman lineage. If we can capture the ship before the meeting tomorrow, Hightower would lose much of his support."

Alex's brow creased as he replied, "I've already looked into that option. If there was some way to recover any of the Asturian shuttles without recourse to violence I would. But I don't se how it can be done without a fight. As commander of the Chameleons, I guaranteed safety for all those who came in peace. I can't break my word Roxanne."

"Alex, we could stop a civil war! Is your word more important then the lives of thousands of people?" Roxanne emphatically whispered.

Sincerely Alex said, "No, but to become a ruler by disregarding a promise is asking for disaster. I told you once, I would follow you any where as long as I kept my honor. That hasn't changed."

They stared at each other angrily. Finally Roxanne snapped, "Pig headed fool! Isn't there anything I can do to change your mind?" She stormed off the bed shaking her luxurious hair aside, "I don't want to rule by fighting my own people."

Alex saw the real pain and horror she felt at the thought of civil war, but he wouldn't change his mind. Then he had a glimmer of an idea, "Roxanne, the *Astor Queen* is carrying a number of different contingents from Asturia. Are any of them loyal to you?"

"One of Count Bonaduce's vassals has a Droid lance on board. Is that important?" She answered.

Alex's expression said, not that frakking Count as he asked rigidly, "How far do you trust him?"

Roxanne reading his thoughts answered, "Your jealousy is unfounded, Tomas wouldn't touch me or the Crown. He's madly in love with Count Castile's daughter. Unfortunately they're traditional enemies.

Alex continued impatiently, "I don't need to know his life story. Can he be trusted?"

Roxanne smiled leaned forward and put her arms around his neck, "Alex I'm your fiancee, not your subordinate. I can ramble if I want to, and besides you needed to know. Yes he can be trusted with my life and yours."

Alex sighed, "I guess I've got a lot to learn about women."

Roxanne only half mockingly replied, "Not women, just me. Now what are we going to do."

Alex with a wily smile replied, "As commander of the Chameleons, I can't attack the *Astor Queen*, but if a contingent aboard the ship were to decide to secure it for you, its rightful owner, I as your fiancee could participate."

Roxanne slipped out of his arms and said, "You and Bonaduce working together?"

Alex slyly replied, "Unless you have a better idea?"

They looked at each other as Roxanne said, "If you weren't risking your life, it would almost be funny.

Alex laughed, "You're going to have to learn to laugh at serious things too Princess, otherwise all the laughter will be gone from your life. I learned that in the mines."

Roxanne looked away then pensively replied, I'll have to come of course. Captain Prebble won't acknowledge your authority without me there." Alex abruptly stopped laughing as Roxanne responded to his expression, "Don't look at me that way. I'm right and you know it." A long silence followed.

Alex knew she was right but still wanting to find some way out asked, "What about your seclusion? Everyone will know you violated it."

Firmly she replied, "My seclusion ends today. It's after midnight. I can't help it if the Counts thought I would remain sequestered until the council meeting."

Alex looked at Roxanne thoughtfully. She had definitely grown up a great deal since he last saw her. This was a more decisive, person. A woman confident in herself and her abilities. He knew she had made her mind up, and like him she wouldn't be denied her place. "All right, but only if you agree to obey my orders to the letter. Is that clear?"

Meekly she replied, "Yes dear." Then she jumped into his arms, "You can't keep me out of danger Alex. Neither of us can rule without taking risks, not on Asturia."

"I know, but you're going to have to let me try to minimize the risk to you." He said as he looked away a moment apprehensively, "Please don't take chances. You mustn't die on me Roxanne. I couldn't bare it!"

She looked at him seriously, then smiled and unbuttoned his already half opened tunic. "That's the nicest thing anyone has ever said to me. But you also mustn't take everything so seriously. After all no one lives forever," then she pushed him back on his bunk playfully.

Alex groaned, "I was kind of hoping to live through this night at least." After a long interlude, "We don't have much time. We have a shuttle to capture.

Alex sighed, "Ah time, its always in such short supply."

Chapter 38

The wavering wraith like outlines progressed jerkily across the cracked spaceport tarmac. Slinking from shadow to shadow, the figures blurred by light distorting Chameleon suits, crossed the field unobserved by the few bored guards stationed around the scattered shuttles. The little group disappeared into a refueling pit not far from the largest shuttle on the field. Then one of the indistinct figures jumped from the pit and sprinted across the last open stretch of Duracrete sliding silently behind a massive shuttle support strut unnoticed. A short while later the guard stationed at the sealed main shuttle ramp flicked his cigar away and wandered lackadaisically on his scheduled round. Like a hunting Otcat, the blurred figure leaped from behind the strut and soundlessly grappled the surprised guard into submission. The way now clear, the rest of the squad dashed across the open stretch of tarmac and joined the figure and its unconscious victim beneath the *Astor Queen*.

"One down two hundred plus to go," Bolithio whispered jestingly, as she finished securing her prisoner.

Alex signaled everyone to hide as he and Bonaduce began scaling the support strut to the port side emergency escape hatch. Bonaduce produced an electronic key and unlocked the small opening. The new Count exuding his annoying boyhood charm said, "That was easy. Now let's rendezvous with my supporters and take this ship."

Alex without responding waved the others up and clambered through the hatch. The squad skulked through the nearly evacuated storage bays, between Droids and tanks interspersed with tons of other equipment. A few off shift techs were laboring away at general maintenance. They were easy to avoid in the cluttered storage areas, particularly since Bonaduce led them on a carefully scouted route. When they reached the main turbo-lift, they found an unconscious Hightower retainer and a dozen Bonaduce vassals hidden behind crates and massive support struts. The Bonaduce partisans immediately bowed down before their new liege and whispered undying support to their Count. Alex cut them off, "We're exposed out here. Count Bonaduce get your people moving. We have to reach the bridge before we're detected."

After some hasty discussion, They split up into two groups, each taking a separate turbo-lift.

The larger group led by Visegrip went down to secure the hopefully unmanned engine room. The remainder of the original group joined by two guides slowly worked their way up towards the bridge. Most of the shuttle's crew and passengers were asleep. With tasers and bindings they quickly immobilized any passengers awake and unlucky enough to get in the way. The little group left a trail of unconscious bodies hidden away in lockers and unused rooms. Alex had made it absolutely clear that lethal force was forbidden on this mission. He hadn't permitted any combat weapons and he knew his team felt naked without them. Their success depended on a bloodless coup and Alex was willing to risk his squad to accomplish that.

They ran into one nearly insurmountable obstacle along the way. A loud, late night card game in the crew's lounge next to the main corridor blocked their path. After a hastily whispered discussion, they formulated a risky plan. One warning and hundreds of sleeping troopers could swarm out of their quarters and capture them. Two of the Bonaduce retainers made their way boldly into the smoke filled room and asked to join the game. When everyone sat back down, one of them faked choking on a chicken wing. Fortunately the tipsy card players fell for the badly, overacted display. The rest of the squad charged in an tasered the distracted night owls. Only a few half uttered screams marked the small action. The squad members held their collective breaths waiting for a reaction. Someone shouted, "Keep it down out there."

Bonaduce replied in an imitation of a drunken slur, "Shud' up yourself." Alex ordered alcohol liberally spilled over the card players and arranged then around the table to appear as drunken sleepers. He ordered the bad actress to stay behind and prevent anyone from investigating the scene too closely.

They reached the bridge soon after. The bridge was the busiest part of the great ship, with a full complement of eight. The numbers weren't the main concern, it was the easy access to help through the communication console. An outbound call would quickly end their little venture. The seven person squad spread out to their prearranged tasks. On Alex's signal, Bolithio activated the quick burst electronic jammer as Bonaduce opened the hatch and Alex threw in a smoke grenade. The two person security detail turned with flachette pistols drawn. Alex, charging through the entrance, fired his taser at the man on the left and tackled the woman on the right in one smooth motion. Bolithio and Bonaduce, right behind him, quickly disabled three crew members, including the woman manning the communications console. Alex had to give the Count credit. He handled his opponent skillfully. The rest of the team covered the remaining members of the crew including Captain Prebble.

Short, stout Captain Prebble, choking on the smoke, coughed, "What is the meaning of this?"

Roxanne removed her gas mask and hood as the smoke dissipated in the powerful ventilators and replied formally, "I, Roxanne Rudnauman, Princess Heir of Asturia, officially take possession of the royal flagship, *Astor Queen* as owner operator. My retainers and I arrived in this unorthodox manner Captain, because we feared illegal opposition to my claim."

Prebble was speechless for a moment before recovering his composure. He bowed politely, then commented dryly, "Welcome aboard your Majesty. I apologize for the appearance of my bridge.", as he waved away the last of the dissipating smoke. "But as you just noted, we weren't notified of your arrival."

Alex jumped into the conversation, "Captain Prebble, the Princess informs me that you and your crew are loyal retainers of the throne. I believe you and your senior officers should demonstrate this by taking fealty oath to the Princess, as vassals secundus. Anyone can choose not to take the oath without coming to harm, but they will be relieved of their duties and detained for a day until certain matters are settled."

Frowning for a moment, Prebble then roared, "I recognize you now Major Kane. You may be an important mercenary commander but you don't have any authority on this bridge, pup. I've captained this ship for four different generations of Asturian royalty and if the crown asks me for a fealty oath, I will submit. But not to you merc." He turned to Roxanne, calming down and politely asked, "Is this your wish Princess?"

Roxanne responded by smiling, leaning over and kissing the suddenly blushing captain, "Yes it is, Uncle Preb. I'm sorry about the Major's remarks." Then she arched her eyebrow at Alex, with that *I told you so* look. "But he is within his authority as Prince Consort to make the request."

The discomforted Prebble paused open mouthed, looking back and forth between Roxanne and Alex. "Well I'll be spaced! I'd heard rumors you two were an item, though I didn't hear it had gone this far."

Roxanne hugging the still blushing, rolly polly captain said, "Consider yourself to be the first Asturian liege to be notified uncle."

Prebble suddenly aware of his crew watching his embarrassment, looked around grimly and snapped at them, "What are you all looking at? Return to your duties and maintain Communication silence until further notice." The crew hid smiles as they returned to interrupted duties with exaggerated fervor. Alex nodded to his squad to release them. He was certain the indomitable Prebble could control his own bridge.

Prebble turned to the Princess and whispered, "Roxanne you are now the Princess Heir, you can't go around calling me Uncle Preb anymore in front of my crew!" Then he knelt before her and swore the ancient Asturian oath of allegiance. Afterwards he rose up and ordered all his senior staff to the bridge to take a similar oath. Up until then he had studiously ignored Alex.

Prebble, turning to Alex, bowed perfunctorily, "Prince Consort, I have over two hundred troopers loyal to Count Highcastle aboard this ship. Once they find out what has happened they will respond. I won't have carnage aboard my ship sir!"

Alex, turning to Bolithio and ordered, "Go to phase two Lieutenant. Have your company take their positions Ms. Bolithio." Alex downgraded Bolithio's rank to follow the ship board convention, that permitted only a vessel's master to be called captain, "Captain Prebble, if you would seal all the critical areas of the ship, my troops will gas the passenger quarters and secure the *Astor Queen* without harming anyone."

Prebble cautiously asked, "Aren't you violating the truce you sponsored Major?"

"Not at all Captain. No one has yet been harmed and Highcastle's men and equipment will be free to depart your ship. I am only taking these measures to maintain the peace and return this vessel to its rightful owner," Alex formally answered.

Prebble was thoughtful for a moment, then turned to the Princess and commented, "Well it seems you're not marrying a fool. Though it will be interesting to see what the Council thinks of all this."

Roxanne laughing as she tucked her arm into Alex's, "Oh, I think the new Prince can handle them now that you approve Uncle Preb."

Hours later Alex awoke in the navigator's seat on the bridge, surprisingly refreshed from a two hour nap. Shocked at his lapse, he hastily determined that Bolithio and Visegrip had secured the ship without mishap and without his help. Everyone, including the doughty Prebble, went out of their way to assure him everything was under control. Alex felt a tremendous sense of relief. The raid had gone far better then he had hoped, Roxanne was happy to have contributed and he was guiltily happy to have caught up on his sleep. Now all they had to do was face down the Counts.

Chapter 39

Roxanne entered the room dressed in a regal, imperial purple, floor length gown, a delicate gold filigree crown studded with sapphires and rubies mounted on her elaborately styled sable hair. A matching necklace draped around her bare neck. The Triarch Marisa, though beautiful in her own right, looked dowdy in comparison, as she escorted the Princess into the great hall. Two of Visegrip's massive troopers, clearly uncomfortable in their colorful royal honor guard tunics, followed the two women. They glowered at the gathered throng, daring anyone to comment at their appearance. The room went silent at the entrance of the little group, some of the Lords bowed, others deliberately ignored any signs of fealty. Roxanne glided imperiously to the temporary throne mounted on a dais at the head of the room, acknowledging Captain Prebble and Count Bonaduce as she passed. Many in the room transferred their evaluating stares to the two men, trying to determine their special relationship, if any, with the Princess. Sitting down stiffly, constrained by the elaborately stylized nature of the royal costume, she appeared completely indifferent to the actions and stares of the room full of nobles.

Alex watched the entire pageant from a hidden closet. He spotted Count Hightower signaling his most powerful ally, Baron Boran, with a barely perceptible nod. Clearly the Count was not going to take the lead in the assault on Roxanne's authority. Alex could understand his reluctance. Historically, those who overthrew young beautiful rulers were not popular. The bulldog Baron, his powerful frame barely concealed by the bulky court garb, strode forward and blared, "You have no authority to wear that crown, you traitoress! You abandoned your vassals on Fairhaven to flee to this ball of dirt. And now you claim the throne!" He marched to within a few feet of her, craggy chin jutting out, and shouted, "Turn the crown over to the High Council Exchequer now, woman, or there will be trouble!"

By his shockingly ill mannered outburst the Baron was the first to declare open opposition to the Princess Heir. The rest of the room breathlessly watched, awaiting her response. Alex admired the brilliance of Hightower's move, while controlling a growing anger at the attack on Roxanne. The not very intelligent Baron's intemperate outburst would make him the lightning rod for Roxanne's supporters, and would make later opposition to her seem moderate and reasonable.

Roxanne however was up to the challenge. She turned to one of her honor guards and commanded, calmly, "Please escort the Baron to his room. He seems to be suffering from distemper."

The big trooper smiled with diabolical pleasure at the Baron. Taking three quick strides forward, he grabbed the open mouthed Baron by cuff and belt, and marched him out the door without so much as a groan. It was an impressive display. The large Baron struggled and squawked like a child in the arms of the genengineered trooper.

Roxanne stood up angrily, all pretense of calm gone, "The decay in good manners among the nobles of the Realm has gone far enough. Asturia has remained civilized because our ancestors established the codes of honor by which we live. I will no longer sit by while those codes are discarded for expediency. Whether this Council chooses to acknowledge me as Princess Heir or not, the proceedings will be conducted in a civilized manner!"

Nostrils flaring, she looked around the room. A surprising number of heads were nodding agreement. Baron Boran's outburst had been too much for them to stomach. Alex was proud of Roxanne. She had handled the situation perfectly.

Hightower, trying to salvage his position, stepped forward and bowed gracefully, "Lady Rudnauman, present members of the Council, let us not forget that we do not have a quorum of the Grand Council here. This is strictly a fact finding session. We need to determine the relationship of Lady Rudnauman with a certain mercenary leader, her alleged status as a Triarch and her culpability, if any, in the defeat on Fairhaven. We all know that Lady Rudnauman was opposed to the invasion from the start and her departure brought chaos into our ranks." Modulating his voice to express concern, "Of course we all recognize the Princess's youth could have caused her to make some mistakes. But given the present dangers, can we afford to have an inexperienced child running the affairs of Asturia. Present members of the Grand Council we must make a decision today. A decision that will alter the future of our nation. We must decide if this woman is the right person to lead Asturia."

Hightower's speech had mesmerized the audience. He had hit on many of their concerns about Roxanne.

It was the unobtrusive Marisa who replied to the Count's innuendo's in a clear and powerful voice. "Members of the council, 'Princess heir' Rudnauman is not a Triarch." Her emphasis on Princess Heir and her statement caused an immediate outburst of noise. She waited until the sound died down, "She is Truzen Triarch! Because of her status she will join the highest rank of the sisterhood and will have the full support of the Triarchy at her command. It has not been our way in the past to enter political discourse directly. But as the Count has already warned, these are perilous times for Asturia. We are fortunate to have a Princess Heir who also happens to be a Truzen Triarch to lead us."

Pandemonium broke out. Some greeted the news with joy other with trepidation as they saw their plans disintegrate. Most were just surprised. Alex noted the sour look on Count Hightower's face. He had not counted on this revelation.

Roxanne had stood throughout the speech. She had been nearly as surprised as the crowd at Marisa's announcement. The Triarch healer had only hinted at the possibility that Roxanne could be Truzen. Roxanne hid her surprise and subtlety signaled Alex to come in. Moments later he entered quietly through the double doors and walked up to Roxanne, knelt and kissed the palm of her hand. A kiss the signaled fealty and intimacy at the same time.

Hightower roared, "What is that mercenary doing here? He has no right to be here. Guards throw him out."

Roxanne, with her hand raised to stop the approaching guards, "You are premature Count. Ladies and gentleman, let me introduce you to Major Alessandro Watanabee Kane, my future Prince Consort."

Pandemonium broke out. Roxanne and Alex stood side by side ignoring the swelling noise until the crowd finally subsided into a murmuring uneasy quiet. Count Castile strode forward bowed politely and spoke, "Princess Rudnauman this man has not gone through the selection process to become a candidate for Prince Consort. You spoke earlier about maintaining the traditions of our ancestors. Yet here you violate one of the most sacred of those traditions and with a foreigner at that!"

Castile was one of the most powerful of the great counts. He had reluctantly joined King Ludvig on his misguided incursion on Fairhaven as his most trusted advisor, and the logistical mastermind of the invasion. He claimed he had no desires for the throne. Unlike many, Alex believed him. Castile was a barely competent CombatJack, and was not particularly combative. The man was certainly smart enough to know he didn't have the temperament to rule his rambunctious warrior nation. A traditionalist, he wanted to choose the next Prince Consort. But only through the established trials of the Grand Council. By referring to Roxanne as Princess, he had acknowledged her right to the throne. But that didn't mean he was about to abrogate any of the privileges of the Grand Council.

Roxanne with a winning smile, "You are correct Count Castile. Had I and the Major had the opportunity, we would have preferred to go through the traditional selection process. I am convinced the Major could pass many of the tests you might require." She paused and scanned the crowd, "But, let us not forget that many times throughout our history, the trial has been bypassed for men who have achieved great deeds and demonstrated leadership." She reached into her purse and raised a parchment, "I have here an agreement negotiated by my future consort with the government of Himalaya. This agreement essentially gives Asturia control of the Crescent Isle and its SymXtend production. It brings enormous wealth into our coffers opens up new trade routes for us and it promises peace between Asturia and both the Vegan Republic and the Imperial Coalition."

She starred at the crowd with the authority and power of a queen and a Triarch. It was an overwhelming combination. "You have all heard of Major Kane's conquest of the Crescent Isle against unbelievable odds. From humble beginnings he has built a formidable mercenary battalion, recruiting some of the most able warriors in known space. Such legendary warriors as Lady Nobunaga, Major Bouchard, Captain Visegrip and Captain Converse, have subordinated themselves to my mate, because they perceived many of the same qualities in him that attracted me, a Truzen Triarch. You have also all heard and some have seen his remarkable personal courage and skills as a warrior. With this agreement he has now brought peace and future prosperity to many worlds. Demonstrating his skill as a negotiator and a player of the great game. Truly could the members of the council devise better tests then these. Count Castille, I ask you and all of you present to forego any trial for my mate in acknowledgment of his contributions to Asturia and his demonstrated abilities.

It was Highcastle who responded first, acidly he shouted "This is ridiculous, I will have no part in it. My man and I are leaving immediately for Asturia. We shall see how the rest of the Council enjoys being ignored."

Alex spoke wryly, "You will have to arrange new transportation Count. The *Astor Queen* is the property of the Rudnauman lineage."

Highcastle smirked, "Your going to have to fight to prevent me leaving aboard the Queen merc. Lets see how good the Chameleons are against a *Hercules* combat shuttle and Asturian CombatJacks."

"No Count, you are going to have to fight your way on board. With Captain Prebble's permission, I now have a full company of Chameleon infantry guarding the *Astor Queen*. Your soldiers and their equipment will be permitted to disembark. I expect they are recovered from the sleep gas they received last night by now. Your men must be off the ship by noon tomorrow, and that goes for any of her other passengers who choose not to support the rightful throne." Alex dropped the bombshell into the disbelieving crowd.

Highcastle snapped, "Impossible!"

"Quite possible. It took a few of Count Bonaduce's retainers and a few of my troopers half an hour to free the ship from your control. Your security procedures were laughable Count. Were any of my subordinates to permit a *Hercules* class shuttle to be captured so easily, I'd demote them to latrine duty for life." Alex continued shaking his head, "And you want to rule Asturia."

Castile trying to suppress a smile at Highcastle's incredible loss of face asked, "You really captured the *Queen* last night? Was anyone hurt? I have some of my troopers on board. How long were you planning this?"

Alex answered politely, "No injuries other then a few bruised skulls, Count. As for the plan, Princess Rudnauman proposed taking control of the *Queen* last night. Count Bonaduce and I formulated the plan within a few minutes. In all fairness to the defenders we did have people inside and I have some of the finest covert equipment in the universe at my disposal."

Castile commented, "Impressive. You are a very decisive man Major. Maybe too quick to a decision. To rule a kingdom one must deal with the slow and sometimes tedious processes of government."

Alex with a quirky smile replied, "I can't agree more Count. That's one of the reasons I recruited Director McCloud to manage key economic aspects of the new Asturian Himalayan confederation. Neither the Princess Heir nor I are experts at running a kingdom. We plan to recruit heavily from the Counts to manage key posts both on Asturia and here. I also want you to know that despite the new treatise Asturia still faces many threats and will need strong decisive leadership. I have stockpiles of Droid upgrade kits to distribute to our CombatJacks. I also have some captured Droids for the best CombatJacks. The Princess Heir in choosing me as consort, has brought to the aid of the kingdom both these valuable supplies, a skilled mercenary battalion and the expertise of my skilled technical and administrative staff."

Castile recognizing the subtle bribes Alex had intimated in his speech, sarcastically said, "It seems you also bring the skills of an orator and politician with you."

Alex from the heart spoke directly to the Count. "I will do what it takes to keep my Princess happy Count Castile as long as I don't compromise my honor. If that means I have to learn new skills like oratory, I will. If it means I have to use my old skills as a CombatJack I will do that also. The princess does not want to gain the throne through civil war, so I will do all that I can to prevent it."

Castile starred at Alex for a moment, then he stepped forward, knelt before Roxanne and pledged the oath of fealty. As he stood back up, he said, "I think you have chosen well Princess Heir."

Roxanne in happy relief answered, "Thank you uncle Max. I know I have."

Count Bonaduce and Captain Lord Prebble followed suite. A steady trickle of others both great and small followed to pledge allegiance to the new Princess Heir. Their reasons varied. Some came for gain, others at the urging of their Triarch healers, others swayed by Roxanne's and Alex's charisma. Some came late out of fear of being left out of the new administration. Other came forward reluctantly fearing the wrath of the grim Consort. When it was over, only Highcastle and a few of his staunchest supporters did not acknowledged the new rulers of Asturia. No one there doubted the absent members of the Grand Council would rubber stamp the decision made here.

Highcastle turned to leave wrapped in his pride. Roxanne rushed forward and caught his arm. "Count Highcastle, please do not leave in anger. You are one of the greatest men of my kingdom, can't you see it in your heart to accept me as Queen? If not for me for the sake of Asturia."

"You expect me to forego my principles and bow down before you and that upstart. Never! Hightower will fight to bring proper leadership to Asturia." Highcastle grimly answered then turned and tried to walk away but Roxanne wouldn't let go of his arm.

Roxanne pleading, "Great Count, I do not ask that you take fealty oath to me if you can't find it in your heart to do so, but I beg you to abide by the consensus of the Council. I do not want a civil war. Please Sir, if not for unity then for your family and vassals."

Highcastle disconcerted by the powerful pleas of a Triarch swore rudely, "Dam it women stop begging! I have daughters your age that do the same thing to me."

"And do they get their way?" Roxanne said with a smile.

Highcastle unable to suppress a responsive smile answered, "Most of the time." For a moment he was mesmerized by the full Charisma of a Truzen Triarch. Then Roxanne released him from her influence. Highcastle stepped back blinking away his daze. "I never doubted you were Triarch. That's why you shouldn't rule. We're a nation of warriors, we need warrior leadership. You will have to much influence over him," Pointing at Alex, "And over the Kingdom. We will get soft."

Roxanne answered regally, "Triarches have influenced Asturia for centuries Count. Has that ever weakened our warriors?"

Alex spoke softly, "Count it was her idea to capture the *Astor Queen*. I was the one objecting to the potential casualties for fear of violating my pledge of safety. The Princess is quite capable of doing what needs to be done to protect her people." Grimly, "She knows how ruthlessly I will deal with a rebellion. Is that not the true measure of a leader?"

Roxanne with a faint smile pleaded softly, "Please Count."

Hightower looked frazzled, then a look of resolve crossed his face. He hesitated for a few tense moments, then snapped, "I don't do things in half measures," As he bowed down and pledged fealty. Roxanne leaned down and hugged and kissed the man in exuberant relief.

Suddenly young Count Bonaduce let out a whoop. Sporadic cheers turned into a full throated roar as Roxanne returned to Alex's side and gave him a passionate kiss. For a moment he was embarrassed, but the deafening roar of their new subjects washed away the feeling.

Roxanne whispered "I love you Prince Consort."

Alex laughingly replied, "I know."